SHADOW & POISON

A detective with strange powers takes on a client whose touch is deadly. . . A torrid, atmospheric fantasy that satisfies on all fronts.

— KIRKUS REVIEWS (STARRED REVIEW)

Gritty and gripping, powerful and sexy, Shadow and Poison *will have your heart racing with each kill and every searing kiss.*

— MAX WATSON, AUTHOR OF *CHAINS OF NURTURE*

This is one of those stories that literally pulled me into it and I couldn't put it down until the end.

— CORRINA LAWSON, AUTHOR OF RISE OF THE FIRESTARTER

Also by J.B. Curry

The Pianos Wild Series

Bad Keys

The Dark Guard Series

Shadow and Poison

The Red World Series

Red Ice—*coming soon*

SHADOW & POISON

THE DARK GUARD: BOOK I

J.B. CURRY

For my family.

I

Confidential sources in Chicago inform me that one of our assets is experimenting with a covert weapon. To protect the nation at home and abroad, I have sent agents to take control of the project by any means necessary.

— FEDERAL BUREAU OF INVESTIGATION
DIRECTOR J. E. H., MEMO, MAY 17, 1933

CHICAGO, 1933

She looked like a long, black calligraphy stroke painted on the air. She was wearing a black mink coat, a black hat with a little brim over her bobbed black curls, black gloves. Only the ivory of her face broke the inky line she made. And what a face. Sculpted cheekbones, elegant nose, full, red mouth. Deep brown eyes with a catlike tilt. Exotic, gorgeous, and dangerous.

He smiled. He could use a little danger.

She was standing on the sidewalk in front of his house, head tipped as if considering whether to walk up the steps to his front door. He watched her from a slit in the curtains over the narrow Gothic windows next to the entrance, his interest stirring for the first time in weeks.

She scanned the facade with surprised eyes, as all the clients did. They came looking for a private detective's office, and instead they found a castle out of a German fairy tale.

His home and office was one of the last mansions left on what used to be Millionaire's Row, the stretch of Prairie Avenue built up with palaces after the Great Fire. But the millionaires had long since fled to the Gold Coast, escaping the tide of slums lapping closer to their walls every year. The big old houses were cut up into apartments, or torn down and replaced with tenements, or just left to rot. All except his castle, looming amid the flophouses and speakeasies.

Sometimes when potential clients first saw the building or the neighborhood, they turned around and marched away. Off to the Pinkerton Agency, no doubt. That was fine with him. Prospective divorcees and fraud victims could move right along. He only wanted people with interesting problems knocking on his door.

Problems like ghosts. Curses. Monsters.

Everyone liked to pretend those things didn't exist, until they got themselves into an otherworldly jam. Then, when they had no other choice, they came looking for him to get them out.

Maybe this girl would be one of them. Would she come in or would she run? The dark power sleeping inside him roused, hungry for her decision.

She stepped up to the massive iron-bound door with *Mark Van Ryn, Private Inquiries* painted on it in gold letters and raised a gloved hand to pull the doorbell.

He let the bell ring, waited several seconds just for the drama, and hit a button that released the door's catch with an ominous sounding creak. He didn't want her to see him just yet though, or he might send her fleeing in terror before he found out what she wanted. So he drew back from the window, away from the light, and unleashed his power.

Shadow poured through him, flooding every cell. His body dissolved into darkness, became part of it, until his whole being was shadow. He was an incorporeal presence in the gloom, watching as the girl pushed open the creaking door and stepped inside.

With her came a wave of intoxicating perfume, wafting through the air to him as her head turned on her graceful neck and she looked around the foyer.

It was a large room, two stories tall, with a stained-glass window in the transom above the door showing a white knight saving a lady from a dragon. The knight, lady, and dragon all looked jaded about the situation, he always thought.

The floor was flagstone, and the paneling on the walls and the beams in the ceiling were heavy oak. An iron chandelier hung suspended in the deep shadows overhead, though all the light bulbs had burned out years ago. Three doors led off into the main part of the house. Doors one and two, opening on the family rooms and the grand staircase to the second floor, were locked. The third stood open, a faint light gleaming from within.

The girl couldn't see him, invisible as he was, though she examined the room carefully. She didn't seem even a little cowed by the darkness, or the massive, decrepit grandeur. She strolled toward the open door, that maddening perfume trailing her. The *click, click* of her heels echoed in the dusty corners.

3

His shadow being followed behind her, invisible and untouchable, a patch of darkness among a thousand others.

She walked into his waiting room, which had once been the house's front parlor. The window blinds were closed, the only light coming from one pale, utilitarian lamp in a far corner.

He slipped through the thick shadow along the walls, watching her.

She didn't sit on any of the chairs set out for his clients, curling those red lips at his threadbare, twenty-year-old furniture. She flicked open the buttons of her coat, revealing a black silk suit belted tight at the waist over a scarlet blouse.

But it was her body underneath the clothes that captured his attention. Long, slim, her hips beautifully curved. An enchantress's body to go with her face. For an instant, rationality fled, and all he could think was that the high, upturned breasts under that silky fabric would exactly fit into the palms of his hands.

She strolled over to the window and tried to open the blinds. They had frozen shut with disuse long ago, but with effort she got a few stripes of pale May sunlight to filter into the room.

He felt himself turning more solid as the patch of shadow containing his presence began shaping itself into flesh. Any kind of light drained his power, but sunlight was the worst. He moved back into the deepest shadows in a far corner, wondering at himself. How had she distracted him enough to almost get caught in the light? Sure, she was beautiful, but he'd seen plenty of beautiful dames, and they meant nothing to him. He tried to study her with his usual detachment.

She was young, though not too young. Mid-twenties, he

guessed. At that age, she ought to be married, but there was no telltale lump of a ring under the glove on her left hand. So, not here about a troublesome husband.

No fear in her relaxed posture, no anxiety in her cool expression. Which left out blackmail, stalking, and missing friends, family, or pets. No feverish glint in those catlike brown eyes betrayed revenge or greed.

She leaned against the windowsill, her long, stocking-clad legs crossing at her slender ankles. Her chin tipped up, and her finely cut nostrils flared a little, as if she was scenting the air. She opened her black handbag and took out a long ivory cigarette holder and a cigarette. "I know you're there," she said, her voice a low purr. And she looked straight at him, as if she could *see* him. "Why don't you come out and give a girl a light?"

2

Shock rippled through the shadows that made up his being. Did she really know? Had he been found out?

Then he realized she wasn't looking at him, but at the wall behind him, paying special attention to the darker squares on the wallpaper where paintings used to hang. After a moment her gaze settled on the closed door between the waiting room and his inner office.

His shadow self shifted in relief. She didn't know. She thought someone was spying on her from a peephole behind the walls. But how had she sensed his presence?

Guess he'd have to put his detective license to use and find out.

His shadow pooled on the floor and slipped through the darkness underneath the door, sliding into the next room. Once his father's study, now Mark's office, it was lit only by a weak lamp set on the old man's Victorian monstrosity of a desk.

With an effort of will, he pulled in his being, separating himself from the dark and turning shadows into flesh and humanity. He felt his suit coat settle onto his shoulders and his tie cinch around his neck. His shoes pressed the floorboards. He was a man once more, a completely human private dick ready to greet his new client.

He stretched out his newly solid hand, the muscles and bones flexing, the blood rushing under the skin as the thrill of his power seeped down into his marrow and hid for now. He grasped the doorknob to open the door between him and the girl. Then he stopped.

He always hated the moment when people first got a good look at him. That flash of shock and revulsion on their faces. And he had a feeling he would hate it even worse this time.

Which was stupid. It didn't matter what anyone thought of his looks, especially some dame.

He shoved open the door and stepped into the waiting room.

The woman's gaze fastened on him, taking him in.

He waited for the usual reaction. She'd stare, maybe smile painfully, and avert her eyes. They always did. To be fair, it wasn't only because people found him ugly. They sensed his power too, and that made them afraid.

But this time, instead of a flinch, he got a bold look from his toes to the top of his head. And then she smiled at him, her dark eyes lighting up like fire behind obsidian. Like she was seeing only his tall, muscular body and handsome features, and not even noticing . . . everything else.

Not once in his life had a woman looked at him that way, without a hint of wariness or repulsion. Or worse, sick fascination. Just a woman sizing up a man and liking what she saw. For an instant he froze, not knowing what to do.

They might have spent all day standing there, staring at each other, but then she blinked, and it was over. Her expression was a sophisticated mask, as before.

He shoved the strange moment aside for now. "How do you do. I'm Mark Van Ryn."

"How do you do, Mr. Van Ryn." She didn't offer her hand or her own name.

"What can I do for you, Miss . . . ?"

She ignored the hint, fitting her cigarette into the holder. "You can take me into your office and offer me a light. I want your help with a sensitive situation."

"You might be in the wrong office. I'm not a very sensitive fellow."

"Oh, I dearly hope not, Mr. Van Ryn."

"Well then, by all means, come in." He held open the door for her.

She straightened up from her lean against the sill in a sinuous movement and walked across the room, her tight black skirt whispering around her legs. Strutted past him, trailing that elusive fragrance. He shut the door behind her harder than he intended.

He turned around to find her waiting by the chair in front of his desk. Remembering his gentlemanly training, he held the chair for her. She sank down into it like a ballerina.

There was something very theatrical about her, the coloring, the clothes, the studied grace of her movements, the sultry expression. Like a vamp in a Hollywood movie. He wondered if she was performing for him, or for herself. Either way, it was one hell of an act. He could appreciate that. He liked to put on a show himself, time to time.

He circled around the desk and seated himself in his creaking desk chair. Folded his hands on the blotter. Gave her a smile. One that, on his face, never failed to disconcert people and get them babbling.

It failed now. She smiled back.

He said, "Let's start off simple. What's your name?"

"Miss Elizaveta Karlova." She spoke with the faintest of accents, Russian maybe, buried deep under an International Money lilt courtesy of the finest finishing schools. He knew that tone of voice well, because he had it himself.

She'd been born rich, then. And judging by her clothes and her attitude, she still was rich, unlike so many people since the Crash four years ago.

She slipped the cigarette holder between her lips and raised her perfect black eyebrows.

He struck a match off the box on his desk and held it to the tip of her cigarette. The scent of burning tobacco mingled with her perfume. He shook out the match and leaned back, eying her through a wisp of gray smoke.

She eyed him in return. "You were watching me, weren't you?"

He didn't bother denying it. "Don't take it personally. I watch everybody."

"Even prospective clients?"

"Especially them. If a gentleman—or a lady—comes in looking like trouble, I might need to take steps."

"Really? What steps would you take if I were trouble, Mr. Van Ryn?"

He just smiled. "What did you want to see me about, Miss Karlova?"

She tapped her cigarette holder against her lips, but she didn't draw on it, letting the smoke wreathe through the air between them. "Amos Mannering, a dear friend of the family, suggested I come to you on a matter of inquiry. A delicate matter."

"The Mannering case wasn't all that delicate, as I recall."

"On the contrary. You rescued Mr. Mannering's silly daughter from that Egyptian death cult *and* preserved her reputation. You've shown exactly the finesse I require."

"Amos told you about that? I thought he was keeping his lip buttoned."

"As I said, he's a dear family friend. He also told me about some of your other exploits, like capturing the zombie master who'd been raiding Rosehill Cemetery for corpses."

"The police made the arrest. I just pointed them in the right direction."

"And about laying the ghost that had been terrorizing that factory on Hermitage Avenue."

"A simple matter of finding her gold ring in the boiler and proving her husband was the killer."

She smiled, a flash of small white teeth. "Brave, clever, and modest. You're perfect." She opened her purse, took out a slip of paper and laid it on the desk in front of him.

He picked it up. Written in an elegant script were five names that looked kind of familiar. A grudging memory clicked. They belonged to five of the richest, most powerful men in the city. High-class fellows who appeared in the society section of the papers. The kind of swells his father would have chummed around with, before he got too busy drinking himself to death. In fact, one of them, Lionel Duke, had bought out the controlling shares in his father's chemical company toward the end.

"I want to learn everything about these gentlemen," Miss Karlova said. "The good and the bad, but mostly the bad. I want you to open up their closets and pull out their skeletons for me. Every secret, every shame, every base, despicable, depraved rumor you can scrounge."

"Why do you want to know all that, Miss Karlova?"

"Because I'm going to marry one of them."

He raised his brows. "Which one?"

"That depends on what you find."

He shoved the paper back at her. "I don't do lonelyheart work."

"Hearts have nothing to do with it," she said coolly.

"And I only take cases that give me a real challenge."

"But this *is* a challenge. These men are rich and well-connected. Prying into their secrets may be dangerous."

In a way, she was right. It had been a few years, but he remembered the particular dangers of the high-class world well.

It was a world of boarding schools, soirees with the "right sort" of people, seats at the opera. All funded by brand new dollars pulled out of Chicago's factories and stockyards, scrubbed down and dressed up to look like some English duke's family fortune.

But wherever it came from, money was money, and power was power, and these men were ruthless in hanging onto theirs. Which made mucking around in their secrets risky, for anyone other than him, at least.

"They're about as dangerous as a sponge cake," Mark said. "Sorry, lady, I don't want the job. I'll get you a list of referrals—"

"I don't want another detective. I only want you."

"You can't have me."

Her lips curved as if she found that highly amusing. "I'll pay you treble your going rate."

Even he had to pause. "That would be sixty dollars a day, plus expenses."

She shrugged at the outrageous sum.

"This is too easy for me," Mark said.

"Then it shouldn't take you long to find the answers to my questions."

"Why me?"

"Because you aren't afraid of anything. I need a man who isn't afraid of anything. This assignment is not without risk. I'm quite dangerous myself, you see." Her smile flattened out, and Mark heard a dark undertone in her voice. She was dead serious about being dangerous.

"Explain, please."

She looked at him through a veil of smoke. "I don't think I will. You're the detective. Discover for yourself why I'm dangerous, if you can."

If that wasn't a gauntlet thrown down, she could paint him yellow and call him a banana.

3

Eliza lounged in her chair and regarded the most intriguing man on five continents with fascination. She'd criss-crossed the globe, met countless men from every walk of life, but never had she seen one like Mark Van Ryn.

Of course, she'd scented him before she saw him. It was one of her talents. The moment she strolled into his dim waiting room, she had breathed in the musk of a healthy man in his prime, a deep, rich, complex perfume, each sepa-rate note of it as unique as a fingerprint. When she opened the blinds on the window, it grew warmer, more intense. As if he was drawing closer to her, or was aroused by something.

That was when she knew he was watching her, no doubt from behind a peephole in his office wall. She couldn't have a man putting her at a disadvantage like that, so naturally, she challenged him to show himself.

Then he stepped through his office door, and she got her first look at him.

Amos Mannering had tried to warn her about what to expect, speaking in hushed tones of Van Ryn's "condition."

But, he assured her, if she overlooked the detective's odd appearance, she would find that he was quite a capable man.

But when she saw him at last, she found she didn't want to overlook his appearance. Quite the contrary.

He was younger than she expected, about her own age of twenty-six. He wore a gray suit and tie, beautifully made, though a few years out of fashion. And the body underneath his clothes put Charles Atlas to shame. Over six feet tall, broad shouldered and lean hipped, with muscular limbs and long-fingered hands, he moved and held himself with controlled energy hidden beneath an easy slouch.

And his face . . . Well. His features were extraordinarily handsome, carved with a perfect balance of strength and grace. He had a straight nose, firm jaw and cheekbones, and a finely molded mouth with an ironic smile tucked into the corners. He wore his thick, wavy hair combed back from a wide forehead.

And all of it, skin and hair, was white. Pure, snow white. The hint of icy blue in his eyes was the only color on him.

He was beautiful, like no other man on earth. And when she first saw him appear among the shadows, something hot woke up in her mind, something sharp twisted low in her body, and she'd smiled at him in a way she'd never smiled before.

It was only a momentary madness, of course. She was here to hire the detective, not to admire him. At that thought, the despair that had never been far from her for seven long years had rushed up to extinguish the stir of heat within her.

Now she studied Van Ryn, keeping only a faint smile on her face.

She longed to ask him why he sounded like an Ivy

League alumnus one minute, and a tenement bruiser the next. Why he lived and worked in this pile of ruined grandeur. He was an educated man, judging by the bookcase against one wall overflowing with well-used books, and yet he'd set up shop as a private detective.

She wanted to solve the puzzle of Mark Van Ryn, but she couldn't afford to let her own mask slip that much. If she didn't keep him at arm's length, he might succumb to her terrible power.

Wherever she went, the inborn scent of her skin poisoned the surrounding air with a perfume that entranced men. If they stayed near her for too long, it made them deathly ill. Her scent affected women far less, and children not at all, but every man who entered her presence became her willing prey.

That wasn't even the worst of it. She shot a glance at the glove on her hand as it rested in her lap. Not the worst by far.

The spike of futile resentment almost caused her to draw on the nasty cigarette. Almost. She really only brandished the foul things about to dilute her scent. If she didn't, the man sitting across the desk from her might fall under her influence far too quickly. And while she might like a more amenable detective than Mark Van Ryn was proving to be, she didn't want a mindless one. She had a job for him to do, after all.

"Do we have an agreement, Mr. Van Ryn?"

He kept his pale yet curiously opaque eyes steady on her for another long moment. He tapped his long, white fingers on his blotter and smiled slightly. "Okay, Miss Karlova. You win. I'll take the job. For sixty a day, plus expenses."

She opened her purse and pulled out a roll of green bills, counted out three of them into a neat pile on the desk, and pushed them over to him. She tucked the rest of the money away.

He sent a sharp glance at her purse.

She realized then how odd it was for her to be walking around Chicago, alone, with hundreds of dollars in cash.

Tchyort. She'd grown lax in the little tricks and deceptions that disguised her as a normal girl. This man, this *detective*, would see through her if she wasn't careful.

She'd dared him to discover her secrets, but only to pique his interest in her case. Letting him get close to the truth was out of the question. As the women in her family had known throughout the ages, discovery meant death.

"I assure you, I'll compensate you well. You needn't think about my money." She flicked her empty hand in a graceful little gesture, wafting a curl of her scent toward him. Not enough to sicken him, just enough to cloud his senses.

His hard, icy gaze didn't soften in the slightest. Interesting. He seemed to have some resistance to her influence. A few men did. But they all succumbed to her eventually.

After a moment, so did Van Ryn, it seemed. He scooped the bills up and locked them away in his desk. "I'll have your information in a few days. Give me an address where I can reach you."

"The Drake Hotel, on Walton. But you needn't contact me. I'll return here soon to learn what you've found."

He tipped his head agreeably. "You're the boss."

She took her time putting her cigarettes away, reluctant to leave him. But the longer she stayed, the higher the risk he would fall under her spell, and she didn't want to enspell this man. Time to go, for his sake. She stood up, walked toward the door, and waited.

For a second, he sat still behind his desk with a devilish

glint in his icy eyes. She wondered if he would leave her standing there like a fool. Finally, his breeding won out. He stood and came to open the door for her, and she breezed through it into the foyer. He followed her a little too close, the heat from his big body warming her back.

At the front entrance, he reached past her to open the door. She stepped outside into the sunlight and turned to face him.

The afternoon light slanted across his white hair, glinting in his pale eyes. *So beautiful.* Terrifyingly beautiful, like an Old Testament angel who might draw a flaming sword and smite her if he deemed it necessary.

She had the sudden mad urge to tell him everything. Her poison. Her curse. Beg him to help her. Offer him anything she had to find a way out of her troubles.

He was brave, strong, wily. He'd taken down a necromancer, banished ghosts, broken up cults. Maybe he could help her, too. Maybe . . .

Sanity returned in a rush. She'd spent the last seven years looking in every corner of the world for a mystic or alchemist who might help her cheat her fate. She'd found dozens of them, but not a single one could save her. And neither could Mark Van Ryn.

She took in a little breath that was almost a sob. Her voice under iron control, she said, "Goodbye, Mr. Van Ryn."

"Goodbye, Miss Karlova." He stepped back into the hallway, a pale gleam among the shadows, and shut the door.

She strolled to the sidewalk, past the cars parked along the curb, and through the decaying remnants of Millionaire's Row. A block away, she paused to smell the air. Pavement, mud, garbage, tobacco, grease, old tires, the odors of the people passing by, and a million other scents that made up the brew of the city.

But nothing of the dark, masculine scent of Mark Van Ryn. He wasn't following her.

Good. She had another call to make this afternoon, one she wanted to keep separate from Van Ryn and her inquiry. Tomorrow, she would face what she had to do, but today she would steal an hour for herself alone.

She strode on toward Michigan Avenue, where she could hail a taxi and be on her way to the Loop, and State Street.

4

Mark shut the door and strode to his office. He got his overcoat and hat off the coat stand and threw them on. It would be the easiest thing in the world to follow his new client. He would track her, spy on her, discover all her secrets.

Find out for yourself why I'm dangerous.

Damn right he would.

He grabbed the list of names off his desk and shoved it in his breast pocket as he rushed back to the front door. He yanked it open and came face to face with a guy.

The guy had his fist up, about to knock on the door just as Mark pulled it open. He dropped the hand and said, "You Mark Van Ryn? The detective?"

He was big, broad, gray faced and flabby-lipped. Even standing still, he looked like he was squirming in his expensive suit. Now, this was trouble of the two-fisted kind, just what he would have liked, if he wasn't barely leashing his need to follow the girl.

"Are you?" the fellow demanded.

"Who wants to know?" Mark said, looking down the

street in the direction she had gone. He glimpsed her long, dark shape turn down Michigan Avenue and vanish.

Damn. He aimed a not-very-friendly look at the obstacle between him and his quarry.

The bruiser stared at him in return, fascination and revulsion warring in his eyes. "Yeah, you gotta be him. Big albino, looks like a damn ghost haunting a castle." His fingers twitched like he wanted to cross himself.

"You got me, smart guy," Mark said. "So who are you, and what do you want?"

"You can call me McGann. I'm an associate of Mr. Camonte. You heard of him?"

"Yeah." Everyone had heard of him. Gabriel "Scarface" Camonte was the king of the Chicago mob. Liquor, girls, gambling, he had a hand in it all. Every day the newspapers blasted out headlines about his nightclubs, his money, his women, and his scores of victims gunned down in the streets.

He'd heard of Jimmy "the Gun" McGann too, come to think of it. Camonte's number one hitter, rumored to be the triggerman behind at least a dozen shootings.

"Mr. Camonte wants to talk to you," McGann said.

"What for?"

"He'll tell you when you see him. I got a car waiting." He jerked his chin toward the street where a big black Lincoln idled, a raw-boned driver hunched behind the wheel. "Let's go."

"Can't. I'm busy." Maybe he could catch up to the Karlova girl after he dusted off this goon.

The goon's face went mean. "I don't think I heard you right. Nobody says no to Mr. Camonte." He pulled a .38 Colt out of a holster under his coat, all casual, and held it near his leg.

Mark grinned in sudden anticipation. Seemed he had to *convince* this dope to get lost. That was okay. Mark could be very convincing. He stepped back from the door, into the shadows.

McGann snorted in contempt. "Where do you think you're going?" He followed Mark inside, grabbing for him with his free hand.

Dark power flooded Mark's body, and he snapped into shadow, sifting right through the grasping fingers. McGann stumbled, thrown off balance.

Mark raced behind him in a blur of darkness, turned solid, and clipped him behind the ear, stunning him. He grabbed his gun hand and yanked it up behind his back, twisting the joints hard, forcing the gangster to his knees.

He snapped the gun out of McGann's limp fingers and stuck it in his pocket. Bent and said into his ear, "Don't ever try that tough guy stuff with me. I'm liable to take it real bad."

"Fuck you," McGann snarled.

He yanked the guy's arm up and leaned on the shoulder joint until he grunted in pain. Mark gave him credit for not screaming. "Now that ain't polite. How about you tell me what Camonte wants with me, and I don't break your arm. Is he trying to shake me down? Shut me up about something? What?" He gave the arm a tweak.

"Aagh! He wants to hire you!"

"Well, why didn't you say so?" Mark turned him loose.

McGann leapt up, red faced and furious. But he was cradling his arm, and there was a healthy shine of fear in his eyes. Mark had shown only a hint of his power, but now the man had an inkling of what he was dealing with.

"You got a death wish, kid?" he blustered, trying to recover.

Mark just laughed at him. "Step in to my office," he said, still chuckling, and sauntered through the inner door.

After a moment, McGann shuffled in behind him.

He sat at his desk, opened a drawer, and took out a bottle of his father's prized Macallan and a tumbler he kept for occasions like this. He poured two fingers of whiskey and shoved the glass across the desk at McGann. "Have a drink. Settle your nerves."

McGann swooped up the glass and guzzled it down like it was bathtub hooch. Which it might well taste like, for all Mark knew. He never touched the stuff himself.

McGann wiped his mouth and glared at him. "How did you pull that trick back there?"

Mark didn't know how he did it. His power over shadows had simply been a part of him, like his white skin, all his life. It was woven through his earliest memories.

One night when he was five years old he made his way downstairs in the dark, looking for his friend Frasier, who lived with his mother and sister in a room off the kitchen. But just as he set his small, bare foot in the hall, his father slammed through the front door, huge and filthy and stinking of alcohol, the light from the street lamps flooding in around him like cold fire.

Mark huddled in a terrified knot against the wall and wished he could hide in the warm, friendly dark so that his father wouldn't see him. The big man stomped past, close enough for Mark to reach out and touch his muddy coat. But he didn't grab Mark and shake him. Didn't scream in his face that he'd killed his mother, that he should never have been born. It was like he didn't see Mark at all. The dark had granted his wish.

Ever since that night, he had the power to blend into the shadows and go unnoticeable. It had saved him countless beatings at home. Later, at boarding school, it had been his first line of defense against the older boys who roamed the dormitories at night intent on torture. And of course, it was useful for him as a detective, when he was surveilling his suspects. Or keeping his clients on their toes.

He smiled at McGann. "I never do tricks."

The guy opened his mouth, shut it, and turned red. "I want my damn gun back."

"I'll take your request under advisement. First, tell me about this job of Camonte's, and it better be good. I've already got a very interesting case."

McGann's liver lips twisted in a smirk. "That dame who was just leaving? Yeah, interesting is right."

He let his power thrill over him, shadows shifting around him, and looked steadily at the man until his color drained. "My other clients are off limits," he said softly.

McGann grunted something foul and sat down stiffly in the client chair. He stuck out his glass.

Mark splashed in more whiskey. "Tell me about the job."

McGann drank, and said, "I'm not supposed to talk about it. I'm just supposed to take you to the boss."

"I don't make house calls. If you won't talk to me, then go on home. Tell your boss if he wants me to do a job, he can come here and ask me himself."

"You really are crazy."

Mark shrugged and waited.

McGann's words dragged out of him. "He can't come here. He can't go anywhere. He don't want to leave his room, see? Someone's after him. Our guys have been dropping dead and no one can figure out who done it, or how. Now the boss, he thinks he's up next."

"He's the biggest crime lord in the city, with an army of

fine gentlemen like you to protect him, and the cops and politicians in his pocket. Why come to me?"

"Because how they died . . . it's weird. Damn weird. Word is, when there's weird stuff, you're the guy to handle it."

"Weird how?"

"Like they've been eaten. From the inside out."

Mark raised his eyebrows. "That *is* weird. I like it. Okay, you got my attention. Tell Camonte I'll come see him this evening, after dark."

McGann shook his head. "Has to be now. There's a lockdown after dark. No one in or out."

Mark steepled his fingertips and considered. No lockdown would keep him from getting in to see Camonte if he wanted. But he tried to avoid terrorizing his clients by sneaking up on them in their homes, usually. And it would be a shame if Camonte got offed before Mark had a chance to investigate this case. His curiosity was killing him.

"Where's he staying?" he asked McGann.

"I'm not supposed to say."

Mark just looked at him.

"The Drake Hotel," the gangster muttered.

"You don't say," Mark said softly. What were the chances that both of his new clients would be living in the same building?

Actually, chances were good, he realized. The Drake was the grandest hotel in Chicago, the perfect place for expensive birds like Camonte and Miss Karlova to roost. Maybe it was simple coincidence. But now he had no choice but to check it out.

"Okay. I'll bend my rules for your poor, scared boss." He

stood up and gestured toward the office door. "Lead on, friend."

"Gimme my gat back first."

"Sure." Mark pulled the revolver out of his pocket, snapped open the chamber and shook out the bullets. He put the bullets in his pocket and tossed the empty gun to its owner.

McGann shot him a filthy look and put the gun away. "Crazy punk freak," he muttered, slugging the rest of his drink. He slammed the glass on the desk, got up and stomped out of the office to the front door. Mark strolled along behind him.

They stepped out into the bright May sunlight pouring down between the canyons of the buildings. Mark winced away from the light, turning to lock his door, taking his time so he could brace himself against the sun.

This was the real reason he rarely made house calls. Going out in daylight stripped him of his defenses. It scoured his skin, lanced through his eyes and pounded his brain to mush. It forced his dark power to hide away in the marrow of his bones. He never left the house until nightfall if he could help it. Until today. He had been ready to tolerate the light to follow the Karlova girl, and now, to meet Camonte. He must really have been bored.

He gritted his teeth, pulled the brim of his fedora low over his eyes, and followed McGann at a careful distance. He wouldn't be able to pull the trick of flickering in and out that had disarmed the man earlier. Any fight would be a fair fight. And if there was one thing Mark hated, it was a fair fight.

But even without his power he could take McGann, easy. He was younger, stronger, and faster. And he knew how to take—and deliver—a beating. Any boy who looked the way he looked and survived seven miserable years of boarding school learned those lessons damned fast. He'd even been the school's champion boxer three years running. McGann wouldn't stand a chance.

But they made it to the Lincoln parked on the curb without incident. McGann got in the front next to the driver. Mark settled into the feeble shadows in the middle of the back seat. The Lincoln started up and rolled down the street to Michigan Avenue, the way Miss Karlova had gone. But she was nowhere in sight now.

He'd find her room after he finished with Camonte, and then he'd learn everything he wanted to know about Elizaveta Karlova. He caught a glimpse of his white face in the car's rear view mirror, his lips spread in a wolfish grin.

5

Eliza got out of the taxi under the clock at Marshall Fields on State Street and looked up and down the avenue at the empty storefronts and half-finished construction. The high-end shopping district had fallen on hard times along with the rest of the city and the country. Still, a few stores were hanging on, supplying the slumlords, factory barons, and bootleggers who still had money with glamor for themselves and their women.

But Eliza wasn't interested in clothes or jewels today. Her goal was a shop selling the most rarified item of all.

There it was, half a block away. A sparkle of crystal in a shop window, a red door, and an elegant sign reading, *Parfumerie DeForest*. Exactly as it was three years ago. She walked toward it slowly at first, then quicker, her heart beating loud in her ears, until the door was there in front of her, the cheerful color welcoming her inside.

She pushed it open to the chime of a silver bell and walked into the shop. A thousand exquisite scents rushed up to welcome her, like long-lost friends. The rows of bottles glinted like jewels on the mirrored shelves surrounding her, as they always had. The girl at the counter looked up and smiled. "Good afternoon."

Eliza smiled back. "How do you do." She looked around, breathing in the scent of . . . well, home wouldn't be the right word, would it? She'd never had a home, so she didn't know what one smelled like.

The counter girl said, "Can I help you Miss? We have soaps, creams, and our pure perfume. We import the most delightful fragrances from France. Or, for a more discerning client, our master perfumer, Mrs. DeForest, can create a unique blend just for her."

"Yes, I know. I'm Eliza Karlova, an old friend of Mrs. DeForest. Is she here?"

Behind the counter girl, the black velvet curtain screening the door to the back room swept aside. A pretty, older lady walked out into the shop with an energetic bustle. She was small but sturdily built, her stylish frock a bit stained at the sleeves, and her silver hair in a practical yet elegant knot. Her skin was lined with decades of smiles. "Eliza? Is that you?" Gray eyes sparkling, the lady walked toward her, hands held out. "My dear! Here you are at last!"

"Mrs. DeForest!" Eliza clasped the strong, slightly gnarled fingers with her gloved ones and kissed the air next to the older woman's cheek. "How good to see you!"

Gwendolyn DeForest flashed a dimpled smile that must have slain men thirty years ago. "You must come in and have a cup of tea. I've so much to discuss with you, I'm at a loss where to begin!" She turned to the counter girl. "Millie, please see that we aren't disturbed."

"Yes Ma'am," Millie said with a placid smile.

"Come with me, dear." She swept Eliza through the curtained doorway and into the back room.

It was a long, low space crammed full of distilling apparatus, measuring pipettes, stacks of vats and kegs, shelves full of bottles and jars. The air was rich with a thousand raw ingredients that went into a finished perfume, from precious ambergris to unassuming violets. Just the same as it was three years ago.

"I've missed this place," she said, before she thought better of it.

"It's missed you too, Eliza. And so have I. I couldn't have wished for a better apprentice." Mrs. DeForest led her through the laboratory to a door leading to a staircase. At the top of the stairs was a small flat, now used as a break room.

They walked through a comfortably shabby sitting area to the galley kitchen. A little table and two chairs stood nearby. Eliza sat in one and watched her old mentor heat water and measure out tea.

A small radio was playing on the formica counter, an announcer trumpeting the World's Fair that was soon to open on the lakeshore near Soldier Field Stadium.

"Come to Chicago's Century of Progress, the spectacular fair beginning on May 27th! People from every corner of the world are coming to see its magic and its marvels of unparalleled ingenuity!

Pleasure seekers in gay attire will wander the beautiful Avenue of Flags, eager participants in a show unmatched in the annals of fair-making!

The Hall of Science is a typical example of the regal architecture that is to be found everywhere on the grounds, creating a skyline of glowing monuments to beauty!

A symphony in steel, a tribute to structural perfection, it is the towering Skyride that offers the major thrill of the fair.

What a view visitors will get from the windows of its rocket riders as they travel across the lagoon!

One sees far below blues and reds and greens and yellows, all fused into a molten fairyland of light, of sights and sounds and hurly-burly, teeming with magicians, sword-swallowers, dragon rides, alligator fighters, Egyptian cha-cha girls, sideshow wonders, a midget village, a conglomeration of freaks and fakirs—

Mrs. DeForest switched the radio off. "It does sound marvelous, doesn't it?"

"You intend to go?"

"Why yes! It's too convenient. Instead of me traveling the world, the world has come to my doorstep. Though, it will be nothing compared to your adventures, to be sure!"

A warm glow infused her as she watched the older woman bring the tea service to the table. Happiness, she realized with a start. Strange it took so long for her to remember the feeling.

Her life had been fortunate, cosseted even. She'd wanted for nothing as a child. She'd had a pleasant social life, the finest education, any luxury a girl might want. And yet, she'd never been happy until the summer she spent with Mrs. DeForest.

She'd been on the run for four years by then, searching the vast realms of Asia for a way to break her curse. Teeming cities in India, mountain shines in Tibet, ancient monasteries in China, and exquisite palaces in Japan, she scoured them all for mystics who might cure her poison.

But after four years and thousands of miles, she'd found no answers.

She redoubled her determination and returned to Europe. If magic couldn't help her, she thought, perhaps science could.

But trusting a doctor or scientist with her secret was out of the question, so she spent the tedious stretches of her journeys teaching herself chemistry. She poured over scientific journals and studied the work of pioneers such as Cannizzaro, Curie, and Haber. She attended lectures and corresponded with experts, all the while developing a new idea for solving her problem. Or rather, a new approach to an old idea. Perfume.

In her youth she'd tried to disguise her scent with fragrance, though it always dissolved the instant it touched her skin. But modern developments in chemistry had revolutionized the ancient art of *parfumerie*. A master *parfumeur* who blended art and science might be able to create a fragrance that would cancel out her poison scent.

She had gone to find one such master in the perfume capitol of the world, Paris. In an old and famous shop in the Rue du Faubourg-Saint-Honoré, she waited hours to see the *nez*, the great *parfumeur* who designed the scents that graced the throats of the royalty of Europe, or what was left of it after the War.

When she was finally allowed into the workroom to see the great man, she found him arguing with a lovely older lady of fashionable dress and strong opinions.

"No, no," the lady said, in American-accented French. "The top notes cannot contain orilo. It is far too delicate a scent for that. Notice how it trills along the middle notes like a xylophone. It doesn't pound them like a timpani. Also, this perfume is the secret recipe of a remote village in Romania. There is no orilo within a thousand miles of Romania! This scent is nothing other than campion!"

The *nez* drew himself up behind his counter full of perfumery equipment like a soldier behind a battlement.

"My dear Madame, my judgment in these matters is beyond question. Might I point out that a lack of experience or lack of talent can lead a nose astray? Or perhaps a fevered imagination?"

"Rubbish," the lady said.

Before she could marshal any further time-consuming arguments, Eliza broke in. "Excuse me, but I believe the scent you refer to is Silena. Maybe the furtive touch of lime flower is confusing the scent."

The lady and the *parfumeur* turned identical looks of shock on her, as if amazed she had the temerity to speak. Then as one they bent their heads over the bottle and sniffed.

After a charged moment of silence, the *nez* straightened and glared at her. "A mere fortunate guess."

But the lady smiled a dazzling smile. "Rather, an amazing gift." She swept Eliza up and carried her off to a nearby *café*, peppering her with quizzes, questions, and compliments the whole way.

Eliza never managed to confer with the *nez*, but she decided it didn't matter. This lady, whose name she learned was Gwendolyn DeForest, might hold the key to her problem, if anyone did.

Over *café au lait*, Mrs. DeForest told her about her shop in Chicago. The most exclusive perfumery in the city, she didn't mind saying. She had come to Paris on a buying trip, and to study Old-world techniques she could combine with New-world innovations. But the venture had turned into a protracted quarrel with the hidebound and clannish *parfumeurs* who couldn't comprehend a new idea if it snapped their noses off.

Nevertheless, Mrs. DeForest said, she would count this

visit a resounding success, for it had brought her to Eliza and her miraculous nose. She had been searching for the ideal apprentice for some time, and now Providence had sent her one. Would Eliza come work with her and learn the art of perfume?

6

And so it was that Eliza found herself in Chicago studying the creation and blending of fragrance. Every day in the workshop, Mrs. DeForest honed and shaped the talent Eliza had always taken for granted. A wondrous new world opened for her every time she stepped through the red shop door.

Her life outside the perfumery was, for once, ordinary. A room in a women's boarding house, plain, sturdy clothes, and regular employment. It was a far cry from her aristocratic upbringing, but she found it marvelous. She was a shop girl like a thousand others, living day by day, her future nothing more than an uneasy dream.

"You still take your tea black, I trust?" Mrs. DeForest asked, pulling Eliza out of her memories. She poured tea from a lovely little pot into two bone-china cups and handed Eliza one.

"Yes, it's perfect. Thank you." Eliza breathed in the steam rising from her cup, and sipped. Mrs. DeForest always had the most delicious blends of tea, naturally.

"Now, where should we begin? It's been three years since you left!" Mrs. DeForest said in gentle reproof.

The fine tea turned bitter on her tongue. "I know," she said. But she'd had no choice but to leave.

As a child, none of her nannies had stayed with her for long as she and her mother moved from city to city. Later, she'd gone from boarding school to boarding school, leaving every friend she'd made behind. Although children were immune to her scent, *Maman* wouldn't risk any teachers getting sick. Eliza was simply too dangerous to stay near ordinary people.

And Mrs. DeForest was elderly, her heart weak. Six months after they'd first met, the older lady fainted in her laboratory. And with that, Eliza's idyll was done.

She'd failed to devise a perfume antidote. After months of study, she was no closer to escaping her fate than she'd ever been. To stay any longer was to risk her friend's health. So she announced she was going on an expedition to discover new ingredients for perfumes, and fled.

"You shouldn't have stayed away so long," Mrs. DeForest continued. "But I did so enjoy your letters. What terribly exciting adventures you've had! And all the samples you sent me, simply breathtaking!"

"I'm so glad you liked them." In this, at least, Eliza had kept faith with her mentor.

In the three years since she left Chicago, she had traveled to even farther-flung corners of the globe than she'd ever reached before. The sweltering jungles of South America, lost islands of the Pacific, the depths of the Congo. Once again, none of the native sorcerers she encountered were able to break her curse, but this time her search for new fragrances drove her onward as well.

She'd sent Mrs. DeForest trunkfuls of roots, barks,

mosses, flowers that bloomed only by night, herbs that grew only on the west slopes of volcanoes, the rarest of orchids.

Then the letter from her grandmother arrived at her hotel in Manaus, Brazil. She must present herself in New York to select a husband at long last. Her quest was over. Her inevitable future had come.

Mustering enough strength for one last show of defiance, she stopped in New York to replenish her wardrobe, and then she ran for Chicago before her grandmother caught her.

She was determined to pay her respects to Mrs. DeForest before the rest of her life began. She owed her that much. After all her encouragement and kindliness, faith in her talents, faith in *her,* Eliza needed to tell her...

Before she could conjure the words, Mrs. DeForest said, "We must have a nice long gossip about your travels, but business first. Now, I wasn't expecting you so soon, or I would have had your paperwork done already. But we'll sort it out quickly enough."

"Paperwork?"

"For putting you back on the payroll, of course. I don't mind telling you it will be a relief to have help in the laboratory at last. Millie is a dear girl, and quite good with the clients, but she has no nose at all, bless her."

"You want me back at the shop?"

"But of course!"

Eliza swallowed the sudden tightness in her throat. "I can't. Though I would like to, very much."

The older lady's face fell. "But in your last letter you said you were coming to Chicago to stay!"

"Yes, but not to work. I'm here to find a husband and settle down."

"But a woman can be both a perfumer and a wife, provided she chooses the right man! My dear Albert was my rock and my light. He believed in me and cherished me until the day he was taken from me." Her eyes turned distant as she spoke, and she absently rubbed her left arm. "Find a man like my Mr. DeForest and stay a perfumer, my dear."

"I don't expect to be as fortunate as you were in your husband. But it's time I had a family of my own." Softly, she admitted her tenderest secret. "I want children."

The longing for a baby, someone to love with all her heart, had grown within her over the years until it was unbearable. And that was the real reason she had given up her quest and capitulated to her grandmother's demands. Because of her own womanly weakness.

Mrs. Deforest's eyes softened with understanding. She had no children of her own, but she must have yearned for them once. Then her jaw firmed. "You are far too young to give up hope for a loving marriage. You deserve to have great work *and* great love in your life."

Heat prickled at the back of her eyes. "I can't."

Mrs. DeForest gave her a stern look, her face pale. "Eliza, a nose like yours is a gift. You mustn't let it go to waste."

"I know, but my family—The future you describe is—is not for the likes of me."

"Your family would understand. If they care about you, they must want you to reach your fullest potential." Her voice wavered on the last word.

"They do, it's only that—Ma'am? Ma'am!"

Mrs. DeForest lurched forward against the table, her right hand clutched white-knuckled on her left arm, her face gray.

Eliza leapt out of her chair and rushed around the table to her side. "Millie!" she cried down to the front of the shop, "Come quickly! Mrs. DeForest is ill!"

The girl clattered up the stairs to the apartment and stood staring at them, wringing her hands. "Oh no! Oh, gee! Not again!"

"Call the doctor!" Eliza snapped out.

The older lady whispered through ashen lips, "No. Pill . . . right pocket."

Eliza felt inside the pocket of her dress and drew out a little box. She opened it with shaking fingers and took out a tablet. She put it to the older lady's lips, and then held her cup of tea for her to drink.

After a long moment, Mrs. DeForest took a wavering breath. "No doctor. It's passed. I'll be all right."

"This is my fault," Eliza said. "I shouldn't have —" *Shouldn't have inflicted your poison on an innocent lady,* the shreds of her conscience whispered. "I shouldn't have tired you," she said instead.

"Don't be silly," Mrs. DeForest said, still shaky but stronger now. "It's merely my old illness. Age catching up to me. Nothing to do with you at all."

"Still, I should let you rest."

"No, you mustn't go yet! I have something important to tell you!"

"Please Ma'am, you shouldn't tire yourself further. We can finish our conversation another time, when you're better."

For a moment, she looked stubborn, but then she sighed and nodded, lids drooping over hollowed eyes. "Soon though. Promise me."

"Soon. I promise," she said, the lie curdling on her

tongue. To Millie, she said, "You'll see her home? Make sure she has everything she needs?"

"Certainly, Miss," the girl said, her good-natured face crumpled in worry.

"I'd take her myself but I—I can't, I'm—I have an appointment elsewhere I cannot miss. I have no choice. I'm so sorry."

"It's all right dear," Mrs. DeForest murmured. "Millie and I will be fine."

Eliza touched her hand where it lay on the table. The bones and skin felt so delicate under her gloved fingers. "Please get well, Ma'am. Please. Goodbye." She ran down the stairs, out of the shop and onto the sidewalk.

A few steps away from the red door she stopped and leaned against the brick wall, fighting back tears.

She must never come back here. Never see Mrs. DeForest or her perfume shop again.

7

The Lincoln took Mark straight up Michigan, the Loop on one side and Grant Park on the other. They crossed the DuSable Bridge and continued to the Gold Coast, where they rolled up to the cream colored Beaux-Arts pile known as the Drake Hotel.

Mark had heard that Gabriel Camonte kept a wife and family tucked away in a bungalow in Park Manor, but for himself, nothing but the best would do. The Drake was where presidents and royalty and movie stars stayed when they graced Chicago with their presence.

Mark and McGann got out at the main entrance and walked through the glass doors and into the marble entryway. Time to remind the gangster that even though they were on his territory, Mark was the one in charge.

The instant he stepped out of the sunlight, he drew his power around him and slipped into half-shadow. There was too much light pouring down from the crystal chandeliers for him to turn invisible and insubstantial, so instead, he dimmed himself enough to be unnoticeable. Eyes would slide off him without registering his presence. He could slip along the walls and spy on his prey without drawing attention if he wished.

McGann stopped inside the lobby, saying, "Gotta pat you down before we go upstairs." He looked around behind him for Mark, brows beetling when he didn't see him. "Van Ryn? Where'd you go?"

Mark slipped around to his front and let his shadows fall away. "Right in front of you."

McGann lurched around, swearing. He got control of himself and said, "I gotta check you for weapons before you talk to the boss." He raised his hands as if to pat Mark's sides.

"You want your other wrist sprained?" Mark asked him idly. Even with the electric light draining him, he could take ten of McGann. "You invited me here. Besides, I don't carry guns. I don't need 'em."

McGann hesitated, then dropped his hands with a snarl and stomped through the foyer. Mark strolled along behind him. They climbed a flight of marble stairs and waded through the ankle-deep carpet in the lobby to an elevator.

The elevator man took them up to the eleventh floor, right below the penthouse. Mark was a little surprised that Camonte wasn't in the best rooms, but then he remembered reading in the newspaper that the first lady and a bunch of politicos were coming to open the World's Fair next week. If anyone could commandeer the presidential suite away from Camonte, it would be the president's wife.

They walked down a hall with plush carpet, tall moldings, and wide-spaced doors. McGann knocked at one door and a butler opened it. If butlers came with crooked noses and hands that hovered close to their pockets, that is. McGann led him through a lavish suite populated by guys dressed in suits and ties who looked like they ought to be wearing dungarees and caps. They gave him the hairy eyeball as he passed. One of them fingered a tommy gun on his lap like he was petting a cat.

McGann led him down a short hall to another door. The tragic sounds of Puccini's *La boheme* drifted through the wood panels. McGann knocked, saying, "Boss, it's me. I got him."

"Come," said a muffled voice in the room beyond.

McGann opened the door. Inside was a bedroom. The shadows were thick, the lamps off, only a little light seeping from behind the window curtains. But Mark, who could see perfectly even in pitch black, took in the whole room at a glance.

It was furnished in an elaborate style and coated in a layer of depravity. Empty bottles of liquor and dishes with spoiling food in them were scattered on every gilded and inlaid surface. The rumpled silk sheets on the bed reeked of sweat and sex. One ormolu table had a mirror laid flat on top of it. On the mirror was a thick scattering of white powder, a razor, and a rolled up hundred-dollar bill.

Near the table was an armchair, and in the armchair was Gab Camonte.

8

The boss of the Outfit had a beefy body wrapped in a brocade dressing gown, a cigar clamped between yellowing teeth, and thin black hair slicked back over a shining pate. He was only in his thirties, but his face was already sallow and bag-eyed. A faded knife scar furrowed his left cheek.

He switched on a bronze table lamp in the shape of a naked woman and looked up at Mark with shrewd black eyes. "Finally. Come in, come in." With a broad move of his arm, he beckoned Mark into the room.

He walked in, McGann following him. The henchman shut the door and stood next to it. "Look out for this one, boss. Guy's crazy."

Camonte took the damp cigar out of his chops. "Maybe I need some crazy about now." To Mark he said, "Sit." He gestured to one of the Louis XIV chairs scattered around the place. Gold rings glinted on his fingers.

Mark pulled up the chair and relaxed into it. Or tried. Louis XIV had damned uncomfortable furniture.

La boheme continued to sing plaintively from the phonograph cabinet as Camonte puffed on the cigar and examined him. He didn't look unduly revolted by Mark's appearance, for which he got a grain or two of credit. After a while he said, "You're not what I was expecting."

Mark let that ride.

"Shamus, are you?"

"That's right."

"I hear you handle the queer stuff. Zombies and ghosts."

"I handle stuff that interests me."

"Then you're in luck. Gabriel Camonte interests everybody," he said with a grin, and Mark saw a glimpse of the ruthless charisma that had made him boss of the Chicago underworld. "I got a mystery for you, shamus. Murders. Three of them."

"I didn't think murder was a mystery for you and your associates," Mark said. "There are a couple of suspects I could pull off the top page of the *Tribune*."

"If you're talking about Sammy Snyder and Jack O'Malley, they ain't responsible."

Snyder and O'Malley were Camonte's main competition in the business of booze, numbers, and girls. "You know that for a fact?"

Camonte showed him a yellowed canine. "I know."

Thinking about the number of beatings and broken bones that must have gone into those two words, Mark raised an eyebrow.

"Besides, wait till you see the bodies. Jimmy, bring shamus here the pictures."

The henchman stomped to a nearby desk and took a folder out of a drawer. He shoved it into Mark's hands and resumed lurking by the door.

Mark opened the folder. Inside were crime scene photographs and coroner's reports. Copies of official police files, it looked like. Not something many citizens could get their hands on, but then, Camonte was no ordinary citizen. Half the police force was on his payroll.

There were reports on three different stiffs, the first dating from three weeks ago and the last five days ago. Each had been killed during the late night or early morning. There were no witnesses.

The first dead guy was sprawled out on a tile floor, the bases of a sink and a toilet showing in a few of the shots. He was dressed in pajamas and was soaking wet. It didn't look alarming at first glance. A slip and fall accident, or maybe a stroke or a heart attack. Only, there was something wrong with his mouth. His lips looked raw, like meat.

"Joey Tomacelli," Camonte said, looking at the picture from the reverse side. "We came up from Brooklyn together. That was three weeks ago."

Mark turned to the coroner's report. No bruising, no heart failure or brain hemorrhaging. Cause of death appeared to be severe damage to the lungs. The tissue had been eaten away. Like the guy had drowned in acid. But there was no acid on the body. The liquid covering him was plain tap water.

He turned to the next report.

"Guido DelMarco," Camonte said. "He owned my favorite restaurant."

The second dead guy was slumped on the floor of a restaurant kitchen. Fully dressed, soaking wet. According to the notes, they found him with his head and shoulders under the sink, a wrench and a flashlight on the floor nearby. He'd been fixing a pipe when he died. He turned to the morgue photographs and stilled. Mark had seen mutilated corpses before, but this was bad.

The photo showed a raw, oozing crater where the

mouth and nose should be. Like the flesh and bone had been dissolved. The coroner's report again said cause of death was severe damage to the lungs. As in, the lungs were gone. Mark turned the page.

The third guy was the worst. Sprawled in a gutter near a storm drain. Soaking wet. What was left of him, anyway. His entire face, throat, and upper torso were an empty pit of raw tissue.

Mark didn't let his expression change as he looked at the picture.

"That was Angel Lombardi. Ran my best casino," Camonte said.

Mark snapped the folder closed. He stared off into the distance, letting his focus drift. Facts and images floated in front of him in a shadowy cloud, each one connected to the others with gossamer threads of causation. After a while a pattern emerged, as clear as a road map.

He blinked and focused on his client. "I can find out who did this, and how. Shouldn't take me more than a week."

Camonte shifted, crouching his bulk closer. "Not good enough. The killer might try to hit us tonight. I need protection right now."

"Protection?"

"You know." He waved his arm. "Woo woo."

"I don't do woo woo. But I can still help you out tonight. And all it'll cost you is sixty dollars a day, plus expenses. Today's pay up front."

The shrewd eyes popped wide. "That's crazy!"

"Told you, boss," McGann said.

"My rates have taken a turn upward lately," Mark said. "And you can afford it, what with all the blood money you've been squeezing out of the city."

Camonte smiled plumply. "Blood money? I don't know what you mean. I'm just a businessman, giving the people what they want."

"Sure, so am I. In my business, I get paid, or I walk. And you don't get the two pieces of advice that'll keep you and your men safe from this creature."

Camonte's cheeks sagged. "Creature?"

Mark nodded. "Want more?"

"Yeah, but what you got to say ain't worth sixty a day."

Mark moved to stand. "You can save it for your funeral."

"Wait."

Mark sat back.

Camonte leaned toward him, lips crooked in a smile. And though his breath was rotten, the smile somehow had the glimmer of charm. "People who help me out, I consider them pals. You like girls? Liquor? Coke? Friends of mine get all they want. You find the sonofabitch who murdered my guys, you help me bring him to justice, and you'll be more than a friend. You'll be family. That's worth more than sixty a day, kid, believe me."

Mark wasn't even slightly tempted. Take that deal, and sooner or later he'd be the one owing Camonte sixty bucks a day. He leaned forward, elbows on his thighs, and returned the gangster's smile. "I don't want friends, or family. And I don't care when two-bit leggers get greased, so I'm not putting my neck on the line for any justice either."

Camonte's face shaped itself into a picture of extravagant hurt. His eyes went shiny and dark with unshed tears. His lips bent in a tragic moue. "I invite you to my home, a house of mourning, and you insult me like this?"

What a fine actor. He should be on stage at the Oriental. Mark grinned. "Yeah. And since I'm the only man in Chicago who can catch this killer, you'll take it and like it."

He saw Camonte consider hitting him. He saw him consider ordering McGann to shoot him. Or march him out to an alley and then shoot him.

Instead, the mob boss threw his head back and laughed, his doughy middle shaking. "You got nuts on you kid, I'll give you that. Pay him," he ordered McGann.

McGann, fuming, walked over and tossed down three bills on the ormolu table, right in the middle of the cocaine on the mirror.

"Hey, thanks. I'll write you a receipt," Mark said. He plucked out the bills with his thumb and forefinger, shook off the cocaine, and put them in his inner coat pocket.

"Now, start talking," Camonte said.

"First, these guys all died near the water system. Bathroom, kitchen sink, sewer. And they were all found covered in water. So this thing attacking your men is coming out of the drains. Second, it avoids light. These attacks took place in the dark."

"How do you know that?"

"It's obvious. A guy gets up at night to take a leak, doesn't bother turning on the light. A guy working underneath his sink puts his flashlight down for a minute. A guy standing in an alley away from the streetlamp for, well, who knows? Anyway, he gets close enough to the open storm drain, and something jumps out of it. Gets into his nose or mouth and burrows inside him. Eats its way out. Runs back down the drain. No trace. See how it works?"

"Eats its way out?" Camonte said, his face gray.

"Yeah. There was no blood or dissolved tissue around the bodies because the creature took the flesh away in its belly. And all that feeding is making it grow. Every attack does more damage than the last."

"So this is some kind of animal?"

"I don't know what it is yet, or who's setting it loose to attack your men. Until I find out, if you want to avoid looking like these poor stiffs," he tapped the folder against his hand, "You'll stay away from the water system, and stay out of the dark."

Camonte stared at him for a full ten seconds. Then he yelled, "McGann! Open those windows and get some fucking lamps in here! And get me the telephone!"

McGann hustled to obey his boss, drawing back the curtains and flicking on the lamps scattered through the room.

Time to drift, Mark thought as the light spiked through him.

He took the papers and photographs out of the file, folded them, and stuck them in his inner pocket to keep Camonte's money company. He stood up to leave, saying, "One more thing. I want you to keep your boys away from me and my investigation until I give you the all-clear."

"Nuts to that," Camonte said, the broken veins in his nose pulsing. "McGann will be keeping an eye on you."

McGann puffed up like a feather bolster.

"Okay. As long as he brings my money with him. If he wants to risk getting eaten, that's his business."

McGann deflated a little.

Mark strolled toward the door.

"Hey," Camonte said.

Mark looked back. The mob boss crouched amid the squalid opulence of his den like a bloated yellowish toad. His black eyes glittered in the harsh light flooding the room. "This stays quiet. We've kept it out of the papers so far, and

I want it to stay that way. I got a reputation to think about."

"I don't rat out my clients."

"Yeah? Maybe you're not so crazy after all." Camonte shoved his neglected cigar back between his teeth, picked up the Bakelite telephone McGann had plunked down at his elbow, and started dialing.

9

Mark left the mob boss's lair and walked past the idling goons in the parlor, McGann trailing his every step.

When they got to the front door, the henchman said, "You better be as good as you think you are, freak. No one takes the Outfit for a ride. I'm keeping you in my sights, and I got plenty more guns."

"Aw, don't be sore, McGann. Go take a nice bath by candlelight so you'll be in a good mood tomorrow when you get the pleasure of my company again."

"Tomorrow? Didn't you hear the boss? I'm going with you tonight."

"Okay," Mark said easily. "But don't you want your bullets back first?" He pulled a handful of McGann's loose bullets out of his pocket and tossed them in his direction.

Swearing, McGann tried to catch them, failed, and bent to chase them as they pinged and rolled across the marble floor.

While he was distracted, Mark pulled his shadows around himself and slipped out the door and down the hall, chuckling softly. But as he made his way to the stairwell, his smile changed into something harder.

A monster was trespassing in his city. Poaching in his territory. He needed to teach this thing who was boss in this town. And his sense of curiosity was flogging him to find out what the hell it was.

He would have gone after the creature no matter what, he thought as he ran down the stairs to the first floor. Getting the king of the mob to pay him for doing what he would have done anyway was gravy. He would start the hunt tonight. There was only one problem—his other client, Elizaveta Karlova.

Checking over Miss Lonelyheart's list of beaus would take too much time. He'd have to give up her case if he wanted to capture this monster before it ate someone else.

He'd find out her room number at the concierge desk, knock on her door, hand her back her sixty clams and say, *sorry doll, find some other chump to do your matchmaking.* Which was what he'd told her in the first place, before she tempted him into going against his better instincts.

Good thing Camonte's pictures had shocked him back into his senses. It never paid to get too curious about dames. He'd just keep his interest in her under strict control next time he saw her, he told himself as he shoved through the door to the lobby.

Then he heard her voice. Just a thread of husky sound coming from an alcove off the lobby containing the concierge desk. ". . . any messages for me?"

She's here. Before he knew what he was doing, Mark sidled up to the opening between the main lobby and the alcove and looked through. A long, graceful black shape lounged against the desk. It was the Karlova bird all right.

The smiling concierge was saying, "Yes, Miss Karlova. One of our new guests left a note for you. She said to deliver it to you the moment you returned."

Her gloved hands clutched the edge of the desk, hard. "A new guest? Here?"

"Yes. Madame la Comtesse de Valois. She said you were expecting her." The man held out a folded paper.

He saw a fine tremor go through her. But she reached out and took the note. She flipped the paper open and read it. "Thank you," she said, her voice muted. She shoved the note into her handbag and turned toward the main lobby. Mark glimpsed a wooden expression on her lovely face before he eased back into the sitting area.

He sat in a chair and took up a newspaper, drawing the shadows close around himself. He was just an anonymous shape. No one important. Unless she knew to look for him, she wouldn't notice him.

Sure enough, she walked right past him through the lobby, trailing her luscious perfume. Her stride, which had a roll and strut to it before, was stiff. Her eyes were distant. She turned into the elevator alcove. The elevator bell rang, and the doors trundled open. "Eleventh floor, please," she said. The same floor Camonte was on.

Mark was out of his chair and into the stairwell the second after the elevator doors clanged shut. He flowed up the stairs, the shadows powering his steps faster than the machine could go.

When he got to the eleventh floor, he waited in the stairwell until he heard the elevator chime and eased the stairwell door open.

Miss Karlova was walking away from him down the hall. He watched carefully as she passed Camonte's door, but she didn't give it a glance. Instead she stopped at a door near the end of the hall and stood for a moment, as if bracing herself. Then she raised a gloved fist and rapped on the wood.

The door opened, and she vanished inside. Mark moved down the corridor after her, still enveloped in half-shadow.

He settled against the door that had swallowed her, his shadowy ear pressed to the crack, and listened for all he was worth.

10

The moment Eliza rapped on the door, a maid opened it. Berte, she thought her name was. Or Gerte. Or Marie. Not that it mattered. The servants in this household were always the same—horse-faced, silent, and devoted to their mistress.

Berte/Gerte ushered her into a softly lit and tastefully furnished sitting parlor. A familiar heavy perfume saturated the air. The scent emanated from a presence enthroned upon a divan at the far end of the room.

The presence wore a lavender frock that Eliza was certain had been designed by Monsieur Worth himself. A heavy gold cross glinted on the bosom. One silk clad arm curved over a needlepoint frame. A pair of pale eyes as sharp as the needle darted up at Eliza as she stepped into the room, pinning her where she stood.

The lady the eyes belonged to was tiny and fair, with bone structure that once, it was rumored, made Degas weep. Her hair was a silver crown on her neatly shaped head. Even at more than seventy years, she was still lovely, and capable of exuding a brilliant charm when she chose. She was also a stone cold dragon. Her name, appropriately or not, was Angelique.

She set aside her needlework. In a light French accent she said, "Élisabeth. Do come in. I've been waiting for you for quite a long time."

"*Grand-mère*." Eliza strolled to the divan, bent and kissed the powdered cheek tilted up toward her.

"Where have you been?"

"Window shopping on State Street," she lied without compunction. The countess was unaware of Mrs. DeForest's existence, and she wanted to keep it that way.

She sat in an armchair nearby in a posture just short of sprawling. "You were wrong, you know," she said as an opening gambit.

Her grandmother regarded her, delicate brows arched.

"The message you left at the desk downstairs. You said I would be expecting you, but in fact, I never dreamed you would come here," she said, pulling off her gloves one finger at a time and setting them aside.

"That was foolish of you," her grandmother replied. "This is the only establishment within five hundred miles providing decent accommodation. Where else would I stay?"

"I meant I didn't expect you to come to Chicago."

"That was even more foolish of you. I intend to see you do your duty, no matter how far I must forge into this uncivilized continent."

"Uncivilized? *Grand-mère*, Chicago isn't the Wild West. There are no desperados riding about, ready to stick you up."

The old lady sniffed. "Just as well for them."

Eliza had to agree. Any gunslinger who went up against

the countess wouldn't live to regret it. She took out her cigarette holder and cigarettes.

"You will not pollute my rooms with those vile objects," her grandmother said. "I do not allow your mother to smoke in my presence and nor will you."

Eliza took her time putting her cigarettes away, content at annoying Angelique without having to smoke the things.

She said, "Where is *Maman* these days?" It had always been too easy for Eliza to lose track of her mother's whereabouts. Alexandrine had spent most of Eliza's childhood jaunting about the Western Hemisphere with her many, many, *many* admirers, leaving her daughter at various boarding schools. She was simply not the motherly type, though she had done the best she could according to her nature, Eliza supposed.

"She is in Istanbul, still," Angelique said.

"Oh, yes. The last letter I had from her was full of her efforts to charm a sheik out of his rubies."

"An Emir. Outrageous of her to get involved with a Musleman, but at least she didn't marry him."

"*Maman* is not the marrying kind." Her mother had had only two husbands, a shocking deviation from family tradition. Eliza, more shocking still, had no husbands at all to her name, even at the advanced age of twenty-six.

"Your mother cares for nothing but her own pleasure. She spares no thought for what she owes her family. But that is my fault. I was too soft with her. A mistake I will no longer make with you."

Eliza controlled her breathing and held her fire.

The maid chose that moment to appear with a tea tray.

When the service was laid, the countess said in German, "That will be all, Helga. You may go to your room. Come back in an hour to help me dress for dinner."

The maid bobbed a curtsy and disappeared. Eliza and her grandmother eyed each other across the teapot like duelists fingering their weapons. The ozone scent of coming battle hung in the air.

Angelique poured the tea, adding cream and sugar to each cup. "I was most disappointed that you left New York without coming to see me, *ma chérie.*"

"Gee, so was I." Eliza took the cup her grandmother passed her, wrinkled her nose at the creamy, sugary tea, and set it aside. "But I had so much shopping to do before I left for Chicago, there wasn't time."

"In fact, I was disappointed you left New York at all."

"I'm afraid I'm very disappointing."

Her grandmother didn't deny it. "I believe I wrote you were to come to the city to select a husband, not to select a wardrobe." She sipped her tea.

"You made it perfectly clear."

"And that I would cut you off without a penny until you came to your senses and did your duty. That was also clear?"

"As a bell."

"Then why," said Angelique, setting down her cup with a click, "Did you attempt to run away again?"

"Who said I was running away? I like Chicago. New York doesn't suit me. And neither does Paris, or London, or Vienna, so don't expect me to go there, either," she added to forestall the next line of attack.

But Angelique said, "No. You mustn't go to Europe now."

A note she had never heard in her grandmother's voice before made her sit up straighter. "Happy as I am not to argue with you, *Grand-mère,* I have to ask. Why not?"

Angelique didn't answer for a moment. Then she said,

"Things have not been the same there since the War. I thought it was a fever that would burn itself out, but . . ." The steel colored eyes flickered uneasily. "The smell of death still lingers in the air. And this new chancellor in Germany, the unrest in Spain . . . I think more trouble is coming. Soon."

Eliza stared hard at the older woman, the hairs at the back of her neck stirring.

The women in her bloodline, along with their other talents, had a nose for self-preservation. Hadn't her mother decamped from Russia years before the Bolsheviks slaughtered her father's depraved family? Hadn't her great-great-grandmother absconded from France well prior to the reign of la Guillotine? Hadn't her ancestresses escaped witch burnings, plagues, sackings, coups, revolutions, and dynastic wars since the days of her foremother Circe herself?

Angelique brushed aside her foreboding with a flick of her fingers, her eyes once again sharp on Eliza's. "I intend for you to come with me to New York at once. I've selected several eligible candidates there for you to choose from."

"I'm sorry you wasted all that effort. You see, I've already picked out several candidates for myself, right here. I'll choose between them in the next few days."

She had taken Angelique by surprise, she saw with grim satisfaction. After a moment to regroup, the older lady said, "I am glad you are making an effort to secure your future at last, *naturellement*. But to be choosing a husband here? In Chicago? No. A thousand times no. This city is full of nothing but millers and butchers."

"Wealthy millers and butchers."

"Wealth is nothing without rank."

"This is America, *Grand-mère*. Wealth and rank are one and the same here."

"More of your republican nonsense. You have no respect for proper bloodlines."

"None whatsoever."

Angelique curved her mouth in a smile as thin as a knife. "One would think you had learned better than to mingle with the vulgar, considering what happened in San Francisco."

Icy shock seared over Eliza's skin. Blood roared in her ears. In an instant, she plunged back into the nightmare of seven years ago. It flashed in front of her eyes and crawled across her skin, as sickening and terrifying as if it were happening to her all over again.

The heavy body crushing her into the dirt. The hand clamped around her throat, stifling her screams. Another hand wrenching at her clothes.

The hideous power boiling up inside of her, sizzling through her fingertips as she clawed at the dark shape above her. And a face in the moonlight, eyes wide, lips blue and frothing, five marks like fingertips blackening the cheek.

She sucked in a breath and blinked hard, forcing her mind away from the past, calming her thundering heart.

The countess was watching her, that sharp smile on her lips. "Do not forget that you are a lamia, *chérie*. It will bring you nothing but disaster."

Fury seared away the last of her lingering horror. Angelique would use any weapon to get what she wanted —Eliza, married and pregnant with her great-grand-daughter.

For uncounted ages, every one of her foremothers had followed the same destiny. Find a rich man of high rank and evil nature, marry him, and wait for him to die, leaving her with a fortune and a daughter to carry on the family legacy.

She had fought the future laid out for her and lost. She was here to surrender.

But by God, she would do it on her own terms. "I know what I am, and what I have to do. But I'll do it my way. I'm staying in Chicago, and I'm choosing my husband myself. You could threaten my finances again, but consider that I'll soon be the wife of a rich man, so I won't need your money."

The older woman's smile withered.

"Cheer up, *Grand-mère*. You're getting what you want. The family will continue, and family is all." She'd meant to sound ironic, but it didn't come out that way. The hunger for a family, the promise of a child to love, was the only reason she was striking this horrid bargain at all.

Angelique took a moment to sip her tea as she mulled things over. "Well. You are quite right. And because family is all, I shall make the sacrifice of remaining here in this city to oversee your nuptials."

At Eliza's expression, Angelique's smile returned. "So you had best make quick work of it, *non*?"

"You'll go back to New York after I'm married?"

Angelique inclined her head.

"Then I'll be married in a week."

"*Merveilleux*. And consider, *chérie*. The sooner you are wed the sooner you shall be a widow."

"Gee, you sure know how to cheer someone up, *Grand-mère*." She leaned her head back and heaved a sigh, suddenly exhausted. She caught a lungful of her grandmother's perfume, tea, furniture polish, and myriad ghostly scents from the surrounding city. And then she smelled a thread of scent weaving through the room. Dark, masculine, and familiar.

Angelique was eyeing her slumped posture with disfavor. "You will kindly sit up straight in my parlor—"

She leapt to her feet, hand out to silence the older woman. Her head turned toward the door.

"What is it?" the countess said, serious and tense.

Eliza whispered, "We're not alone."

The older lady's eyes widened, and she tipped her head up, scenting the air. Eliza signaled her to stay still and stalked toward the suite's door. She knew exactly who was standing behind it.

II

Mark had just enough time to peel his ear off the door before it was yanked open. Miss Karlova appeared in front of him, mouth set and eyes narrowed.

Caught. His half-shadow trick wouldn't hide him when someone knew he was there and was looking straight at him. He let his power slip away. He had been holding his hat in his hand, and now he put it on, tipped the brim at her and grinned. "Miss Karlova."

An older woman's voice called from the room behind her. "Who is it, Élisabeth?"

"One moment *Grand-mère.*" She stepped into the hall and closed the door, still glaring at him. She had taken off her hat, coat, and gloves, and stood before him in her sleek black silk suit. "Why are you spying on me?"

"It's not spying, it's detecting. I'm a detective, you know."

"Oh? Why don't you detect your way back downstairs and get working on my case instead of eavesdropping on my private conversations?"

"But they're such fascinating conversations." Actually,

he hadn't heard much. The door was too thick and the women's voices were too quiet. He only caught a few tantalizing scraps, like *vile objects* and *what I have to do* and *the sooner you shall be a widow.*

But she wasn't sure how much he'd heard. Her dark eyes took on a wary cast. Interesting.

Not. Not interesting. He had a real case now, one that would be far more of a challenge than checking out a few society bachelors. What had he decided, just a few minutes ago in the lobby? Right.

He said, "Listen, I came up here to tell you I'm dropping your case. Another client has an emergency. Men's lives are on the line. I can't waste my time husband hunting for you. I'll give you your money back and a referral and say so long." He put a hand to his inner coat pocket for the sixty greenbacks Camonte had paid him.

"Don't be ridiculous. You're not dropping my case."

He lowered his hand. "And why not?"

Her lashes veiled her eyes and her lips turned up in a crimson curve. With a whisper of silk she moved toward him. Her perfume curled around him, as delicate and rich as a rare flower.

"Because you don't want to." Her voice was a velvety rasp. "You want to stay on my case. You want to help me, don't you? That's the real reason you're here." She reached out one fingertip and brushed it lightly down the outside of his hand to the tip of his little finger.

Desire shocked through him as fierce as a lightning strike. He drew a quick, hard breath as his blood rushed across his skin and heated his groin.

No. Unacceptable. He refused to get hard over a smile and a touch like some stupid kid. He ground his teeth and forced himself under control, narrowing his eyes at Karlova. This girl didn't realize what she was messing with.

But damn if she wasn't right. He did want stay to on her case, desperately. His curiosity about Elizaveta Karlova had him in the grip of compulsion. It was pointless to pretend otherwise. But he gave it his best shot. He gestured to the door behind her. "Why don't we go in your room and talk."

She blinked at him, as if he'd surprised her. "We can't. This isn't my room."

And you don't want your family to see me. "Well, where is your room?"

"None of your business."

"Maybe I should ask your grandmother." He reached past her for the doorknob.

The girl darted sideways to block him. "All right," she said with an exasperated huff. "It's room 505. Meet me there in half an hour, and we'll talk. Now go!" She opened the door, whisked through, and shut it with a snap.

Through the door, he heard a muffled sentence in a sharp questioning tone. Then Miss Karlova's voice, "Nobody. Just a message from someone I hired to do a little research for me."

Nobody. That's me, nobody.

A few minutes later, he was standing in front of room 505.

He took a slender case of lock-picks out of his overcoat pocket and set to work on the lock. When it was dark enough, he could turn fully shadow and slip under doors or through keyholes, but when there was too much light to use his power, he had his backup skills.

He got the door open in less than a minute and slipped through, shutting and re-locking it behind him. The curtains were drawn, casting the room into murk. He didn't bother turning on a lamp as he looked the place over.

It was a humble abode, for the Drake Hotel. Fancy bed, well-stuffed sitting area, a door to a bathroom tucked discreetly in one corner. He saw a furtive movement, but quickly realized it was only his reflection in a full-length mirror standing against a wall.

He walked to the closet and opened it, examining the contents. On the floor were neat rows of shoes and two scuffed suitcases that had been through the ports of half the world, judging by the stamps. A shelf above contained stacks of hatboxes. Hanging on the rod were dresses and coats, hand tailored to mold perfectly to Elizaveta's taut, slender body. Some were wrapped and tagged as if they'd never been worn. He ran his fingers carefully over each of the garments, feeling the fine materials for suspicious lumps sewn into seams, or tucked into hat linings, or stuffed into shoes. But he found nothing.

He shut the closet and moved on to the dresser to sift through the drawers. He found gloves and handkerchiefs. Stockings. Nightgowns. Underwear. The delicate cloth slipped through his probing fingers, silky and lacy, and scented with that subtle, luscious perfume.

There was nothing hidden under the slippery folds of fabric. He shut the drawer harder than he had to and turned toward the desk.

In the desk drawers he found routine correspondence from a bank and a solicitor in New York, a journal in an indecipherable shorthand, a packet of personal letters from a Mrs. DeForest, and an invitation to a soiree at the home of Amos Mannering in Edgewater, scheduled for tomorrow night.

Underneath the desk was a locked wooden chest. He

made short work of the simple lock and opened the lid. Inside were narrow velvet lined compartments, each holding a small bottle of yellowish liquid. He took one out and unstoppered it. Cautiously, he held it to his nose.

Fragrance flooded his senses. Delicate yet earthy, like sunlight on dewdrops. Perfume. He looked down into the case at the identical bottles. An entire trunk full of perfume.

Thoughtfully he put the bottle back, re-locked the trunk and tucked it away where he found it. He was about to search the bathroom when he heard a soft footstep outside the door and a scrape of a key in a lock.

Damn. She'd finished up with the grandmother much sooner than he expected. He snapped into full shadow, hiding his presence in the darkness of the heavily curtained room, invisible and intangible.

The door opened and Elizaveta's shape appeared, silhouetted against the light from the hall. Her hat was on her head and her coat slung over her shoulders. He waited, resigned, for her to step into the room and flick on the lights. When that happened, it would force him out of the shadow, his body growing solid and visible. The girl would see him and instantly realize he'd been rifling through her things.

Maybe he'd get lucky, and she'd fire him on the spot. Then he'd start work on Camonte's case with no distractions. But damn, his pride would take a beating. He'd never been caught snooping before, but today he'd been caught twice by the same woman. *Getting sloppy over her,* he thought as he braced himself for the glare of electric light.

It never came.

12

The girl's eyes narrowed. She tipped her head up slightly and her nostrils flared, as if she were scenting the air. Hadn't she made the same gesture earlier today at his office?

She stood in the doorway, eyes gleaming. Her hands were out of her pockets and bare of gloves. She stepped inside and shut the door. Ignoring the light switch on the wall, she moved further into the room with a predatory grace.

Now was his chance. He could shift past her though the darkness, slip his shadow self out underneath the door, and walk off down the hall. She would never know he had been in her room.

He should leave. But he didn't. He drifted slowly through the shadows along the walls, watching her.

She opened her closet with a snap and looked into it for a moment before she took off her coat and hat and hung them up. Still in the darkness, she walked past the open door of the darkened bathroom, lingering just slightly before continuing on across the room to the tall, luxurious bed. With a swift movement she knelt and looked under it.

He watched her, fascinated. Was she looking for an intruder? But if she suspected someone was hiding in her room, wouldn't she be more nervous? Instead she seemed as self-assured as a cat stalking a mouse. And she must see in the dark like a cat, too, since she hadn't turned on the light.

She stood up, a line between her brows, and tipped her nose to the air again. Slowly she walked to the full-length mirror standing against the wall.

She faced the dim shape of her reflection in the glass, and Mark saw a smile on her full mouth.

Riveted, he watched her reach for the belt at her waist. She took it off slowly, held it out in one hand, and let the black length slip through her white fingers to the floor. She lifted her hands to her throat and trailed them down to the jacket buttons nestled between her breasts. Slowly, one after another, she popped them free. When the jacket was loose, she shimmied it off her shoulders and let it fall at her feet. Her crimson blouse was next, falling silkily atop the jacket. Her hands went to the fastening of her skirt. With a twitch of her hips, the black fabric slid down her long legs to pool around the black pumps on her slender feet.

He watched her move in the mirror, long, slim curves shifting under a black slip and stockings.

He shouldn't be doing this. It was wrong. He had to go, now. But he couldn't move. He could only look, helpless, a statue made of shadow.

It had been years since he'd succumbed to his baser instincts like this. For one terrible period when he was nineteen he had stalked the night streets in his shadow form, slipping through keyholes and under doors, sliding up the walls of buildings at night to reach the open windows. Ghosting inside darkened rooms. Settling into shadowed corners to spy on people. From the darkness he watched them talking and fighting and drinking. And having sex.

Mostly, he spied on women. Clothed and naked, awake and asleep. Taking men into their beds and into their bodies. He watched their moving breasts, their twining limbs, their soft skin. Faces lost in mysterious female pleasure.

Night after night. Torturing himself with what he would never have.

And seeing it now, this unattainable vision, was just as incredible and painful as it was then.

It was one of the worst parts of his power that even when his body was intangible, he lusted. He could touch nothing, and nothing could touch him, but that didn't matter. He wanted Elizaveta Karlova. Need tore at the substance of his being like a riptide in the darkness.

He drifted closer, captivated. His presence shivered through the space around her, the shadows growing denser and thicker.

The shifting, roiling darkness might have raised the hackles on another woman. Not Elizaveta. She was gazing into the glass again, but not at herself. Instead her eyes fastened on the reflection of the room over her shoulder at the exact place his presence occupied in the shadows behind her. As if she saw him standing there, watching her. *Impossible.*

He saw her lips move in the mirror. In her low, purring voice she said, "I know you're here. Somehow, you're here, watching me. You like to look at me, don't you? Wouldn't you like to touch me?" She raised her hands and slid the straps of her chemise off her shoulders. The silk poured down her tiny waist, over the sweet flare of her hips, into a pool of black at her feet. Brassiere, panties, stockings and garters. Black silk on even silkier white skin. Black lace over the taut curves of her bottom, her firm, high breasts. "Show yourself and you can touch me."

She knew he was there. How? He forgot the question the next instant as she bent at the waist and untied her garters. She rolled her stockings down her long, slim legs one by one, her rounded bottom tipped up, luring the clasp of a man's hands.

In the mirror past her upturned bottom, he saw a pale glimmer in the air where his face would be. His shadow self was taking on substance and reality, his desire for her wrenching his control away. In seconds his power would fail him and she would see him.

Her stockings and shoes gone, she straightened up and stretched in a luxuriant arc. She twined her slender arms over her head, then slowly lowered them, reaching behind her back to the fastening of her brassiere. In the mirror he saw her perfect breasts jutting out, her eyes once again on the shadow where his presence hid.

"Mark." She shaped his name on a breath.

He broke. He bolted past her through the shadow to the door and forced his intangible being through the gap underneath it. The overhead lights in the hallway forced him back into solid flesh and he materialized already running. He hurried to the stairs and didn't stop until he hit the street.

He stood panting on the sidewalk outside the hotel. The sun was going down, sliding behind the tall, purple shapes of the buildings. The day had waned fast since he'd stepped through the doors of the Drake. He strode away down the street, his newly shaped flesh still throbbing with desire. He found a telephone booth in a drugstore a few blocks south. He put in his nickel and had the operator connect him with the Drake hotel.

When the desk man answered he said, "I want you to take a message up to Miss Karlova in room 505. No, I don't want you to connect me with her room telephone. Just send up a note saying Van Ryn can't make the appointment today but he'll be in contact." He hung up. He was far too rattled to spar with the girl any more tonight. He was still half hard from watching her, his organ pulsing thickly between his legs.

But battling with the heat was shame, and fury at himself. He wasn't a half-crazed boy of nineteen anymore, recklessly spying on anyone and everyone. He was a grown man, who knew how to act civilized. When he came to his senses seven years ago, he swore he would never abuse his power like that again, like Dr. Jekyll swearing off Mr. Hyde. He would spy only in the course of legitimate investigations, never to titillate his own disgraceful lusts. And he'd succeeded in taming himself, until tonight.

But mere seconds in Elizaveta's presence had destroyed every shred of discipline and self-respect he possessed.

He had to control himself. He had to think. How had she known he was there? A few images jumbled through his mind. A case full of perfume. Her face tipped up, her nostrils flaring, as if she was scenting the air.

That was it. Scent. She'd smelled him. It seemed crazy, but it was the only explanation. She had senses acute enough to smell a shadow. She was something *different* from other people. Like him. *Find out why I'm dangerous*, she'd said. That was why.

But she didn't really understand Mark's power. She'd

made a guess, nothing more. His secret was safe, though she'd gotten far too close to it for comfort.

It was impossible for him to give up Elizaveta's case now. If his suspicions about her powerful senses were right, she might be dangerous indeed. He couldn't afford to let her out of his sight.

Even if you wanted to, his desire whispered to him.

But he still had to work his other job tonight. Camonte's case wouldn't wait. If he had to deal with Karlova too, he needed backup. He put another nickel in the telephone and started dialing.

When a familiar voice answered, he said, "It's me. Meet me at Florian's."

13

Mark had lied to Camonte when he said he had no friends or family. In fact, he had one. A friend, and the closest thing to a brother he'd ever get.

He got out of a cab on Grand Boulevard in Bronzeville, at a door with a discrete painted sign that said *Florian's*. He pushed through the entrance and stepped into a long, narrow room stretching back into the building. A scuffed wooden bar took up one of the long walls and tables crowded the rest of the space. It was dim and cool, half-full of people. Chatter and tobacco smoke filled the air.

As he walked into the place, faces turned toward him, all in shades of brown. The room abruptly went silent.

Florian's wasn't one of the colored clubs glammed up to attract white people out for a wild night on the town. This was a low-key place where a black man could a get a decent meal and a beer after his shift. They knew him here, but his arrival always drew stares.

A young man sitting at a table in the back looked over at him and grinned, white teeth flashing in a handsome, dark-skinned face. He was a lean, high-cheekboned fellow with big brown eyes and a generous mouth. Standing, he would be on the tall side, though not as tall as Mark. He looked self-assured and smart in a respectable brown suit, like life had been treating him well.

Mark let himself smile back as he strode through the restaurant to his table. In his wake, the babble of conversation resumed, though more muted than before.

"Hello Frasier," he said, sliding into the seat across from the man.

"Mark, my brother. Good to see you."

"Likewise," Mark said, meaning it.

Mark, Frasier, and Frasier's older sister Opal had grown up together in the Van Ryn house, raised by Frasier's widowed mother, the housekeeper. Mama Elnore was kindly enough, but life had knocked the personality out of her long before her kids and Mark entered the picture. Still, Mark was fond of her, and of Opal.

But he and Frasier had a deeper bond. They'd lied for each other and spied for each other and taken beatings for each other. They'd shared secrets and dreams. Frasier was the only person who understood Mark's power.

He'd been Mark's constant companion and ally against the world until the year they both turned twelve and Mark's father shipped him off to boarding school in Pennsylvania. He didn't come home again for seven years, but Frasier wrote to him faithfully all that time. And when he'd finally escaped the school, only to see his world fall apart, it was Frasier who helped him find a reason to keep going.

Frasier had two glasses of beer on the table in front of him. Pushing one over to Mark, he said, "I was glad to get your call. It's been a while since I heard from you. Weeks."

Mark took a mouthful of beer, to be polite. "I've been

real busy. Listen, I need to talk to Florian. I want his help with a case."

"You have a new case? What is it?"

"I'll tell you and Florian together. Save some time."

"Then let's go see him. You've got me curious." Frasier stood and walked over to talk to the fellow at the bar.

The barman, a wiry old bird in a vest and white shirt-sleeves, was methodically polishing glasses. Frasier leaned across the bar and spoke to him. The fellow flicked a glance at Mark, thought for a minute, and nodded.

Frasier looked over at Mark and jerked his chin.

Mark got up and followed his friend around the bar to a door leading into the back rooms. A couple of toughs leaning their chairs against the wall nearby watched them go in, but said nothing.

They walked down a carpeted L-shaped hallway to a wooden door, standing cracked open.

Frasier knocked on the doorframe. A deep voice with a Southern accent said, "Come in."

Frasier pushed open the door and stepped inside, Mark on his heels.

The room was small and dark, the high windows casting a gray light across two straight-backed chairs, a set of filing cabinets, and a hard-working desk.

Behind the desk sat a man reading a ledger. He closed his book and watched them come in with eyes that had long ago lost any expression of surprise or curiosity. They were very dark eyes, to go with his very dark skin lined with fifty-odd years of hard living. He wore a respectable brown suit, and some extra weight around the middle, but under-neath was the toughness of a fighter who'd somehow made it out of his youth alive.

He was the owner of several businesses and properties

in Bronzeville, some reputable, some very much not, but all fronts for his various rackets. The colored aldermen danced to his tune at city hall, and no wonder. Florian—and he had no other name that anyone knew of—was a man to fear.

Or so Mark would think, if he ever feared anyone.

"Mr. Florian," Frasier said with a careful nod.

"Mr. Robinson," the older man drawled, "and Mr. Van Ryn. Well now." He gestured to the chairs in front of his desk with a hand full of scarred-up knuckles.

When they sat, he leaned back in his desk chair and smiled with a flash of gold teeth. "It's been a while since I've seen you in these parts, Mr. Van Ryn."

"I've been around, Mr. Florian," Mark said.

At night when the darkness was thickest, he would unleash his power and go roving through the streets and alleys of Chicago, invisible and untouchable. He slipped into bars and theaters and casinos and brothels, Florian's joints included. But he only dropped the shadow and let himself be seen if he was stopping a beating or a robbery.

So, yeah, he'd been around, only no one had seen him.

Florian said, "So what brings you boys to visit me?"

"My friend here wants to ask a favor," Frasier said.

Florian blinked sleepily. "That so?"

"I'm looking for information on some people," Mark said. He took Karlova's list of playmates out of his pocket and pushed it across the desk.

Florian glanced it over. "And who are these fellas?"

"Classy mugs with big wallets and big houses. The kind who don't notice the hired help." Which made them perfect targets for Florian's network of informants.

People of color worked in every important establishment in Chicago as waiters, cooks, and maids. They had eyes and ears everywhere, and since they were nearly invisible to the whites they served, they had no trouble finding out all kinds of juicy secrets. And then those secrets, like everything else that wasn't quite legal in the black community, found their way to Florian.

The older man said, "What do you want to know about these classy boys?"

"Scandals. Rumors. Dirty secrets. Anything you've got."

"And what would you do with that information?"

"I'm investigating them for a client. I can't say more about that, but I can pledge any information you give me will stay confidential. And there's one other name I want to add to the list. A Miss Elizaveta Karlova."

Out of the corner of his eye, he saw Frasier look at him sharply.

He continued, "Another high roller, new in town. Staying at the Drake Hotel. I want to know where she goes and who she sees."

"Anything else?"

"That's all. I'll pay a good price for any tips that pan out."

"Well, I'm sure you will, Mr. Van Ryn. You've always been a righteous man. Don't think I've forgotten."

No, he didn't think Florian had forgotten how he'd proved himself on the zombie master. In fact, he was counting on it.

The year Mark turned nineteen was a landmark in his life for many reasons. That was the year his ability to turn full shadow manifested. And it was the year that set him on the road to becoming a private detective when Frasier brought him his first case.

Colored men in Frasier's neighborhood, young and healthy men, had started sickening and dying. And then their corpses vanished from the cemetery and the morgue.

The police were making no progress and weren't trying to. Fear started to grow.

In desperation, Frasier turned to his strange and powerful friend for help. Frasier had always known about Mark's affinity for shadow, though they never spoke about it. It was just something his friend accepted about him, like his skin and hair. But Frasier believed that Mark was the only match for the curse gripping Bronzeville.

Mark had been in the middle of the worst time of his life when Frasier had come to him. Staying in his shadow form most of his waking hours, wandering invisible through the streets at night, slipping into darkened rooms to watch strangers from the corners, as desperate for human contact as a drunk for a bottle. Wallowing in adolescent misery. He'd figured helping his friend would be a better way to spend his time. Anything would be. He was heartily bored with himself by then.

So he'd done it. He'd tracked the corpse thief down. It turned out to be a white doctor. Under the pretense of running a charity clinic, he was dosing colored men with an experimental drug. When they died, he stole their corpses and kept on experimenting. He claimed he was trying to reanimate them. And he'd been having some success, from what Mark had seen when he cornered him in his lair.

Mark got him locked up in an insane asylum.

That was seven years ago. But the black community hadn't forgotten. He'd earned a lot of favors with that case, including from Florian. His brother-in-law had been one of the victims.

But that debt only got him in the door. Florian was a businessman, not a sentimental fool. He said, "I appreciate your offer of monetary compensation, I surely do. But an agreement between gentlemen needs something more. A show of trust."

"Well then, let me give you some advice, gentleman to gentleman. Keep everyone you can away from Gabriel Camonte for now. Him, and all his top boys."

Camonte mostly left the colored neighborhoods to themselves, but Florian still had to buy his beer and liquor from Camonte's Outfit, like everyone else in Chicago. And if the thing targeting the Outfit was getting bigger and stronger, Mark wanted innocent people out of its way. And even the not-so-innocent.

Florian raised his eyebrows. "That all?"

"All I can say. But I'm dead serious. Keep as far away as you can."

Florian nodded thoughtfully. "To tell you the truth, I've heard about a few questionable events involving those fellas in recent days. I believe that's good advice you gave me, son. I'll put the word around about the fancy boys on that list."

"And Elizaveta Karlova," he said. Then he wished he hadn't.

Florian flashed another gold-edged smile. "And your flossy twist too, by all means."

Mark kept his mouth shut this time.

"I'll be seeing you boys," Florian said. He opened up the ledger on his desk again and bent over it.

14

Mark and Frasier took their cue and left the office, walking back down the hall.

"I've got to get going," Mark said as they neared the door back to the bar.

"Why don't you come join me for dinner? You're always welcome around here," Frasier said.

Mark knew this was a polite lie. He was tolerated in most places, but welcomed nowhere.

The high-class society he'd been born into looked at him with disgust and pity, and the working class added superstitious fear.

The colored people he knew treated him better than most, since they were still grateful to him for capturing the zombie master. They even felt sorry for him, a little. But he'd never belong with them.

He said, "I can't. I've got to get to work."

Frasier stopped and said seriously, "You need to tell me more about this, Mark."

Mark rubbed a knuckle over his top lip, thinking.

"You're right, I do. I'll need your help. Your professional help."

Frasier's eyes brightened. "No kidding? With the case about the dame or the one about Camonte?"

Mark didn't answer.

"Mark!"

"It's only a hunch right now. I expect I'll have more in a day or two. I'll come by your office then."

"You do that," he grumbled. "But about this Karlova cutie—"

"How do you know she's a cutie? Maybe she's sixty-eight, with a squint and a limp."

"Please. The way you said her name back there? She's a honey all right, and she sounds like trouble."

"Of course she's trouble. She's a dame. But you don't have to worry she'll get a hook in me, Frasier, if that's what's bugging you. You know the skirts aren't my line." He saw Frasier was about to argue, so he said, "Speaking of which, how's Opal?"

His friend glared at him, then sighed. "She's fine. She's expecting a new baby in a few months."

"That's great. Congratulations. Your mother must be thrilled."

And he? He was happy for her. He really was. It had been a long time since the summer Frasier's sister had broken his heart.

At nineteen, back home after graduating from the boarding school, Mark had found himself suddenly thrust into the exotic world of females. He'd been cloistered away from them in the wilds of Pennsylvania for seven years, but now suddenly they were everywhere. Soft little fragrant, giggling creatures he had no idea what to do with.

Because of his father's social connections and wealth, Mark had been invited to a few parties for debutants in search of fiancées. Young girls had been offered up for him to dance with or stammer pleasantries to, like maidens sacrificed to an ogre.

They stared at him with frozen smiles, murmured politely, and skipped off as fast as they could to whisper and laugh to each other, occasionally darting looks at him with shiny eyes. It was hideous.

But at home, there was Frasier's sister, Opal. She was still living there with her mother, taking on more and more of Mama Elnore's housekeeping duties. Whenever she saw him, she smiled at him and took his hand. She even kissed his cheek when he first came back to his father's house. And she was so familiar yet changed, so pretty and so kind that he had trembled at the touch of her fingers and her lips with all the violence of first love. Looking back, he could only laugh at what a damn chucklehead he was.

A few weeks after he got home, his father finally succeeded in drinking himself to death. When the will was read, Mark learned that he was a lot poorer than he thought. The family chemical manufacturing company, once the finest in Chicago, had been sold, the proceeds gone to pay his father's debts. All that was left was money for college, a small annuity from his mother's estate, a car, and the house. The party invitations ceased.

Mark didn't care. In romantic fashion that would have done Rudolph Valentino proud, he asked Opal to marry him, storming and ranting and making grandiose plans. It didn't matter what anyone thought of them! He would take her to Paris and marry her there. That free-thinking city would accept them in a way no city in the States would.

They could live out their love, with fluffy clouds and cherubs and everything. Only, he figured out too late that it was his dream, not hers.

Opal's dream was a nice normal life with a nice normal boy. Not exile with a white freak. He'd mistaken her pity for something more. Finding that out was a real kick in the gut.

He'd brought it on himself, though. That night after he proposed to her he'd wrapped himself in his half-shadow and listened at the kitchen door as Opal talked about him to Mama Elnore.

He could hear her words now, like a record on a phonograph. *"Of course I won't marry him Mama. You know I feel sorry for him, but I could never love him. I can't stand the thought of him touching me. And it's not just the way he looks. There's something wrong about him. There always has been. He scares me."*

But she'd done him a favor, really. She'd opened his eyes to the truth about himself. He was a monster, and he would be alone for the rest of his life.

Except for Frasier, who stubbornly wouldn't let him go.

His friend said, "Mama will tell you all about it when you come to Sunday dinner." Mama Elnore had moved in with Opal when she got married to a normal boy years ago. Frasier had his own place in Bronzeville, and so Mark was alone in his father's mansion. But Frasier still dragged Mark to his family's Sunday dinners from time to time, the obstinate son-of-a-gun.

Mark said, "I'll try, but I'm really busy with these cases."

Frasier pressed his lips together. But he said, "All right. See you soon, brother."

Mark nodded and strode out of the bar. He heard an

eager murmur of voices rise behind him just before the door swung shut.

Out on the street, he stopped at the edge of a pool of light cast by a buzzing streetlamp. The sky was full dark, the sun gone beyond the curve of the earth. Shadow poured into him like water into parched ground. He tipped his head up toward the blackening sky and parted his lips a little. He could almost taste the darkness curling over his tongue.

The power in his bones stirred, reaching for the darkness beyond the city lights, beyond the earth, all the way out between the stars. *Come,* it whispered. *Fall into the ocean of night and let it bear you away from pain, fear, loneliness, grief. Come into the loving darkness.* He'd heard that whisper all his life, and he'd always known that if he yielded to it, he would be lost to the real world forever.

That was why he always stayed close to the ground when he used his power, why he took to sliding over floors or along walls in his shadow form. Without solid objects to ground him, he knew he would lose himself in the dark. His body would dissolve into shadow and vanish as if he'd never been.

But thanks to Frasier, he'd found a reason to stay in the real world. He had puzzles to solve, questions to answer, battles to fight. A job to do. And he'd better get to it.

He had to talk to another guy tonight, though this one would be far less happy to see him than Frasier.

He grinned in anticipation and walked away from the light of the streetlamp, into the night. Between one step and the next he let the power loose and burst into shadow. One second he was there, and the next he was a black wind sweeping through the city, down bustling streets and smoking alleys, over paperboys and hustlers and bankers, past skyscrapers, tenements, hooch parlors, drugstores, concrete packed with human flesh and roaring cars, night pricked with cold lights, all the way to Chicago Police Head-quarters.

15

Police Headquarters was a fifteen-story brick building in the Loop at 11th and State. It had just been finished five years ago, remarkably only a little over time and over budget and with only the usual amount of corruption. When Mark shoved through the brass and glass front doors, the cut marble lobby was almost empty. The bustle of cops, lawyers, and clerks slowed at night, but there were still a few people around to rubberneck at him.

The lights above were weak enough for him to hide in half-shadow, but he didn't bother, tipping his chin at the cops manning the desk as he strolled past them to the elevators. The desk cops, a fat one on the edge of his pension and a skinny rookie, whispered to each other and stared. They knew who he was. Everyone in the building knew. And he knew them, much better than they thought.

When he first fell into detective work, he decided he'd better get some training. He shadowed cops on their beats and detectives out on cases and learned police business, like who was grafting, and how to beat a confession out of a guy with a rubber hose. And along the way, he picked up a point or two on catching criminals.

He got to know the police pretty well, though he rarely let them see him. He'd saved a cop from getting gunned in the back once, and run down a few thieves for them, broken up plenty of fights and stopped some bank robberies. But usually, he stayed in the shadows. Unless he wanted to remind them he was out there in the dark, watching.

He grinned cheerily at the desk cops as he stepped into the elevator and got to see the rookie go pale before the doors closed.

The elevator was a sharp, modern, high-speed contraption that took him down to the sub-basement level with the push of a button.

He walked out of the elevator and through a web of corridors to a kind of blister off of a hallway that had a set of filing cabinets and a desk crammed into it.

At the desk sat a rawboned man in his late thirties, sucking down a cigarette. There was a mountain of ashes in the tray by his elbow and a mess of files on his blotter. He was reading over the top level of paper with a sour frown. His gray suit was as lank as his hair.

He looked up and saw Mark coming. His sallow cheeks quivered. "Great," he said through a thick cloud of smoke. "Just what I needed tonight. I got a medium scam and a ghost dog to deal with already, so do me a favor and get lost, freak."

"Nice to see you too, O'Bannion. How's the lumbago?"

"Go to hell."

"I've been there already," Mark deadpanned. "It's not so bad. You'll fit right in someday."

O'Bannion squinted at him, maybe half wondering if Mark was serious.

Detective Lloyd O'Bannion was the unlucky bastard the police had sent to take the zombie master off Mark's hands once he'd caught him. But after the doctor was straight-jacketed and the mobile corpses incinerated, the Police Commissioner's main concern was to quarantine the madness. He made O'Bannion Mark's official police contact, moved him to the night shift, and put him in charge of all the weird shit the Department wanted to pretend never happened.

Whenever a fortune-teller got robbed or a couple of circus geeks tried to knife each other, O'Bannion's desk was where they landed. Whenever Mark had a curse to break or a cult to destroy, O'Bannion had to haul the villains off to the clink.

And since the other cops now avoided him like a hooker with the clap, he'd probably be stuck on weird shit duty for the rest of his career.

"What do you want?" the cop growled.

"I need to get into some old case files," Mark said.

"What cases?"

He reeled off the names of Camonte's dead men. Camonte had given him the police reports on their deaths, but not their arrest records and legal files, which Mark bet were thick as encyclopedias.

He intended to look for files on Karlova's boyfriends too, but O'Bannion didn't need to know that.

The cop made a show of looking confused. "Who are these mooks?"

Mark eyed him thoughtfully. The police reports Camonte had shown him hadn't mentioned O'Bannion, though he had to have been looped in on the slayings from the first. The dead men were too notorious, and the way they died too bizarre. So why was he faking ignorance? In fact, why was he in his office grumbling over mediums and ghost dogs instead of pounding the streets to get the killer?

He said, "Those mooks are gangsters. Dead gangsters. Worked for Gab Camonte, before they got eaten from the inside out. Sound familiar?"

The cop stared at him and blew smoke out of his nose.

"Anyway, I've been hired to find the killer."

"Hired by who? Camonte?"

Mark tipped his head.

O'Bannion smiled nastily. "Then you're out of luck. Camonte and his boys are on their own. No more special consideration from the Department. That's the word from the top."

Mark raised his eyebrows. "Since when? I thought Camonte had city hall by the short hairs."

"Times change. Prohibition's on the way out. No more need for bootleggers. Camonte's little empire is coming down, and everyone knows it. If the hoods start dropping dead for us, who's going to complain?"

Mark leaned a hand on the cop's desk. "It won't just be hoods dropping dead, O'Bannion. There's a monster loose out there. If someone doesn't stop it, innocent people will get hurt. The ones you're supposed to serve and protect, remember?"

"You think I need your help to do my job?" O'Bannion tapped his cigarette at his ashtray, somehow missing his aim and scattering hot ashes over Mark's hand.

Mark didn't so much as twitch. He stared the other man down. "Yes. You need me to catch this thing before it eats some kid or a little old lady. And to do that, I need those files."

O'Bannion lowered his eyes. "Nothing I can do."

Mark took his hand away from the desk, flicking the ashes off. "If Camonte's on his way out, then who's on his way in? Who's giving the orders to cut the Outfit loose?"

"None of your concern, boyo. Now piss off."

Mark turned and sauntered back the way he came.

O'Bannion said, "Wait."

Mark stopped and cast a bored glance over his shoulder.

"The World's Fair is starting in a few days. Thousands of hayseeds are coming to town to spend their money, and Chicago needs every cent. The big boys aren't going to tolerate any freak business fucking up the fair, so watch yourself. Don't make trouble."

"I don't cause problems, O'Bannion. I solve them. But it's sweet of you to care."

The cop looked like he wanted to throw the ashtray at him.

Mark laughed and walked on down the hall. He turned a corner, stopped. Waited and listened.

He heard the man swear under his breath, shifting in his seat and shuffling paper. When he went quiet, Mark pulled shadow around himself and silently drifted back around the corner and down the hall, right past O'Bannion.

If the cop looked directly at Mark, he would see him. But his eyes stayed clamped on his paperwork.

Mark made it down the hallway and around the next corner. He wove through a network of corridors he'd come to know well over the years, empty except for a few straggling clerks. They walked past him without a look, his shadows sliding him right through their tired awareness.

He came to the archive room, locked tight. His lock

picks took care of that quickly. Past the door was a huge, low space full of filing cabinets, an empty clerk's desk to one side. He locked the door behind him and set to work hunting through the files.

16

By three o'clock, Mark was finished with the police files. He left the building and made his way to his favorite all-night diner on Mulry Street for breakfast. The counterman, whose name he never tried to learn in return for the same, silently brought him his usual ham and eggs and left him alone as he poured over his notes.

After breakfast, he headed home. It was that brief, silent time after the drunks and the hookers had found beds to get into but before the early morning laborers got out of theirs. Only a few people wove furtively under the street-lamps. Only a few cars growled through the echoing streets.

One of them, a Buick, tore past him down the road a couple of blocks from his house. He got an impression of three men in the car, two big brutes and one scrawny figure with a pale, lopsided face.

What's their hurry, he wondered. But when he got to his house, he found something else to think about.

It seemed he had visitors. Two big black Lincolns were parked on the curb and his front door had been rudely smashed in.

He gathered his shadows and slipped around the house to the back lot. He checked over the garage, but the intruders hadn't made it that far yet. The doors were closed and locked, and through the grimy window he could see the long shape of his car still shrouded in its tarpaulin.

He turned back to the house. On the corner near the kitchen was the old coal chute, unused and padlocked shut. He slipped his shadow self through the narrow crack in the slanted doors and down the concrete ramp into the basement.

He stole up from the basement to the first floor. The place had been tossed. In the kitchen, food and crockery was in a pile on the floor, the cabinets and icebox gaping open. In the formal ballroom he had converted into a gymnasium, his barbell rack was shoved over and his punching bag was slashed open, leaking stuffing.

He heard sounds of movement coming from his office and waiting room. He slipped up to the inner waiting room door. It too was broken open.

The dim lamp in the corner was switched on. Three men were in there, one standing, two sitting. Hands on their guns.

He slid past them through the shadows along the wall to his office and looked inside. His desk and file cabinets had been ransacked. His radio was smashed, his books torn off the shelves. Drifts of paper covered the floor. McGann stood near the desk, prodding a pile of loose files with his shoe.

The thugs looked settled in. They would keep while he cleared the rest of the house.

He raced silently up the main staircase to the second story and glanced through the upstairs rooms. Empty, as always. He'd gotten rid of the furniture in the bedrooms years ago, except for his own room and one other.

When he got to his room he found his bed knifed up, clothes ripped out of the closet and the dresser. Without a second's pause, he raced down the hall to his mother's room.

The locked door had been smashed open. He stood on the threshold for a long moment, looking in. Like his father before him, he'd kept this room untouched, just as it was twenty-six years ago, the day he'd been born and she had died. But now, the beautiful, faded room lay in ruins.

He bared his teeth and let the dark power take him. In a rush of shadow he was down the stairs. Another rush, and he was in the sitting room where the intruders were waiting for him.

He turned solid, his power rippling over him and through every muscle and nerve. He picked up the nearest man out of his chair and threw him on top of the second. He flicked back into shadow as the third guy leapt up and aimed his .38 at him. He rushed close, materialized again next to the gunman and slammed a fist into his temple. As the man crumpled, he yanked the gun out of his hands.

The first two guys were scrambling to get up and draw their own guns, but Mark threw the .38 into the face of one of them, then plowed his left fist into the face of the other. Both of them collapsed.

McGann appeared in the office doorway, waving his revolver. Mark snapped into shadow and turned solid with his hand around the wrist of his gun hand. He yanked and twisted, and the revolver crashed to the floor. He hurled McGann away from the door and into the wall, following it up with a hook to the gut. He kept him from doubling over with a forearm shoved hard into his thick neck, pinning him against the wall.

He let the shadows seethe around him as he leaned into McGann, close enough to see the writhing darkness reflected in the man's terrified eyes. Very quietly, he said, "I didn't think you were stupid enough to come into my house twice, McGann. Tell me why I shouldn't kill you right now."

"It wasn't us!" McGann choked out. "We just got here! We found the dump like this! The door was broke, so we came in here lookin' for you!"

"If it wasn't you, then who?"

"How the hell should I know?" He started yanking at Mark's arm, some of his fight returning. "You gotta have a million enemies, freak! We saw some guys run out and get in a Buick, that's all!"

Mark's mind flashed on the Buick he'd seen tearing down the street away from his house. Too late to follow them now. Damn. Who the hell were they? And what did they want? To send a message? Or were they looking for something?

"Say I believe you. What are you doing here?"

"The boss sent us. There's been another murder."

Mark stepped back and let McGann go. The guy shoved himself off the wall and furiously straightened his clothes. "You're asking for a bullet in the back, freak."

Mark paid him no attention, wheeling on the pile of gangsters lying on the floor and groaning. He grabbed the youngest-looking one by his coat, hauled him to his feet, and dragged him out of the waiting room, through the hall and out the broken front door. He planted the kid on his front stoop and said into his terrified, gawping face, "Stay right here and make sure no one else gets into the house. If you do a runner before I come back, I'll hunt you down. And when I find you, I won't be happy. Got it?"

The gunsel nodded frantically.

McGann and his boys had limped out after him. "Well?" Mark said to them. "Don't stand there like idiots. We've got a murder to solve." He strode off to the cars.

17

McGann and his banged-up crew didn't drive Mark back to the Drake. Instead, the two cars sped north across the river to Old Town. They turned into a street off of Wells lined with Queen Anne houses that had decayed into tenements a decade ago and were now spending their afterlives as brothels.

The two Lincolns pulled up in front of a house that had an apple-cheeked young beat cop standing in front of it. The gangsters slowly and painfully piled out of the cars and limped past the cop to the door, Mark following along at a leisurely pace.

Inside were a few half-naked girls draped across the parlor furniture, but they looked more terrified and exhausted than alluring.

Mark made a point of ignoring the women. He'd seen their wares plenty of times before. Hell, back during his crazy period seven years ago he'd watched hookers servicing their clients from the shadows just about every night. Though he never showed himself to them in the flesh, let alone tried to buy their services.

Because he'd also watched them pour hatred and contemptuous laughter over their johns the second the brothel doors closed behind them. And he knew exactly how revolting they would find him, no matter how much money he paid them to pretend otherwise. He could see it in their faces now, in how they shrank away from him as he walked past.

The two goons headed straight for the bar in one corner of the parlor, but McGann led Mark up a staircase and along a hall to a closed door. Camonte and a police detective Mark hadn't met stood in front of it, talking in low tones. The detective's clothes were buttoned crooked, and he wavered on his feet. Stone drunk, by the smell. He could be safely ignored.

No sign of the coroner yet. Looked like the wheels of justice were turning extra slow tonight.

Camonte rounded on him as he approached. "Where the hell have you been?" He wore pajamas and a smoking jacket. His face was yellow-gray, sweat beading on his scalp.

Mark ignored his question. "What are you doing here?"

"What do you think? I'm hiding. Too many people knew I was staying at the Drake. After you left, I came out here on the down-low. Fat lot of good it did me."

"I hear you got another dead guy."

"Frankie Torelli. My driver."

"Same thing that killed the others?"

"You tell me." He knocked open the door.

Inside was a bathroom. A pool of water covered the grubby tile floor. In front of the toilet were trousers pooled around a pair of men's shoes, toes pointed out, like they would be if a fellow were sitting on the toilet seat. Sticking up from the shoes were a pair of hairy lower legs ending in a gristly flesh-and-bone mess just below where the knees ought to be. The rest of the body was nowhere to be seen.

Mark's gaze moved to the toilet bowl where the water rippled gently. He had a pretty good idea where the rest of poor Frankie Torelli had gone.

"About two hours ago, we all heard a loud sucking noise coming from in there. We ran in and found . . . that," Camonte said.

"Nuts."

"That's all you got to say?"

Mark glanced at him and shrugged. "I told you to tell your people to stay away from drains."

Camonte turned purple.

Before he exploded, Mark said, "Was the light on when you came in?" He pointed to the flickering overhead bulb.

"Yeah. Why?"

"This creature is getting stronger. It's able to tolerate the light when it attacks. That's bad news."

"Tell me something I don't know."

"I need to take a sample." Mark glanced at the police detective, who was leaning against the wall and lightly snoring. Then he turned to McGann. "Get me a jar with a lid."

"I ain't your errand boy," McGann snarled.

Camonte wheeled on him. "Get him a fucking jar!"

McGann stomped off, swearing under his breath.

After he left, Mark said to Camonte, "Who knew you were coming here tonight?"

"Frankie, McGann, and a few of McGann's guys. You met three of them already, the ones who came to get you."

"Yeah, we met," Mark said drily. "Did anyone here make any telephone calls after you arrived?"

"Couldn't have. We disconnected the telephone line

when we got here, to be sure the girls didn't get chatty." He started pacing in tight circles.

"Anyone leave or enter?"

"Of course not. We posted guards."

"Guards can get distracted in a place like this."

"Not unless they want to see the bottom of the Chicago River."

"Is it possible you were followed from the Drake?"

"Not likely. Frankie's a good driver. Was." He stopped pacing and squinted at Mark. "You think it's one of my guys, don't you. One of them wants to bump off me and my *consigliores* and take over as *capo*."

"Hold your horses. I'm looking at all possible leads. Maybe one of your boys is a squealer, but I think you got bigger problems."

"Like what?"

"The cops, for one. They sent you a green kid and a drunk twit." He jerked his chin at the detective propping up the wall.

"He-ey," the detective slurred in protest.

"That tells you how seriously they're taking your case. And you've been having trouble with the mayor's office and the city council lately, right?"

Camonte said nothing.

Mark nodded. "Like I thought. You've got a politician after you."

"Who is it?" Camonte said softly.

"You don't have any ideas?"

"That's what I'm paying you for, kid."

"Here's an idea. Why don't you and your boys take off for Florida? That's where you usually go to let the heat die down, isn't it?"

He barked a short laugh. "What I wouldn't give to be in

Florida, under the palms, with a nice rum. But I'm in a delicate position. If I let this killer run me off now, I'll never get back in again."

"You'd have your life. And Chicago wouldn't miss you."

The boss's eyes glinted hard and shiny. "Chicago is mine."

McGann reappeared, stomping up to him and shoving a glass jar into his hand.

He took the lid off and stepped into the bathroom, splashing through the puddle on the floor to the toilet.

Avoiding the stumps of the legs, he scooped up some of the water from the bowl into the jar. He straightened and examined the it through the glass. Looked ordinary enough to him. He sniffed it. Smelled ordinary, too. He screwed the lid on tight.

"What are you going to do with that water?" McGann said.

Mark *could* tell him he was going to have it analyzed in a laboratory by one of the best scientists in the business. Instead he gave the man a toothy grin. "Do you really want to know?"

McGann shuddered and looked away.

He splashed out of the bathroom to the hallway. "I'll be in touch," he said to Camonte, and started to leave.

"That's it? That's all you've got?"

"I'm working on it. I'll have information for you after I follow up a few leads. Until then, buy a chamber pot and stay the hell away from the water system."

Camonte stepped closer and grasped his shoulder with a soft yet meaty hand. "Listen, if any more of my men die, I'm going down. And if I go down, I'm taking you with me. That's a promise from Gab Camonte."

Mark smiled. "Don't threaten me." He reached up, took

the hand off his shoulder, and dropped it. "And don't forget, I'm your only hope now that city hall gave you the kiss-off."

Camonte took a cigar out of his breast pocket and shoved it in his chops. "Just find the guy who's doing this," he said around the butt.

"Oh, I will, as long as you keep paying me. Speaking of which, I'll take my sixty bucks for today." He stuck out the hand that wasn't holding the jar.

Camonte snorted softly. "Take him where he wants to go and pay him. And don't lose him this time," he told McGann. He stumped off down the hall.

"I'm only going home for some shut-eye," Mark said to the henchman. "And I'll find my own way there. So I'll take my money now."

McGann got out a roll of dough and held between his fingers. He leveled vicious eyes at Mark. "You heard the boss, freak. Finger this killer or you're going down with the rest of us."

Mark leaned forward and let his shadow swirl across his face and behind his eyes. "I'm beginning to think you want me to hurt you, McGann. Pay me my money, or I'll grant you your wish."

McGann wisely shut up and slapped the bills into his hand.

Mark went down the stairs, past the cringing hookers, and out the front door. The rookie cop stationed outside edged away as he passed him. He started down the sidewalk at a quick pace. One more stop to make tonight before he dealt with the disaster at his house.

When he no longer felt the cop's eyes boring into his back, he let his shadow loose and vanished into the waning darkness.

He flowed through the city on a black wind, across the river, down along the Loop and back into South Side. He materialized in front of a neatly kept bungalow a couple blocks off of Cottage Grove. He knocked on the freshly painted door and kept on knocking until it was yanked open. In the doorway stood Frasier, in pajamas, robe, and slippers. He blinked at Mark with puffy eyelids. "Mark."

"Good morning, Frasier."

"Do you realize what time it is? No, forget it. Stupid question. You'd better come in and have some coffee." He started to move back to let Mark in.

"Can't. It's almost dawn. Listen, I came to ask a favor. I need you to analyze this." He held up the jar of toilet water.

Frasier rubbed his eyes and peered at the jar. "What is that?"

"Evidence." He shoved the jar into Frasier's hand. "Can you do it by tomorrow?"

"Yes, but—"

"Swell. I'll come by your office then."

"But what's this all about?"

"Sorry, gotta scram. I'll tell you everything when I see you next."

"Bless it, Mark!"

But Mark was already gone into the shadow.

18

The horizon was a pale line across the lake as Mark raced to his house. He reached his street just as the first rays of the sun shot between the buildings, forcing him out of the shadows and prickling over his newly formed skin. He winced and hunched away toward his door.

The gunsel he'd left to watch his house was still standing on the stoop where Mark put him an hour ago. The boy started like a rabbit when he stepped up to him.

"Anything happen while I was out?"

He gulped and shook his head.

"Swell. Now beat it."

The gunsel darted past Mark and took off down the street at a dead run.

Mark went inside, slammed the ruined door shut behind him, and got to work.

He spent the morning cleaning up the mess downstairs and overseeing the carpenter he hired to fix his door. He had to pay him a good chunk of the sixty bucks McGann gave him, but his house was secure again at least.

When the workman was gone, he steeled himself and

climbed the stairs to the second floor, trash bin in hand. He walked down the hall to his mother's room.

Her door was still open, and he drifted through it. He stopped in the middle of the soft carpet and surveyed the damage. The invaders had torn open his mother's closets and dumped her clothes on the floor. They had tipped over her dressing table, smashing the contents. The ghosts of scent from her broken perfume bottles hung in the air. They had stripped the bed and cut the mattress. The photograph of her and his father, taken shortly after their wedding, was torn off the wall, its frame in splinters

He knelt and picked up the photograph, carefully brushing off the slivers of glass and wood. In the picture, his mother was tiny and lovely, no more than twenty, with a sweet, round face. She was sitting posed in a chair, his father standing behind her, one hand cupping her shoulder with a tenderness Mark had never seen him show toward anyone when he was alive.

The couple in the picture was young, healthy, and plainly in love, a golden future before them. Or so they thought then. Before Mark came.

He laid the photograph aside and started picking up the pieces of the broken frame. When he got his hands on the men who did this, he vowed, he would do to them what they had done to his mother's room. He would tear them apart.

His fingers clenched at his furious thoughts. A small pain made him look at his left hand. A nail from the frame had sliced open his fingertip. Blood welled up, ruby-red against his white skin. Immediately, shadow rippled around him, wisps of darkness spiraling out of the air toward his finger, vanishing into the cut. The bleeding stopped, and the skin around the injury took on a healthy pinkish tone and started closing as the shadow healed him.

Just another thing that made him a freak, his fast healing. But it was a lucky talent to have, growing up in his father's house. Even after all the beatings, all the whiskey bottles thrown at him, his skin had no marks on it. Lucky, that was him.

He got back to work. When he'd swept up the broken stuff and hauled it out, and his mother's bed was made and her clothes hung back in her closet, only then did he allow himself to fall onto his own slashed up mattress for a few hours' sleep.

He still had plenty to do, but he needed the rest to be at his best tonight. He had a cocktail party to crash and a tricky dame to hunt down.

19

Eliza, champagne in one gloved hand and a smoldering cigarette in the other, strolled through the crowded grand salon of the Mannering House, the hem of her black silk gown frothing around her ankles. The laughter and chatter of well-liquored party guests swirled about her. The soiree to introduce her to Chicago society was in full swing, but it was time for a breath of air. Husband hunting was hard work.

She made her way to the long gallery of windows stretching across the front of the house overlooking Lincoln Park. A light evening breeze was coming in through the opened panes, caressing the bare skin of her throat and shoulders. She found Amos Mannering himself standing near one window. He was a rosy-cheeked, round-bellied man of sixty, with an avuncular smile on his face and a glass of whiskey in his hand. "Ah, the young lady of the hour," he said as she approached. "Are you enjoying yourself, my dear?"

She put on a smile and said, "Yes indeed, Amos. You're a darling to throw me such a splendid party."

"My pleasure, sweetheart. You must allow me to stand in the place of your father while you're with us. I'm sure dear Alexandrine would want it that way." A wistful note crept into his voice when he spoke her mother's name.

"*Maman* always said you were the best of men," she murmured.

Mannering was not, in fact, the best of men. No one could climb to the pinnacle of Chicago's finance industry without a great deal of underhanded ruthlessness. Unlike some of his colleagues, he didn't jump out a window after the Crash four years ago, but instead capitalized on the misfortunes of others and built a financial empire amid the ruins.

However, Mannering was not exactly a bad man either, which made him unmarriageable from her mother's perspective.

Besides, he had a harmless featherhead of a wife already, and it was family policy never to offend wives by stealing their husbands. Women were far more resistant to her family's poison than men, and it was stupid to make enemies of them.

But *Maman* had other uses for rich and powerful men besides marriage. She kept a collection of gentlemen scattered throughout the world whose purpose in life was to lay their wealth and connections at her feet. When Alexandrine had met Amos Mannering on holiday in Monte Carlo several years ago, she quickly made him one of her cavaliers.

And so, when Eliza came to Chicago, she decided to put her mother's local conquest to use. She ambushed Mannering at his office, and then it was the work of a moment to persuade him to throw a party introducing her to eligible bachelors.

"How do you like the company?" Mannering asked.

"Very well. I've met several interesting people." Especially the five prospective husbands on her list. She'd made sure that Mannering invited them, knowing for certain that they would come. When the greatest financier in the American Middle-West invited you to his home, you went.

She'd spent the evening flirting with each candidate in turn. Only one showed any hint of resistance to her, but even he would succumb after another couple of evenings exposed to her scent, she estimated. At any rate, she would have no trouble securing one of them for a husband, as soon as her detective determined which man was the worst.

Her detective . . . He'd been lingering at the back of her mind all day. Had he really been in her room last evening, watching her take off her clothes in front of the mirror? Or had she imagined his dark scent wreathing through the shadows near her bed?

Her nose had never been wrong before. And she already knew he had some hidden talent, some uncanny ability that allowed him to hunt eldritch creatures in a way no ordinary man could. She didn't know what shape his power took, but that he *had* power was beyond question. And her nose told her that he'd used it to spy on her last night, just as he'd spied on her when she came to his office.

His scent had grown richer and stronger as she took off her clothes until it abruptly vanished, leaving her alone in the dark, and feeling aroused, frustrated, and quite silly. It hadn't been some mad erotic delusion, had it? She took a sip of her champagne to hide her sudden blush.

"You're quite the social success tonight, my dear," Mannering said, drawing her out of her heated thoughts.

"You should have let us arrange a party for you when you were in town last. Three years ago, was it?"

"It was, but back then I wasn't ready to give up my bachelor girl ways."

"Yes, you were busy playing shopkeeper with that lady perfumer. What was her name? DeForest? How is the old girl?"

"She's well," Eliza said, with more hope than truth. She'd called the perfumery just this morning to ask after her, but only Millie had answered. She said the older lady was at home, resting, but had asked for Eliza to come visit her.

Eliza said she would call, but avoided promising a visit. The familiar guilt settled like lead in her heart and she took a gulp of her champagne, wishing alcohol had some effect on her. But no drink or drug known to man could affect a lamia.

"Good, good," Mannering said. "The lady is opinionated, as I recall, but she makes lovely fragrances. My wife likes them, at any rate." He gestured with his whisky glass. Eliza glanced that way and saw the faded blonde woman across the room, paying court to none other than Eliza's grandmother. Her mood soured further.

The countess had invited herself along to supervise Eliza's courtship, and the Mannerings were only too thrilled to have her. Titles were very impressive things to Americans.

"Mrs. Mannering is a saint to humor my grandmother." The poor woman was fluttering like a bird under the paw of a cat as Angelique spoke to her.

"Not at all," Amos said. "Delightful lady. Honored to have her. The more the merrier, I always say."

At that moment a powerful engine roared out on the

street, coming to a low, steady growl in front of the mansion. Throughout the salon, heads turned toward the wide front windows. Eliza looked out through the glass as a fire red Duesenberg slid up to the curb. It was monstrously long and gleaming with chrome and glass, the red paint and white wheels polished to a mirror gloss. It was an outrageous honey of a car. Exactly what she would have bought for herself to tour around the California hills, before her years in exile.

A clarion call blasted from the horns at the front, making a gawping valet leap off his stool. People started to gravitate toward the windows to look out at the new arrival. A murmur rippled through the assembled guests.

The driver got out, a striking figure in a sharp black suit, a black hat tipped low on his head. Under the shadow of the brim she caught a flash of snow-white skin. She almost dropped her glass in shock. *Mark.*

20

Mark van Ryn tossed a quarter to the valet and strolled up toward the mansion's front door.

"What the devil is he doing here?" Mannering said.

Excellent question, Eliza thought. How did he find out about this party? The invitation she'd left on her desk flashed across her mind. He *had* been in her room!

"Amos, I'm afraid this is my fault. I hired him to make an inquiry for me, remember? I think he's here to play detective."

"Oh, no. Not in my house. Not tonight." Mannering gestured to his butler, who had been hovering nearby. The man put down his tray of glasses and proceeded through the arch to the front entryway. Mannering stalked after him. Eliza set down her drink and hurried behind.

The doorbell rang.

At a gesture from Mannering, the butler opened the door. Mark stood on the stoop, his shoulders relaxed, a hint of a smile on his angel's face.

"Your invitation, sir?" the butler said, his voice glacial.

"I don't need one to drop in on an old friend." Mark

swept off his hat and shoved it into the butler's hands, his eyes already looking past him as if he were invisible. He caught sight of Mannering and his smile widened. "Isn't that right, Amos?"

Then his pale gaze landed on her like an electrical wire. "Miss Karlova."

She fought down a blush as she studied him in return. Up close she noticed that his suit, though it looked almost unworn, was several years out of date, cut in a tight-waisted style that had been replaced by the boxy modern fashions. It was also a fraction short in the sleeves and cuffs and straining across his bulky shoulders. Mark had grown since the last time he'd worn these clothes. Perhaps, like nearly everyone else since the Crash, he'd fallen on hard times and couldn't afford to update his wardrobe.

And yet, he was clearly the scion of old money. It was there in the way he wore his fine fabrics with careless ease, in the way he treated the butler like a mobile hat rack, and in the way he walked into the finest mansion in Chicago like he'd been there a hundred times before.

Invited or not, he belonged at parties like this. Even Mannering seemed to feel it. "What brings you here, Mark?" he said, a trifle subdued.

"I'm working a case for the lovely new client you sent me," he said, nodding his head at Eliza. "I'm going to circulate among your guests and see what I can see."

"Out of the question," Mannering said. "This is a social gathering, not an inquest."

"Don't worry, I'm better house-trained than my father, your old chum. I won't fall down drunk and vomit in the garden, at any rate. Why, you'll hardly even notice I'm here."

"I'm sorry, Mark, but you cannot—"

"How's your daughter these days?" That would be the daughter he'd rescued from a pack of sorcerers who were trying to reincarnate the spirit of a mummified Egyptian princess. Mannering had told Eliza all about it.

Mannering's eyes turned small. "She's quite well. In her second year at Vassar."

"So she's recovered from that drugging and brain-washing business? Must be a relief for her friends and family. But then, they don't know about it, do they?" He let the threat hang in the air.

"You wouldn't dare! You guaranteed client confidentiality!"

"I have a new client now. My loyalty is to her, as long as she pays me."

"You'd ruin my innocent daughter to get your way?"

"She didn't seem so innocent when I dragged her out of that orgy."

Mannering flushed in rage.

Mark said, "Anyway, this is business, nothing personal. Just like when you wouldn't finance Dad's debts anymore, even though he was your good friend."

Time for her to intervene. She stepped up to the older man and touched his arm. "Amos, would you allow me to talk to Mr. Van Ryn in private?" She let her scent wreathe through the air.

His eyes glazed over and his spine slackened. "Of course, Eliza my dear," he said. "Anything you like."

"Thank you, Amos." She turned to Mark. "Mr. Van Ryn, would you come with me please?"

Mark had been eying her steadily. He said, "Don't mind if I do," and strolled past Mannering to her side.

She led him through the arch into the salon. A low mutter and a ripple of sidelong looks among the party guests greeted them. An older woman in a moth-eaten sable stole edged away from Mark. Two younger matrons whispered to each other, shooting him quick glances. The men ignored him. Eliza heard a whisper come from somewhere, "Albino."

Anger on his behalf flushed over her cheeks. But Mark seemed unaffected. He sauntered into the crowd, a half-smile on his face.

Eliza suddenly realized that it wasn't only his coloring that was making people uneasy. He had an aura of sheer uncanny power, a current of unseen force running through him. His very presence disturbed and excited everyone he came near. Even the shadows seemed to shift and play around him.

She led him toward a doorway to Mannering's study off the far end of the salon. But halfway there, he took her elbow in a firm grip. Fortunately she was wearing long gloves, so his hand never touched her bare skin.

"Let's not go off alone together," he said. "I'll buy you a drink instead." He tugged her toward the bar at one side of the room.

"The drinks are free," she said, letting him steer her by her elbow.

"In that case, you can buy me a drink." To the bartender, he said, "Whiskey, neat. And for the lady . . . ?" He arched an eyebrow at her.

"Champagne."

"Of course." He took the glass the bartender gave him and sniffed the contents. "Ah, the real stuff. Just like my dad used to drink." He didn't sip it, she noticed.

She took her own drink and, glass in one hand and cigarette in the other, led him to a quieter corner of the room, where she leveled a look at him. "Now then. What are you doing here?"

"I'm investigating the targets you gave me."

"I'd hoped for more discretion."

"You'll get over the embarrassment of being seen with me."

"Don't be ridiculous, darling. I'm more concerned that the gentlemen will realize they're being inspected. I don't' want you to frighten them off."

"I won't. I'll drift around and see what I can pick up. I'll be subtle."

"You call that entrance you made subtle?"

He grinned. "No, that was just plain fun. But trust me, I can be practically invisible when I want."

She looked into his eyes, thinking of what she'd done in front of the mirror last night, surrounded by the scent of an invisible watcher. "Can you? Can you turn invisible and watch people, Mark?"

A flash of heat lit his ice-blue gaze and a red flush ran over his snowy skin. The hot smell of masculine arousal flooded her nose.

Her mouth curved in triumph. It was true. Somehow, he had been in her room yesterday. He had seen her. And he wanted what he saw.

They looked at each other, the shared memory coming alive. Awareness hummed between them like an electric cable, rippling over her skin, twisting through her body. And she would bet everything she had that he felt the same.

The next moment his face was impassive again, his eyes flat as ice. "I don't know what you mean. I just do my job. Excuse me." He walked off toward the nearest knot of people.

As she watched him go, she saw something strange

happen. The shadows cast by the light of the crystal chandeliers seemed to bend and shiver around him. She still smelled him, but her eyes kept sliding off him as his shape blurred and faded into the air.

And it wasn't only *her* vision that was clouded. He stopped right next to the woman in the sable stole, but she didn't look at him or pause an instant in her conversation. The lady wasn't shunning him, Eliza realized. She didn't seem to see him there at all.

He was hiding himself in the middle of a crowd. What an amazing ability. It must make him an excellent detective.

Across the room, Angelique caught Eliza's eyes and summoned her with the twitch of a finger.

Eliza obeyed. At her approach, poor Mrs. Mannering, trapped at Angelique's side all this time, whispered some excuse and scurried off. She and the countess were left in a little eddy of privacy.

"Are you enjoying the party?" Eliza asked, coming to lounge against the sofa next to her.

"I'm being as tolerant as I can. Who is that odd looking young man? He smells familiar. Is he the one who came to my hotel room yesterday?"

"Yes. He's the detective I told you about. The one I hired to investigate my candidates for me."

Angelique watched him wander through the clusters of people, close enough to eavesdrop on their conversations, though they never seemed to see him. Her finely cut nostrils flared again. "There's something about him . . ." The steel colored eyes narrowed. "He's concealing himself."

"Yes. He's different, like us."

"How?"

"I'm not sure," Eliza said. She'd bite her own tongue off

before she told her grandmother that he'd spied on her last night, and how she'd tried to lure him into the open.

Angelique turned her sharp gaze on Eliza.

Eliza had a nervous thought the older lady somehow read the hot, sinful memory written on her face.

"Be careful, *ma fille*," the countess said.

"I'm always careful, *Grand-mère*. I've spent the last seven years dealing with witches and shamans across five continents. I can handle an American detective."

"Do not remind me of your past gypsy ways," Angelique said tartly. "Now, go talk to your candidates. Remember, you pledged to secure one within a week."

"And you promised to go away as soon as I did," Eliza said, lighting up a fresh cigarette. "I'll keep my promise if you keep yours."

21

Eliza did as her grandmother told her. She made the rounds of her five prospective husbands again, flirting with each as she wove her scent around them. But Mark Van Ryn invariably eased up to listen in on their conversations. He studied the men carefully, but as often as not, he seemed to study *her*. She had a hard time ignoring him, but none of the men ever noticed him.

One of them, an oaf named Monroe, grabbed her around the waist as she came near and slurred into her cleavage, "You're a foxy dame. I love foxy dames. How's about we go for a drive?"

She clasped his shoulder and saturated the air with her poison. "I think rather you should sit down for a bit, darling."

Monroe's eyes glassed over. His arm dropped from her waist and he turned and shuffled off to a nearby sofa without a word. He never even noticed Mark's hands inches away from his collar.

That was an extreme case, but none of the other men

she spoke to paid any attention to Mark either. Except for one, a chemical manufacturer named Lionel Duke.

Duke was the candidate most resistant to her perfume, and also the one she most disliked. She could almost say he made her uneasy. Perhaps it was his scent. Whereas the other men smelled only of liquor, sweat, and hair-oil, Duke's scent had an odd taint like corroded metal.

But aside from that, he was a very eligible bachelor. A millionaire, forty years old, handsome and powerfully built, with a head of tawny hair and a small Clark Gable mustache. He was wearing a white dinner jacket and gesturing with a champagne flute in one callused hand as he held forth on the splendors of the upcoming World's Fair.

"'A Century of Progress' is a marvelous concept," he said. "I'll take some credit for it myself, if I may. Duke Chemical was instrumental in planning and funding the enterprise. And what better way to press onward toward the future than with an exposition focused on science, the engine driving America on to its destiny? What better way to showcase Chicago, the city at the leading edge of the scientific frontier?"

"None, I'm sure," Eliza said. Around her a small circle of Duke's admirers, who had gathered to listen to him lionize, murmured agreement.

"And what better company to demonstrate our advancement than Duke Chemical?" he continued. "Our display will be the crown jewel of the fair."

"Will you have a pavilion of your own? Like General Electric, or Chrysler?" she asked.

Duke said a bit stiffly, "We have no need for one. We shall have pride of place in the Hall of Science."

"Of course, the Hall of Science!" she said. "I can't wait to see it! How I long for a glimpse of the future!"

Duke smiled. "Indeed, my dear, we are seeing the future arrive before our eyes. When I was at Oxford back in 'seventeen, I saw firsthand how science won the War for us against the Jerrys. How the magnificent weapons we devised carried the day. What other miracles might we create if we can seize the tools to challenge Nature for her supremacy!" The hand at his side curled into a fist. "What conquests we shall make! What battles we shall fight!"

"My, how martial," Eliza said, irony creeping into her tone.

His face turned deadly cold for an instant. But then the look vanished, leaving nothing but a suave smile. "You must forgive me. I get carried away when contemplating the endless potential of science. Not a fit subject for young ladies, I daresay."

Out of the corner of her eye, Eliza saw Mark's indistinct shape easing up to the circle of people around Duke. He was intent on eavesdropping on another of her conversations. She resolutely did not look at him. "Oh, science is splendid," she said with a brainless trill of laughter. "Your exhibit is certain to be a tremendous success, Lionel."

"Indeed. The fair will be a golden moment for those of us who must guide Chicago into the future. The first lady herself will be here on opening night, along with many other government dignitaries. We must show them what our city is capable of."

He turned his head to look directly at Mark. "Wouldn't you agree, Mr. Van Ryn?"

Eliza almost started. Duke had been watching Mark's movements, like she had.

The vague, shadowy cloak that covered Mark wavered and fell away.

The other partygoers standing near him startled back, as if they only just realized he was standing next to them.

Mark paid them no attention. He smiled at Duke, his pose relaxed, still-full whiskey glass held negligently in his hand. His only sign of surprise was a hard glint in his eyes. "I'm afraid I don't agree, Mr. Duke. I know exactly what Chicago is capable of, what with the men begging for work and freezing in the streets and dying in the factories. I doubt you want to show the first lady any of that."

Duke arched a smooth brow. "How cynical of you, Mark. I heard you're scraping by as a private detective these days. No doubt it's made you overly familiar with the squalid side of life."

"I'm no more familiar with Chicago's filth than, say, an average fellow who grew up in Back of the Yards."

Duke's fingers tightened on his wineglass at the mention of the infamous slum. Eliza stared at his hand, and something clicked in her mind. It was a rough, muscular hand, a workingman's hand. He might be rich now, but Duke hadn't grown up in wealth and luxury.

And now that she considered it, other things about him didn't ring true either. Like the way he spoke, just a little too mannered. Or his white dinner jacket, a finely tailored garment of the latest fashion, but perhaps too formal for cocktails. Or the way he let drop the fact that he had gone to university at Oxford. It all added up to the impression that he was trying too hard.

He made a striking contrast with Mark, who wasn't trying at all, and was still every inch the arrogant aristocrat.

Duke tried another sally. "What brings you to this little gathering, Mark? I thought you had given up the social scene. I haven't seen you at a party since your father's wake."

"Parties usually bore me."

"Ah yes, I understand people of fragile constitutions such as yours often suffer from ennui."

"Ennui? That's a mighty fancy word. You pick it up at Oxford?"

Duke's smile grew a shade brittle. "Quite. If you had attended university, you would undoubtedly have learned it too."

"Yeah," Mark said with a grin. "I got my education in a different school, you might say."

Duke swirled his champagne in its glass. "You never answered my question, Mark. Why did you come here tonight?"

"I'm interested in the company Amos keeps these days."

Duke looked amused. "And the company is certainly interested in you." He flicked a glance around the room at the heads bent together, whispering, shooting sidelong looks at Mark now that they could see him once again.

"They must have heard I'm a private detective," Mark said easily. "Private dicks are fascinating, I'm told."

Duke laughed. "Yes. That must be why they're staring at you like an exhibit in a zoo."

"Why, Mr. Van Ryn," Eliza broke in. "You never mentioned you were acquainted with Mr. Duke."

Mark shrugged. "Ancient history. See, he used to work for my father. Right-hand man at his chemical plant. But then he forced the old man to sell him the controlling shares of the company before he died. Got an excellent deal for himself, as I recall."

"Yes," Duke said, regarding Mark through heavy-lidded eyes. "I put the lessons your father taught me to good use.

Never let personal feelings get in the way of business. Unfortunately, Edward Van Ryn didn't take his own advice. He was driving the company into the ground with his . . . foibles."

"That he was," Mark said genially.

"And, an excellent deal or not, I paid a pretty penny for Van Ryn Chemical, now Duke Chemical. It was unfortunate that the proceeds of the sale had to go toward Edward's debts instead of to his son and heir, but *c'est la vie.*" His French accent was dreadful.

"*Exactement. C'est la vie,*" Mark said, his French accent considerably better.

Duke smiled a satisfied smile. "No hard feelings, son?"

"Not at all, pops. My father may have been a drunk, but he wasn't an idiot. He knew what kind of jackal you were when he plucked you out of the gutter in the Back of the Yards. Oh, sorry, I meant when he plucked you out of *Oxford*. Anyway, he expected you'd turn on him once you got the smell of blood in your nose. He just didn't care. So why should I?"

Duke's expression didn't change, but he went a little white around the mouth. "Why indeed, when it turned out for the best? I daresay your delicate health couldn't withstand the rigors of business. Why, you may yet be forced to spend your remaining years in a hospital ward."

"I promise you I can look after my health, Lionel. You just worry about yours."

22

Once, in India, Eliza had seen a cobra and a mongoose sizing each other up for battle. She could smell the same animal menace in the air between the two men now. Time to intervene. "Darling," she said to Duke, slipping her gloved hand around his elbow, "Would you go freshen up my drink for me while I walk Mr. Van Ryn to the door? He mentioned earlier that he couldn't stay for long. I'm sure he's ready to be on his way."

Duke tore his focus away from Mark and glanced down at her. She flooded the air with her scent, but she saw none of the telltale haze in his eyes. He really was resistant to her poison.

But he took her glass and said, "Certainly, my dear. Mark, always a pleasure."

"*Jusqu'a ce que nous nous revoyions,*" Mark said. *Until we meet again.*

Duke hesitated, gave a hard smile, and walked off toward the bar.

Eliza threaded her arm through Mark's and started

edging him to the front door. "What did you learn from studying my gentlemen?"

He set his glass of whiskey down on a table and let her pull him along. "How do you know I was studying them?" he said.

"Because I was studying you."

"I knew you were watching me."

"And I knew you knew. What a pair we make, knowing so much about each other." She was clouding the air with her scent to influence him, and he was strolling along with her toward the entryway easily enough, but she had the unsettling feeling that he was humoring her. He, like Duke, was resisting her power.

He slanted his ice-colored eyes down at her, a smile edging his mouth. "You think you've got a handle on all my secrets, do you?"

"Not all. Just the fact that you're different."

"Like you?"

She didn't answer that.

They had reached the front door. She released his arm and looked at him squarely. "I'd like to hear what you've learned tonight, Mr. Van Ryn."

Just then the butler appeared to give Mark his hat and open the door. Mark angled his black fedora over his eyes. He said to Eliza, "Step outside with me for a moment."

She glanced over her shoulder at the crowd, but no one was watching her, except Angelique. She turned her shoulder against her grandmother's cold, disapproving stare. "All right," she said, and walked out into the night. Mark followed her, a warm presence at her back.

They strolled down the walkway to where the valet was dozing on his stool. Mark sent the man off to bring his car around. When they were alone again, he looked down into her eyes. "Come to my office tomorrow at ten."

"You'll have the information ready for me then?"

He nodded. "In return for sixty dollars, and the answers to a few questions."

"Those weren't the terms of our agreement."

"I'm renegotiating."

"That doesn't seem fair."

"Life's not fair, angel."

The valet slid the Duesenberg up to the curb. Mark gave him another quarter and slid behind the wheel.

Eliza stepped up to the passenger side and ran an envious hand along the gleaming hood.

Mark grinned at her through the window. "You like the car?"

"Darling, I love this car."

"If you're a good girl, maybe I'll take you for a spin."

"If you're a bad boy, maybe I'll let you." With one last stroke of the red paint, she stood back from the road.

He laughed, eyes gleaming blue. "Ten tomorrow, angel." He tipped his hat to her, blasted his horns, and roared away into the dark. Eliza looked down the road after him, wondering if they had played some sort of game, and if so, who had won.

23

Mark drove back to his house and put the car away in the garage. Then he went to his room to strip off his evening clothes and throw on a gray suit. The instant his hat was on his head he unleashed the shadow, racing out into the city. He had a lot of work to do tonight, and he was hungry to get started.

He was more determined than ever to solve the mystery of Eliza Karlova. She had claimed to be dangerous and he had a pretty good notion of why. Every smile, every gesture, and the incredible perfume she wore were all calculated to drive a man mad. Tonight he had watched her work over the men who came near her, weaving her spell until they obeyed her every whim. He was almost ready to fall at her feet himself.

Just look at him, wasting time when he should be working on the Camonte case. He had a monster to catch, after all. But dammit, he would make time.

His first stop was back north across the river, at a Venetian style skyscraper near Lincoln Park where Lionel Duke had an apartment.

He had gotten Duke's address and those of Eliza's other bachelors from the police and city records last night. He would search all their homes and offices tonight, but Duke had earned the first and hardest look.

When he'd first seen Duke's name on Eliza's list, he'd thought nothing of it. The few times Mark had met him, he seemed to be an insufferable prick, but other than that, he was merely one face among many from the life he'd left years ago.

But Duke had certainly caught his attention tonight. He was one of the few people who had ever noticed Mark when he was in half-shadow. And then there were his barely veiled threats. Mark had gotten used to casual cruelty by the time he was old enough to talk, and it never bothered him any more. But Duke's insults had a personal edge. This wasn't just another asshole. This was an enemy. But why?

Duke would probably be out of his apartment for hours yet. Plenty of time to look for answers.

When he got to Duke's apartment building, he stood in the shadows under one of the ornamental trees lining the street and looked the place over. The white stone façade was brightly lit, the grand entrance guarded by a liveried doorman. Mark didn't bother with it. Instead he slipped around the side of the building to the alley behind it.

His shadow presence flowed up and over the rear wall and across the service courtyard. The fire escape ladder was fifteen feet above the ground but Mark didn't need it. He slid straight up the wall next to the metal staircase.

Duke's apartment took up the entire fourteenth floor. When he got to the right level, he found the fire escape's access window and probed along the edges until he found a crack in the casement. He slipped his shadow being through it like a stream of dark smoke.

Inside was a kitchen, very modern, clean, and cold. The lights were off, the domestic servants having gone home hours ago. Mark moved to the kitchen door and listened. He heard nothing but the silence of an empty apartment.

He let himself go solid and pushed through the swinging door into a dining room beyond. He spared it a glance, saw enough silver and mahogany to give an auctioneer the vapors, and passed on into the grand parlor.

More fine furniture, crystal, gilding, and a marble fireplace set up with birch logs. Duke might be a believer in modernism and science and progress, but his home sure didn't show it. No chromium, no Bakelite, not one sleek Art Deco line to be found. Everything looked like an heirloom handed down from his family estate. Which, as Mark knew from his father's caustic rambling, was in reality a tenement near the slaughterhouses.

He didn't bother searching the parlor, but headed toward the corridor leading to the bedrooms and the study. He took the study first. It was decorated in grand men's club style, and was fitted with an attached washroom. He opened the washroom window a crack, so he had a quick escape route out into the night in case Duke returned.

He jimmied open the desk and scanned through the correspondence he found there. Household bills, notes from a few old chums and a few mistresses, and a packet of letters from a sister.

He scanned the letters quickly. The sister, it seemed, had never married. Her brother supported her in a villa in Wisconsin. She had been raising his son since his birth five years ago, when the mother had died.

Poor kid, Mark thought before he stopped himself. He read on.

The sister was extremely upset that Duke had taken the

boy away from her about three months ago and put him in the care of a doctor and a nurse. Whatever malady the child suffered from she didn't say.

So Duke might be ill-treating his son. Further proof that the man was a bastard, but it wasn't illegal, or even scandalous by society's lights. Mark knew that firsthand.

He put the correspondence back as he found it and relocked the desk. He'd have to ransack Duke's business office and his lawyer's office to get any serious dirt.

He was about to head toward the bedrooms when he heard the quiet snick of a key in a lock and the creak of hinges on the front door. He turned full shadow and slipped back into the washroom with the open window. But he didn't escape just yet, lingering in the dark and listening.

He heard two sets of footsteps coming down the hall. The office door creaked open, the overhead light clicked on, and the footsteps entered. No one spoke. The desk chair squeaked, and there was the sound of another chair being shifted.

Mark looked through the crack between the hinge side of the door and the frame, ready to dive for the window on an instant. After the way Duke had seen through his half-shadow at the party, he had to be extra cautious. The man was more sensitive than he'd given him credit for.

But the two people in the office were focused solely on each other. Duke had assumed a relaxed pose, seated behind his desk. The other man was perched on the smaller client chair. He was a spindly, twitchy little fellow of about fifty, with a few lank strands of hair combed over his pate, and a musty tweed suit.

There was something strange about his face. The left side of it looked deformed, the eye larger and shinier than normal and frozen in place. A glass eye, he realized.

Mark was certain he had never seen the man before, and yet something about him seemed familiar.

"Well, my insomniac friend?" Duke began. "What was so important that you had to track me down at a party to tell me about it?"

"I am not an insomniac." The little man's voice was as dry as sand. "It is best to conduct the Project Plasma experiments at night, as I have told you. But that is not why I am here. I wish to discuss my other experiment."

Duke's shoulders tensed. "Which other experiment?"

"Subject A."

"Ah yes. Dear old Subject A." Duke rested his elbows on the chair arms, gripping the ends. He seemed at once relieved and almost angry.

The doctor continued, "I wish to bring it in for testing. Observing it in the field does not yield enough data. It is too elusive. I must examine it under controlled conditions."

"All in good time, doctor. Our current endeavor is having such great success, I don't want to dilute your attention. We are on the brink of creating an unmatched weapon that will win wars for America."

"The War is over."

Duke smiled coldly. "War will never be over. War is the means by which great men shape the world to their liking. Do you not yet see, doctor? The future belongs to the man with the power to reach out and seize it!" He suited action to his words, raising one calloused hand and making a fist. "A man with strength of will, and a mind unclouded by sentimental weakness. A man who will not hesitate to use every tool at hand to fulfill his destiny."

The doctor sniffed impatiently.

Duke went on, "Think of the place we shall have in the affairs of the country when we demonstrate our new weapon to our friends from Washington. Nothing must interfere with the project's completion."

The doctor made an impatient buzzing sound, like an insect in a glass jar. "Project Plasma *is* complete. The creature is ready. It is unworthy of my abilities to perform this drudgery any longer. We agreed—"

"We agreed that my money had the final say on the matter. And my money likes the growth potential of Project Plasma. The results have proved far more dependable than your other experiments."

"That is because you will not give me the resources to test them!" The little man leaned forward, mismatched eyes gleaming. "My contacts in Washington want to see Subject A now. They've already begun their own inquiries. If you don't bring it in, they will."

Duke's smug smile faded. "What contacts? Who have you been talking to? It isn't the general. I'd know."

"You have your connections and I have mine. People who know where their priorities should lie. People who appreciate my work and are eager to acquire my services."

"Are you threatening to renege on our contract?" Duke said softly. "Don't forget I hold your life in my hand, doctor."

The little man twitched. "And I hold the key to the creature in mine."

Duke's eyes narrowed. "So is it to be war between us? I warn you, I always win."

"There is no need for such hastiness. It would be inefficient to tamper with our successful partnership. Merely allow me to bring in Subject A for testing, and you will continue to get the full benefit of my research."

Duke frowned into the air.

"And I'll remind you that Subject A will be highly lucrative for you, since I know you are concerned about such matters," the doctor added.

"Very well. Prepare the laboratory. I'll make the arrangements."

The glass eye glinted. "Excellent! When—"

"At my discretion. I have my own reasons for granting your request, and I will do it my way."

"Your own reasons," the doctor repeated softly.

Duke's face darkened. "Time for you to get back to work. We're scheduled for a field test of the new formula soon, are we not?"

"Further testing is unnecessary."

Duke smiled. "But it *is* necessary. The tests are accomplishing exactly what I need them to accomplish. They are reshaping the power structure of this city and cleansing it of its undesirable elements. If you poked your nose into a newspaper now and then, you'd know that."

"I do not wish to concern myself with sordid politics. I am a man of pure science."

Duke laughed outright. "Your notion of purity amuses me." His smile dropped. "But don't push it. You've carried your point. If I were you I'd get out while the getting is good."

Without another word, the little man rose from his chair and scuttled out of the room.

Mark backed away from the door and sent his shadow being flowing through the open window into the night.

24

Mark slid his presence down the side of the building to the ground. He slipped across an alley and settled into the shadows near a wall where he had a good view of the doors of Duke's building. The doctor would come out any second now.

After the conversation he'd just heard, with all the talk of "experiments" on a "creature," even the dimmest detective would guess he had stumbled on the very killers who had sent a monster after Camonte's men. And Mark liked to think he wasn't quite that dim.

So he'd solved the mystery of who was responsible for the attacks. But now he had a host of new questions, like where they were keeping this thing, how they were controlling it, and what exactly it was. Not to mention how to destroy it. He'd find the answers as soon as he followed the doctor to his laboratory.

But there was another, even more disturbing implication in the discussion he'd overheard. There was a second monster somewhere loose in the city, the "Subject A" that

Duke and the scientist were eager to capture. One was bad enough, but two?

And what were the chances that Eliza Karlova's most prominent beau would be the very killer he was hunting for Camonte? Mark didn't like the coincidence.

All the more reason to find out what secrets the other men on her list might be hiding. The police files he'd read about the four other suitors contained evidence of various sordid crimes, but nothing uncanny. But then, there was nothing like this in Duke's file either.

The scientist stepped out of the building, his scrawny shape instantly recognizable. He started down the street at a limping walk. Mark followed him close behind, like a second shadow.

Mark had pursued hundreds of people in his full shadow form, and only a handful had ever suspected they were being watched. But the doctor seemed ill at ease, glancing over his shoulders, his good eye darting about. He scurried through the dark spaces between the street lamps, moving from island of light to island of light. Mark kept pace with him, slipping through the edges of shadow.

The little man got to a lamppost and stopped and spun on his heel, the glare from above pouring over him. He drove a hand into his pocket and pulled out a knife. No, not a knife, a scalpel, Mark realized. The razor-sharp edge caught a shard of yellow light.

"Who is there?" The doctor's voice rang shrill against the brick and concrete.

Mark kept his shadow presence still, waiting. The scientist twitched, peering into the dark. After a long moment, he hid the scalpel in his pocket and hurried onward. Mark followed him, farther back than before, but twice as curious. Either the little man was paranoid, or he had some sensitivity to the unnatural. Or both.

The doctor hailed a passing cab and got in, heading south on Lake Shore Drive. Mark easily kept pace with the taxi.

After about ten blocks, the car turned off of Lake Shore and wove through some streets until it pulled up in front of the Knickerbocker Hotel. Which was right across the street from the Drake Hotel, where Karlova and Camonte both had rooms. It was a hell of another coincidence.

The scientist got out of the taxi and scurried into the Knickerbocker. The lights inside were bright enough to force Mark out of his full-shadow form, so he hung back long enough to let his quarry get ahead of him and relax his guard before entering the hotel himself.

It was still early enough so that the marble lobby and attached lounge were churning with guests out for a night on the town. But the scientist was nowhere among them. Mark wove through the crowd in half-shadow form toward the elevator.

One elevator was going up, the needle in the dial above it coming to rest on number seven. Mark found the stairs and ran up them, speeding through the shadows to the seventh floor in mere seconds. But when he eased open the stairwell door and looked through, he saw only a young, plump, and dapper fellow step out of the elevator. There were no other passengers.

Damn. Had he somehow missed him in the lobby? He raced back downstairs and sifted through the milling guests. Nothing. He ran outside and scanned up and down the street. Nothing.

Suddenly he remembered that the Knickerbocker had one other place he hadn't looked. He rushed back inside to the lounge, where he found a door with a sliding Judas-hole tucked away in a corner behind a potted palm. There was too much light for Mark to slide under the door in full shadow, and there was no chance the guard waiting behind it would willingly let him in, so he had to wait impatiently for the right moment, his half-shadow seething around him.

After a few tense minutes, a fellow in a sharp suit approached the door with a special knock and a C-note in his fingers. He didn't see Mark's lurking shadow, his gaze already focused on the delights to be found inside.

The Judas slid open to show a pair of eyes, then slid shut. The door clicked and swung inward. Mark drifted in like the sharp-suit man's shadow, slipping past him and the bouncer as the money changed hands.

He ran silently down a set of carpeted stairs to the basement level. He entered a long, low-ceilinged room done in plush golden carpet, wine-red silk wallpaper, and dim lights. It was full of men in tuxedos and women in glittering dresses gathered around felted tables or whirling roulette wheels, drinks in their gloved hands. The air was thick with smoke, perfume, and acrid sweat. A furtive murmur of voices rippled underneath the clink of glasses, the shuffle of cards and the clack of dice. He was in the Knickerbocker's very expensive and very discreet hooch parlor and casino.

In such suave company a twitchy little man in an awful suit ought to stick out like a flare, but Mark still didn't see him. He wove through the craps tables and blackjack games, scanning for his prey. He kept himself in half-shadow, though the gamblers were so intent on their labor they wouldn't have noticed him, anyway. It was no use. The scientist wasn't here.

He entered the warren of service rooms behind the bar

and searched those. Again, he found nothing, except another steel door off the boiler room standing ajar. Behind the door was a concrete staircase leading down, and at the bottom of that was a landing with a set of trolley tracks through a tunnel stretching away in either direction. The air reeked with smoke and the cold smell of dank clay.

Mark swore. This was the tunnel trolley, a huge network of underground utility rails that spread throughout the Loop and a considerable way beyond. It had stops at every major hotel and office for delivering coal and taking away garbage. If the scientist had access to a trolley, he had enough of a head start on Mark to be anywhere in the city by now.

He listened hard, but heard no sounds telling him which way the man had gone. He picked a direction at random and raced along it for a way hoping he might stumble over his quarry by sheer luck, but it was no use. The scientist had slipped away as slick as a rat down a hole.

Cursing to himself, Mark retraced his steps, slipping back up through the casino and lobby out to the street. There was nothing to be done about Duke's scientist now. He had four other men to investigate tonight, and the dark hours were already passing. But he would catch the little creep later, he vowed. No one outsmarted him on his own turf.

Furious, he vanished into shadow and sped into the night.

25

Mark finished his breaking and entering jobs at the homes and offices of Eliza's suitors without much trouble and got home at the crack of dawn once again. And just like yesterday, someone was waiting for him. His front door was in one piece this time, but he found a small figure sitting against it.

As Mark walked to the stoop, the figure bounced up and smiled brashly, a flash of white teeth in a brown-skinned face. It was a kid of about twelve, with quick hands and quick eyes. He looked familiar. One of Frasier's relatives, he thought.

The boy took a letter out of his pocket. "From Mr. Florian, sir."

Mark took the letter. "Thanks. What's your name, son?"

"Jeremiah Stickles."

"Okay, Mr. Stickles. Give this to Florian." He handed the kid three twenty-dollar bills. Then he delved into his pocket and flipped him a quarter. "And keep that for yourself."

The boy snatched the coin out of the air and made all

the money disappear. "Thanks Mr. Shadow!" He tipped his cap and took off running.

Mark chuckled. *Mr. Shadow. That's a new one.*

He let himself inside and went straight to his office. He sat at his desk and opened the letter. It was four pages in Florian's careful handwriting detailing all the gossip about Eliza and her suitors. He read it through twice carefully, and added the information in it to his files on the five men. Then he struck a match under the corner of the letter and burned it to gray flakes in his ashtray.

He caught two hours of sleep, and when he woke, he still had an hour before Eliza was supposed to arrive. He had some thinking to do about everything he'd learned, so he put on his boxing trunks and walked barefoot to his gymnasium.

He'd set up his equipment in the house's former ball-room. The parquet floors were covered in pads, his weights were stacked up along one white-paneled wall, and his heavy bag dangled from the gilt ceiling on the other side.

Replacing the bag the invaders had cut up yesterday was one of the first things he'd done, even before fixing the radio or putting his books back on the shelves. He could do without a radio, even without his books, but he couldn't do without his bag.

Some nights, when the darkness became too alluring and the black ocean was tearing him away little by little, he would go at his bag until his fists were bloody and his heart was bursting, just to remind himself that he was a flesh-and-blood man, not a ghost. He needed to feel *something* to keep him in the real world, and pain and exhaustion worked just fine.

He wrapped up his fists in tape and started in with a few easy jabs and combinations, circling his target, staying light on the balls of his feet. He sank his knuckles into the canvas again and again, relishing the impact traveling up his arms and throughout every inch of muscle and bone.

As his body worked, his thoughts cleared. He sifted the patterns of what he had learned and started putting them together into a guess at the truth.

He fell into an easy rhythm, mind and body moving as one. Until something strange and new suddenly rippled across his senses. A hint of movement, a waft of delicious perfume. *She* was here, watching him from the doorway, her eyes burning across the naked skin of his back.

Usually he was the one spying on people, but somehow Eliza Karlova kept getting the drop on him. Maybe because he was letting her. Maybe because some stupid-kid part of him *wanted* her to see him.

He landed one last punch on the canvas and wiped the sweat off his forehead with the back of his taped hand. Then he turned and looked straight at the long graceful shape of her standing in the shadows of the doorway. "You're early."

She walked toward him, moving as quietly as a cat. Her eyes gleamed in the shadows as they flickered over his bare chest and stomach. When her gaze returned to his it was studiously blank. But her cheeks were a delicate shade of pink.

Once or twice, he'd encountered women who would sidle up to him furtively, shamefully, the way one approaches the object of a sick fetish. That always left him feeling coated in filth. But Eliza reacted to him like she was seeing a man, not a thing. He was quickly becoming addicted to that look.

She said, "My apologies for the intrusion. Your door was unlocked. I came in when no one answered my ring."

"Sorry, the doorbell's broken."

"A lot of things in this house appear to be broken." She looked around pointedly.

"That's because the place got robbed."

Her gaze flew to his. "When?"

"The night you hired me. Some coincidence."

"Yes," she said, a troubled frown creasing her brow.

"So, as you were saying. You came in to my house, and then you came looking for me because . . . ?"

"I heard noises. Blows being struck. When I saw the broken doors and furniture I became concerned, so I thought I'd see if you needed help."

A smile tipped his mouth. "You thought I was getting a beating, so you came to rescue me?"

Her eyes were suddenly dancing. "Why not? Don't you think I can lick a dozen men?" She struck a muscleman pose, flexing her right arm.

He laughed. "I don't know. Let's see what you've got." He stepped behind the heavy bag and clasped it, holding it for her. "Come on. Hit the bag."

She let out a surprised laugh. "Don't be absurd, darling."

He reached out and took her slender, black-gloved right hand in his. The silk over her fingers was cool on his heated skin. He folded her hand into a fist. "Thumb tight over the fingers. Keep your wrist straight. Put your shoulder into it. Got it?"

Eyes wide, she nodded.

"Good. Now hit it." He held the bag for her again.

She wound up and punched the bag with a surprising amount of conviction. He actually felt a slight thump through the stuffing. She was strong for a woman.

"Not bad," he said.

"Ouch." She stepped back and shook out her fingers. "I think I prefer my own methods of defense."

"And what might those be?"

"Why, my womanly wiles, of course."

"Formidable weapons."

"You have no idea."

He suddenly realized that he was getting hard, and had been since the moment she stepped through the door. It was a mistake to let her get so close. "Why don't you tell me about it in my office, after I have a chance to clean up?" he said quickly.

She smiled. "Perhaps I will. I'll wait for you there." She turned and vanished through the door as smoothly and silently as she came.

26

Mark ran up the stairs to his room, where he quickly cleaned the sweat off his body, threw on a fresh suit and combed his hair. He took a look in the shaving mirror. The same white face as always stared back at him. Was that really the man who had just bantered with a gorgeous woman while wearing nothing but trunks?

He returned to his office wondering if he had imagined the whole episode.

But she was there, real as could be. She was standing at his bookshelf, a book in one hand and a smoldering cigarette in the other, her legs posed at dangerous angles.

Without looking up, she said, "*Brave New World*? How shocking of you Mr. Van Ryn."

"So you've read it then."

She slid a smile at him. "But of course."

"You're a daring lady. Whatever would the Mannerings think?" He sat down behind his desk. On the blotter in front of him were three fresh twenty-dollar bills. He put the money in a drawer and said, "This is a good start on my bill, but you still owe me some answers, angel. Like you promised last night."

She returned the scandalous book to the shelf and came to sit in the client chair, crossing her long legs at the knees. "Very well, since you insist, I'll answer some of your questions. But," she tapped her cigarette in his ashtray, "you're a gentleman, and you know the rules. Ladies first."

"Where did you ever get the notion I'm a gentleman?"

She merely smiled. "What have you found for me, detective?"

"I investigated each name on your list thoroughly and I feel safe in saying that you don't want to marry any of these men. All five of them are cads who would make the worst husbands imaginable. But then, you knew that already, or guessed it. Right?"

She gave a tiny shrug.

"So what's the real reason you wasted my time with this investigation? Were you going to use these files to get your grandmother off your back about marrying?"

"Not at all. I fully intend to marry one of these men. I hired you to help me select the right candidate."

"I can't help you find the best one of these fellows. They're all mutts."

"But I don't want the best. I want the worst."

"The worst? Why . . . " The old lady's words suddenly echoed in his head. *The sooner you'll be a widow.*

He steepled his fingers, looking at her over the tips. "Okay, angel. Are you planning on killing your husband once you're married?"

He saw her take a slow breath. "My, you *are* direct. But, you don't really want to discuss such things with a client, do you?" She made a dismissive little gesture toward him with her fingers, sending a waft of perfume to him.

"I'm afraid I do. See, I have a private detective license I want to keep. I may skirt around the edges of the law time to time, but there are lines I won't cross. So you're going to have to answer my question before I go any farther."

She blinked. "An ultimatum. How novel." She put out her cigarette in the ashtray. "I assure you, I'm not planning to commit any act of violence."

"That was a very carefully phrased denial, but not quite convincing. Maybe I need to go visit your grandmother to get my question answered. She looked like a reasonable lady when I saw her at the party last night."

She didn't like that. "For your own good, I wouldn't attempt it. The countess is not a person even you would want to cross."

He struggled to keep a straight face, and said gravely, "I might have to risk it. Unless you give me a real answer."

She busied herself lighting up another cigarette, rolling the ivory holder between her fingers.

He waited.

Eventually, she said, "My family—the women in my family—we believe that we live under a . . . well, a curse. That when we marry, our husbands are doomed to die an early death. For many years, we've kept a tradition of only marrying the most wicked of men, so that when the curse falls, the blood of an innocent will not stain our hands." She paused, waiting for him to comment.

He merely lifted an eyebrow.

"Since we're being direct, I'll tell you directly. I don't plan to kill my husband. I simply believe he will die." Again, she spoke a little too carefully. He didn't think she was lying, but she was leaving a lot out.

Mark didn't know what to think of her explanation, except that on a deep, visceral level, he hated it. He said, a

148

little sharply, "If evil was your big requirement in a husband, why not go down to the local drunk tank and marry the first fellow who can stand up in front of a Justice of the Peace?"

She smiled faintly. "Because wealth and rank are also considerations for us, as they are for any woman. But the moral and the practical need not be in opposition. There are, after all, many evil men with money. And the more money a man has, the more evil he can do, no?"

"You don't seriously believe in this curse, do you? Enough to marry a pervert or a criminal?"

"I didn't expect to find a man in your line of work skeptical on the matter of family curses."

"In my experience, most families make their own curses without the need for witchcraft. I'd be remiss in my duty as your consultant if I didn't tell you that marrying one of these mutts out of some old superstition would be a terrible mistake."

"I'm paying you for information on my prospective spouses, not to judge my motives. But take heart, Mr. Van Ryn. If this curse of mine is so much nonsense, then you need not worry about the fate of the man I marry."

"That's not what worries me," he said, before he thought better of it.

Her lips curved. "Gee, are you worried about me?"

"I'm always concerned for the welfare of my clients."

"You needn't be. I assure you I can look after myself. Now, are you going to give me the information, or are you going to moralize at me some more?"

He yanked open the hot file drawer of his desk and pulled out the five reports he had written up this morning. He slapped three of them down in front of him, holding up the last two files. "Monroe and Witcliffe are your basic drunken brutes. Assault, theft, property damage, public intoxication, etcetera. They've each been able to buy their way out of any real trouble, but that won't last much longer. They're burning through their money at a fast clip and not bringing any in, because they're worthless." He tossed those files on his desk and took up the next one on the pile.

"Jameson was slightly more interesting, but you should know that he's not the marrying kind. He's more the 'sleep with other men and then blackmail them for it' kind. That's how he keeps his fortunes up. But with the kinds of games he's playing, it won't be long before he ends up with broken legs in an alley. If he's lucky." He laid aside the file and took up another.

"Munch is a gambler, and a bad one. He's taken to torching stables, laming horses, and beating up jockeys to try to stem his losses. He's also an opium addict and a patron of exotic brothels." He set the file down on top of the others.

She said coolly, "This is quite disappointing. None of these gentlemen have real money?"

"None but my last subject. Duke is rolling in cash. But he's got a taste for blood."

She leaned forward, interest sparking in her eyes. "You aren't prejudiced, are you, because of what happened with your father's company?"

"You better believe I am, but that doesn't mean what I tell you isn't the truth."

"All right, go on."

"He fought in the War, in the trenches at first. His specialty was gas. He got so good at killing Germans with it, he was sent to the war scientists at Avon-mouth in England help them make the stuff more deadly. That was as close as he ever got to Oxford, by the way.

"When he came home, he did well for himself, got a job with my father, married an heiress. Then his wife died when his son was born. The mother's father left all his money to his grandson when he died about three months ago. Shortly after that, the boy supposedly fell ill. But no one knows what his illness is. He's been kept locked up with only a nurse and a doctor allowed to see him."

A line appeared between her brows. "Does the boy have no other family?"

"One aunt, a Miss Martha Duke. He was living with her until three months ago."

"Poor child," she said softly. "What's his name?"

"Steven. Don't tell me you're interested in the boy."

"Why? Is it so incredible that a woman like me would care for children?"

He heard a faint but definite quaver in her voice, which made him look at her carefully. Suddenly, a vision sprang up in his mind, amazingly clear, of her long, slender shape turned soft and ripe with child. "No. No, it isn't incredible at all," he murmured.

She veiled her eyes with her lashes.

He cleared his throat. "There are also rumors of mysterious deaths in Duke's factories. Union organizers who disappeared, business rivals who suffered fatal accidents. There were a couple of investigations, but nothing was ever proved. Coincidentally, the police doing the investigating each got nice big deposits in their bank accounts courtesy of distant relatives at about the same time."

"How very lucky."

"The same luck that brought you to me. The non-luck variety. Isn't that right?"

She tilted her head at him. "You've lost me, darling."

"Duke has a connection to another case of mine. One devil of a coincidence. Only, I don't believe in coincidence."

"What else can it be?" There was nothing but confusion and curiosity on her face. She was good.

He took a photograph out of his desk and tossed it down in front of her. "What do you know about the death of this man?"

She leaned forward to look at the picture closely, but didn't touch it. It was the snapshot of the first of Camonte's men to die, the one with the least damage to his face and body. He wanted to shock Eliza, but not too much. Not yet.

He watched her closely, but only a frown of concentration showed between her brows. "I've never seen him. Who was he?"

"Just a guy who got eaten from the inside out."

She looked up at him, lips parted in shock. "How awful. You say he was eaten? By what?"

"That's a good question. One I'll be asking your boyfriend sooner or later."

"Are you saying that Lionel Duke may have somehow killed this man?"

"Yeah. And maybe Duke guessed I'd be on his trail, and sent you here to spy for him."

For a moment she looked as if she didn't understand him. Then her face changed, and in a voice tight with incredulity, she said, "How dare you think that *I* would stoop to being any man's spy!"

Confusion, he would have scoffed at. Tears, he would have laughed at. But sheer indignation? That he believed, coming from her. She was the cat, not the cat's paw. He started to relax, but quickly put his guard up again. One thing still didn't make sense.

He looked hard into her eyes. "Why did you choose me? Really. Any number of private dicks could have checked up on these mugs. Why me?"

"Because you're *different*. You have power. Whenever I come to a new place I sniff out the people who are different and I get them to help me."

"Help you? With what?" he asked skeptically. The only people he had ever met who had eldritch power either tried to kill him or enslave him. Or both at once.

"Research, mostly. I've travelled all over the world in the last seven years, looking for ingredients for perfumes. The local mystics and witch doctors were always fonts of information. They helped me devise the most glorious scents." She flashed a smile. "But then, you've seen my diary and my trunk. You already know all that."

He didn't rise to her bait. "You were only making perfumes? Not magic potions?"

Her smile came again. "They're the same thing, aren't they? They both get men to do whatever a woman wants." She tapped out her cigarette, not having drawn on it once. "I'm a perfumer by trade, and I've learned a fair bit of chemistry. But the affinity with scent is natural to me."

"And that's how you're *different*, is it?" he said, an idea springing into his head.

After a beat, she admitted, "Yes. That, and the curse."

He waved the ridiculous "curse" aside. "Then I want you to meet somebody who's helping me in my other investigation. I can take you to him right now."

She raised her eyebrows. "Are you mad?"

"You'd be perfectly safe with me," he assured her.

"I'm sure I would. But I'd still need a reason to go."

"You could help me solve a few murders."

He saw a flash of curiosity in her face, but she said coolly, "And why would I want to do that?"

"You get to experience the thrilling life of a private detective first hand. Besides, this case affects you directly. If I'm right, your favorite boyfriend is the very killer I'm looking for. Something I think you'd want to know before you marry him."

"True," she said, regarding him with a measuring eye.

He played his ace. "I'll drive you in my car."

She grinned. "Darling! That's all you had to say!"

27

Eliza stepped to the curb as Mark pulled the Duesenberg around. She didn't wait for him to get out and open the door for her, but pulled it open herself and slid onto the cream leather seat with a purr. "Lovely. Now, where are we going?"

"To meet with my secret weapon." He slipped on a pair of dark glasses and revved the engine.

"Good enough," she said. *Swept away by a mysterious man to a mysterious destination. How exciting.*

She shouldn't be wasting time like this, when she should be preparing for her date with Lionel Duke this evening.

After Mark had left the party last night, Duke had promised to escort her to what he said was the best jazz club in Chicago. Shortly after that, Mannering's butler had brought him a note, and he had abruptly taken his leave.

She wondered briefly if the message had something to do with the murder case, but set it aside. She didn't want to think about Duke right now. She would rather think about the man next to her.

Finding him in his gymnasium that morning had been a revelation. He was even more muscular than she'd imagined, and perfectly proportioned, like a Greek statue come to life. Every chiseled inch of his naked flesh gleamed with sweat as he shifted and danced around his punching bag, landing blow after blow with ferocious speed. His massive shoulders bunched, his tight buttocks flexed, his stomach rippled. Muscle rolled down his long arms and legs. Every movement of his fists and feet was a study in graceful precision and feral power.

And when he'd turned to look at her, head up, nostrils flaring, like a stag startled by a huntress in a clearing, the hot, rich scent of him luring her closer . . . She blushed and stole a sidelong glance at him.

He grinned at her lazily, one powerful hand on the wheel and the other working the gear. "Hold on, angel," he said, and stepped on the gas. The car roared and leapt down the street.

It was a fine, clear day, beautiful for driving. They turned on to State Street and cruised toward the Loop, the big car prowling through the canyons of the city like a great jungle beast. They passed under the L tracks just as a train rattled and howled over their heads.

Mark drove down a side street a few blocks off of State and pulled up at the curb. She looked out her window at a nondescript, four-story brick building that had all the hallmarks of a den of municipal bureaucracy. Which might be harrowing in its way, she supposed, but was nevertheless a bit disappointing as a solution to a mystery. "Your secret weapon is in there? I expected a more exotic destination. A gambling den with a smuggler's tunnel, perhaps."

Mark looked amused. "You've been reading too much Black Mask." He got out of the car and went around to open her door for her, all gentleman. "We're going to see a friend of mine who has an office and laboratory here. He's consulting with me on this murder case."

Eliza was intrigued. "Did you say laboratory?" she asked as she got out of the car.

"That's right. He's a brilliant water engineer."

They walked into the building lobby, past a counter clerk who eyed them warily, and down a wide, marble-floored hall. A door with a sign in gold lettering that said, *Harvey Daley, Chief Engineer, Chicago Department of Water Management* opened just as they approached and a plump little man in tweeds stepped out, whistling to himself. But when he caught sight of Mark he yelped and jumped back against the doorframe. "You!"

"'Morning, Harvey. Taking an early lunch?" Mark said.

"What are you doing here?" His beady eyes ran around the hall, barely even pausing to take Eliza in.

"I came to consult with Mr. Frasier Robinson. Your assistant. Remember him?"

The fat man blinked owlishly. "Of course, of course. I believe you'll find him in his office."

"Which is still hidden down in the basement, is it?" Mark said softly.

He gulped, his chins jiggling. "Y-yes."

"That's what I thought. Say, while I'm here, why don't you and I have a little chat, too."

"No! I-I mean, I can't, terribly sorry. I have a lunch meeting with the County Commissioner."

"Suppose I joined you at your meeting? You think the Commissioner would mind?"

Harvey dug a handkerchief out of his pocket and mopped his face. "Well—"

"Or maybe I'll come to your house tonight. You can tell

your wife to expect me at, say, two a.m. Or tell your mistress in that apartment up in Old Town."

"No," the man said miserably. "Now is fine."

"Swell. I'll see you in your office in a few minutes, after I'm done talking to my friend. Why don't you go back in and wait for me?"

Without a word, Harvey fumbled the door open and edged inside, never taking his eyes off of Mark until it snapped shut.

Mark turned to Eliza. "Shall we?" He started down the hallway to the stairwell.

"What was all that about?" she asked.

"I have to administer a dose of terror to that idiot every so often to keep him from firing Frasier."

"Your friend the brilliant water engineer?"

"That's the one." He opened the door to the stairwell for her. She walked through and waited for him to lead the way down. The steps were worn, but clean enough, she noted.

"And why would he want to fire your friend, if he's so brilliant?" she asked as they went down the stairs.

"I told you, Harvey's an idiot," Mark said, his voice echoing up to her.

"An idiot? But he's the chief engineer of the Chicago water system."

He let out a bark of laughter. "Old Harvey is no engineer. He's the nephew of some alderman who pulled strings for him." He opened the door at the bottom of the stairs and ushered her through. They walked down a hallway that was low and dimly lit, but as clean as the staircase.

Mark continued, "Harvey needed someone who could do his job for him, so he picked Frasier, sight unseen, because he graduated from Oberlin University *summa cum laude*. Frasier got this job strictly on his own merit, you see. I simply remind Harvey of that fact from time to time."

She was about to ask another question when Mark stopped in front of a scuffed wooden door with no nameplate. It looked like a large utility closet, but Mark rapped on it, saying, "Frasier, it's me."

"Come in," said a muffled voice behind the door.

Mark pushed through. Eliza followed him.

28

Eliza wasn't sure what to expect, but when Mark opened the door she saw a cramped office lined with bookshelves, the center taken up by a massive drawing table and lamp. A man bent over a set of blueprints on the table, a frown of concentration on his forehead. He straightened as they came into the room, his coffee brown face splitting into a grin. "Finally decided to show up, did you?" As he spoke, his eyes fastened on Eliza, and his smile faded.

"Good morning, Frasier," Mark said. "Are we interrupting something?" He gestured to the plans.

"No." The man came out from behind the table. "I'm just finishing a design for the filtration system in the new South Side plant, if it ever gets built." He shot an inquiring look at Eliza.

"Frasier, this is Miss Elizaveta Karlova. Miss Karlova, this is Mr. Frasier Robinson," Mark said, watching her carefully.

"How do you do," Frasier said. He stuck out his hand, his face blank.

"How do you do," Eliza returned, taking his hand in her gloved one and shaking it.

He blinked, as if surprised that she observed basic etiquette toward him.

She looked over at Mark, who was smiling, an approving glint in his eyes. Apparently she'd passed a test.

Americans, she thought. *Always taking such absurd attitudes.* Eliza had met far too many kinds of people to be shocked by the sight of a man of color who was a scientist, as they clearly expected her to be.

"Miss Karlova," Frasier said. "Mark mentioned your name before. You're a client of his, I believe?"

"That's right," she said.

"And the sample Mark had me analyze is related to your case, is it?"

"No, only indirectly," Mark cut in. "This is about my other client."

"You mean Ca—" Frasier stopped himself, shooting another suspicious look at Eliza.

"Yeah," Mark said smoothly. "I'm looking for a creature that killed at least four men. That sample I gave you was found at the scene of one of the murders. A guy who got too close to the water system and was eaten from the inside out."

Frasier seemed shocked for an instant, but that was replaced by a thoughtful expression. "I see. So what's Miss Karlova's role in this?"

Mark said, "She has a background in chemistry. I want her to take a look at what you found in that sample. Did you finish the analysis?"

"Of course. The liquid was ordinary tap water, but there is one unusual thing about it."

"What?"

"Why don't I show you?"

He led them out of his office to another door across the hall. Inside was a narrow room mirroring the first, this one stuffed with laboratory equipment. Bottles and jars full of chemicals and several gleaming machines crowded shelves and lined two counters, one on either side. There was a beaker full of soup bubbling gently over a Bunsen burner on one counter, and the other contained a microscope, slides and pipettes.

"My lunch," Frasier said wryly, pointing to the Bunsen burner. He beckoned them over to the microscope.

As they wedged between the counters, Mark said, "I can't believe Daley still has you trapped in this basement."

"I like my basement," Frasier said. "No one bothers me here. I run my projects without any interference. I never even have to talk to the city planners. I simply hand over my work to Mr. Daley, and he takes it from there."

"And takes all the credit."

"Small price for the freedom to do exactly what I like and get paid for it. And before you ask, no, Daley isn't skimming my paycheck. Something has him afraid to even think about it," he said with a grin.

Eliza was concerned about the smallness of the laboratory as well, but for a different reason. In such cramped quarters, she might overwhelm the men with her scent, whether she tried to or not. "Do you mind if I smoke?" she asked, taking out her holder and cigarettes.

Frasier eyed her with a deepening disapproval. "Please try to refrain. Some of this equipment is delicate. Tobacco smoke can prove damaging to it. I hope you understand."

"Certainly," she murmured, putting the things away again. She leaned against a counter, as far away from the men as she could get.

Frasier set a slide on the microscope and looked into it, adjusting a few knobs. He drew back, gesturing for Mark to look into the eyepiece. "Tell me what you see."

Mark bent down and applied his eye to the lens. "It looks like a bunch of little pieces of tissue." He straightened up and beckoned Eliza over.

Reluctantly, she walked over and peered into the microscope. She saw a drop of water with a few translucent membranes floating in it. "These appear to be fragments of cells, but I can't tell what kind of organism." She drew its scent into her nose and held it there, concentrating.

There was a faint chemical tinge, but under that was an earthy smell that was strangely familiar, as if she'd smelled it all her life but never noticed it before.

"Those are fragments of slime mold cells," Frasier said as Eliza straightened up. "The water is remarkably clean otherwise. It's as if the slime mold absorbed all the microorganisms that are usually found in a water sample. Those cells were the only biological material I found."

"What's a slime mold?" Mark asked.

Frasier smiled a professorial smile. "A slime mold is an extremely common yet overlooked life form that is neither a plant, nor a fungus, nor an animal. It is instead a colony of microscopic amoeba-like cells that live dispersed in soil or water. But when resources grow scarce the individual cells can congregate together to form a single, larger organism that can move around to seek food."

"What kind of food does it eat?" Mark asked.

"Well, most slime molds are scavengers. They absorb dead tissue. However, some have been known to be predatory, though mostly on a microscopic scale."

"So this thing lives spread out through the water as a

bunch of little creatures and then globs together to form a larger creature when it wants to eat," Mark said. "How much larger are we talking about?"

"The biggest slime molds I'm aware of are only a few cubic inches in volume. But . . ." He shook his head, a frown creasing his brow. "The sample you brought me appears to be a species that has not yet been documented. At least, it isn't mentioned in any of the literature I've studied." He gestured toward the shelves crammed with scientific tomes in the office across the hall.

"If indeed this is a previously unknown species, characteristics like size would be equally unknown. And there's something else." He hesitated, as if what he was about to say made him uncomfortable.

"I'm listening," Mark said.

Frasier looked at Eliza.

"Do go on. This is fascinating," she said.

Frasier grimaced. "Well. The drainage systems around the Chicago River and Lake Michigan have been inundated with chemicals from the factories for nearly a century now. It's well understood that organisms exposed to strong chemicals mutate in various ways. And the more primitive they are, the stronger the mutation."

"So what are you saying?" Mark asked.

"It's possible that this slime mold has been warped beyond nature by industrial waste. Its capabilities might be impossible to predict."

"I think we have our killer," Mark said, his pale eyes gleaming. "Or, actually, our weapon. This creature's attacks aren't random, but it can't pick and choose specific victims by itself, right? It can't plan a sophisticated attack on a crime syndicate, for instance."

Frasier somehow nodded, shrugged, and shook his head all at once. "No, it can't. Slime molds don't have brains. They're not capable of anything but feeding and reproduction. The individual cells stay dispersed in their habitat until the chemical signals in the environment tell them to congregate."

"So someone is driving it," Mark said. "But who? And how?"

Eliza spoke up. "The how, you already know. Mr. Robinson just told you. Chemical signals in the environment."

Both of them turned toward her, startled.

She smiled at Mark. "Scent, darling. How all creatures navigate feeding and reproduction. Someone is giving this thing the scents of his targets and then turning it loose in the drain system to hunt down its victims like a bloodhound."

"I think you're right," Mark said.

"Do you?" Frasier said, his mouth flat. "I wonder how a rich debutante could know anything at all about chemical scent."

"Frasier," Mark said sharply.

She locked eyes with him. "If the debutante had studied the recent work of von Frisch and Butenandt, in which they demonstrate that scent is the key to animal behavior, then, she would know."

Frasier turned away, shoulders stiff. He said to Mark, "Be that as it may, I think you can rule out mystical methods of controlling this creature. It appears to be a natural, not a supernatural phenomenon. It must obey the laws of science. Which means the one guiding these attacks must have a biology or chemistry laboratory, and the skills to use it."

Mark met her eyes. "It just so happens I know a man who fits that description."

"Who do you mean?" Frasier asked.

"Lionel Duke," Mark said.

Frasier was looking back and forth between her and Mark. "But isn't he the one who—"

"That's right. The fellow who took over dear old Dad's chemical factory." Mark's face was thoughtful, verging on crafty. "I have to make a telephone call. Can you look after our guest for a moment, Frasier?"

"Of course."

"I'll be back in two shakes," Mark said, and left.

Eliza and Frasier sized each other up.

29

"Would you care to sit?" Frasier said, pulling out a stool tucked under the counter.

"Thank you," she said, taking the seat. "Please, carry on with your work if you like. I don't mean to inconvenience you."

"It's no inconvenience. You may as well get comfortable, since we might be waiting for a while. Mark will probably make a short stop at my boss's office," Frasier said with a mischievous grin as he pulled out another stool and sat. "I'm glad for the chance to speak to you."

"Oh? About what?" she said.

"If I may ask, what is the nature of your case with Mark?"

"It's merely to look into the backgrounds of a few gentlemen I know socially."

"Really?" Frasier looked skeptical. "Mark doesn't usually do background checks."

"He made an exception for me."

"Ah. And is your case going well?"

"Yes, in fact, it's all but over. Mr. Van Ryn gave me his report this morning."

Frasier seemed to relax a bit at that. "Then I suppose you won't be seeing much of him in the future."

"I suppose not," she said, fending off a pang of regret.

But Frasier looked happy at her response.

"You seem to know Mr. Van Ryn quite well. Tell me about him." She let her scent waft around him. Not much, just enough to make him say more than he normally would. "How did the two of you become friends?"

He blinked hazily. "We were raised together. My mother was his father's housekeeper. I've known him since we were babies."

She smiled, picturing Mark, the avenging angel, as a little white cherub with skinned knees and a smudge on his nose. "What was he like as a boy?"

"The same as he is now. Smart, tough, loyal." Frasier's eyes were taking on the unfocused quality that showed her poison was working on him. "He could have turned his back on me. Any other white boy would have. Instead he paid for my schooling with his own college money. When I asked him to help catch the zombie master, he helped, no questions asked. I'll always protect him. That's been my job ever since I can remember."

"Protect him from what?"

"The world. Other children. His bastard of a father."

"Did his father mistreat you?"

Frasier made a caustic sound. "He barely knew I existed. Which was lucky for me. Not so lucky for Mark. Mark, he hated."

"He hated his own son?" she whispered.

"He blamed him for his mother's death when he was born. And he despised him for the way he looks."

"That's awful!"

"That's been his life. Everyone he ever cared about has rejected him, except for me."

"He never had anyone special in his life? No woman?" she asked.

"Never. He tried to court my sister once, and it was a disaster. He doesn't let himself get attached to people anymore, especially his clients." He blinked, like he was struggling to focus. "Why are you different?"

"What do you mean? You think he's becoming attached to *me*?" She poured more scent into the air. She had to know the answer.

Frasier sank deeper into his trance. "I think he's falling for you. But I don't want Mark involved with someone who's going to yank him around and then throw him away. He loved my sister, and it almost destroyed him."

A strange sensation twisted through her heart. "You needn't worry about me. Our paths won't likely cross again after today."

His eyes were still unfocused, but his voice had an edge to it. "Good. Whatever your real scheme is, please, leave my friend out of it. Let him be."

Eliza bit her lip, hard. Standing, she said, "You know, I think I'll go out and smoke my cigarette in the hallway while I wait. Excuse me."

"Sure," Frasier said dreamily.

"And why don't we forget this conversation ever happened?"

"Okay."

She withdrew to the hallway before he passed out and lit a cigarette with shaking hands, wishing she'd kept her questions to herself after all.

But now, at least, she knew what she had to do. She had

to cloud Mark's memory. It would be simple, just as it had been with Frasier. She'd clouded men's minds many times before. All she had to do was contrive a way to touch his skin to deliver a dose of poison strong enough to overwhelm his resistance. And then she would tell him to forget her.

Because she couldn't have him falling for her. She couldn't bear the guilt. Or the shame. It might break her heart.

30

From the telephone booth in the lobby, Mark rang up a number he kept for cases just like this. Somewhere deep in the bullpen of the Chicago Tribune, the other end of the line clicked.

"Alvin Tracy," said a voice that sounded like it came from between teeth clenching a pipe. A typewriter chattered away in the background.

"Hello Alvin. It's Mark Van Ryn."

The typewriter ceased. "Van Ryn!" the voice was abruptly clear and there was a tension in it, eagerness with an edge of nervousness. "Long time since I heard your voice. How are things in spooksville?"

"Busy," Mark said. "Maybe you heard?"

"Heard what?" The caution in the reporter's voice was swamped by curiosity.

Mark said, "There's a dangerous science experiment going on at the Duke Chemical Company."

"You don't say." There was a rustle of paper and the scribble of a pencil.

He briefly told Tracy about the slime monster in the

sewer, let loose on Chicago by none other than the politically connected millionaire Lionel Duke. "It's already resulted in the deaths of at least four men," he finished.

"Which men? What's your evidence?"

"I can't name the victims. And the evidence is circumstantial at this point."

"In other words, you got nothing." Tracy sounded disgusted. "You don't think I'm actually going to write a story tying a man like Lionel Duke to crazy tales of monsters and murder with no proof, do you?"

"Of course not. I don't want anything published yet. All I want is for you to know what's happening and who's responsible when the rumble starts. If you want a front row seat on the action, watch Lionel Duke."

"Come on, you gotta give me something more than that," the reporter coaxed.

"I'll call you when I have anything solid, in return for our usual deal. You keep me out of it."

"You're the only private dick in the world who doesn't want his name in the paper, you know that, right?"

"Anyone who needs me can find me just fine. I don't want publicity. If I get any, I'm coming to talk to you personally."

"Swell, as long as you stand still so I can take your picture."

Mark hung up, pretty well satisfied. A little added pressure on Duke from the press was just the ticket. Who knew what a shameless muckraker like Tracy might dig up?

Next, he stopped at Harvey Daley's office for a quick chat. It followed the same script as all their chats, with Mark explaining how unhappy he'd be if Frasier wasn't treated right, and Harvey sweating, shaking and blubbering promises.

A few minutes later, when he went back downstairs to Frasier's laboratory, he found Eliza standing in the hallway outside his door. She was staring pensively at the smoke curling up from the cigarette in the holder between her fingers. She looked up as he approached, a reserve in her expression that hadn't been there when he left. "Hello," she said quietly.

"You look like you're ready to go."

She smiled, a forced, polite curve of her lips. "No, I merely stepped out to have a cigarette away from the equipment."

"Why don't you smoke it then, instead of staring at it?"

"I'm finished," she said, stubbing out the butt in a nearby ashcan.

The laboratory door opened and Frasier stepped out, looking around vaguely. "Mark. There you are. Where did you go?"

"To the telephone booth. I had to make a call, remember?"

"Oh. Right." He lifted a hand to his temple. "Sorry. I don't know what got into me. I have a bit of a headache all of a sudden."

"We should let you have your lunch," Eliza said. "No doubt you'll feel better after you've eaten."

"Yes," Frasier said, blinking hard. "No doubt."

Mark said, "All right, I can take a hint. Thanks for your help, Frasier. I'll let you know if I need anything else."

"You do that," Frasier said, his old grin returning. "And don't think I'm not going to call you about this later."

"Do what you got to do," Mark said, grinning back. They shook hands, and Frasier nodded to Eliza and wandered back into his laboratory.

Mark and Eliza walked to the stairwell and climbed back up to the first floor.

As they stepped into the lobby, he said, "Frasier isn't the only one who needs lunch. Come on, I'll buy you a red hot."

She stopped short in the middle of the lobby. "I beg your pardon. A red hot? With you?"

He stopped too. "I want to talk over the case while we eat. You had a good insight back there, about this monster using scent to hunt its victims. I bet you've got some more useful ideas floating around under your hat. What do you say?"

"Well, I don't know . . ."

"Don't tell me. A lady like you doesn't eat chili dogs."

"For your information, I adore chili dogs."

He grinned. "Then you shall have one."

31

Mark escorted Eliza into the car and they cruised through the city, nice and easy. Mark had never much liked his father's car until today. But for the first time in his life, he knew how it felt to drive a powerful machine with a gorgeous woman by his side. He glanced over at her as looked out the window at the streets at the buildings sliding past, imprinting her profile in his memory. The exquisite lines of her face glowed with warm May sunlight. The glare was jabbing at him through the windows, but not even the headache spiking through his temples could spoil his mood.

He spotted a likely hot dog stand tucked in a street across Lake Shore from the Field Museum and pulled up to the curb. They got sausages smothered in chili and wrapped in grease paper.

Eliza took hers with an eager smile. "Thank you. Care to go to sit in the park near the fair while we eat?"

Mark's immediate impulse was to say no. Even here, in the shadows of the buildings, the daylight was draining his strength. Out in the open space near the fair, exposed to direct sunlight, he would be completely defenseless. But as he looked down into Eliza's sparkling eyes, he found himself saying, "Sure."

They strolled toward Lake Shore Drive and crossed over the road on the walkway to Grant Park, where they found a bench with a view.

Past the Field Museum and the stadium were the grounds of the World's Fair, only days from opening. A tall fence shielded the fair from the curious eyes of passersby, but the tops of the pavilions reared above the barrier. They were modern, sleek monuments to the future, each in a different combination of red, white, yellow, green and blue. And above it all towered the Skyride, two towers of steel struts rising high above the shore, a cable for the gondolas strung across the lagoon between them.

From where they sat, they could see the small shapes of workers hanging long red flags from the modernist flag-poles slanting over the main promenade. Beyond the flags rose the blue-and-white tower of the grandest building in the fair, the Hall of Science.

Next week, half of Chicago was going to be streaming through that flag-lined street, eager to catch a glimpse of the marvelous future of the Twentieth Century.

They ate as they looked out over the peaceful view of the fairgrounds and the park. A nanny strolled with a baby in a perambulator, a spinster trotted by with crumbs for the birds, and two men walked slowly past, a tall beefy one and a lean whippy one, their heads bent together in conversation. There was something familiar about the last pair, but he filed them away for later and focused on Eliza.

She was, he learned, the only person in the world who managed to look elegant while eating a red hot. But she seemed to be enjoying herself, taking her dainty little bites with enthusiasm.

Next time, though, he'd have to buy her caviar and lobster. Or moonbeams and dewdrops. Or whatever angels ate.

She glanced up at him as she chewed, eyes smiling in pleasure. She touched her lip with her little pink tongue.

All thought of angels evaporated in a flood of heat. He cleared his throat and looked away from her. "So. Keen to go to the fair, are you?"

"Definitely. It'll be a grand time. I'm especially eager to try the Skyride." She pointed to the two metal spires with girlish excitement. Underneath that cool, jaded façade was clearly a woman eager for thrills. "And you?" she asked. "Will you be going to the fair, Mark?"

"Sure. I'll need to keep an eye on the place in case it goes kablooey."

"Why? What could happen?"

He shrugged. "Anything. World Fairs tend to attract the weirdos. Like the madman who built the Murder House down in Englewood and killed all those tourists during the last world's fair."

"I've heard stories about that."

"They're all true. One of my first jobs was to track down the bones of a couple of the girls he murdered. The owners of the lot where the house stood wanted to build an apartment block on the site, but ghosts were haunting the place. Couldn't have tenants running away screaming."

"And did you find them? The girls?"

"Yeah. I got them buried properly, and the hauntings stopped. Turns out, though, the ghosts weren't the real problem. No one wants to live on that lot, haunted or not.

So now the only thing standing there is a post office. The Federal Government isn't sentimental."

"You have the most fascinating stories, Mr. Van Ryn."

He might have felt flattered, if he hadn't heard her say pretty much the same thing to five other men just last night. And how did they get on this topic, anyway? *She* was the one who was supposed to be talking. He said, "Not nearly as exciting as yours, I'll bet. You've been all over the world lately, haven't you?"

"You would know, since you've seen the stamps on my luggage."

He merely arched an eyebrow at her. "Tell me about your travels. I'm interested."

"Well, I rode an elephant through Burma, and a camel through the Sahara, and a river boat up the Amazon. Oh, and I was nearly thrown into a volcano in Java . . ." She sighed. "The truth is, travel isn't nearly as interesting as one would think. Mostly it's tedious and uncomfortable."

"Why did you do it, then?"

She turned her face away. "I was looking for something."

"Looking for what?"

"Perfumes. I've been in pursuit of exotic scents."

"Huh." He thought for a moment. "In all your travels, have you ever smelled something like the sample in the microscope?"

At her startled glance, he said, "I saw you take a sniff in the laboratory."

"You're very observant."

"That's why they pay me the big bucks. So what did you smell?"

"Something I've smelled a million times before, but

never really noticed until now. It's simply part of the ambient odors of soil and water."

"What's it like?"

"It's hard to put a scent like that into words. There are thousands of comparisons to what it smelled like."

"Why don't you make it real simple for me."

"All right. It smelled like mushrooms and blood, with an acid taint. It was the acid that caught my attention. It makes me think your friend Mr. Robinson was right, that this slime mold creature has been altered by chemicals. It's no longer completely natural."

"I see." He brushed his fingers over his brows as his headache gave a twinge. "Would you be able to recognize the scent if you smelled it again?"

"Certainly, now that I know what I'm looking for. Why?"

"Because maybe I want to call on that nose of yours to help solve this case."

He saw interest flash in her face, but then she shook her head. "I don't want to get involved in detective work. Especially if your client is the likes of Gabriel Camonte."

He shot her a narrow glance. "Now, what made you bring that name up?"

"You said that the monster was attacking a 'crime syndicate.' And Camonte is the only crime syndicate boss I know."

"So you do know Camonte. What's your relationship with him?"

"Why, none. He tried to charm me in the hotel lobby a few days ago, but it won't surprise you to learn that I sent him on his way."

"Actually, I *am* surprised. Why wasn't he on that

husband list of yours? He fits your requirements. Rich, evil."

"Don't be ridiculous, darling. He's already married. And even if he weren't, I wouldn't touch him with the tip of my shoe. He stinks of disease."

He stared at her, nonplussed.

She smiled faintly. "Too direct? Forgive me. I forgot to cater to a gentleman's delicate sensibilities."

"There you go, thinking I'm a gentleman again." He grinned at her, but with more difficulty than before. Pain was cinching around his skull like a vise. He was reaching the limit of how much light he could tolerate. He got his dark glasses out of his pocket and put them on, but it didn't help much.

Eliza was watching him more carefully than he liked. "Are you all right, Mr. Van Ryn?"

"I'm fine," he said, his voice clipped.

"Ah, good. Well, I believe I'd like to go back to my hotel, now. Would you kindly take me?" She stood up.

Mark stood too, trying to hide a wave of dizziness. "Sure. It will be my pleasure."

They crossed over the street back into the canyons of the buildings. He almost sighed when the thin shade enveloped him. His headache subsided to a dull throb. Eliza was still sending him considering looks.

"Sure you want to go back to your hotel?" he said to distract her. Maybe he could take her to an ice cream parlor instead, keep talking to her—

"Yes," she said. "I need to get ready for this evening. Lionel Duke is taking me to hear jazz at the Green Mill."

32

"You're seeing Duke tonight?" he said, incredulous. "After everything I've told you? You can't be serious!"

She faltered, but recovered quickly. "But of course I am. He's exactly the kind of man I came here to marry—wealthy and corrupt."

He took a moment to calm himself down. "Have you considered that I might put him in jail for murder before you can get him to the altar?"

"You don't know he's your killer."

"It's him. I'm sure of it."

"But you have no proof. And furthermore, if the facts you discovered about his past life are true, Duke doesn't have the science background to control this creature."

"No, but he has a scientist working for him," he said, thinking of the scrawny little man who gave him the slip in the trolley tunnels. "When I find the scientist, I'll have Duke. It won't take me long."

"Another reason to marry him soon," she said quietly, as though half to herself.

"Why are you so sure he'll marry you? He's been a

widower for five years. He's shown no signs of looking for a wife."

"I don't think you'd like to hear my methods for tempting a man into wedlock."

He bit his tongue. She was right. He would hate it. And at the same time, he was on fire to hear about her "methods".

They had reached the car. He opened the door for her. "I'd prefer not to discuss this further," she said as she slid into the seat.

"Yes, Ma'am," he said shortly, and closed the door.

He drove them back up Lake Shore, but the fun was gone. *You aren't supposed to be having fun, fool. This is a job.*

As he pulled around in front of the Drake and parked at the curb, he saw her stripping off her gloves, slowly tugging one finger at a time. He couldn't decipher her expression.

"Thanks for the outing, and for lunch," she said.

A bellhop came to open the car door for her, but Mark took off his dark glasses and sent him a glare that had him beating a hasty retreat. He turned in his seat to look at Eliza square on.

He said, "I gave you my best information in my report. What you do with it is up to you. But I'll throw in some free advice. Stay away from Duke."

"You know what they say about things you get for free."

He ground his teeth. "Take it as a warning, then. Don't get in my way when I'm investigating this case. Because if you're not my client any more, and you're lying to me about your involvement in these murders, you'll be my suspect, and I'll be your worst nightmare."

Her eyes fell to the gloves she held in her hands. "I thought you trusted me more than that."

"I don't trust anyone, angel."

"Well, I trust you, Mr. Van Ryn," she said with a half-smile. "And I enjoyed myself this morning. You treat me like a real person. You have no idea how much I appreciate that."

She stowed her gloves in her purse and looked up at him, eyes wide and clear, yet somehow sad. "You do wish me well, don't you?"

"Of course I do," he said quietly.

"In that case, won't you kiss the bride, for luck?" With an arch of her neck, she turned the soft curve of her cheek toward him.

He knew what he was supposed to do. What a *gentleman* would do. He'd kiss her and be done with it.

He took off his hat. Slowly he bent his head and brushed his lips against her cheek. Her skin was soft as a flower petal and smelled a thousand times as wonderful. He could only draw back a few inches.

Her eyes flickered up to his. He was aware that she had raised her hand to his neck, her fingers hovering near his collar.

But pure, animal need had taken him over. The heat from her body was searing him, her scent driving him out of his mind. He had no experience to draw on, so he acted on sheer instinct. He cupped her face in his hands and slanted his mouth over hers.

She stiffened in shock, but he didn't let that stop him. He caressed her lips with his, and when she gasped in outrage, he merely deepened the kiss. He slipped his tongue between her lips and . . . *God*. She was hot and wet inside, her flavor exquisite. He plundered her with his mouth as he slipped his hands down to her waist and pulled her toward him. She was amazingly slender and soft against his bigger, harder body.

And yet, she was the one in control. If she pushed him away, if she shrank back in revulsion, she would destroy him. But she didn't. The hand that had been hovering at his neck fell to his shoulder. The slender fingers clenched in the fabric of his coat, and she kissed him back. Her body shaped itself to his, as lush and slender as a flowering vine twining around a tree. Her mouth was fever hot, her lips and tongue tangling with his. A low moan sounded in her throat, vibrating deep in his own body.

It lasted for a second out of eternity, as deep and endless as the night. And then he felt the panic in her, the withdrawal. She moved back, the end of the kiss leaving him cold. But her fingertips were touching his neck above his collar. "Forget me," she said unevenly.

"What?" he said, his voice rough.

She pressed the pads of her fingers to his neck, and there was a slight tingling sensation where she touched him. She said, "Go home, and forget me. Forget my case. Everything. You never saw me. We never—" she broke off.

He had no idea what to do or what to say. His lips still burned from her kiss. His heart was hammering, his shaft was hard as steel. His breath was coming in time with hers. But she said . . . she said . . .

His hands fell from her waist of their own accord, and he drew back in his seat. She took her fingers away from his neck and bowed her head. She wouldn't look at him. "Eliza," he wanted to say, but her name turned to ash in his throat.

She spun toward the door and grabbed the handle. "I'll remember for both of us." He saw a teardrop fall on her naked hand before she wrenched the door open and escaped into the sunlight.

33

Eliza fled to the hotel as if the devil was after her.

Her first real kiss had been a glorious, dreadful revelation. Now she knew what true desire could be. She had learned the savage pleasure to be found in the arms of a man she really wanted. And she would never have that perfect moment again, only the memory of it haunting the rest of her days.

But at least it wouldn't haunt him, not now that she'd used her poison to cloud his mind.

It's better this way, she told herself, blotting her eyes with the back of her hand. Mark's life would go back bear the burden of the longing between them.

But he would still remember his other client, Gabriel Camonte, and his other case. And so she would take his warning about Duke to heart. She would have to marry the man as soon as possible, before his enemies closed in on him. When he took her out to the Green Mill tonight, she would get him to propose.

Perhaps there would even be a silver lining to the cloud of intrigue she found herself in. Perhaps Camonte would take Duke down before her poison did. Even if he was as evil as Mark claimed, she didn't want his blood on her hands. She never wanted to be responsible for a man's death again.

The bellhop opened the hotel door for her and she rushed inside, desperate for the privacy of her room. But when she climbed the grand staircase to the hotel lobby, a gaunt figure in a severe black frock rose up out of a chair and stepped squarely into Eliza's path. Her grandmother's maidservant, Helga. "What is it?" she said shortly.

"Mistress says you are to come up directly," the maid said in a thick German accent. "She wants to speak with you."

Eliza was tempted to send the woman back with nothing but a biting retort, but she would have to face the inevitable sooner or later. So she gritted her teeth and followed the maid's thin back up the elevator and down the plush hallway to her grandmother's suite.

The parlor was much as it had been two days ago. Angelique was once again on her settee, lavender frock perfect, embroidery in hand. This time the silver tea tray was already set out in front of her. "So you are here at last."

Eliza raised an eyebrow coolly. "As you see, *Grand-mère*."

The countess flicked a finger at Helga, and the maid left without a word. She set aside her needlework and lifted her teacup. "Where have you been?"

"Meeting with the detective I hired to investigate the backgrounds of my candidates. You saw him last night, remember?"

"Yes, I remember." She took a dainty sip from her china cup. "And why did this detective leave his scent all over you?" Her voice was needle sharp.

Eliza turned toward the entryway mirror to take off her hat and coat. "It must have happened when I clouded his memory. He's very resistant to my influence. I had to touch him to dose him with enough poison."

"Hmm." She felt her grandmother's steely regard prickling over her. "But you did manage to cloud his mind, did you not?"

"Yes, of course." She kept her dry eyes on the mirror as she fluffed her hair. "I have no more use for him. Most likely we will never meet again, but if we do, he won't remember me."

"Very well. Did he at least discover the information you wanted?"

Eliza released a silent breath in relief. "Yes. I know enough now to make my choice." At last, she turned to face the older woman. "Lionel Duke."

Angelique considered that, tapping a fingertip on her teacup. "Well. His birth is decidedly below yours. But he is the wealthiest of your candidates, if the gossip I heard from the Mannering woman is correct."

"He is. He's also the worst of them, I'm told. He may be a murderer."

"Yes, I suspect he is. All four of my husbands were murderers, you know. One gets to know the type."

Eliza studied the older woman for a moment. Sometimes, she was forced to remember that Angelique had had four husbands, each one of the vilest men imaginable, and each dead by her poison. She had to wonder what that must have done to her . . .

"*Grand-mère.*" She sat on a chair near the settee and looked into her grandmother's beautiful, finely lined face. "Didn't you ever wonder if it were possible to *not* live the way we've been living? To . . . to make our way in the world with our skills and talents alone, and not by preying upon other people, no matter how evil they are?"

The countess looked back at her, as impassive as a Madonna in an ikon. Her gold cross glinted at her throat. "Foolish girl. You should not talk of such things. Who are you to question the ways of our ancestresses? Who are you to question the will of God?" she said, her voice rising as she spoke.

She paused for a beat and then said more calmly, "We are what we are. It is our place in this fallen world to punish wicked men. As you have already done once. Do keep that in mind, *chérie*."

Eliza managed not to flinch at the cruel little jab about the man in San Francisco.

"Besides," Angelique continued, "low breeding aside, you could do far worse in a husband than the one you have chosen. Duke is neither old nor ugly. Consider yourself fortunate in that regard."

"Yes," she said in a low voice. But though other people might find Duke handsome and charismatic, she felt no attraction to him. Certainly none of the heat she had felt with Mark from the first moment she saw him.

Last night at the party, when Duke invited her to the Green Mill, he had smiled smugly and slipped his hand around her waist, his disturbing, metallic scent enveloping her.

She had smiled and let him touch her, but she felt nothing but distaste. Fortunately, the butler had interrupted them to tell Duke that a visitor was at the door looking for him. He had left the party soon after that, so he didn't have a chance to touch her further, thank heaven.

What would she have done if he had kissed her the way Mark kissed her? She could hardly bear to think about it.

But she would have to find a way to tolerate his kiss, and much more than that.

Angelique was watching her with sharp eyes. "This detective you hired. What is his power?" she suddenly asked.

She shrugged and said in a disinterested tone, "He has an affinity for darkness. I believe he can hide within it, and can draw strength from it. And I think light has the opposite effect."

The old woman's eyes glimmered in thought. "Light weakens him? *Très intéressant.*"

Eliza had meant only to convince Angelique that Mark was no danger to them, but now she wondered if she had said too much. She didn't like her grandmother's considering expression.

She hastily stood up and said, "Not to cut this delightful chat short, but I'd like to rest. I intend to get Duke to propose this evening."

"See that you do." Angelique set down her cup and took up her needlepoint again. "Sleep well."

34

When Eliza got to her room, rest was the last thing on her mind. She had a call to make, and she'd been avoiding it long enough. She picked up the telephone on a small table and put it to her ear, clicking the call button. "Could you connect me please," she said to the operator, and gave her a number she knew by heart.

The telephone rang long enough for her to grow worried, but at last, there was a click. "Hello," said Mrs. DeForest.

"Hello, it's Eliza."

"My dear! I'm so glad you called! How are you?"

"I'm well, but how are *you*? Are you better?"

"Indeed I am," the older woman said cheerfully. "Why, I'm fit as a fiddle! The only reason I'm here at home instead of at the shop is because my doctor insisted that I rest for a few days, the dear old fool. When he visits tomorrow, I shall tell him he must allow me to go back to work or I'll run mad."

"Oh, do be careful! You mustn't tire yourself."

"Nonsense. There is far too much for me to be doing

before I can take a proper holiday. Which reminds me, we still need to have our talk, you and I. I intend to persuade you to come back to the shop."

Her heart plummeted. "I can't. I'm so sorry."

"Will you at least discuss it with me? I'm certain we can work out whatever is troubling you, my dear."

"Mrs. DeForest . . ."

"Come to tea tomorrow, won't you? We can talk things over then." She sounded so affectionate and eager that Eliza's resistance broke.

"Of course I will." Her poison wouldn't hurt the older lady if she only spent a few minutes with her, surely.

"Wonderful, dearest. One o'clock, sharp."

She smiled. "One o'clock sharp."

After she ended the call, Eliza was still restless. Ordinarily at this time of the day, she would be trekking through a pathless jungle in search of a rare flower, not idling in a luxurious room. The silk-lined walls and soft bedding felt smothering when she was used to a cot in a tent. It was harder than she'd thought to adjust to the habits of a lady of leisure.

She prowled toward the window. As she wandered past the trunk of perfumes, she glanced down at it and stopped. On impulse, she knelt on the floor next to it and opened the lid. As always, a little thrill of pride ran over her at the sight of the glass vials full of her own original creations. She took them out one by one and sniffed them, critically analyzing each nuance of scent. Not bad work, if she did say so herself.

Perhaps it was only her imagination, but this time one of the blends reminded her a bit of Mark. Rich, subtle musk with top notes as pure as a clear evening sky. She cradled the vial in her hands, breathing it in. If she were to manufacture it as a cologne, she would name it *l'Ange blanc,* she decided. Her would-be guardian angel. He really had wanted to keep her safe. And she had clouded his memory to keep *him* safe. The irony was bitter.

His warning about Duke echoed in her mind, nagging her. If Duke was indeed the man behind the monster attacks, maybe she should take measures to protect herself.

Perhaps she could recreate the scent of the water sample in Frasier Robinson's laboratory. If her theory was right, and Duke was controlling the monster with chemical scents, then she might be able to counter it with her own formula.

She gathered up a notebook and pen, perfume, pipettes, and a bottle. She sniffed the essence, measured drops into the bottle, scribbled in her book, thought, sniffed, dropped, and scribbled. Hours ticked by, the daylight behind the curtains falling into dusk. When six o'clock struck, she had a page full of a written formula and a bottle full of scent that had begun to mimic the fetid chemical signature of the monster. It wasn't nearly finished, but it was a start.

She stood and stretched. It was past time she dressed for the evening. She took off her day dress, hung it in the closet, and started to pull on her dressing gown when she caught sight of herself in the full-length mirror. She turned to look into it fully. Her eyes drifted to the place behind her reflection where she had scented Mark's presence the day they met. Warmth flooded over her as she remembered the way she'd teased him. Luring him to touch her. And it hadn't been merely a ploy to get him to show himself. Part of her had wanted his touch, badly.

She closed her eyes and raised a hand to her throat, trailing it over the delicate skin there, imagining it was Mark's hand. Her fingers smoothed lower to the swell of her breast. She touched the hard-beading nipple through the silk of her undergarments, then pinched it, gasping at the pleasure. Her other hand pressed the place between her thighs that was suddenly pulsing with need. She pretended it was Mark's broad, callused palm rubbing her there. The folds of her sex were wet and slippery beneath the fabric, her bud swollen, her opening aching for something to fill its emptiness.

"Mark," she whispered. Wild thoughts rose up in her. Perhaps he had thrown off her poison and followed her again. Perhaps he was here, watching her now, about to come out of the shadows and touch her, take her, put himself inside her. She breathed in deeply, searching for his scent on the air. But there was nothing.

She forced her hands away from her body and grabbed the mirror frame. She lifted her lids and stared into her reflection's bleak eyes.

She shouldn't think of Mark any more. It seemed impossible to do, but she had to try, or else go shrieking mad. She had promised to be married, and Mark had forgotten all about her.

35

Forget her? Like hell. Mark slammed his fist into the heavy bag. He'd done nothing but think of her for the last eight hours. He hadn't slept. Hadn't eaten. He'd lifted weights until his tendons creaked and hit his bag until his knuckles were raw. But he couldn't pound his body into submission. Ever since that kiss, he'd had an iron-hard erection that would not quit.

He wanted Eliza like he'd never wanted anything in his life. His craving for her flesh against his was like a monster inside him. For the last seven years, he had kept his lust buried in a deep slumber, but she had aroused it, darker and fiercer than ever before. And now one way or another, he had to get it out before it drove him mad.

He went at the bag in a flurry of fists until his heart was thundering and sweat was trickling down the naked skin of his back. Canvas streaked with his blood swam before his eyes. He landed one last punch and sank to his knees, his chest heaving, his breath sawing out of his lungs. *No good.* He couldn't function like this. He had to do what he had to do. He stripped the boxer's tape off his hands with a few quick jerks and grabbed his towel, spreading it out on the floor in front of him.

He didn't like to do this often. He was afraid that if he got in the habit, he would spend his days doing nothing else. But right now he simply had no choice. He had a load of seed in his balls that would not be denied.

He eased the waistband of his boxing shorts over his straining shaft. It arched up fiercely between his thighs, its veins throbbing with need. He fisted himself, biting down on a groan. A drop of pearly liquid beaded out of the swollen head.

He knelt over the towel, stroking down the length of his cock with one hand, rubbing the sensitive tip with the other. He groaned again and his eyes slid shut. On the back of his lids he saw Eliza, standing at her mirror in her underwear, just as she had been in her hotel room the other night. "You like to look at me, don't you? Wouldn't you like to touch me?" she said, her voice a soft purr. In the reflection, her back arched and her hands lifted to the hooks of her brassiere.

This time, in Mark's vision, he didn't run off. He came out of the shadows and stood behind her, feeling the heat of her body against his naked skin as he drank in her image in the mirror. His eyes met hers in the reflection. She smiled at him and unfastened her brassiere. Black silk and lace whispered over her skin as it fell away from her breasts. In his mind he saw them perfectly, high, firm, and beautifully shaped. Her skin gleamed like satin and her nipples were as tight and rosy as little berries. "Touch me," she said to him.

He saw himself move behind her, sliding his hands up the curve of her waist and around her front to fit those gorgeous breasts to his palms. He weighed them, rubbing the hard points between his fingers and thumbs until she arched them harder into his grip, her silky head falling back against his shoulder. He bent his head and raked his lips up the curve of her throat, nipping and licking her, and she tasted as delicious as she smelled. She turned her head as he swept a kiss over her jaw, and her lips tangled with his, kissing, sucking, lapping, biting, until she was moaning into his mouth. He moved his hand down, over her flat stomach to the vee of her legs, and palmed her through the black silk of her panties as she cried out in pleasure.

He gasped at his vision, his fist flying over his shaft. In his fantasy, He saw himself stroke down the fine skin of her arms, lifting her hands to brace them on the mirror. He broke the kiss and leaned her forward, drawing his fingers down the sleek line of her back to the cleavage at the swell of her bottom, hidden by her panties.

He tore the last flimsy scrap of silk off of her and ran his hands greedily over the lush curves he exposed. Her sex was pink, and tight, and gleaming with wetness for him. He put his cock to that hot little opening and shoved it inside in one hard, fast thrust. She was soft and tight, hot and wet, and he forged into her all the way to his root. She cried out at his invasion, a breathy, needy moan. He pulled his glistening cock out almost all the way and shoved it in again, and again, and again. He watched her in the mirror, her breasts bouncing and shimmering, her skin flushing, her lips parting in pleasure. He grabbed her hips and slammed her back into him and she cried out again.

In the real world he was pumping his cock faster and faster through his fingers. He cupped his balls as they grew hard and tight, flexing his buttocks, straining toward his orgasm. In his dream, she looked over her shoulder at him, her eyes shining. "Mark!" she whispered.

That was it for him. He snarled as his seed exploded out of him in a volcanic rush, on and on until he saw white.

Gasping, Mark slumped back on his haunches and grabbed onto the heavy bag to keep from falling over. He eased his hand away from his pulsing shaft and tried to slow his heart. He closed his eyes, not wanting to see the evidence of his shame on the towel. He felt drained, empty, and furious at himself.

He should be getting ready to track down the monster's lair tonight. Instead, he was going to go chasing after the twist who'd tied his cock in a knot. She'd told him that she and Lionel Duke would be at the Green Mill, so that was where Mark was going to be. In this too, he had no choice.

36

When he could move again, he grabbed his soiled towel and got to his feet. He stumbled off to the shower.

He scrubbed himself down, shaved, and got dressed for battle. The Green Mill had a black-tie dress code, so he pulled a tuxedo out of his closet. He planned on letting himself be seen this evening, and his clothes might buy him a few extra minutes before the bouncers tried to throw him out.

By the time he stepped outside his front door it was fully dark, the dim streetlights flickering to life, the city stirring with the hard energy of early night.

At that very moment, two familiar black Lincolns pulled up at the curb. Mark locked his door and stood waiting on the stoop for McGann and his boys to climb out of the cars. The same gang as before, but now sporting some colorful new bruises.

He shoved his hands into his pockets and said with a half-smile, "Hiya fellas. Those are some nice shiners."

McGann stumped up to him. His arm was in a sling, his gun hand wrapped tightly. He looked over Mark's clothes and sneered. "Where the hell are you going in that monkey suit?"

"Monster hunting, where else?"

"Yeah? Well, we're going with you. The boss has had enough of your stalling. He paid you good money, and he wants answers. Or you're gonna pay him back with interest."

Mark heaved a sigh. "Do you need another gimp wrist to remind you not to threaten me?"

McGann flushed. "You're going to pay for that, too, punk, but later. Tonight you're helping us stop this . . . this *thing*."

Mark scratched his chin thoughtfully. "As it happens, I'm going to allow you to take me where I'm going. Come on." He pushed through the small clump of gangsters to the first Lincoln and yanked open the rear door.

"Take you where?" McGann called after him.

Mark set a foot on the running board and grinned at him. "Your very own nightclub, the Green Mill." He got into the car and shut the door.

Swearing, McGann scrambled into the front seat next to his driver and glared at Mark over his shoulder. "You think the . . . thing is gonna attack our place tonight?"

"Could be. I need to do some investigating."

"You're not investigating our club!"

"Is this about your bootlegging tunnels? Don't worry, I already know them all."

McGann snorted in fury.

Mark said, "I'm catching this monster with or without your help. If you want to be useful, all you've got to do is walk in with me all friendly-like, and let everyone know what good pals we are. After that, keep your people out of my way so no one gets hurt. Simple. So let's go."

"Wait one damn minute," McGann said. "Me and my guys ain't dressed right. We gotta go change."

"The Outfit owns the place, McGann. You can dress any way you want. Besides, if someone there gets eaten tonight, they're not going to care what you're wearing."

McGann clenched his jaw, but he barked out, "The Green Mill, boys."

They drove up through the Loop, under the rattling L, and across the river to North Side. The Uptown clubs and restaurants were hopping, the Riviera Theater was crowded with people buying tickets for the new *King Kong* movie, and the Aragon Ballroom was milling with arriving dancers. The Green Mill was bustling too. The Outfit's unofficial jazz club was in a low building under a green neon sign in the shape of a windmill, aiming to be the Moulin Rouge in Paris and not quite getting there.

As the Lincolns pulled up at the curb, Mark could already hear a muffled wail of jazz horns coming from inside the place. He and the mobsters got out and pushed through the green wooden door into the club as the bouncers all but bowed to them.

Inside was a long, low-lit room with green wallpaper and gilded acanthus leaves everywhere. A bar snaked along one side and a stage occupied by a jazz band took up the far end. The stage lights gleamed off of the musicians' white jackets as they played. Tables and chairs full of jazz fans filled up the remaining space, except for a narrow slice of floor cleared for dancing. The air was full of cigarette smoke and music.

Mark only dimly registered this, because the instant he set foot in the place, all he saw was *her*. She was sitting at a cozy table by the wall, looking bored and fashionable in a glimmering black gown cut low over her ripe breasts and silk gloves cut high over her slender arms.

He'd done her a disservice when he'd thought she was pretending to be Greta Garbo or Marlene Deitrich, he thought. She wasn't copying the femmes-fatale from the movies. *They* were copying *her*. She was the original seductress who led men gladly to their doom. The others all tried, and failed, to be Eliza.

And right now Lionel Duke was getting the full force of her charm. Mark saw the man's handsome profile crease in a self-satisfied smile as he leaned toward her and murmured in her ear. She tossed her head and said something in return, a dimple flashing on her cheek. Then she stiffened.

As he watched, he saw her do that gesture of hers again, tipping her nose up to scent the air. She looked carefully around the room and caught sight of him standing in the group by the door. For an instant their eyes locked. Then she smoothly turned back to her companion.

But by then Duke and the rest of the patrons were looking at them too. A lull fell over the room as the band struck up "Rhapsody in Blue". Mark had heard they played that song whenever Camonte's gang walked through the door. But after a few bars they trailed off in a confusion of notes.

They must be quite a sight, Mark thought gleefully. Banged-up, badly dressed mobsters limping into their own joint with Mark, of all people, in tow.

The gangsters slouched toward their usual table in the center of the room between the bar and the dance floor looking thoroughly disgruntled.

Mark peeled off from the group and strolled to the bar. "Whiskey. Put it on McGann's tab," he said to the barman.

After a long look at him and another long look at the Outfit boys, the guy poured him his drink.

The band shook off their awkward moment and started up a slow dance number. A few couples drifted to the dance floor and the murmur of conversation swelled again.

Whiskey in hand, Mark leaned an elbow on the bar and glanced around the room. He caught the eye of a fellow bussing tables. A lean man with mahogany skin and a white waiter's jacket. Johnson, he thought his name was. Frasier had introduced him a few years ago.

Mark caught the man's eye and nodded.

Johnson nodded back and vanished into the back room with a tray full of glasses.

He turned his attention on the patrons, but saw nothing but the usual bunch of shady types and slummers. No one in the place pinged his senses except Eliza and her date.

37

Eliza's face was carefully turned away from him as she cuddled up next to Duke. Pretending that if she couldn't see him, he couldn't see her, maybe.

That never works, sweetheart. Drink in hand, he ambled across the room toward the darling couple.

Duke watched him coming with a half-smile. "Mark," he drawled. "We seem to be meeting everywhere nowadays. I see neither hide nor hair of you for years, and now here you are. Again."

"Funny coincidence, eh Lionel?"

"Indeed." He slid a glance at McGann and his boys, who were eyeing them right back. "Interesting friends you've made."

"I might say the same for you," Mark returned, his eyes on Eliza.

"Ah, where are my manners?" Duke said with a little laugh. "You remember Miss Karlova."

She held out her hand in a languid gesture. "How do you do," she said, with a polite, distant smile on her lips. As if those lips hadn't been locked on his a few hours ago.

A hard smile edged his own mouth as he took her hand in his. "Yeah," he said. "Eliza isn't the kind of lady a man forgets. Thank you for the lovely morning we spent together, by the way. I hope you enjoyed the red hot sausage." He brought her hand to his lips and brushed a kiss over her gloved fingertips.

Her face drained of color as she stared at him, wide-eyed. She all but snatched her hand away from him. "You—you remember."

Duke arched an eyebrow at her. "What's this? You spent the morning with Mark? Why, how charitable of you to visit with a poor invalid, my dear."

"Yeah, she's a regular angel of mercy." Mark kept his eyes on Eliza. "We could talk about the reason you came to see me, or we can dance. What do you say angel?"

"I . . . I . . ." she said.

"Speechless with delight, I guess." He plopped his whiskey glass down on the table and all but scooped Eliza up out of her chair. "You don't mind, do you old fellow?" he said to Duke. Without waiting for a reply he swept Eliza onto the dance floor.

It had been a long time since he'd danced with a woman. Not since the fluffy little debutantes of his youth. But she made it easy. She was a smooth, graceful dancer, responding to the lightest touch as he moved her around the floor. Her gloved hand rested light as smoke on his shoulder, the fingers of the other clasping his softly.

But though her body moved beautifully with his, from the neck up, she wasn't happy with him at all. Her eyes were narrowed, her lush red lips drawn tight. "What are you doing?" she murmured. "Why are you trying to convince Duke you're courting me?"

"Would you rather I told him you hired me to spy on him?"

"I would rather you hadn't come here at all. What do you think you're about, interfering with my plans like this?"

"It isn't about you, sweetheart. I'm on a job. It's just your bad luck if I accidentally wreck your chance to nab a murderer for a husband."

"For your information, you can't destroy my chance to 'nab' Duke, no matter what you do. You're only making a fool of yourself, Mr. Van Ryn."

"Since our lips got to know each other so well this morning, I think you can call me Mark."

Her cheeks turned pink. "So you remember that too."

"If you think I'd forget a kiss like that just because you tell me to, you don't know me very well, Eliza." He slipped his hand down her back an inch and squeezed her softly.

She sucked in a breath and her blush deepened. "Stop that. What do you want, Mark? Really."

"I want to know what Duke told you about his pet monster."

"Nothing. The only topic we've discussed is the World's Fair."

"That's all?"

"That, and all the important politicians who will be there on opening day. Lionel wants very badly to impress them."

"So it's Lionel, is it?"

"Yes. What else should I call my future fiancé?"

"The defendant?"

"Hilarious." The band started winding up its tune. "Now that you've got what you came for, you can take me back to my table."

"I haven't got everything I want yet, angel, but I will."

She didn't dignify that with a reply, but pivoted, chin in the air, and marched off the dance floor, barely waiting for him to escort her.

Duke was watching them with hooded eyes. He got up lazily as they approached and held out his hand to Eliza. "You dance beautifully, my dear. All you need is a partner worthy of you, and you would be without peer."

"I'm already without peer, darling, but I wouldn't mind another dance," she said with a saucy smile.

Duke immediately took her in his arms and danced her off as a new tune began.

"Have fun kids," Mark said. The sight of Eliza in Duke's arms did something nasty to his insides, so he turned away and went back to the bar. He ignored McGann's meaningful glare as he passed by their table and put his foot on the rail and his elbow on the counter. "Gimme another whiskey," he said to the barkeep.

As the man poured his drink, McGann got up and huffed over next to him. "What's going on? You're not here to make time with some twist."

He looked away from McGann, staring into the long mirror behind the bar. His own ghost-white face stared back at him. Behind his reflection, Eliza and Duke danced past. "I know what I'm doing," he said. "This is all part of the plan."

"What plan?"

Out of the corner of his eye, he saw the bartender standing a few feet away from him, staring down into a sink behind the counter. He craned his neck for a better look and saw water bubbling up out of the pipes. The guy took a piece of wire out from underneath the counter and stuck it into the drain, probing around.

The hair at the back of Mark's neck stirred.

"Did you hear what I said, punk?" McGann barked. "What's your plan to catch this thing?"

In the mirror, Mark saw Eliza stop short in the middle of the dance floor. She pulled away from Duke and spun toward the bar, nostrils flaring, eyes wide.

"Damn!" Mark lunged for McGann. "Get back!"

A fountain of greasy water exploded from the sink, sending the bartender tumbling. A tentacle like a long rope of jelly lashed out of the drain straight for McGann's face. Mark got a fist in the gangster's collar and yanked him away from the thing, but he wasn't quite fast enough.

The tip of the tentacle whipped across McGann's chin, leaving a wide red streak like an acid burn. One touch of that thing dissolved human flesh. Mark released McGann and he flailed away, pulling out his gun.

Mark was dimly aware of the screams erupting around him, the Outfit boys leaping to their feet and drawing their heaters, people in a mad stampede toward the doors.

But all his focus was on the slime pouring itself out of the drain, across the bar and onto the floor. It was a rubbery, pulsing, roiling mass of greenish jelly that quickly formed a viscous blob three times as big as a man. Tendrils of slime shot out of the main body, probing around like long tongues licking the air, and then sucking themselves back in with an awful slurping sound.

There you are at last, you ugly bastard. He gathered his shadow and got ready for a brawl.

38

Gunfire exploded through the room as the gangsters emptied their rounds into the monster, pulling the triggers until the barrels were smoking. But slime just oozed over the bullet holes in its gelatinous body. After a second, the bullets popped right out again and clinked to the floor. The blob was completely unharmed. It started slithering toward the gunners, moving in a fast, pulsing crawl. Its tentacles waved through the air, tasting for its prey.

"It wants McGann!" Mark yelled. "Get him out of here!" He grabbed the man and shoved him toward the others. The horrified mobsters didn't wait but scrambled for the back door behind the stage.

He saw Johnson standing by the door already, on the edge of bolting. "Get the house lights!" Mark roared. Johnson sent him a stark glance and disappeared.

He grabbed a barstool as the monster made a lunge for the fleeing gangsters, lashing out its tentacles. Mark darted in and brought the stool smashing down on the fingers of slime.

The tentacles shattered into thick chunks of jelly and

fell quivering to the floor. They instantly dissolved into a puddle of liquid that streamed across the floorboards toward the larger mass of the creature to be reabsorbed into the roiling bulk.

More ropes of slime slithered out of the thing. The wooden legs of Mark's stool were half dissolved with its venom. He tossed it aside.

The slime was in the middle of the room now, the wooden floorboards hissing and bubbling underneath it. Its deadly tentacles snaked through the air.

The bar had emptied out except for a knot of dancers who had been caught in a corner away from the doors when the monster had lunged after the Outfit boys. They'd have to get past the thing to get out.

There were six people huddled against the wall. Two of them were Eliza and Duke.

Eliza looked as terrified as the others, but Duke was watching the creature with a fascinated, almost lustful expression, like a pyromaniac watching a fire.

He saw all of this in a flash, before the tentacles suddenly turned and slashed toward Eliza. She screamed and clutched at Duke.

Mark couldn't think. He could only act. He snapped into full shadow and tore past the slime to Eliza. He turned solid long enough to grab her arm and yank her away from Duke, into the shadows with him. The deadly finger of slime missed her by a mere fraction of an inch, lashing through the air where she had been.

Mark carried Eliza's shadow presence with him as he rushed away from the monster across the room to the now-empty stage.

He pulled himself out of shadow with her in his arms. Her face was stark white and her eyes were wild, but he had no time to calm her panic. He set her on her feet and ran to a spotlight on a stand at the edge of the stage. Grabbing the light, he spun it around and trained the beam on the monster.

The instant the light hit the slime it writhed back, shrinking from the ray in a rubbery quake.

At that moment, the house lights blazed on. Johnson had come through. Mark flinched at the light, but so did the creature. The beam of light he was pointing at it drilled into its substance. The jelly oozed away from the glare. He chased it with the beam, raking the quivering thing with light. The slime cringed away and slithered back toward the sink behind the bar. A rope of slime shot out of the central mass and dove into the drain.

The pipes shrieked and broke, water spraying into the air as the huge blob of slime funneled itself back down the drain like a fountain in reverse. In mere seconds it was gone, leaving only a trail of half-dissolved wood across the floor and the bar. Mark trained the light on the broken sink, in case the thing tried to come back out. He stepped back and took stock.

The entire attack had lasted less than three minutes, but that was enough time to empty out the place, except for the dancers who had been trapped in the corner. They were still cringing against the wall, except Duke.

He stood straight, his feet braced apart like a fighter, his eyes burning into Mark from across the room. There was no trace of fear or shock on his face, only absolute fury. If Mark hadn't already known it was Duke driving the monster, he would have figured it out then.

He heard the wail of sirens in the distance. He glanced through the windows at the front of the club and saw people massing on the sidewalk. One man was wearing a tan hat with a paisley hatband. He'd know that piece of foppery anywhere. Alvin Tracy was here. The reporter was following Mark's tip about watching Duke a little too well. He wheeled toward Eliza and grabbed her arm again. "We've got to get you out of here," he said. "They're coming."

She blinked at him as if struggling to focus. "Who? The police?"

"Worse, the press. They'll be flooding the place any second now."

She looked nearly as horrified as when the slime monster attacked.

"Come on!" He ran with her to the backstage door that let out onto an alley.

They burst out onto the pavement and came face-to-face with a cop, a scrub-face rookie younger than Mark. He jumped back, eyes popping. "You!"

Mark lifted his hands. "Hey, it's okay," he said to the kid.

But the rookie drew his gun. "Stop right there! Put your hands up!"

Mark didn't want to sucker-punch a cop, but he had to get Eliza out of here before Duke caught up to them. Reluctantly, he gathered his power.

But then Eliza glided toward the man in a rush of intoxicating perfume, gloved hands outstretched. "Oh, officer! Thank goodness you're here!"

The young cop lowered his gun, confusion washing over his face.

Eliza clutched his arm, looking beseechingly at him. "There's been an attack! You should go help the poor people inside right away. You'll be a hero!" To Mark's surprise, the cop went perfectly still, his face slack. And then without a word he marched straight past them to the Green Mill's back door and pushed inside.

Mark watched the man go and then looked hard at Eliza.

She didn't meet his gaze.

"We've got to talk, angel face, but not here," he said. He looked around. Crowds of rubberneckers and reporters milled through the streets and alleys nearby. More cops would be coming soon. And Duke would be after them any second now. It was going to be hard to get her out without being spotted. Unless . . .

What if he carried her through the shadows again? It had been so easy before. He had to try it. He stepped close to her and wrapped an arm around her waist, like he was taking her for a waltz.

She looked up into his face, her soft red lips parted on a little gasp. "What—"

He stopped her by leaning down and pressing those lips quickly with his. "Hold on to me." He let the power flow through him and exploded into shadow, taking her with him into the darkness.

39

Clasping her shadow-self to him, he swept her through the crowds, down the streets, past the lights and buildings, all the way to the other side of town. Within seconds he was standing on the sidewalk near his favorite all-night diner, Eliza still cradled in his arms. *I did it!* he thought, elated.

She pushed back unsteadily, and looked around, blinking. "Where are we?"

"South Side, not far from my house."

"But . . . how did we get here?"

"I'll explain it in the diner," he said, guiding her to the door with a hand on her lower back. "Come on. You look like you could use a sandwich." He squired her inside.

A counter took up half the place, with a few scarred tables and chairs crammed into the corners. It was nearly empty, except for a dozing drunk on a stool and the cook behind the counter. "Couple of sandwiches and coffee," he said to the counterman.

As usual, the guy seemed to be entirely uninterested in his customers, bless his soul. Mark in his tuxedo and Eliza in her silk gown and long gloves might be the strangest pair ever to set foot in his joint, but he gave them only the briefest of glances before silently going off to fill the order.

Mark took Eliza to his usual table and sat her down. The food came quickly and he fell on his, suddenly ravenous. Having her safe by his side once again had somehow brought his appetite roaring back.

Eliza was quiet and dazed at first, but by the time she had nibbled on half a roast-beef sandwich, her face had cleared and her eyes had taken on an ominous sparkle.

"All right, let's talk," she said, pushing aside her plate. She took her cigarettes and holder out of the little beaded purse she had looped around her wrist.

Mark finished his sandwich in one bite and gulped some coffee. "Yes, let's. You didn't come clean with me about your power this morning."

"Nor did you. But perhaps it's time we both laid our cards on the table." They watched each other for a long moment, tension thickening in the air between them.

He said, "Why don't we take turns asking each other questions again, just like before. But this time, we answer fully."

She considered and nodded once. "All right."

"Great. I'll go first," he said, ignoring her exasperated look. "Now, I already know your sense of smell is amazing. But that's not all, is it? You give off a chemical, a perfume. Not one you've made. An all-natural one that comes off your skin. A scent that can put a guy in a trance, like Mannering, and that cop outside the club tonight. That's why you're so sure you can get Duke to marry you." He gestured to her cigarette. "It's why you wave those things around without ever smoking them. You're masking your scent. Am I right?"

She stared at him. "You're very clever."

"Flattery will get you nowhere, doll. And neither will your mind control perfume. You tried to put the whammy on me right after we kissed, but it didn't work, did it?"

"No." Distractedly, she put away her cigarette and holder. "You're the only man I've ever met who seems to be immune to it." She sounded a little scared. She'd always had the upper hand with men before, he realized. For maybe the first time in her life, she was vulnerable. He sensed wariness rising up around her. Even her perfume took on a sharp tang.

"I would never hurt you," he said quietly. "I'll do everything in my power to protect you."

She searched his eyes. "Why?"

"Because you're my client."

"But I fired you, remember?"

He shrugged. "It didn't take."

Her mouth curved. "So I'm still your boss?"

"You're the boss."

"In that case, you can answer my question now. What is this power that lets you make a ghost of yourself and whisk away poor unsuspecting girls?"

He opened his mouth. Closed it. Turned his coffee cup around. He'd never talked about his power before. Not even with Frasier. But for some crazy reason he was sure to regret, he wanted to tell *her*. He tried to sort out a few words. She waited, her oblique brown eyes watching him.

"How about this," he said recklessly. "I'll show you mine if you show me yours."

"What? No!"

"Yes. I'll do my parlor trick for you. Then I'll watch you do yours."

"I couldn't," she said.

"Sure you could." He leaned closer to her and lowered

his voice. "You know you want to. You like it when I watch you."

Red bloomed on her cheeks, but her eyes sparked in challenge. "And you like watching."

"Yeah," he said softly. "So, are we going to do this?"

She regarded him a little longer, tapping her gloved fingers on the table. "All right. Show me."

He cast a glance at the dented light fixture above their heads. "Not here. There's too much light. Come on." He got up and threw some money on the table.

They left the diner and walked down the sidewalk. At a patch of darkness between streetlamps, he stopped and turned to face her. "You can see well in the dark, right?"

"Yes," she said. "Very well indeed."

"Then watch." He held up his hand, palm out, and slowly unleashed his power. His fingertips melted into the dark, then his hand and arm. The wave of shadow washed down his body and up over his head until only his eyes were visible.

She watched him turn without the slightest hint of fear, a soft smile of wonder appearing on her face.

He winked at her and vanished completely. His physical form melded with the darkness until he was a being of mind, shadow, and desire.

"Incredible." She stepped forward into the place occupied by his presence. He moved his shadow self around her, enveloping her. "I can still smell you, but I can't see you or touch you. You're here, but you're not here. Am I standing inside you right now? Or are you inside of me?"

He materialized right behind her, his body a breath away from hers, and said close to her ear, "That's not how it works. I can't move through solid objects."

She whirled to face him but he snapped into shadow

and swept around her to her back. He turned solid and said in her other ear, "I can move around you, and over you, but not inside you. I haven't figured out a way to do that yet."

She didn't try to turn around this time. He saw a smile curve her cheek as he stood behind her, so close one deep breath would press his chest against her slender back. He took that breath. Her perfume filled his lungs, amazingly sweet. He was fully erect, he realized. He stepped back before she felt that too.

But she knew. She looked over her shoulder at him, eyes dancing. "Amazing,"

"Not frightening?"

She tossed her head. "Do I look scared?" She started walking down the street with that rolling strut of hers.

He fell in at her side. "You did, a little, back when I grabbed you and took you into the shadow with me at the Green Mill."

"Yes, well it was rather startling."

"What was it like for you? Going through the shadow?"

"Like . . . like black chaos. Everything all at once, and nothing. No sight, no sound, no feeling, only rushing darkness. If I hadn't been able to smell the world around me, and you, I suppose I might have been frightened indeed. Isn't that the usual experience?"

"Not for me. I always see and hear when I'm in shadow. I don't know about other people. I've never taken anyone with me until tonight. I had no idea I even could. When I saw that thing lunge for you, I just reacted. But I'm sorry I scared you."

"All things considered, I'd rather be scared than eaten by a slime monster." She added quietly, "Thank you for saving me."

"It was my pleasure," he murmured.

"How are you able to do this, Mark? Where does your ability come from?"

He shrugged "Just lucky I guess."

"It's not part of your family inheritance?"

"No," he said shortly.

"How long have you had your power, then?"

"All my life, but I didn't fully turn into shadow until I was nineteen."

"Nineteen? That's when I—when I first used my talents too."

"About these talents of yours. A deal's a deal. I showed you mine, now you show me yours."

She was silent for a few steps. Eventually she said, "First, answer me one more question. Why are you a detective?"

He glanced at her in surprise and shrugged. "Got to pay the bills somehow."

"I don't believe that's the reason. You have no need to work for money. You could simply take it whenever you please. You could rob more banks than John Dillinger. You could steal the *Mona Lisa*, or the diamonds off of King George's crown, if you liked."

He stiffened. "What do you take me for, a common thief?"

She laughed. "No, no. You're one of those rare aristocratic types too proud to stoop to criminal behavior. However, I'm certain you could put your talents to other uses if you chose. So why do this?"

"Because it interests me. I'm dead bored when I don't have a puzzle to solve."

"You don't do it to help people? To sere justice, perhaps?"

He laughed. "Not a chance. I'm in it strictly for my own

entertainment. And because I don't like monsters and wizards operating in my city."

"I see. I myself always wanted to use my abilities for good. To *be* good. But I can't, and I'm not. My power is not like yours."

He stopped her with a hand at her elbow and drew her close until she had to tip her head back to look at him. "Show me. I dare you."

She licked her lips. "All right. You deserve to know, after saving me." She straightened her back, her eyes going hard. "What's the worst part of town? The most dangerous place, where no woman should ever go alone?"

"That would be one of the neighborhoods the Italian street gangs took over. Cabrini Green, maybe."

"Take me there, and I'll show you what you want to see."

"No cabs will take us to Cabrini Green at this time of night."

She smiled at him. "We don't need a cab, darling. Why don't you carry me there, right now?"

"You mean . . ."

"Take me through the shadows with you."

He started to grin. "Are you sure?"

"Absolutely."

"All right, then." He wrapped his hands around her tiny waist and pulled her close. "Hold on." Shadow poured through them and swept them away through the dark streets.

40

They sped north through Old Town, into more and more derelict neighborhoods until they came to the warren of tenements and boarded-up shops of Cabrini Green. He materialized with her in the deep shadow at the mouth of a trash-strewn alley. He set her on her feet and examined her for any sign of panic at being snatched up and rushed through the darkness again. Incredibly, she didn't seem rattled by her journey at all. She looked around, eyes bright, getting her bearings.

He watched her take in the ramshackle wood and brick buildings rising around them. Smoke from barrel fires and the stench of raw sewage tainted the air. In this wasteland, the lights were few and far between, but the darkness was thick with roving shapes and voices of men.

She tipped her head up to scent the air and smiled grimly. "This will do." She started stripping off her long satin gloves.

"What are you going to do?"

"I'm going to go for a walk, alone. You may watch, but don't interfere."

"Are you sure?"

"Positive, darling. I've been in far deadlier places than this." She handed him her gloves and her little purse. "Hold these for me, please."

He put her things in the pocket of his tuxedo coat. "Remember, I'll be here you if you get in over your head." He dissolved into the darkness and vanished from sight.

She scented the air again and stepped out of the alley into the street, her long gown swirling around her ankles. She moved along the cracked pavement with a silky, predatory stride, bold as a tigress prowling her jungle. He kept his presence as close to her as a second shadow.

A few of the figures in the dark watched her stroll past. Soon two of the shapes detached from the rest and started following her, muttering to each other, their shoes clomping as they sped up to catch her. But her stride never altered. When she came to a lonely streetlamp she stopped, turned on her high heel, and waited. The hard light glinted off the silk of her dress and the black curls of her hair. Her eyes gleamed in her ivory face. Her perfume coiled lazily through the air.

The two men stalking her stopped, looking confused, maybe even a little wary. Maybe some animal instinct warned them that they were in the presence of a creature far more dangerous than they were. But stupidity and lust soon got the better of them. They sauntered up to her, leering. The beefier of the two men said, "Look at what we got here, Freddy. What's a fancy broad like her doing on our turf? Maybe she's looking for a little fun. We're a couple of fun guys, aren't we Freddy?"

His friend sniggered.

Eliza's voice rang like cut crystal. "Leave me alone or I'll make you regret it. This is your only warning." The perfume in the air grew thick and deadly sweet.

"Oh-ho! We got us a snooty bitch here Freddy. Thinks she's too good for a working man. Come here, bitch, and don't gimme no lip." He lunged for her, grabbing her bare arm with one hand and raising his other hand to strike her.

Mark almost snapped out of the shadows to tear the bastard apart, but he stopped himself at the last second. The thug had frozen the instant he touched Eliza's skin. His raised hand dropped limply to his side and his face went slack.

His friend stopped giggling. "Bruno? What's going on?"

Eliza turned a gaze on him like a big cat staring down her prey. She beckoned him with her finger. Already under the influence of her scent, he shuffled forward, confusion on his face. Eliza slipped one bare fingertip underneath his chin, and his eyes went blank. "Flap your wings and squawk like a chicken," she told him.

The man started waving his arms up and down. "*Bawk! Bawk! Bawk!*" burst out of his mouth.

Eliza took her arm out of the limp grip of the first man. Mark saw that his fingers and palm were red and blistered where he had touched her skin. "And you. Get down on the ground and grunt like a pig." The man instantly fell to his hands and knees, snorting and squealing.

Eliza watched them for a moment, then turned her back on the beast-men and continued on down the street, her heels snapping on the pavement, her mouth set in a cruel red line.

Mark materialized next to her. "That was a amazing." *And terrifying*, he thought to himself.

"I gave them fair warning."

"So you did." He looked back over his shoulder. The

two would-be rapists were still going at it, barnyard noises echoing through the buildings and alleys. "How long are they going to be like that?" Not that he cared. He saw the red mark that thug had left on Eliza's arm when he grabbed her and had the strong urge to go back and kick him.

"A few weeks, perhaps. They'll recover eventually. Probably."

"Do you make a habit of brainwashing people?"

"No. Usually I'm far more subtle. I prefer to influence a man with a very light dose of my scent, so that he thinks whatever I want him to do is his own idea. Too much of my poison can lead to . . ."

"Yes?"

"Undesirable results."

"Like what?"

She rubbed her hands over her bare arms. "Like drawing too much attention. I'm not powerful enough to control a mob bent on stoning a witch to death, for instance."

He had the feeling that wasn't what she first meant to say, that she had another "undesirable result" in mind. There had to be a reason she called her scent, the perfume in her skin, "poison."

"Can your perfume kill a man?" he asked bluntly.

She started, but covered it with another shiver. "It's possible."

"Wait." He stopped her next to the brick wall of a decaying apartment building. "You're cold. Here." He stripped off his jacket and draped it over her shoulders.

Her eyes widened. "Thank you."

He adjusted the collar and said conversationally, "So now I know why you're determined to marry a total bastard like Lionel Duke. The family curse you told

223

me about is your scent. You think the chemical you give off will kill your husband."

She was silent for a long moment. Her pale, slender hand came out to hold the coat closed at her bosom. "I don't think it. I know it."

He waited.

"We call ourselves the Lamia. Poison ladies."

"We? There are others who have your abilities?"

She didn't answer.

"Of course, your grandmother."

"And every female ancestor before her. We are an ancient family, cursed by God to take the lives of wicked men. Or so my grandmother believes."

"And what do you believe?"

"Only what I know happened to my father, and grandfather, and every other man who ever took one of us for a bride. The moment I give myself to a man, he is doomed. It might take a few months, but it always happens. No man has ever been able to withstand our power."

"Except me."

She looked up at him with dark eyes. "I never gave you the full dose."

"Do it now." He held out his hand, palm up.

She jolted back. "Are you mad? I tell you I come from an ancient line of killers, and you offer yourself up as a victim?"

"You won't hurt me."

"You don't know that!"

"I'll show you. Do it."

"Never! D'you hear me?" Her cheeks were almost as white as his.

He dropped his hand. "You're a scientist, aren't you? Why not conduct the experiment?"

"Because I don't want to risk your life, you fool."

"Worried for me?" He eased a half step closer to her.

She stepped back until her shoulders were against the wall. She tipped her chin up. "I would never endanger any man's life for the sake of an experiment."

"You won't endanger me. I'm hard to kill." He moved closer again.

"So arrogant."

"Just telling the truth." He stood a handbreadth away from her and looked down into her face. "Touch me. Your perfume can't harm me."

Her voice husky, she said, "You can't be certain."

But he was certain. He felt it deep in his bones, where his shadow lived. It yearned for her just as the rest of him did. She was the one for him. They were the same. But he couldn't tell her so and make her believe it. He'd have to show her.

41

Eliza was trapped between Mark's body and the wall, but strangely, there was none of the panic she might have expected from being so vulnerable. Instead, she felt . . . anticipation. She settled into the warmth of his coat and waited to see what he would do next.

His eyes on hers, he reached up to his throat. Slowly, he loosened the knot of his tie, and pulled it off in a whisper of silk. He shoved the tie into his pocket and raised his hands to his collar. He undid his top button, revealing the strong, smooth column of his throat. He slipped another button free, and another. The hollow between the graceful wings of his collarbones appeared, and the beginning swell of his chest muscles.

Her breath stuttered in her throat.

Slowly, gently, he curved his big, callused hand around hers, the one that was holding the jacket closed. He lifted it to the opening of his shirt and placed it against the firm flesh there, pressing her palm against him.

She stopped breathing altogether. It was incredible to touch another person with her bare hand like this, not to influence him with her poison, but simply to feel his skin. Warm, and smooth as silk over muscle as hard as steel. Beneath her palm, his heart beat a fast, hard rhythm.

"You see? You can touch me."

"I'm not using my power," she whispered.

The muscles of his chest moved as he shrugged. "Doesn't matter."

She ought to pull away. This wasn't right, no matter how delicious it felt.

But his eyes held her captive, his white lashes half-veiling irises the color of melting ice. She stroked her fingertips over him. His chest heaved in an unsteady breath. "You like touching me, don't you?" His voice was a velvety rasp.

"I . . ."

Slowly, he moved their clasped hands down, away from his throat, over his chest. The buttons of his shirt pressed against her palm. His flesh was like a furnace beneath the thin cloth. Slabs of muscle over heavy bone, and under that, the quiet storm of his breath and the thunder of his heart.

He pushed her hand lower, down the iron ridges of his stomach. She marveled at how strong he was. But he wasn't using his strength against her as he gently pressed her hand to his body. She knew he would let her break away at any time.

She should. She should stop this right now. But she didn't want to.

His eyes flashed as he sensed her yielding. He pushed her hand down, over the cool, complicated shape of his belt buckle. And then her palm was on something else, a long, thick shape as hard and hot as an iron bar straight out of a forge.

She gasped, her knees going liquid as shocking desire twisted through her belly. Her fingers tightened instinctively around him, making him hiss. The scent of desire perfumed the air.

She tried to rein in her careening thoughts, but it was impossible. She could feel that he wasn't wearing any briefs, only the thin wool of his pants separating her hand from his naked flesh. She wanted to see it, touch it. She wanted . . . wanted . . .

Good God, what was she doing? She tore her hand away from his grip. He let her, but then he placed his palms on the wall above her shoulders and bowed his head down until his lips were only a breath away from hers. "You're so beautiful, you drive me crazy. After you left me today, I couldn't sleep. I couldn't eat. All I could think of was kissing you again, Eliza . . ."

"N-not here. Someone will see."

He shook his head. "No one can see us." The surrounding darkness rippled with his power. He was drawing the shadows around them, she realized, hiding them from prying eyes. "Kiss me," he said, his voice low and rough.

"Not here," she said again, trying to regain her scattered wits. Not on a filthy street in the middle of a slum.

Without a word he scooped her up in his arms. The shadow rushed through her, sweeping her up into the storm of darkness. An instant later the real world closed around her again. She blinked hard, trying to orient herself. She was high in the air on top of a building, perched on the roof. She looked down into the deep shadows below and realized that five stories down was the street she had been standing on mere seconds ago. Mark had brought them straight up the wall she had been leaning against.

His arms were still around her, steadying her. She looked up into his face. "Goodness," she managed to say.

He grinned. "Is this more like it, angel?"

She looked out over the rooftops marching off into the night, the canyons of the streets dimly glowing. A cool wind swirled over the roof, washing away the stink of smoke and concrete with the scent of the lake. She tipped her face up to breathe it in. Through half-closed eyes she saw the crescent moon sailing high overhead, and even a few brave stars pierced the city night.

She looked back at Mark. He was as wild and beautiful as a white tiger, hair ruffled in the wind, clothes half-undone, eyes full of hunger. His hands were still wrapped around her waist, holding her safe. "Amazing," she said. And she didn't know if she meant the city below them, or him.

"Yeah. I like to come up on the roofs sometimes and look out over it all."

"Master of all you survey?"

He grinned. "Something like that." He flexed his fingers over her hips. "Is this a better place for a kiss?"

"What if I say no? What if I ask you to take me home instead?"

His smile dimmed, but his eyes stayed keen on hers. "I'll do whatever you say."

"Because I'm the boss?"

"You're the boss."

She smiled. Her hands stole up to his shoulders, his flesh fever hot against her palms. "What if I say I don't want to kiss you here? Will you take me somewhere else?"

"Where do you want to go?"

"Surprise me."

His eyes sparked at her challenge. He wrapped his arms around her again and the world shifted into a chaos of shadows.

42

When she blinked open her eyes, she was on a building even higher than before, cold fingers of wind combing through her hair. She and Mark stood on a metal catwalk, a vast plain of buildings flung out before her in a grid of black and gold. She turned her head and caught a glimpse of the moon-dappled expanse of water. She looked down along the slope of a vast peaked copper roof to the well of light and darkness below. The roar of the wind filled the night. Twisting around to look up over her shoulder, she saw that they stood at the foot of a gigantic bronze goddess holding up an ear of grain at the building's apex.

She laughed in delight as she realized where they were. "The Board of Trade Building!"

"Right you are, angel."

He'd brought her to the top of the tallest skyscraper in Chicago. She stepped to the railing, looking out over the mighty city under the night sky, the black squares of the buildings like islands amid rushing rivers of light along the streets. The wind was fierce, and she gathered Mark's coat around her. "How did we get up here? Did we fly?"

"No," he said. "I simply climbed the tower very fast. I don't fly."

"Don't? Not can't?"

He came to stand by her side at the railing, his body throwing off heat like a furnace. He seemed completely immune to the sheering wind, his shirt still half-buttoned and rippling over his chest. "I need to stay in contact with solid surfaces. The darkness, it—" He paused for a moment. "It's too easy to get lost. If I lose contact with the real world, even for an instant, I might never find my way back to it again. I'd vanish into the dark like I never existed."

She gazed at his profile as he looked out into the night, as remote and lonely as a carved angel on a cathedral. A thrill like fear moved over her skin. A gust of wind made her curl into his body for shelter, and she blurted out, "I'm glad you're here in the real world with me, Mark."

He switched his attention away from the city, back to her again. He smiled into her eyes, and her heart almost broke at how beautiful he was. He leaned his head down toward her. "Does that mean I get a kiss?"

She tossed her head, her curls dancing in the air. "It's a fabulous view, darling, but a bit too windy for kissing."

"Swing and a miss. I'd better try again." He gathered her into his arms and took her into shadow.

When she came out of the darkness this time, she found herself in a maze of white chambers lined with paintings and statuary. Mark released her and she walked down the gallery, looking around, her steps echoing along the silent marble halls. "Are we in the Art Institute?"

"That's right," Mark's voice rumbled through the shadows in reply.

"Lovely. But ought we to be trespassing?"

"I'm not trespassing. The Institute is a client of mine."

"You work for them?" she said skeptically.

"Sure. I keep an eye on the place at night. Got to protect it against art thieves, you know."

"And do the museum directors know what you're up to?"

"If they did, I'm sure they'd be grateful."

She laughed and walked further along the gallery, examining the paintings on the walls more closely. Manet, Monet, Renoir. Pictures of water-lilies, haystacks, girls taking tea, couples walking in the park. Scenes of ordinary people and ordinary things, soaked in light.

"You like the Impressionists?" she asked, turning back to look at him.

He had fastened his eyes on one painting, a study done in feathery white brushstrokes of a young woman putting up her golden hair. He shrugged. "Sure. I grew up with them. Some of these pictures used to belong to my dad. Had to sell them off to pay his debts."

There was something on his face as he looked at the painting that was darkening to melancholy. She couldn't have that. She slipped her hand into his.

He looked at her, startled.

She smiled up at him. "I like them very much, but I can't kiss you in front of them. I'd feel like all these fine ladies and gentlemen were watching us."

The banked heat flared in his eyes. "Strike two. One more chance before I'm out." He swept her into his arms again and dark rushed over them.

The next moment they were in a garden, in the middle of a wooden bridge over a fishpond. On the shore across from them stood a serene Japanese pagoda, the sweep of the roof like silvery wings in the moonlight. Water rippled crystal and black below their feet. Wind hushed through the cherry trees on the bank, carrying the sweet green scent of leaves.

"Where are we now?" she asked. She stepped to the railing to look around.

He let her go, but stood close to her shoulder and murmured, "The Garden of the Phoenix in Jackson Park. It was built for the last world's fair, the Columbian Exposition. After the fair closed, they decided to keep it."

"I'm glad they did. It's beautiful."

"And it's not too windy. And we're all alone."

She smiled. "Yes."

"Does that mean this is the place?"

She turned and looked up at his beautiful face, at the desire written there. She laid her suddenly shaking hand on his chest. His skin was hot beneath the fine fabric of his shirt. "You want me to kiss you?"

"I want it more than I want to live." His heart was pounding beneath her palm.

She moistened her lips and tried to steady her breath. "Well then. To save your life, I can't say no, can I?"

43

Mark's eyes flashed. He started to reach for her, but she pressed her hand against his chest, stopping him. "Am I still the boss?"

"Yes," he grated.

"Will you let me do what I want?"

"Anything. Do anything to me. Just do it."

"All—all right." Summoning up her courage, she did what she'd been wanting to do all night. She bent her head toward the opening of his shirt where his strong throat sloped into his shoulders, until her face was a mere breath away from his skin. She drank in the rich, dark perfume of his flesh until she simply had to close the last bit of distance between them. She pressed her mouth to where the tempting swell of muscle began at the base of his throat. His skin was hot and salty against her lips. He made a startled sound, but he didn't move, letting her do as she liked. Emboldened, she slipped the tip of her tongue out to taste him. She almost moaned, he was so delicious.

His breath stuttered, and his hands flew to her waist.

Eager for more of him, she brushed her lips over his collarbone, up the fine skin of his throat to drop tiny kisses along his jaw. She rubbed her cheek against his. Then she touched her lips to his as soft as a breath.

Mark took over, slanting his mouth over hers and caressing her lips with his in a long, fierce kiss.

She had lost control of the situation, but she no longer cared. She slipped her hands up to his head, sinking her fingers into his hair. His hands moved up her waist, spreading his fingers out over her ribcage. His thumbs caressed the lower curves of her breasts.

His coat fell off her shoulders to her feet, but the night air didn't touch her. There was only the heat of his hands moving over her body, down with a slow, easy glide over her hips and bottom, leaving a trail of fire along her skin. He pulled her lower body against his, and she felt it again, the long, thick shaft pulsing hot against her belly. A soft sound of desire broke from her throat. She pressed herself into him, kissing him with all she had.

And he returned each kiss ruthlessly, slowly, every luxurious caress of his mouth heating her until she was liquid with desire, need twisting through her body and pulsing in her veins. He made her as hot and soft as wax under a flame, until he could bend her any way he wanted, touch her any way he liked. She was enspelled by his hands and his lips, the big, muscular body rubbing against hers. She pressed against him harder, her skin hungry for his under the thin layers of his clothes.

He held her captive in a timeless dream of desire until suddenly he broke the kiss with a low growl and looked up at the eastern sky, now taking on a pearly glow.

She blinked up at him, dazed. His lips were pink, his skin gleaming in the early light. His blue eyes turned back to hers with a look soft and wondering. He brushed the backs of his fingers down her cheek and throat. "Eliza," he said, his voice rough. "Eliza." Just her name, but she knew what he was asking.

She drew back a little, not sure how much farther she wanted to let this go. The reasons for stopping it once and for all were the same as ever. But they seemed so distant now, with Mark solid and warm in her arms.

She whispered, "Take me back to my hotel, Mark."

He swept his coat up off the ground and draped it around her again, trembling eagerness in his fingers. When he took her into his arms, she felt the deep quaking there too.

Darkness rushed over them, and then they were standing in a pool of shadow close against the wall of the hotel.

Mark said, "Last stop of the evening, the Drake . . ." He staggered, leaning a hand against the wall to steady himself. Wisps of shadow swirled around him and tore themselves into nothing.

"Mark!" She reached for him, and for an instant his body under her hand seemed insubstantial, like her fingers might pass right through him. Then the strange moment was over, so quickly she nearly wondered if she had imagined it. "Are you all right?"

"Sure," he said, curtly, straightening away from her hand.

She studied him. Of course he would say he was fine rather than display a moment's weakness. It was foolish of her to even ask. But he must have expended a lot of energy tonight bringing her through the shadows all around the city. And his power, like hers, wasn't limitless.

But she wanted to hold on to the spell of this night with him a little while longer, so she said nothing.

They walked into the hotel, up the stairs and through the lobby to the elevator. The colored elevator man was as professionally deaf and blind to their presence as if Mark had made them invisible. Eliza was profoundly grateful for his discretion.

She had decided to invite Mark into her room. And then she'd—she'd see what happened. A distant warning sounded in her head. *You're not thinking this through!*

She didn't want to think. She wanted to feel, for once. She wouldn't let things go too far, of course, but she simply couldn't let the night end. Not yet.

They walked down the hall together in silence.

When they came to her door, she found her little beaded bag in his coat pocket and opened it to get her key. She turned her face up to his, looking into his eyes. "Thank you for coming to my rescue tonight."

"Any time, angel." He didn't move.

She moistened her lips. "Would you care to come in for a cup of tea? We still haven't discussed the slime creature. Perhaps I can help you think of a way to fight it."

"Yeah," he said softly. "Tea sounds grand."

Her hands were shaking so that she fumbled the room key and dropped it. They both bent down to get it, and somehow got tangled up in each other. They stood up blushing and laughing a little, Mark with the key in his fingers. He leaned around her to unlock the door, his face only inches from hers, his body almost pressing into her. On impulse, she closed the last bit of distance to kiss his lips. Which turned into another kiss, then more, until they were grappling desperately in the hall against the door.

Mark somehow got the door open between kisses and they tumbled into the room.

A familiar scent hit her like an icy wave. "What an illuminating sight," said a voice in the darkness.

They froze. Eliza found her voice. "*Grand-mère*."

44

She pushed away from Mark as a light switched on. Angelique sat in an armchair, settled in as if she had been waiting for a long time.

"What are you doing here?" Eliza was horrified to hear her voice crack.

The countess said, "Your Mr. Duke came to my suite looking for you after you disappeared from the nightclub. We had quite an interesting chat. You'll be happy to know that I told him you were well out of harm's way, and that he would see you again tomorrow. I sent him home and came to wait for you here. I had foolishly assumed you had a good reason for vanishing." The old lady rose and glided toward them. "I admit my mistake. I am entirely taken by surprise to find you with this—this creature."

Mark stiffened beside her.

"Don't call him that!" Eliza snapped.

"You told me you had clouded his mind. Was this a lie?"

"Oh, she tried," Mark said. "Only, your mind-control perfume doesn't work on this creature, old lady."

She turned her steel-colored eyes on Mark. "*C'est vrai?* Let us put it to the test." She held out her bare, blue veined hand to him.

He moved to take it, but Eliza grabbed his arm. "Don't! She'll poison you!"

"It's all right." Mark gently took Eliza's fingers off his sleeve and reached for her grandmother's hand.

She threw herself against him, sending him staggering back a step. "*Nyet! Non!* Don't hurt him!" She stood between the countess and Mark, her hands out, keeping them apart.

"It is not I who would hurt him, *petit fou.*" Angelique tucked her hand back against her body. "It is you who are too eager to become a killer again."

Eliza sucked in a breath in icy shock.

"Again? What does that mean?" Mark said.

Angelique's eyes lit. She turned a sharp smile on Eliza. "You haven't told him, have you?"

"Told me what?" Suddenly his eyes had the same hard glint in them as when he interrogated her about Duke.

"Shall I tell him?" said the countess.

"No!" She shut her eyes and whispered, "Seven years ago. When I was nineteen. There was a man." The riptide of memory rushed over her again, pulling her down into its depths.

The Nineteen-Twenties had been in full roar, and the future mapped out for her by her mother and grandmother was nothing but a distant, troubling story. Newly released from the cloisters of a Swiss finishing school, she had come to stay with *Maman* and her dissipated timber baron husband in San Francisco. She threw herself into everything the brash American city had to offer, dancing all night, laughter, dares and mayhem. Drinking too, even though the power in her blood meant that booze had no effect on her.

And there was flirting. Discovering the fascinating world of young men. For the first time in her life, she talked and smiled and danced with them in spite of her mother's warnings. It made her giddy. Foolish. Reckless.

One night, she went with some friends to a dance hall high up in the hills around the city. She sipped gin out of a flask, laughed with strangers over nothing at all, and danced the Charleston until her legs were wobbly.

Lingering caution usually made her avoid spending too much time with just one boy, on the chance that her scent might enslave the poor fellow. But that night she selected one man out of the hordes in the dance hall. Older, dark haired, with a knowing smirk that made her think he might be a good kisser. Because she wanted to have her first kiss, at long last. She let him take her outside, down a path to into the woods.

She didn't notice the way the trees closed in on her, blocking out the light of the moon, muffling the sounds of drunken revelry in the building a few hundred yards away.

What happened next, she remembered in flashes of pain and fear burned on her mind.

A shove. Falling hard onto the gravel path, the stones scoring her skin like little knives. A heavy body coming down on her, squeezing the air out of her lungs. The stench of gin and aggression. A knee forcing her legs apart. Rough hands pawing her skirt, ripping at her underwear. A voice snarling terrible, hateful things. The clutch of fingers at her throat, sending her spiraling into blackness.

And for the first time, it happened. Poison flooded

through her veins, boiling out of her fingers. She flailed, clawing at the face of the man forcing her down.

He screamed in pain. His weight wrenched off of her, and she scrabbled away, the gravel tearing her hands and knees. She staggered to her feet, gasping, sobbing, hideous power still sizzling in her fingertips. A horrible shape writhed on the ground before her.

It made a terrible, wet, strangled noise, twitched violently, and stilled.

In the silence, a curious numbness descended on her, as cold and quiet as a snowfall. She heard the harsh sawing of her breath echo from a great distance. She felt strangely light, and wondered if she might float away into the night with the first gust of wind. Instead she found herself drifting closer to the still form in the dirt and looking down at it. At the face lit by the cold moon.

His lips were peeled back from his teeth. Foam bubbles popped on his chin. The skin around his mouth was already turning blue. There were five blackened finger-marks on his cheek.

The vision of that dead face was etched against the back of her lids, as clear to her now as it was then. "It was an accident." Her ragged whisper sounded far away in her own ears. "He attacked me and I—I panicked. He died." She forced her eyes open.

Mark's expression hadn't changed at all. "I see."

Her heart crumpled. Now he knew.

She drew her remaining scraps of dignity around her. She might not be able to save her heart, but at least she would save her pride. "Mark, I'd like to speak with my grandmother alone. Good evening." She took his jacket off and held it out to him.

243

He stared hard at her for a long moment. Then he took his coat from her and pulled it on. He turned toward the door without a word.

As he reached for the doorknob, raw pain twisted through her. "Mark!"

He stopped.

"Thank you for—for everything."

He looked over his shoulder. "Anything to keep my clients happy. We'll talk tomorrow, boss."

She nodded, not meeting his eyes.

He shot a last, hard look at her grandmother, and then he left. The soft snap of the door behind him echoed through the room. She could smell him for several long moments, lingering in the hall outside her door. But finally he walked down the hall, his scent fading away.

She and the countess stood in silence, watching each other. Then her grandmother took two swift steps forward and slapped her across the face.

Eliza stumbled back, hand pressed to her burning cheek, and stared wide-eyed at the old woman.

"How dare you pollute yourself with that creature!" Angelique spat.

"Don't call him that," she said, her voice a dry croak. "He's not a creature, he's a man! A good man!"

"Even if that were true, we do not dally with *good men*. You have already selected a victim, and quite the eager murderer he is."

"You know for certain that Duke is a murderer?"

"I know it all. He and I had a long *tête-à-tête* this evening while you were out playing the strumpet. I made him confess everything."

"Everything? Including his pet monster?"

"That, and much more."

"His creature almost killed me tonight. Did he mention that?"

"Nonsense. You are in no danger from Duke. I entranced him readily. A skill you seem to have forgotten."

"I tried to influence Mark and failed! He may truly be immune to our poison!"

"Why, then, did you not allow him to take my hand?"

She didn't answer.

"No matter. Even if he were immune to us, is he immune to bullets? Or fists, or fire?"

Eliza sucked in a breath. "You wouldn't!"

"Oh, wouldn't I? It would be simple. A creature such as he only lives in society on tolerance. How long do you think he'd last if I turned the whole of Chicago against him? A hint dropped in the mayor's ear, and he could be branded an outlaw, to be shot on sight. A word to the newspaper publishers, and a mob could be burning his house down and hunting him through the streets. Is that what you want?"

"No!"

"Then do your duty! Unless you want to destroy him, as you destroyed another!"

Eliza's knees trembled. She sank into an armchair, her eyes blurring.

Angelique glided closer. "Lionel Duke will be at my suite at four o'clock to ask for your hand in marriage. You will be there to receive him, and you will answer yes. This is the marriage you have chosen, and by God, you will honor it."

Eliza struggled to swallow a harsh sob. She felt withered fingers pass over her hair. It was the first time her grandmother had touched her like that since she was a small child, if she had ever done so at all.

"Stop fighting, Élisabeth, *ma petite*," Angelique crooned. "You are what you are. There is no escape. It is as God wills it. You are the scourge of wicked men. Submit yourself to your fate. It is the only way you will find peace."

45

Mark shoved through the hotel doors into the hot glare of morning. The sun had risen while he'd been sparring with the dragon upstairs.

Eliza had ordered him to go, and he had promised to do what she asked. But it took every ounce of his control not to turn around and march back to her room to snatch her away into the shadow. He'd take her to his house and keep her there until they'd finished what they started.

Too late now, he thought, squinting into the light. He drove his hands into his coat pockets and found Eliza's satin gloves. He fisted the smooth lengths of fabric. *Damn her.* She was tormenting him on purpose. When he got home, he was going to wrap those gloves around his aching shaft and get some relief from the torture.

He started hunting down the street for a cab. But before he got two steps away from the door, a black bulletproof limousine pulled up next to him. The rear door opened and a yellowish, toadlike face appeared. "Get in," Gabriel Camonte ordered him.

Mark looked into the car and saw a driver and another

guy up front and a couple of triggermen in back with the boss, hats down, guns in their laps.

He considered briefly. On one hand, out here in broad daylight he would have a hard time taking on five men with guns if this conversation turned bad. On the other hand, he figured a ride in a limousine surely beat walking in the sunshine. He climbed in and sat down next to one of the goons on the bench seat across from Camonte, pulling the door shut behind him.

"Go," the boss ordered his driver. The car moved into traffic and cruised down Michigan Avenue.

"Draw the blinds, Lou," Camonte told the man sitting next to him. He obediently pulled the cloth blinds over all the windows in the limousine. Awfully obliging of them, Mark thought, relaxing into the shadow.

Camonte examined Mark over a cigar he had clenched in his teeth. "Where have you been? Me and my guys have been looking for you all night!"

"I've been doing my job," Mark lied. "Cultivating an informant."

The mob boss raked his eyes over Mark's rumpled clothing, his lip curling. He got the nasty feeling the man saw every kiss Eliza had left on his skin. "My boys say you were dogging after a twist before the monster attacked. That who you been *cultivating*?"

Mark bared his teeth. "My methods are confidential. All you need to know are the results."

"You haven't got results! You've given me nothing so far!"

"I saved McGann's life last night."

"Not before that thing took a chunk out of his face!"

Mark shrugged. "He was ugly enough already that no one's going to notice."

Camonte looked like he wanted to strangle him, but controlled himself, barely. "Have you seen the papers this morning?" He grabbed a pile of newsprint off the seat next to him and flung it in Mark's lap.

On the front page a headline screamed, "Crime Boss Stalked By Slime Fiend!" Mark snatched up the paper and scanned the story. Written in Al Tracy's sensationalistic prose, it described the monster attack at the nightclub from witness interviews and hinted that Camonte's associates were dropping dead under mysterious circumstances. Luckily for Tracy, he had kept Mark's name out of it. But he did mention Lionel Duke.

Mark smiled, imagining Duke's disgust at landing in the middle of a crime report instead of the society pages.

Camonte said, "It's out. Now everyone knows what's been happening to us. I gotta make an example of the guy who's behind this, or I'm done. And that means you're done."

"He's getting arrogant to attack so openly," Mark said to himself, ignoring Camonte's threat.

"Who? You got a name?" Camonte said.

Mark looked up from the paper and considered him, saying nothing.

Camonte leaned forward and said in a toneless mutter, "Listen kid. I paid you to do a job. You owe me what you promised, and I always collect my debts. Now tell me who it is."

Mark still didn't know where the monster's lair was, and he still had no proof that Duke was controlling it. But Camonte was right. He had taken the job. He owed his client the truth. "Lionel Duke."

Camonte squinted. "Duke of Duke Chemical? The

industrialist? Guy who's been throwing his weight around with the World's Fair?"

"That's the one. I overheard his conversation with a scientist he has working for him. Duke wants to develop weapons for the United States military, something that can be used for targeted assassinations. He plans to demonstrate his creature to the brass while they're in town for the fair. Your men are the lab rats in his experiment. He thinks the government will let him get away with it, and he might be right. The city politicians are already in his pocket."

The black eyes turned distant and calculating. "I see."

"What are you going to do?"

Camonte looked at him strangely. "I'm going to kill Duke, of course. Him, and his friends, and his family, and his neighbors, and his lawyer, and his grocer, and his fucking paper boy. Then I'm going to burn his place to the ground and piss on the ashes. What did you think?"

"I think I don't want a war in this city. I won't interfere with you protecting yourself, but hurting innocent people isn't in my line. Besides, I still haven't tracked down where Duke's keeping the monster."

"A few hours with my boys and a rubber hose should get him to talk."

"Or, maybe I just find it for you, and save you a lot of grief down the line."

"What are you talking about?"

"This is a new age, Camonte. The outlaw days are numbered. You're not going to be able to fight city hall forever, so why not use them instead? If you get solid proof against Duke, you can force the law to do your work for you. Make the cops capture him. Make the judge execute him. You get to show the politicians who's boss, and there's no need for killing paper boys."

Camonte chewed on his cigar, contemplating.

"Give me one more day," Mark pressed. "I'll track down the creature and have Duke arrested, nice and neat."

"You got until tomorrow," Camonte said. "After that, we do it the old way."

"Swell. Now that's settled, I'll take my sixty bucks for the day."

"Fuck you. You'll get your money when I get Duke." He knocked on the glass between them and the driver. "Pull over!"

The car stopped. One of the goons flung open the door to let in the glare of the sun. "Out," Camonte ordered.

Mark climbed out, and immediately the light hammered into his skull. He squinted and looked around. He was standing on the corner of Randolph and Halstead. "This is West Side."

"Yeah, so?"

"My office is in South Side," Mark said.

Camonte showed his eyetooth in a grin. "Then I guess you'd better start walking." His goon slammed the door shut, and the limousine peeled away.

Mark stared after it, then tipped his head back and laughed. "Bastard."

46

At noon, Eliza dragged herself out of bed after a few hours of fitful sleep. She was due for tea at Mrs. DeForest's home at one o'clock.

She dressed in a fresh black suit and regarded herself in the mirror. Not all the powder in the world could hide the dark circles under her eyes or the pallor of her cheeks, she thought.

Downstairs she got a cab and ordered it to Mrs. DeForest's North Side address. But she made a brief stop at a florist along the way where she found a bouquet of fragrant yellow lilies for her hostess.

A few minutes later her taxi pulled up in front of a respectable North Side townhome. The street looked much as it had three years ago. Neat brick buildings with well-trimmed front gardens and polished brass fixtures. At the same time, there was something, some subtle difference with her memories that she couldn't quite name.

She walked slowly up the tidy path and knocked on the door. After a moment, a portly older gentleman smelling of iodine and licorice drops opened it. Eliza had never met him before, she was certain. She stared at him, her fingers clenching on the bouquet of lilies.

"Can I help you?" the man said in a somber voice.

"I've come to take tea with Mrs. DeForest. She invited me yesterday."

"Are you Miss Karlova?"

She nodded.

"I was just about to telephone you. I'm Dr. Mills, Mrs. DeForest's physician. Won't you come in?" He stood aside, holding the door for her.

She stepped into her mentor's pretty parlor. The room was dark, the chintz curtains drawn. Two people were there already, a thin, elderly man with a starched collar sitting at a delicate writing table, and Millie, the shop girl in a damask armchair. Millie was dabbing her eyes with a handkerchief and the old gentleman was reading a sheaf of papers. Eliza barely noticed them, because a terrible thread of scent wound to her nose from somewhere in the house.

She spun to face the doctor, who had followed her in.

"Would you care to sit?" he said.

She shook her head in a convulsive little jerk. She felt her mouth wobbling "Please," she said, though she didn't know what she was asking for.

The doctor regarded her sadly. "I'm sorry, my dear. Mrs. DeForest passed away in her sleep last night."

Before she knew what was happening, the doctor was pressing her down into one of the comfortable armchairs. The flowers scattered in her lap.

There was a confused babble of voices for a while. Eliza heard herself ask when the funeral was to be. In four days, she was told. The reading of the Will was to be the day after that. But the thin old gentleman, who she learned was Mrs. DeForest's lawyer, was authorized to give Eliza a personal letter in the event of her death. The envelope he handed her had a flat, key-shaped lump inside it. She put it in her purse. To read it at this moment was impossible.

She asked, "May I see her?"

"They've already taken her away. But you can see her at the viewing," The lawyer said kindly.

"And what of her shop?"

"Closed," Millie said. "For good, I guess." She folded and unfolded her handkerchief. "But I know she'll have done something to help tide me over until I find another job. She was a—a real fine lady."

"Yes, she was," Eliza whispered.

47

When Eliza got back to the hotel, it was past four o'clock. She should be accepting Duke's proposal right now, she thought distantly. She felt a bit like she was floating, only a cushion of thin air preventing her from falling and shattering on the floor. She drifted into the elevator and up to her grandmother's suite. Helga opened the door for her and led her into the parlor.

Duke was sitting in an armchair near Angelique's divan, conversing with her in low tones. When Eliza entered the room, he rose to his feet, fingering his small mustache.

"There you are at last," Angelique said, her voice light, but with the faintest thread of warning. Her scent wreathed through the air.

"Do forgive me. I've been out for a walk," Eliza said. She held out her gloved hand to Duke. "Good afternoon, Lionel."

"Good afternoon, my dear." He took her hand and held it clasped between his, tightly, and tugged her toward him. His metallic odor enveloped her. "I'm glad to see you've recovered from the unpleasant business of last night. You look ravishing."

"Thank you." She forced her smile wider and looked him in the face. His eyes displayed little of the telltale haziness her grandmother's poison produced. His resistance might prove to be a problem, she thought with detachment.

She said, "But last night wasn't entirely unpleasant. In fact, parts of it were wonderful. Magical." Her mind flashed on Mark as he stood at the top of the Board of Trade Building, a sternly beautiful white silhouette against the black city sky. She thought of his strong arms around her, his mouth urgent on hers.

Duke, of course, thought she was talking about her date with him. His smile widened into a smirk. "They certainly were. My dear, I've decided it's time I married again. A man in my position needs a suitable helpmeet, and I believe that, with your beauty and breeding, you will serve quite well."

"Of course, Lionel."

"Marvelous." He took a velvet box out of his pocket and opened it. Inside was a ring set with a diamond the size of a pigeon's egg. He grabbed her left hand and stripped her glove off, holding her fingers in an almost painfully strong grip. This was the first time she had ever touched his bare flesh, and she all but cringed away from the feel of it. His skin was cool and unpleasantly moist. He felt nothing at all like Mark.

He slipped the ring on her third finger. "There you are dearest. Shall we seal the agreement with a kiss?" He pulled her forward, bent his head, and covered her mouth with his. His lips were clammy, the taste of him harsh and metallic, but she allowed the kiss until she felt the tip of his wet probing tongue.

She pulled back, smiling up at him for all she was worth. "Lionel, I am overcome!"

He chuckled and pinched her chin, his thumb pressing hard. "Why then, you must strengthen your nerves. When you're mine, I'll require you to be the perfect wife both in public and in the bedroom."

"Mr. Duke," Angelique said sharply, "Perhaps you might tell your bride about the engagement party we've arranged?"

"Yes." Duke released her chin. "A garden party at my country house at noon tomorrow. For tonight, dinner here at the hotel, and then dancing at the Triannon Ballroom."

"My, how delightful!" Her bubble of calm was about to shatter. She had to get away this instant. She let her scent rise up around her. "You must allow me to change for dinner."

"Of course. I'll collect you in the lobby at seven," he said.

"Splendid. Until tonight, darling," she said, and made her escape.

She took the elevator down to her floor and drifted along the hall and through the door to her room, shutting it carefully behind her. Then, at last, she collapsed on the bed, buried her face in her arms, and wept.

48

When Mark finally got back to his house, he forced himself to eat and bathe, but sleep was out of the question. He didn't want to miss Eliza's call. But the morning passed without a ring on his telephone or a knock on his door. A strange and terrible restlessness began to grip him, winding him tighter and tighter as the time ticked down to nightfall.

Tonight, he would search Duke's factory out past the edge of the city in Chicago Heights. He might find the monster there, or at least some evidence of it. He'd already searched Duke's city office and his lawyer's office when he was investigating him for Eliza, but there were no clues there. He needed a new lead.

He combed through his notes again, looking for angles he'd missed, but his concentration was wrecked. And he knew who's fault that was.

He wandered from room to room in his house. He tried to read Agatha Christie's latest murder mystery. He listened to an episode of *The Adventures of Charlie Chan* on his new radio. He boxed his heavy bag and lifted weights until his tendons creaked. All useless.

Finally he gave in and telephoned Eliza's room. She didn't answer. He left a message for her with the concierge and tried to work at his desk, a weight settling in his chest.

Finally, just after the sun set, the telephone rang. He made himself let it ring three times before picking it up. "Hello."

"Hello," a man's voice said. "This Van Ryn?"

"Maybe," Mark said, pushing away his disappointment. "Who's this?"

"Name's Peters. I'm a bellhop at the Drake Hotel. Florian says you'll pay for information on a lady who's staying here name of Karlova."

He felt something in him go tight. "What have you got?"

"She just got engaged to a rich fellow named Duke."

"Engaged."

"That's right. I heard 'em talking about it when they was gettin' in their limousine. She had on a big ol' diamond ring, too."

After a long moment, he said in a level voice, "Where were they going?"

"I heard him tell the driver the Trianon Ballroom."

"When did they leave?"

"Ten minutes ago."

"Thanks. You'll have your money tomorrow." He hung up and walked to the window, staring without seeing through a crack in the blinds.

After he showed her his deepest secrets, after she put her arms around him and kissed him with such passion, she'd given herself to another man.

He had to be cool and rational about this. He had to consider all the angles. Ignore the pain cinching around his chest. Admit that he'd been a pathetic, desperate, self-deluded fool. He'd actually thought last night meant something.

He laughed at himself, a forced, rusty sound in his throat. The view of the street out the window blurred a little.

Outside, night had fallen at last. Time to get to work and find this creature once and for all. No more letting some dame distract him.

He threw on his hat and coat and unleashed his shadows, racing out of his house and down the street. But instead of going to Duke's chemical factory in Chicago Heights, he found himself headed for the Trianon Ballroom in Woodlawn. And somewhere along the way, the pain inside him morphed into fury, and the growing certainty that he'd been a sap. That she'd been spying for Lionel Duke the whole time, feeding him the lines he wanted to hear.

Well, Eliza was going to answer a few more questions before he took Duke down tonight, and God help her if she tried to yank him around again.

Since Eliza and Duke had only left the Drake ten minutes ago, he got to the dance hall before they arrived, with plenty of time to scout out the place. The Trianon was the most luxurious ballroom in Chicago, half the size of a football field and done up in golden French curlicues and a mountain's worth of marble. At the curb under the tall electric sign, swarms of men in dinner jackets and ladies in jewel-colored gowns were getting out of cars and sweeping through the gilded doors into the marble lobby.

Mark pulled enough shadow around himself to ensure the ticket-takers wouldn't notice him and slipped inside with the rest of the crowd. Invisible, he climbed the grand staircase to the ballroom.

The huge oval dance floor was ringed with marble pillars and a gallery full of chairs and tables. Hundreds of people waltzed to the strains of the orchestra or milled about in the gallery, chatting and laughing under the blazing crystal chandeliers and the painted nymphs cavorting on the ceiling.

Not Mark's kind of place at all. The light was strong enough that even maintaining his cloak of half-shadow was hard work. And it was a bad spot for a confrontation. Too crowded and too wide open. But at least it was safe from a slime attack. Too much light, and no drains.

He returned to the lobby downstairs to keep an eye on the street, leaning a shoulder against a baroque column near the doors. A few more parties of dancers arrived, piling out of touring cars and sports cars. Then, a limousine purred up to the curb.

Mark straightened from his lean against the pillar.

The liveried driver got out and opened the rear door. Lionel Duke climbed out of the back seat, his white evening coat perfect and his oiled hair gleaming. He reached into the car to take the gloved hand of a lady. Her massive diamond ring glinted in the electric lights.

Eliza set a delicate dance slipper onto the pavement and let Duke help her out of the limousine. She wore a black, low-cut gown, the beaded bodice painted on her slender body like the jeweled scales of a beautiful serpent. Two straps crossed the ivory skin of her naked back. Silk skirts swirled around her legs as she turned toward the doors. Her bobbed ringlets gleamed. Her red lips were set in a smile.

He found himself grinding his teeth. He might be

immune to her perfume, but one look at her hurt him just as bad. And that made him even more furious.

The doorman flung open the doors for the glamorous couple, and as they walked through them, Mark came out of half-shadow and stepped right in their path. "Lionel! And Miss Karlova. Fancy meeting you here."

They stopped in their tracks. Eliza turned pale, and Duke flushed, his eyes narrowing. Then he smiled deliberately. "Mark. What a surprise." He walked past Mark, pulling Eliza silently along.

Mark fell into step with them on Eliza's other side. "Funny, you don't look too surprised."

"I'm getting rather used to you following me about like a spaniel."

"I was here first. Maybe you're the one following me." He turned a smile on Eliza. "*Are* you following me, Miss Karlova?"

"No, Mr. Van Ryn." She kept walking, not looking at him.

"How are feeling after your terrible ordeal last night?"

"I'm well, thank you."

She and Duke started climbing the stairs, Mark sticking with them tight as a tick.

"And you, Lionel? You must have been terrified."

The man's cheeks darkened. "Quite," he said. A waiter met them at the top of the stairs and led them to a reserved table with a view of the band. Duke held Eliza's chair for her.

Mark pulled up a chair and sat without asking.

Eliza busied herself lighting up a cigarette.

Duke sat down himself and snapped his fingers for the hovering waiter. "A bottle of champagne and two—no, make it three glasses." The man disappeared, and Duke smiled at Mark with lazy eyes. "Why don't you join us in a drink. We're celebrating tonight, you see. Miss Karlova has just agreed to become my wife."

Mark's hand fisted under the table. "Congratulations." He turned his head and looked at Eliza. "You must be terribly happy."

She lifted her chin, finally looking him in the face. "Terribly."

"Lucky me, I can be the first to dance with the bride. What do you say?"

She set her cigarette holder on the ashtray. "That would be lovely," she said, a sharp edge to each word. Duke stirred, and she placed her hand on his. "Lionel, please."

"As you like, my dear," he said after a moment.

Mark claimed her other hand. He helped her up and led her to the dance floor. Duke watched them go, his heavy-lidded smile never wavering.

49

He clasped her lithe waist, his other hand enfolding hers as he drew her close, her luscious scent invading his mind. The heat from his body tangled with hers as he moved her into the dance. He waltzed her away from Duke, into the middle of the swirling crowd.

The other dancers shot them wide-eyed glances and edged away, leaving a space around them.

The instant they were out of earshot, she murmured, "Mark, you have to leave."

"I'll leave when I get the answers to a few questions, angel, not before."

"What questions?"

"What have you told Duke about me? About my—my shadow."

"Nothing. I haven't mentioned you once, and nor has he. Whatever you may think of me, I would never betray your confidence, Mark."

"You talk about betrayal!" He got hold of himself. "Listen to me. Duke is dangerous. He's already murdered four men at least. What if his pet tries to eat you again?"

"I can handle Duke."

"You can't marry him. He's a killer."

"You forget, so am I. Perhaps Duke and I deserve each other."

"Don't give me that. What you did was in self-defense. Any man who attacks you deserves what he gets in my book."

For an instant, her veneer of calm cracked. "You ran off quickly enough last night when I told you about it."

"I left because you asked me to go! I was trying to be a *gentleman*. Last time I do something that dumb. If I'd taken you back to my house the way I wanted to, your grandmother wouldn't have talked you into this crazy marriage. What kind of hold does she have over you?"

"None! I'm doing this of my own free will."

The sidelong looks from the other dancers were turning into outright stares.

"Then what's your game, angel?" he said in an ireful whisper. "Tell me the truth. Why did you spend last night kissing me stupid, and the very next day get engaged to another man?"

Red washed over her cheeks. "Kissing is all well and good, but I must marry someone, and far better Duke than you."

That was the last straw. They had waltzed around the ballroom and were near the doors. Mark swept her through them and towed her down the hall to the coat-check room. He pulled some shadow around them and they slipped past the bored-looking girl at the counter. He tugged Eliza deep into the closet until they were surrounded by hanging coats. The rich, musky smell of wool, fur, and perfume enfolded them.

He looked down into her beautiful, sulky face. She'd let

him drag her away into a closet without a sound. She wanted to fight this out as much as he did. "Why? Why not marry me?"

"Because I'm trying to save you, you dolt!"

"I'm immune to your perfume, remember?"

"You don't know that for sure. And my grandmother—"

"Forget your grandmother. If she hadn't been there, I would have had you last night, perfume or not, and we both know it. You're hot for me, angel. Me, not him. I can feel it, right now."

She drew a shaky breath, her face blooming pink with either anger or desire. "You–you're trying to shock me."

He crowded her up against the wall between the coats. "Yeah. But you like it when I shock you, don't you?"

"You cannot treat me this way. I'm—"

"You're a lady, I know." He grabbed her hips and pulled her against him. The sharp little beads of her dress pressed into his flesh. He was hard already, his arousal nudging against her. "But I'm done being a gentleman for you. Admit it. You don't want him. You want me."

"I can't have what I want!" she said, shoving at his chest with trembling hands.

"Yes you can. I know exactly what you want, angel, and I'm going to give it to you."

50

Her lips parted in shock, and he took advantage. He cupped her face in his hands and kissed her, invading her mouth with his tongue.

She froze for an instant, then she pounded his shoulders, wrenching away from him, her eyes flashing. "What are you—"

He captured her lips with his again as she made a furious sound. Captured her little fists in one of his, pinning them against the wall above her head. Pinned her body against the wall with his body. Her breasts crushed up softly against his chest, her nipples tight, hot points beneath the thin layers of her clothing. Her long lean belly quivered against his. Her sleek thighs parted as he shoved his own thigh between them. His cock was an iron spike in his pants, pulsing against her hip.

He cradled her delicate jaw in his free hand and kissed her fiercely. And then a moan rose deep in her throat, instantly suppressed, but there just the same. She bit him, hard, on his lower lip.

He pulled back an inch, looking into her furious eyes.

"You want me. Say it."

She was panting in rage. Her eyes burned into his. He was about to release her wrists and step back, but then she leaned forward and kissed him.

Good enough. He groaned and slid his hand down her body, over her hip and around. He palmed her bottom, squeezing and kneading the firm, ripe flesh through the glass beads and silky cloth. She was sharp, and soft, and so sweet. He rocked his hips into her, growling into her mouth. He grabbed the hem of her skirt and pulled a handful of fabric up to her waist.

She made that angry sound again, bucking against him, twisting her wrists under his hand. He kept his grip, careful not to hurt her, only to render her absolutely helpless.

He drew his fingers up her leg, past the top of her stocking to the silky skin on the inside of her thigh. He braced her legs apart with his knee and stroked over the delicate lace of her underwear. When she gasped, he thrust the lace aside with his fingers. He stroked over her again, and this time he touched silky hair. Then below . . .

It was his turn to gasp. She was satiny. Hot. Sopping wet against his fingers. He drew his hand through her folds, amazed.

She squealed and tried to bite him again. But he swirled his fingers through her wetness, touching and rubbing, drawing them up to the very top of her sex where he found a hard, hot little nub. When he touched it, she jolted against him, and let out a new sound, deeper, throatier, that shot straight down to the root of his cock.

He rubbed her again, full of wonder, swirling his finger around and over the place that made her thighs quiver around his hand, made her head fall back against the wall, her eyes going hazy, her lips trembling against his.

He drove his fingers downward, searching, and this time her breath stuttered. Her hips squirmed, trying to get his fingers back on that spot again. But he found her plush, wet opening and drove a finger inside. He cupped her sex hard with his palm, rubbing her with the heel of his hand as he penetrated her with one finger. Then two.

She cried out again, deep in her throat. He broke the kiss to move his lips down to the bodice of her dress.

Her hands, which had somehow gotten loose from his grip, clutched his hair and his back, holding him to her now.

The hard little beads on her dress burned cold against his lips. Underneath them was the even harder little bead of her nipple. Turn about was fair play. He bit her, just enough to force a cry out of her. She bucked against him again, this time not to throw him off.

He kissed his way back up her throat, over her jaw to her ear. "You're so wet for me. So hot for me. I'm the one you want inside you." He twisted his fingers, making her moan.

"Forget about Duke. Come home with me. I'll take you to my bed and rip these clothes off you. I'll spread you wide open and have you until you scream for mercy. Then I'll put you on your hands and knees and have you some more until we pass out from coming. And when we wake up, I'll do it again. I'll—"

She buried her face in the crook of his neck, her lips hot against his throat as she bit him again, an animal groan coming from deep inside her. Her hips were pumping against his hand, her sheath clenching around his fingers. Her hands twisted in his hair, pulling it to the edge of pain.

Her whole body, strung tight as a bow, shuddered against him for an endless moment, and slowly melted soft against him. He drew his hand out of her and wrapped her in his arms, holding her up as her legs trembled. Her breath was coming fast, her heart pounding hard against his breastbone. Or perhaps it was his heart. Her hands released his hair and drifted to his shoulders.

She drew her face away from his neck and tipped her head up at him slowly. He looked down into her eyes, speechless, awed by her pleasure. He wanted to do it again and never stop.

Her lips were soft and trembling, her eyes starry. She was the most magnificent creature he had ever seen. His cock lunged hungrily for her, demanding more of her. Always more, of her sweetness, her softness, her hot, wet body, her moans and cries, her fire, her life. He bent his head to kiss her again.

She drew back her hand and slapped him.

His head snapped around and he actually staggered a little. Woman had a hell of an arm on her. He reached up and moved his jaw back and forth to make sure it still worked. He looked down at her and grinned. "You're welcome."

She shoved past him and stormed toward the door, heels snapping on the floor. At the entrance she spun on him, her teeth bared, eyes flashing. "You stay the hell away from me!" she hissed. Then she shoved aside the curtain and was gone.

He let out a harsh breath. "That wasn't quite what I planned," he said to the empty closet. He must have gone out of his mind.

After a few minutes he stumbled to the door and took a shaky step out into the hallway. He caught sight of a mirror on one wall for ladies to check themselves before their grand entrances. The man he saw in the reflection was a wreck. There was a bright red handprint blooming across the white skin of his cheek. Another red bite mark on his neck. His lips were swollen and smeared with her lipstick.

In the mirror, he saw himself put his hand to his hair, ruffled from where she had sunk her fingers into it. "A fine upstanding citizen, you are," the guy in the mirror said. He got out his handkerchief and rubbed the lipstick.

Beyond the doors he heard the band start up again.

He couldn't possibly go in there like this. Not to be seen. The poor coat-check girl was already staring at him in horror. He walked away from her and gathered his half-shadow around him as he eased up to the ballroom doors.

He looked for Eliza at her table, but it was empty. Had she gone home? Had she . . . He caught a glitter of black on the dance floor. She was there, waltzing with Duke.

Somehow, in the few minutes since she left him, she had fixed the hair and clothes he had mussed up, calmed the heat that had rushed over her skin when she trembled in his arms, and become the ice-cold society lady once again.

He saw Duke smile down at her composed face and murmur something to her. She replied with a sparkling laugh. Duke turned her gracefully on the dance floor and she flicked a glance like a whip cut over his shoulder at Mark.

She knew he was there watching her. Watching them together.

A shocking pain seared his heart.

To hell with her. He turned on his heel and marched back to the street doors, his hands shaking, the skin on his back cold. He'd wasted enough time here. He had a job to do. Tonight, he was taking Duke down. And he was saving Eliza in spite of herself.

51

Mark raced through the shadows to Duke's chemical factory out past the edge of the city proper in Chicago Heights. It was a large compound, the main building five stories tall with plenty of outbuildings and towering metal vats connected by snarls of pipes. He slipped through the wire fencing and past the security guards easily enough. In no time he was touring the factory from the fifth floor offices to the main laboratories to the sub-basement.

He looked in every barrel and every test tube. He rifled through every paper in the offices. But he found not one shred of evidence that the slime monster even existed. He spent almost an hour cracking the safe in Duke's office, but inside were only financial and legal documents related to Duke's legitimate business. Not a word about Project Plasma, as he and his scrawny scientist had called it.

He put everything in Duke's office back the way he found it and slipped out of the factory just as gray predawn light crept across the eastern sky. He had wasted the night with nothing to show for it.

Camonte had only given him one day to break the case, and even that deadline he didn't trust. The vengeful, erratic mob boss might bring out the guns at any time. Unless he kidnapped Duke and took him to Camonte.

He turned the idea over in his mind. Slipping into Duke's home while he was asleep, snatching him into the darkness and dropping him at Camonte's feet. If he could carry Eliza through the shadows, surely he could carry Duke.

He didn't like going outside the law. He always roped the cops into his cases whenever possible, if only to make Detective O'Bannion's life more difficult. But if he took Duke to the police they wouldn't arrest him, not without proof. He'd simply walk free, and Camonte would go to war.

If he delivered Duke to Camonte, on the other hand, at least he would avoid any more deaths. And it would be justice, of a kind.

And then, there was Eliza. He had to protect her, whether she wanted him to or not.

Camonte it is. He raced through the dark city to Duke's Gold Coast apartment. He scaled the back wall to the kitchen window and sifted his shadow self through the crack in the frame. The second after he entered the kitchen, his instinct told him the place was empty. He sped through the shadows inside every room, hunting for his quarry, but Duke was nowhere to be found.

Where the hell was he? Mark didn't have time to rumble every bar and brothel in the city, not before morning came. Unless . . . He had a sudden, terrible thought. He tore out of Duke's apartment in a rush of shadow, speeding through the streets to the Drake Hotel.

He slipped up the outside of the building to Eliza's room on the fifth floor.

He eased his presence against her window, darkness pressing against the glass. There was a sliver of an opening between the drapes. He looked inside, dreading what he might see. If he found Duke there, Camonte would never get his revenge, because Mark would kill the man himself.

But when his gaze found Eliza's satin covered bed, he saw only one dark head on the pillow, one slender shape curled under the counterpane. She was alone. He was so relieved he almost turned solid, right there against the side of the building five stories in the air.

He wouldn't go in her room. He didn't dare. He wanted her too much. Still, he stayed, his shadow-self roiling with frustration.

Eliza's head turned on her pillow, and he saw the sparkle of her eyes opening in the darkness as if she sensed his presence. Instantly he slipped away down the building to the street.

He turned solid, shaken to his core once again. He had to get a grip. Dawn was coming. He needed a lead on Duke.

He walked to the hotel's main entrance and pushed through the glass doors. There were two liveried bellhops on stools behind the service counter. One was a young man who had his eyes closed, chin on his chest, snoring lightly. The other was a short, wiry fellow with light brown skin and an attitude of fixed wakefulness. When Mark walked through the doors, his eyes snapped wider.

"Peters?" Mark said. "Fellow I talked to earlier?"

The man nodded once.

"I got something I need your help with outside." He held up a five-dollar bill, turned and strode back through the doors. Peters got off his stool and followed along behind. He stopped in a patch of shadow along the hotel's side wall. "What else can you tell me about Miss Karlova and Lionel Duke? Did you see them when they came back here?"

"Yeah. Heard 'em too," Peters said.

"What did they say?"

"They were talkin' about an engagement party tomorrow at noon. A garden party."

"Where?"

"Mr. Duke's country place in Forest Park."

Mark knew about that house. He had seen the address in Duke's lawyer's files, but he hadn't had a chance to search it yet. "Thanks." He handed over the fin.

Peters made the money disappear, and then he himself disappeared back into the hotel. Mark walked down the street, cursing his stupidity.

He'd played this all wrong from the first. He should have grabbed Duke at the beginning and delivered him to Camonte to deal with. Instead he'd spent the last three days letting a twist lead him around by the balls. Now Duke was in the wind, the sun was already edging along the horizon, and a pack of violent mobsters was in a safe house somewhere cleaning their guns.

But he could still salvage the situation. He might not know where Duke was right now, but he knew where he'd be in a few hours.

It looked like Mark would be attending a garden party.

He didn't dare wait until tonight to go to Duke's country estate. He had to be on hand today in case Camonte attacked, or Eliza and innocent bystanders might get hurt. And he still might have time to search the house for evidence.

But if he couldn't find enough proof to force the cops to

act, he'd grab the bastard and take him to Camonte when night fell. He had to keep the Outfit from going to war, whatever it took.

And he had to get Eliza out of this engagement one way or another.

Sure, he was going in half-cocked. Sure, it was reckless and stupid. It was the perfect plan in other words. Only one problem with it. He couldn't get to Forest Park through the shadows in the few minutes before dawn, and he couldn't drive the full two hours it would take to get there in the daylight. He had to save his energy to withstand the sun at this damn garden party. He needed a driver.

Putting the last scraps of predawn darkness to use, he snapped into full shadow and raced south.

He came out of the shadow at the house in Bronzeville and pounded on the door. Frasier answered in slippers and a robe again. This time he just growled, "Coffee," and refused to let Mark say another word until he'd led him into his kitchen and put on the coffeepot. He started pulling out eggs and bacon. "Okay. Now talk."

Mark sat down at the wooden kitchen table and told him the predicament he had landed himself in. "So," he finished, "I have to crash this engagement party if I'm going to stop a bloodbath."

Frasier plopped down coffee and plates full of breakfast and eyed him shrewdly. "Are you sure you're not going there because of that dame?"

"It's not about her. It's about catching this monster and saving lives," Mark said tightly.

Frasier cast him a skeptical glance. He sat down and slugged his coffee. "I want to go on the record saying I hate this plan of yours."

"Noted. I could really use your help, though, Frasier."

"What do you need me to do?"

"Drive me to Forest Park."

Finally, a grin split his face. "I get to drive your car? Brother, that's all you had to say!"

52

At ten o'clock sharp, Eliza, her grandmother, and Helga drove up the winding private road to Lionel Duke's country estate. They passed a wood, a meadow, and another wood, which opened onto a formal park. A French chateau stood resplendent amid the rolling acres. All that was missing were the thatched huts for the peasants.

As their driver pulled the hired car into the broad circular driveway, Duke came out to greet them. He was wearing a white linen suit, and a little smile. He had left the city for his estate immediately after escorting her back to her hotel last night, saying he wanted to be on hand to supervise a few last details early in the morning.

Eliza had been profoundly relieved he hadn't tried to escort her to her room. After that incredible encounter with Mark at the Triannon, it had taken every ounce of her resolve simply to get through the rest of the evening in Duke's company without a weeping fit.

Last night, as she lay sleepless in bed, she had scented Mark's presence near her for an all-too-brief moment, and her heart had leapt with joy and fury in equal measure. He made her wild, wanton, so that she barely knew herself anymore. He had destroyed whatever peace she might have had forever. She leapt out of bed ready to fight him, or to throw herself into his arms. But then he was gone again like the memory of a dream.

Since that moment, the numb, floating calm from yesterday had descended on her again. Passively, she allowed Angelique to sweep her along, into the car and off to her engagement party in the country.

The numbness persisted as Duke opened the car door for them and handed them out, saying all the right things about welcoming them to his home. Eliza said the right things back, allowing him to hold on to her hand after he helped her out of the car. Angelique announced that she would go to her room immediately. Duke summoned the butler hovering in the doorway. Angelique and Helga followed the man inside. Eliza was alone with her fiancé. She tried not to shiver.

He brushed a fingertip over his mustache as he looked down at her, his eyes heavy-lidded and smug. "You look ravishing, my dear." His harsh, metallic scent enveloped her as he leaned down to kiss her cheek. His cold, moist lips brushed her skin, and she wanted to scrub her hand over the spot they had touched.

She smiled up at him instead. "Thank you, darling."

"Welcome to your future home. I trust you will find it all you wish for, and more." He grasped her elbow in his too-hard grip and led her past the marble columns flanking the entrance and through the massive carved door.

Inside, a parquet floor gleamed under a crystal chandelier. Large oil paintings glimmered on the walls. A grand staircase swept up to a gallery above. "It's marvelous," Eliza said dutifully.

"Yes, isn't it?" Duke said with a small smile. "I shall give you the grand tour." He led the way through the sprawling rooms and salons of the ground floor. They were built on a baronial scale, but were so crammed with furniture and decorations they seemed close and stuffy. Every stick of wood was carved and gilded. Every scrap of fabric was brocaded. Silk gleamed on the walls. Plaster cherubs fluttered along the ceiling. Persian carpets covered the floor. Bouquets of hothouse roses perfumed the air.

Eliza made sure to say, "Splendid!" and, "Lovely!" several times. Duke seemed satisfied. He threw open door after door until all the rooms had been examined. Except one door tucked into a corner of the hall which stayed closed.

Before she could ask Duke about it, he led her up a wide, curving staircase to the second story. He showed her over the bedrooms, including the one she was to be using tonight. It was a low, dark chamber, and the air was hot and dense with the scent of yet more roses. The bed and curtains were stiff with white satin.

"This will be your room when we are married," Duke said. "You can see the adjoining door there, which leads to my room."

"It's charming!" she said brightly.

Duke reached out and pinched her chin. "Perhaps you'd like to try out the bed?"

"Oh, I shall!" She took the hand off her chin and held it in both gloved hands. "But I'm longing to see the gardens now. Do take me through them, Lionel." She had to get a breath of fresh air. Had to.

His eyes narrowed, but he said, "Certainly." He took her arm once again in his hard grip and led her down the staircase and out a set of French doors to the garden. The caterers were setting up awnings and banquet tables near the turquoise swimming pool. She thought of the slime monster's fondness for water and resolved to stay well back from the pool herself.

Duke took her along the flower beds and over an endless green lawn. They passed through an arbor that led to a formal rose garden surrounded by high boxwood hedges. Past that was a dovecote folly, a stone tower with a tall cupola, its wooden door standing ajar. Beyond the folly the woods resumed.

"What do you think of your new home, my dear?" he said as they walked back to the house.

"It's lovely so far," she said. "But I haven't seen everything, have I? Or rather, everyone?"

He looked at her sharply. "What do you mean?"

"Why, your son Steven! He lives here, doesn't he?"

"Yes, but unfortunately my son is an invalid. He is not fit for visitors at this time."

There was a warning in the tone of his voice, which Eliza ignored. Mark had told her in so many words that the child wasn't safe with his father. She was determined to see him for herself.

"But I'm not a visitor, Lionel. I'm to be his stepmother. I should at least meet him. I won't tire him, I promise."

Duke's expression remained cool. "My dear—"

She touched his arm and smiled up at him through her lashes, letting her poison weave around him again. "Please, take me to him, Lionel."

His eyes didn't glaze over instantly, so she dosed him some more. Finally, he said, "Very well." He led her back into the house and up a narrow, dark staircase leading to a door to the fourth floor attic. The cramped hallway beyond ended in another door. He opened that, too.

Inside was a large, nursery-style bedroom with a child's bed against one wall. A small boy of about five sat there among the pillows. In a rocker near him was a middle-aged woman with a dull slab of a face.

A spindly little man sat on the side of the boy's bed. Something metallic glinted in the man's hand. A syringe. In a flash of instinct, Eliza took a step forward to stop him from plunging the needle into the boy's flesh. But as she and Duke came into the room the man jerked around, startled.

Duke seemed surprised to see him. With an edge to his voice, he said, "Dr. Smalley. We had not yet discussed Steven's treatment."

"I was merely drawing a blood sample. Nothing out of the ordinary."

"I wish to speak with you for a moment, doctor. Now." He stepped aside from the door and gestured Dr. Smalley out of the room.

The doctor stowed his syringe away in his case with sharp, impatient movements and stalked to the door. He slowed down as he neared Eliza, flicking a glance at her.

She almost stepped back as he approached. A visceral loathing had seized her the instant she had seen him. Something in the way he hunched over the boy, and the strange glitter of his eyes. Or eye, rather. Up close, she could tell that his left eye was made of glass. He smelled of metal and old blood. As he approached, her power rose up around her in instinctive defense, but he merely scuttled past her out of the room.

Duke shut the door behind them.

She turned her attention to the boy. He didn't seem disturbed or frightened at all. Indeed, he had sat up eagerly when they came in the room.

He was a remarkably handsome child, though he didn't much resemble his father. His skin was fair and his hair was black and wavy. Though his features still had a baby-softness, they showed the promise of sharply chiseled beauty when he was older. His eyes were a striking light gray color, but there was a silvery sheen over the pupils that nearly made them vanish within the light circles of his irises.

His pale, blank gaze seemed to be fixed on her. Then his small face lit with the most heartbreaking smile she had ever seen. "It's you!" he said, as if he'd been waiting for her. He scrambled out of the bed. His small body was swimming in blue striped pajamas. She was relieved to see that though he was perhaps a little too pale, he had no visible injuries. He started to walk in her direction, his cuffs dragging.

The nurse lumbered up from her rocker and caught him in a rough grip. "Where do you think you're going? You want to fall on your face?"

"Please," Eliza said. "I'm to be his new stepmother. Let me speak to him for a moment."

Grudgingly, the woman walked the child forward, hand still on his arm. The boy was blind, Eliza realized. He came to stand in front of her and tipped his face up toward her.

"Hello, Steven. My name is Eliza," she said. "I'm to marry your father and come live with you."

His eerie, sightless eyes seemed to sparkle with silver. "You call me Stevie." He reached out and slipped his hand into hers, as naturally as if he'd done it a hundred times before.

She was startled, but not worried about his touch. She was wearing white cotton gloves, and anyway, he was far too young for her poison to sicken him. A lamia's perfume affected only adult men.

As she looked down into his small face, forking lines of

283

light flashed across his eyes. He said, "You'll keep me safe, but the monster might eat you. Watch out for the masks."

Eliza caught her breath.

"That's enough of that crazy talk," the nurse snapped, pulling the boy away from her. She propelled him back to his bed and lifted him into it, none too gently.

"It's all right," Eliza said.

But the woman looked mulish. "Mustn't tire him. Doctor's orders."

Duke entered the room. "We must let Steven rest now," he said to Eliza. To his son he said, "Be a good boy, Steven."

The child's silver eyes turned on his father and again she saw the sparkle of light within them. His small face drained of all expression. "Goodbye, father."

"Goodbye Stevie," Eliza said as Duke took her elbow.

"You'll see me soon," the boy replied.

53

Duke nearly pulled her out of Stevie's room. He shut the door and escorted her firmly down the hallway. That Dr. Smalley was nowhere to be seen, thank heaven.

"Stevie is delightful," she said. "I'm looking forward to being his stepmother."

Duke grunted.

"He seems healthy and active. Why must he stay in bed?"

"He's undergoing a medical treatment."

"For what?"

"He suffers from a nervous disorder. His imaginative nature and his blindness have led his mind astray. Sometimes he says very odd things. You must pay them no attention."

Eliza didn't believe him for a second. The boy wasn't mad, he was *different*, just as Mark was different. And Duke either didn't understand that, or he understood it all too well. She wondered what his "medical treatment" entailed. Whatever it was, she would put a stop to it immediately. If there was one good thing about this dreadful marriage, it was that she had a chance to help that little boy. She didn't trust Duke with him, or that Dr. Smalley, not one inch.

She walked toward her room. "I need to freshen up before lunch."

He followed her and leaned against her doorframe, smiling lazily, his son apparently forgotten. "Why don't we skip lunch. We have some time before my guests arrive and you look good enough to eat, my dear." He reached out and took her elbow, his grip hugely strong. Drawing her to him inexorably, he bent his head.

She turned her cheek to him, casting about for a new distraction. "On second thought, there's one more thing I'd like to see," she blurted. "That room downstairs, the last door on the left. You never showed it to me."

"That? That's nothing but my private study," he said, cold lips trailing wetly over her skin.

"How fascinating! I'd like to see it."

He drew back slightly and looked at her. "No one goes in that room but me."

Her instincts prickled. She had only asked about it as a diversion, but now she had to know what he was keeping so private. It wasn't the monster. She would have smelled its presence the moment she came through the front door. But perhaps it was evidence of another sort. "You won't even allow your wife in? Why? Is it quite a Bluebeard's chamber?"

He laughed lightly, a fey expression creeping over his face. "Perhaps it is. Perhaps it's crammed with the bodies of my victims. Do you still want to look?"

"Oh, I simply must!"

"Then by all means, come and see my study." He coiled his arm around her shoulders and almost dragged her through the hall and down the stairs to the forbidden room.

Duke unlocked the door and shoved it open. The air that rushed out smelled of awful chemicals and old rot. He thrust her inside and stepped in after her, switching on the lights.

They were in not a study, but a trophy room. It was windowless and painted stark white, lit from spotlights on the floor. In the center of the room was a glass case holding a dummy dressed in a U.S. Army uniform, medals glinting on the chest. Dull metal gas canisters stood in regimented rows along the walls. Dozens of them. Above them were mounted more than fifty dummy heads, each one wearing a long-snouted gas mask. The circles of the eyepieces seemed to glint at her as she stared back at them.

"Mementos of the War," Duke whispered in her ear. He clutched her shoulders from behind, his fingers digging into her flesh. "Each canister, each mask taken from the scene of a triumph in the field."

Her skin turned cold. The masks were stained with rusty patches, she saw. He had looted them off of enemy corpses. She maintained her composure with an act of will. "There are so many of them. You must be terribly proud."

"Yes. Proud as only a survivor, a winner, can be. You must be proud yourself, to be chosen by a man such as I." He spun her around and yanked her to him.

A vein of panic began to pulse inside her. His grasp was inescapable, his fingers digging in as he crushed her against his body, his harsh scent invading her. *Wrong!* She tried to pull away, but his mouth came down on hers, his lips writhing and sucking, forcing her lips apart, his tongue wriggling inside. It was wet and cold, like a slug. She nearly gagged.

Her poison rushed up to the surface of her skin and she saw it again, the dead blue face in the moonlight. She struggled to tear her mouth away. "We have to stop!"

He trailed his moist, cold lips over her neck. "I don't want to stop. You are delicious." She felt the graze of sharp teeth on her skin.

"We must!" His hands were painful. His smell suffocated her. She couldn't bear the touch of his mouth another second. "Stop!" Power boiled through her skin, barely held in check.

The wet slither of his lips slowed as her poison worked on him. He pushed her away slightly, but his hands clenched tight around her upper arms. His eyes were hard, as if he were fighting her compulsion.

She smiled until her face almost cracked. "We aren't married yet, darling," she said. "We must wait a few more days, for our wedding night."

"I take what I want, when I want," he said softly. "I don't wait for anyone." She saw the gleam of his teeth behind his parted lips.

A spark of fear leapt in her. What if he was like Mark, resistant to her poison? What if he had been toying with her all this time? What if she couldn't control him?

"Élisabeth!" An upright figure appeared in the doorway, the lavender silk of her frock rustling.

Duke's hands loosened, and Eliza struggled out of them. "*Grand-mère!*" She had never been so happy to see Angelique in her life.

The countess said, "I have rested from our journey. I wish to speak to you *tête-à-tête* as you prepare for this afternoon." She directed a stare at Duke, her perfume cloying the air. "You will excuse us, *Monsieur*."

Duke eyed them both for a fraction of a second too long. "Certainly." He lifted a hand to an imaginary hat and saluted them with a hint of mockery. "I'll find you later, dearest," he said to Eliza, an amused slant to his eyelids.

She escaped the horrid room, her heart pounding, and all but ran through the hall and up the stairs to her bedroom.

The countess followed at a more sedate pace. When she reached Eliza's chamber, she settled herself in a dainty chair as Eliza closed the door. "You will be happy to know that the preparations for this party are complete," Angelique said. "I myself will ensure that nothing goes wrong today, even should Mark Van Ryn appear."

"There's no need to concern yourself with him." Eliza moved to the mirror over the gilded dresser and tried to refresh her lipstick with an unsteady hand. Her cheeks were ashen, she saw.

"On the contrary, there appears to be the greatest need. He is likely to disrupt the party, and when he does, you will have only one chance to save him."

Eliza watched her grandmother in the mirror, the older woman's hourglass figure as still as a spider in the center of her web. "What do you mean?"

"If you do not finally send him away for good, I will be forced to act. I will see to it that he has a target on his back and a mob at his door."

"I told you, I can't cloud his mind!" She spun around to face the countess, her hands fisted against her thighs.

"Then you must break his heart."

"How can I?" she cried.

Angelique smiled. "Why, it is simple. Hold out what he wants most in the world, and when he reaches out to take it, snatch it away from him and destroy it utterly. You understand. You are a lamia."

"I can't hurt him. I can't."

"Do it. Break his heart. Or else I will break him."

"You're a monster."

"*Oui, ma petite*. We both are."

54

Mark and Frasier caught the trolley from Bronzeville to Millionaire's Row. The weather was perfect, warm and breezy, not a cloud to be seen in the pale blue sky. In short, it was a gorgeous day for a garden party. Which made it pure hell for Mark. A vicious headache was already drilling into his skull as he got the Duesenberg out of his garage and settled into the passenger seat.

Frasier slid behind the wheel with unconcealed glee. He tuned the car's radio to a jazz station, and they peeled out of the driveway and down the street as Louis Armstrong blasted a fiery riff on the cornet. "This detective gig isn't so bad, is it?" he said with a grin.

Mark grunted. "It has its moments." He pulled his hat down over his eyes and tried to doze as the road rumbled beneath the tires, taking them north. The tall buildings on either side gradually turned into houses and spread farther apart. The powerful car ate up the miles until they were among trees and fields and sprawling country houses.

After a few consultations with a map, they found the driveway to the Longacres Estate, as Duke called his place.

They wound up a paved drive to an overdone French country chateau, painted white. Mark had expected nothing less. The party must already have started, because a fleet of shiny cars were parked along the side of the drive-way. Frasier eased the Duesenberg among them and shut off the engine.

"Frasier," Mark said as his friend reached for the door handle, "maybe you should take the car back to my house. I'll find my own way home."

"Let you go in that place alone? You crazy?" Frasier got out of the car.

Mark followed suit. He came around to stand next to his friend, and they sized up the immaculate house. "You sure you want to do this? It won't be pleasant. Might be dangerous."

"That's why you need someone to watch your back." Frasier set his Fedora at a rakish angle. "Let's go crash a party. It'll be like sneaking into Wrigley Field to see the ball game when we were kids, remember?"

Mark couldn't find any words, so instead he clapped his friend on the shoulder and they started walking up the drive toward the house, past the line of parked cars.

One of the cars had a couple of men sitting in the front seat. The guy behind the wheel was nattily dressed in a linen suit, had a white hat with a paisley hatband tilted over his gingery hair, and was watching them in the side mirror with guileless blue eyes.

"Al Tracy," Mark said as they came up on his open window. He was starting to regret tipping Tracy off. The reporter was doing his job a little too well. Mark glanced at the other guy slouched in the passenger seat, a hat over his face and a large black camera on his knees.

"Van Ryn," Tracy said. "Didn't expect to see you at a garden party."

"Likewise. The society page is out of your wheelhouse, isn't it Tracy?"

"Wouldn't you know it, the society columnist called in sick at the last minute. I stepped in to take her place, because I'm a gentleman like that."

"But Duke didn't buy it."

"Nah. We got bounced in three minutes flat. I bet you and your friend don't even make it one. What do you say Orwin?" He turned to the photographer beside him. "Want to give me odds?"

"Umph," the photographer said from behind his hat.

To Mark, the reporter said, "We're waiting to get some photos when the swells stagger out. Say," his voice turned wheedling, "how about Orwin here takes *your* picture for the society pages?"

"How about I make you eat that hatband of yours?" Mark said.

Tracy laughed a bit nervously, and Mark and Frasier continued up the drive. Faint voices and strains of music drifted from the back gardens. They followed the sounds around the side of the building and found a brick path that led past a glass conservatory attached to the house. Beyond was a shrubbery that screened the partygoers in the gardens from view.

As they stepped on to the bricks, a door in the conservatory squeaked open, and a small shape appeared in the doorway. It was a dark-haired boy of about five. He was dressed in floppy striped pajamas and his small feet were bare. He tilted his face toward them. His eyes were like two silver coins.

Mark stopped short, staring into that strange gaze. "Hey kid."

"Mr. Van Ryn!" the boy said, his face lighting up with a smile. "I've been waiting for you!" He turned his silver eyes on Frasier. "Hello, Mr. Robinson."

"How did you know my name?" Frasier said.

The boy shrugged. "We go in the car, and you take me to Aunt Martha." He took a few steps toward them. He kept his hand on the conservatory wall and walked with a careful, toe-tapping gait. The child was blind, Mark realized.

"You're Mr. Duke's son, Steven, aren't you?"

"I'm his exp—experiment."

The back of Mark's neck started prickling. "What experiment?"

"A scientific experiment. They're trying to make me see the future. But I can't!" His soft voice grew frustrated. "I only see people. Where they've been, and where they're going."

"Can you see me?"

The strange eyes suddenly looked up directly into his, and Mark saw light sparkle across the silver. "Yes, I see you really well, 'cause we were both made by Dr. Smalley."

"Who is Dr. Smalley?"

"The one-eyed man. The man with needles and knives. He made us." The child suddenly turned his wide, blank stare down the path toward the garden. "I have to go." He reached out and grasped Mark's hand with his soft little paw. He tugged it, saying seriously, "The bad men are in the roses. We'll come get you."

He let go and quickly felt his way back along the wall to the door. An instant later he had vanished into the house.

"What in the world was that about?" Frasier murmured.

Mark was more rattled than he wanted to admit. He stared down the path where the boy had cast his blind gaze, his muscles coiling in readiness as he heard footsteps approaching. But what appeared around the corner of the hedge wasn't a gang of bad men but an old woman. Eliza's grandmother, the countess.

She walked toward him, her paces deliberate and her small form erect. Her sharp eyes locked on Mark. She didn't spare Frasier so much as a glance. She stopped in the middle of the path, an arm span away from him. "You were foolish to come. Do you want to tempt fate, boy?"

"Sure. I was born lucky." He held out his hand to her with an insolent half-bow.

Quick as a striking viper, she clutched his wrist in her bony claw. Cloying perfume flooded the air as she let loose her poison.

Out of the corner of his eye, he saw Frasier sway on his feet, already affected by the scent. But Mark felt only a slight tingling in his hand where her fingers dug in.

He smiled at her, deliberately pulled away, and dusted his hands off.

She stumbled backward, blue veins pulsing under the papery skin of her face.

"Maybe you'd better sit down," Mark said, reaching for her elbow.

She recoiled. "*Bête*. Do not presume to touch me."

He raised his fingers to his hat instead and sauntered past her down the path to the garden. Frasier followed him silently, one wary eye on the old woman.

They walked through an arbor onto an acre of velvety green lawn soaked in May sunshine. Party-goers in spring fashions milled about the lavish refreshment table, or sat on benches by the flower beds, or putted balls about a croquet course. White-jacketed waiters wove between them. A band on the patio played a vigorous jazz line. A few dark-suited men roamed the periphery of the lawn, their hands ready and their eyes watchful. The host and his bride-to-be stood together under an awning near the swimming pool.

Eliza's beauty fell on him like a blow, pain that was getting all too familiar. She was dressed in a black and pink chiffon frock that fluttered around her legs with the lightest breath of air. Her long, sleek body curved gracefully toward Duke and her face was tipped up at his. The very picture of a devoted bride, except for the brittle smile and too-bright eyes.

Duke seemed relaxed enough as he held court with his guests. Dressed in a perfect white linen suit, he gestured expansively with the cocktail glass in his hand as he spoke to the partygoers gathered around him, playing lord of the manor to the hilt.

Then the pair of them looked over and caught sight of Mark.

55

The blood drained from Eliza's cheeks and then rushed back again when she saw Mark's tall shape striding through the arbor. *He came*, she thought with an unbearable mixture of elation and despair.

"Here at last," Duke murmured beside her.

Frasier Robinson came out after Mark. The pair of them started walking across the lawn. Socialites and their swains turned their heads to stare as they passed.

One of Duke's hired men strode toward them, his hand up. "This is a private party. You got an invitation?"

Mark stopped and took off his hat. The sunlight glinted off his hair like spun glass. He aimed a half-smile over the bouncer's shoulder at her. "Miss Karlova invited us at the last minute. Isn't that right?"

"Yes, of course," she said, her voice dry in her throat.

The bouncer flicked a glance at his boss. Duke gave the slightest nod, smiling under his mustache. "Your driver can wait in the kitchen with the others," the man said to Mark.

"My *friend* goes where I go," Mark said.

Duke called, "It's all right Bert."

Mark and Frasier brushed past the man and walked up to stand face to face with her and Duke.

"Well, well," Duke said. "I can't say I'm surprised to see you here, Mark."

"You know me, I'm a sucker for garden parties. Your begonias are splendid." He looked at Eliza. "Good afternoon Miss Karlova."

She held out her hand to him, safely sheathed in a white cotton glove. "Good afternoon, Mark."

He clasped her fingers in his. She shook his hand once and pulled away.

She said, "And you, Frasier." She held out her hand to his friend too.

Frasier took it with a startled look. There was an audible gasp from the party guests eavesdropping on them.

"You must be in need of refreshments," she said. "Come this way, won't you?" Without daring to glance at her fiancé, she led them toward the buffet table.

Duke let her go without a word.

She saw a glimmer of lavender silk in the corner of her eye. Her grandmother was watching them from the arched veranda that ran along the back of the house, her face a mask of stone.

As they walked, Mark murmured to her, "We have to talk. Let's go into the house." He put his hat back on and pulled it low over his eyes. His temples were beading with perspiration. The sunlight must be hurting him already.

She stole another glance at the countess, standing in the shadows near the French doors into the house. "No, not there." She thought quickly. "I know a place we can be alone."

To Frasier, she said, "Mr. Robinson, why don't you help

yourself to a canapé while I show Mark around the garden?"

"I go where Mark goes, remember?"

"It's all right," Mark said to him.

"But—"

"Frasier."

He shut his jaw. "Fine. I'll be here, with the canapés."

Eliza said to Mark, "Come with me." She led him across the lawn to the arbor through the boxwood hedge and onto the path through the rose garden. The scent of the flowers hung in the air. The midday sun poured light over them as they walked through the glossy, thorny shrubs.

Mark's lips were thinned, his eyes sunk in dark circles.

"Just a little farther." She took his hand and tugged him toward the stone dovecote folly. "In here." She pulled him through the door and shut them inside the circular room lit by only a cupola above. She heard him let out a soft breath of relief as the cool dimness washed over him.

She released his hand and walked to the curving wall. Leaning her back against it, she looked at him. "What did you want to speak with me about?"

He fixed her with his intense blue gaze. "You and the rest of the guests need to leave this place as soon as possible. It isn't safe here. Camonte knows Duke is the man controlling the slime. He might attack at any moment."

"Already?"

"Yes." He moved toward her. "Call off this engagement. Get far away from Duke."

"I can't. I have to marry him."

"Why?" He took her arms, lifting her off the wall. His eyes burned into her face, his mouth fierce. "Did you sleep with him?"

She twisted away. "That's none of your business!"

"You are my business, boss!" He grabbed her hands and stripped her white cotton gloves off, gently but ruthlessly. His gaze caught on the diamond ring Duke had placed on her left hand, but he gripped her naked fingers in his and looked into her eyes, his irises like pale embers in the dimness.

"Don't you remember the way you touched me? The way I touched you?"

Fury overtook her. He thought to enslave her with his touch, did he? She twisted her hands in his grip, until she laid them on his chest, right over his heart. "Yes, I remember." She pushed sharply enough that he stumbled back against the wall.

His eyes opened wide. "Eliza, what—"

She silenced him by pressing her body against his. Wrapping her arms around his neck, she kissed him. Softly, deeply, her lips and tongue stroking him, her nails running over his nape.

His hat fell off and rolled on the floor. After a frozen instant, his hands flew to her hips, and he clutched her body to him, growling as his tongue moved inside her mouth.

She trailed her hands over his shoulders and down to the firm muscles in his chest. Her fingers found the circle of a nipple and she stroked it through his shirt. She was suddenly wild, her heart beating fiercely. She pressed her thighs together to ease the empty ache between them. She moved her kiss over his cheek to whisper in his ear, "It's my turn. I want to touch you. Let me . . . let me . . ." *Let me give you this*. She nipped at his earlobe and rubbed the tips of her breasts against him.

His breath stuttered, and he nodded his head, his lips trembling against her skin.

Her hands slipped down his stomach, the muscles rippling beneath her fingers. Then she eased her hands lower to the iron-hard bulge between his legs.

He widened them for her.

She touched him the way he'd showed her before, the night of their first kiss. She cupped his long shaft through the cloth of his pants, running her palm along the curving ridge.

He groaned and moved his hips, shoving himself more firmly into her grip.

She was trembling with lust for the flesh in her palm. She wanted to see it. She wanted to taste it. Fumbling open his belt buckle and trouser buttons, she slipped her hand inside his pants and found his organ, skin to skin. It was so big she couldn't close her fingers around it, and so hot it scorched her palm.

Daring to look down, she saw a long, thick column of flesh curving toward his belly, its crown as ripe as a plum. She had never seen or touched a man like this before in her life. She pulled her trembling hand up the length of his shaft, marveling at the sensation. Hard as rock and yet soft as velvet, the knotted veins pulsing fiercely.

He groaned as she stroked him. A crystal bead of his excitement welled from the dimpled slit at the tip. Fascinated, she ran her thumb over it until the whole plump head was slick and glistening.

His hips were pulsing slowly in and out, his shaft sliding through her fingers. She tightened her fist, and he made a sharp sound of encouragement. She stroked down and back up again, watching the long ruddy shaft, then looking up to his face, dazed and dreamy and utterly gorgeous. His hands trembled along her back.

Emboldened, she slipped her other hand between his

legs, cupping the tight sack she found there. She stroked her fingers in feather light touches against the soft skin around it, the crisp hair and quivering muscles of his thighs.

He groaned again, a frustrated note in his voice this time, and his hands closed over hers, guiding her, showing her what he needed.

She was shocked at how tight he made her squeeze his shaft as he forced it through their joined hands. She looked into his face, afraid of seeing pain there, but he threw his head back, his throat arching in pleasure, his lips pulling back from his teeth in fierce need.

His hips moved in a fast rhythm, forcing his shaft in and out of their clasped fingers. Every muscle in his body was flexing and straining against her.

"Oh! Oh God! Eliza!" His agonized cry echoed off the stone walls. She watched his seed explode out of him, scattering on the ground like ropes of pearl.

He froze, holding her hands still as ecstasy washed over his angel's face. His trembling fingers fell away, and he collapsed against the wall, breathing hard. His eyes were closed, his lashes fanning over his cheeks.

Eliza released his shaft and touched her fingers to her lips, her tongue darting out to catch the last drop of his seed. She moaned at the taste, pressing against his body, her thighs trembling as she almost came herself.

She took a deep, shaking breath. With trembling fingers she closed his trousers over his half-hard organ, doing up his buttons and belt. When she looked up into his face again he was watching her. She stilled, looking into icy-blue eyes melting with tenderness and wonder.

He brought his hands up to cup her head and kissed

her, moving his mouth softly over hers, gratitude and praise in his touch and in every line of his body. He broke the kiss and leaned his forehead against hers. They stood there, quiet, sharing breath.

His voice low and rough, he said, "I'm in love with you, Eliza. Come home with me. Marry me. I'll slay your dragons and lay their hearts at your feet. I'll give you everything. Everything." His lips touched hers again, achingly tender and passionate, like it was the most beautiful moment of his life.

Which made what she was going to do now even more monstrous. But what of it? She was a monster. More of one than he would ever be.

She broke away from his hands and lips with a little jerk of her head. "I can't go home with you," she said. She pushed back from him where he leaned against the wall. "I have to go announce my engagement to Lionel Duke."

His hands fell. He stilled, his eyes not moving from her face.

She drew on the iron-hard will she had earned these last seven years, and she smiled. "Did you really think I'd call it off? Marry you instead? Live as an outcast from society, with no money, no standing, in that ruin of a house?" She laughed lightly.

He flinched as if she'd hit him.

She said, "I thought you had more sense, darling. The sorry fact is you have nothing to offer me. You're an amusing plaything, to be sure, but you could never be anything more to me. Surely you see that."

His eyes were empty, his expression was blank. He didn't make a sound.

"You should leave now," she said, her voice soft

and cold. "And don't come back. We've had our fun, but I can't have your sort ruining my parties anymore."

She turned her back on him and walked away, out of the dovecote and down the path. She did not look back. The only sound was the crunch of her footsteps in the gravel.

56

When Eliza was out of Mark's sight, she staggered and leaned against a tree for support, stifling a gasp at the pain stabbing under her ribs. Hating herself more than she had ever hated anything on earth.

But Mark would go now and be safe. And that was all that mattered.

She forced herself to continue up the path. She entered the rose garden and was hit by a wave of deadly sweet perfume that did not come from the roses.

The countess was standing in the middle of the gravel walk, her back straight as a sword.

"*Grand-mère*." Her voice, she was pleased to note, was ice cold. "I've been convincing our unwanted guest to leave."

Angelique's delicate nose tipped up to the air, nostrils flaring. Her lip curled in disgust. "I know exactly what you were doing. I will not have it, girl!"

Eliza dug a compact out of her pocket and repaired the damage to her makeup. "I sent him away, *Grand-mère*. I did as you told me. Aren't you proud? I broke his heart. He hates me now. He'll never come near me again." Her face in the mirror was as blank as marble.

"Very well," Angelique said. "Return to your fiancé this instant. People are beginning to talk."

Eliza put her compact away. She had left her gloves in the folly, she realized. No getting them back now. She strolled past Angelique through the gate in the tall hedge that led to the lawn. She walked across the green expanse toward the jazz music and the murmur of the party guests, every step ratcheting her tension higher, like a wire stretched to the breaking point.

She scanned the crowd. Frasier was no longer standing by the buffet table. He must have gone back to wait for Mark at his car. She didn't blame him one bit. Eyes peered sideways at her with ready malice as she approached the group around Lionel Duke.

Her fiancé was holding forth to a gaggle of admirers. "Once the criminal element has been subdued, we can strive onward toward our national destiny," he was saying. "When great men are free of the shackles imposed on them by the weak and corrupt, we will conquer the new frontiers of science and industry, and the United States will take its place as the mightiest country on earth!"

"Hear hear!" A red-faced man said, lifting his glass of bootlegged rum. "When are you going into politics Lionel?"

"All in good time."

"Duke for mayor! No, governor of Illinois!" another fellow slurred.

Duke smiled. "Why stop there? Chicago got the new president elected. Why not the next one as well?"

Everyone laughed, but Eliza got the feeling he wasn't joking at all.

As she drew close, he turned an urbane smile on her.

"Ah, there you are, my dear. I was beginning to feel neglected." He stroked the neat line of his mustache with a finger.

Eliza stepped up to him, close enough to smell his strange, metallic scent. *Wrong!* Her mind shrieked. But her face smiled and smiled. "Never, darling. I was merely seeing off one of our guests. Mr. Van Ryn was not able to stay long. He sends his regrets."

Duke looked highly amused. "Yes," he drawled. "I thought that might be the case." He reached out and curled a cool, moist finger under her chin, his hooded eyes examining her critically. "You'll do," he finally said.

And something inside her snapped. She couldn't do this. She had to leave, to run as far and as fast as possible.

She would go this very night. She would get back to the city and get on a train across the country. Tomorrow she would be in Denver. Then Los Angeles. Then, perhaps, Hong Kong. Then some island on the other end of the world. Away from Duke, and Mark. Away from herself.

57

Mark stood in the darkness of the folly for a long time, waiting for the shadow to take the pain away as it always did when he got hurt bad. But his power wouldn't heal him now. Because this time it wasn't his body that had been savaged. Just his heart.

Come to me. The faintest whisper in his mind. *Come to me and leave the pain forever.* Shadow writhed through the air around him. He reached out his hand and saw shreds of darkness peel off of it and vanish into nothing. *Let go.*

No. Not yet. He still had a job to do. The monster. He had to get inside the house and search for a lead on the monster.

Finally, with a clumsy shove, he opened the folly door. The sunlight blasted him as he stepped out. *She* was nowhere in sight. He started up the path through the rose garden, his footsteps crunching on the pebbles as he made his way toward the entrance to the lawn.

It was hot and still in the enclosed space, the perfume of the flowers a sickly sweet spike in his nose. Sunlight poured over the thorny bushes, glittering on the gravel, pummeling his skin and his eyes. He'd left his hat in the folly, he realized. He really had gone out of his mind. *Get to the house.*

Beyond the boxwood hedge, the jazz band was playing loud and fast, something with horns and drums. The sun scorched him. The smell of roses overpowered him. He staggered a little, his vision wavering. Stevie's voice flickered across his memory. *The bad men are in the roses.*

He stopped short just as two figures stepped through the arbor that led through the hedge to the lawn. A couple of Duke's black-jacketed bouncers, spreading out between him and the opening.

Mark spun half-way and looked behind him. Three more men were coming through the opening to the wood.

He was a stone-cold fool. He'd followed his prick and look where it led him. Caught in the open, without his power.

Hell with it. He bared his teeth in a grin. "Only five of you boys? Who's going to clean up the bodies?"

As the men closed in around him another figure appeared from the arbor. A short, scrawny man with a lopsided face. The scientist he'd seen in Duke's apartment. He held a strangely shaped gun cradled against his bony chest. His glass eye glinted at Mark. "Hold it steady, and do not damage it," he told the men.

They all rushed him at once. Mark whipped his body to the left, slamming his elbow into the gut of a man behind him who was trying to grab his arm. On the recoil he drove his left fist into a face in front of him. The thug staggered into the rose bushes and fell over backward. Another guy got hold of his arm from behind and sank a fist into his kidney. He arched in pain but used it to whip his head back. His skull crashed against a set of teeth.

Another man dove for his other arm. "Yes! Hold it!" the doctor said, training the dart gun on him.

The guy he'd punched was heading straight for him. He kicked out and planted a foot in his balls. The man folded wheezing to the ground. The force of his kick sent him and the men on his arms lurching into the rose bushes. Thorns clawed at his skin and the stink of crushed roses filled the air.

Mark braced his feet and dipped his shoulder, slamming his body into the man holding his left arm. The guy stumbled backwards over a bush, lost his grip and fell on his ass.

Mark had yanked the man on his right arm off balance. He gave him a jab to the gut and an uppercut to the chin, and the thug collapsed to the ground.

Two men standing, getting their footing and coming at him again. Above him the sun blazed white. He staggered, shaking sweat out of his eyes. He got his fists up, but too late.

An ugly mug got in close, sending hard jabs at his head. His vision exploded into white as fists laid open his cheeks and bloodied his nose.

He put his head down and hit back hard. When he felt his fist break through cartilage, he pivoted toward the second goon. He powered off of his back foot, launching a straight right as the guy lunged at him. The man's face plowed into Mark's fist and he dropped like a rock.

"Fools! I'll do it myself!" a voice hissed. Mark whipped his head up, blood flying off his face, and saw the barrel of the doctor's gun gleaming silver in the sunlight. Too far away to reach the doctor before he fired. One chance.

He spun and ran, zigzagging left and right, arms pumping, trying to get to the thin shadow of the woods past the stone folly. He heard *thwppp thwppp thwppp thwppp* behind him. Pain stabbed the back of his thigh. Icy numbness rushed through his body from the wound, and his leg collapsed, pitching him forward onto his face.

He clawed at the ground with rapidly numbing fingers and dragged himself forward an inch. Behind him he heard men groaning, cursing, struggling upright, footsteps crunching toward him. He tried to kick out at the approaching legs, but his limbs had gone dead. He wanted to howl in rage but his mouth was full of mud and the blood pouring from his face.

Steel-toed shoes kicked him over onto his back, and then kicked him again for the fun of it. He heard a rib snap, but he couldn't feel it. He tried to keep his eyes open but all he saw was the merciless white sun filling the sky above him, cooking him.

"I said do not damage it!" the doctor said. "Get it to the car. We are taking it to the laboratory."

His last thought before the white consumed him was that *he* was the monster the scientist and Duke had been talking about at Duke's apartment. He'd overheard them plot his own kidnapping. He was Subject A.

He would have started laughing, but a boot came down on his face, and he was gone.

58

Eliza had held her smile for so long she thought her face might shatter. An older couple, friends of the Mannerings, were congratulating her on her engagement, talking about the flower show they were hosting next week. She answered them by rote, still smiling and smiling.

She had to get rid of these people. Then she had to get out of here.

She had managed to drift away from Duke and his toadies and was now across the yard from him. But she kept a careful eye on him.

One of the hard-looking security guards she had seen lurking about all day appeared at Duke's side, speaking into his ear. She caught a whiff of scent from him, like sweat and blood and . . . roses? But she was too far away to overhear what they were saying. Duke spoke a few terse words, and the henchman walked quickly toward the garage.

Duke looked around and saw her. He strolled over, interrupting the elderly couple nattering about their hydrangeas. "Unfortunate news, dearest," he said. "There's been a mishap at the factory."

"Nothing too serious, I hope," she said.

"No, no, nothing that will affect quarterly profits. Still, one must keep on top of such things. The real disaster is that I must leave our party. You'll be able to carry on without me, I trust?"

"Certainly." This was perfect. She would send the guests off as soon as his back was turned and get a ride back to town with one of them. Then she would be on a train, gone.

Duke smiled under his little mustache. "I knew I could depend on you." He darted a kiss over her cheek. It took everything she had not to cringe away.

He took leave of a few more people before following his guard to the garage. The moment his Chrysler roared away, Eliza set about convincing the guests to go home, using touches of her scent to speed them along.

She was aided by the weather off the lake. A bank of low, dark clouds had begun massing along the horizon, flickers of lightning dancing among them. Like a herd of cattle, the partygoers started moving toward their cars in the driveway.

She shook a few hands, waved a few goodbyes, and ran upstairs to her room. She tore Duke's diamond ring off her hand and threw it on the dresser before packing a valise and hurrying out. Quickly she crept down the stair to the ground floor and stole through the hall toward the front door. But then she stopped, looking down the back hallway toward the cramped little stair that led to Stevie's room.

Could she leave him at his father's mercy? Or Camonte's? But what choice did she have? She couldn't bring him with her. But she had to at least tell his nurse to take him away from here before Camonte attacked. She took a step toward the stairs.

"I knew it," the cool, elegant voice rang through the hall.

Eliza whirled to see her grandmother descending the grand staircase, lavender skirts clasped gracefully in her hand. "I knew you would bolt. You're a disgrace. You disobey me, and you disobey God."

She swallowed, breathed hard, and said, "I'm leaving. You have to leave too, *Grand-mère*. This place may come under attack."

"Foolishness. If you mean the threat posed by that gangster, I assure you that Duke will snuff it out tonight. He told me that he wants the city cleansed of its criminal element by the time he welcomes the Washington people to the World's Fair. As soon as he wins his *coup*, you shall marry him, the most powerful man in Chicago."

She faced the other woman squarely. "No. I won't marry him. I'm going, Angelique."

The countess stilled upon the stairs, watching her. Their scents were roaring through the air in invisible battle.

Just then, the main doors swung open. She spun to see a tall, slim figure silhouetted in the doorway. She caught the smell of books and chemicals. "Where's Mark?" the figure said.

"Frasier? What are you still doing here?"

He stepped into the hall. His eyes were blazing and his face was drawn tight. "Tell me what you did with him!"

A faint note of dread sounded in her mind. "I don't understand. I thought you both left."

"Don't lie to me. I saw the torn up rose garden. I saw the trail they made when they dragged him through the woods, and the tire tracks on the access road."

She dropped her bag. "What?" She whirled on Angelique. "What have you done?"

The old woman looked down at her from the stair. "I did only what I had to do. The evening you didn't come back until dawn, Duke and I had a long talk. I told him that Van Ryn was making a nuisance of himself and needed to be removed. He agreed. Apparently, he has his own reasons for wanting the creature gone. We devised the plan to use his vulnerability to the sun against him. Your engagement party was a trap, and you were the bait. And he fell into it beautifully."

"But I did what you asked! I sent him away!"

"No matter. It was too dangerous to leave him alive. And I . . . failed. I was unable to kill him myself. He is too powerful. I had to enlist Duke's help to capture him."

"Where did they take him?"

"I do not know. Most likely someplace extremely unpleasant. They may kill him, or they may keep him alive, for a time. I believe Duke and his scientific friend are most interested in studying his abilities."

"Damn you!" Frasier said, voice shaking.

Angelique cast Frasier a disgusted glance. "How like a man to overlook the creature's servant."

Frasier sagged against the doorjamb, overcome with the scent of two lamia. His head was lolling, but he gasped a breath and said, "Not a servant, old woman."

Angelique blinked at him, as if surprised he managed to speak. Then she smiled. "You are now, boy. Come here." She snapped her fingers as if calling a dog to heel.

Frasier staggered toward her, his eyes going blank.

"No! Frasier, run!" She put all her power into a wave of scent that crashed over him, battling her grandmother's poison for control of his mind.

Frasier stumbled in a circle and wove out the double doors.

Eliza backed away after him. "I'm leaving. I'm finding Mark, and then I'm gone. You'll never see me again."

"I had hoped you would not attempt another foolish escape, but I was prepared for the worst." Raising her voice, she said, "Alvin! Carl! Come!"

Two men burst from a doorway above and pounded down the stairs. Each of them wore a gas mask from Duke's trophy room. Behind the terrifying circles of the goggles, their eyes were wide and blank. Angelique had enspelled them, but she had made sure to guard them from Eliza's power. Their hands were covered by medical gloves.

The old woman said, "Take her to her room and lock her in. Gently. If you harm so much as a hair on her head, I will make you cut out your own livers."

Eliza bolted for the door, but the goons were too fast for her. They seized her, one on each arm, dragging her back toward the stairs as she thrashed, helpless.

No! Never helpless again!

She screamed as the power she'd kept chained for seven years rose up within her and broke free. The air boiled with deadly scent as the poison surged through her blood and poured out of her flesh, bubbling and hissing on the gloves of the men holding her, eating the rubber away until there was nothing between their skin and hers.

The men shrieked behind their masks. They let go of her arms and fell to the floor, convulsing and gasping.

59

Angelique staggered back, tumbling to sit upon the stairs, her eyes huge in her thin face.

Not sparing a glance for the fallen men, Eliza spun and ran outside to look for Frasier. She found him half-collapsed against the wall near the door. He looked up blearily as she approached. "Head hurts."

"Frasier, I need you to fight it. We have to find Mark. Duke and a doctor named Smalley have taken him to their secret laboratory."

"Where?" he said.

"I don't know." *Tchyort.* The two guards she had poisoned were the only ones who might know where Duke had gone.

"We'll have to wait until one of Duke's men comes to his senses. Then—"

"No! Can't stay here. If Mark doesn't get Duke arrested, the Outfit will go to war. Have to get back to the city. Find Mark."

She looked down the driveway and saw Mark's Duesenberg parked to one side. She grabbed Frasier's arm and

317

pulled it around her shoulders. She hauled him to his feet, and they staggered over the gravel to the car. She got him in the passenger seat and cranked the window down. "Wait here," she told him. "I have to take care of something."

She ran back inside the house. The countess was still half-sitting on the steps, her hand over her heart. Helga had appeared and was clasping her mistress's shoulders. She shot Eliza a burning look of reproach.

"Élisabeth!" her grandmother said, reaching for her.

Eliza walked toward the old woman. "You must leave this place at once," she said. "There may be an attack. Go back to the hotel and stay there for now."

Angelique's bony fingers grasped at hers. "Do not do this! Do not betray your destiny! We are the scourge of wicked men!" Her other hand fumbled for the gold cross at her throat.

She carefully took the old hand off of her. "I'm making a new destiny, *Grand-mère*."

She said to Helga, "Tell the household staff that they may be in danger and they are to leave. Then take the countess back to her hotel and look after her."

The servant's long face was pale and drawn. She nodded, her eyes fastened on her mistress, her arms supporting her.

That only left Stevie. She started down the corridor to the back stairway when she heard a light, sweet voice behind her. "Miss Eliza!"

Eliza whirled to see a small shape framed in a doorway off of the main hall.

"Stevie!" She hurried toward him. He was still in his pajamas, and barefoot. "Where's your nurse?"

"She took my medicine and now she's asleep upstairs."

"You're all alone?" Eliza said, furious at the woman.

"You have to be away from here!"

"Yes. You'll take me. I'll show you the way to find Mark."

She stared at the boy. "Do you know where he is? Did you hear the men who took him say something?"

His eerie sightless gaze fastened on her face, and again she saw the silver glitter across his pupils. "No," he said, "I *saw* them. I saw where they went." He pointed out the door, toward the southeast. "We'll follow their trail. I'll show you."

Gooseflesh flooded over her skin. This boy had power. She smelled it on him as clearly as his sweet, childish scent. Perhaps he really could lead her to Mark.

Stevie held his hand out for hers, a sweet smile on his face, as if he already knew she was going to take him with her.

She clasped his hand and led him to the door, snatching up her valise off the floor as she passed.

"Élisabeth!" her grandmother called out behind her.

She didn't listen. Before she left, she glanced quickly at the two men she had poisoned, lying crumpled on the tiles. They were still alive, but there was nothing she could do for them now. Duke's thugs would have to take their chances. She walked Stevie quickly down the drive to the Duesenberg and lifted him into the rumble seat, stowing her case next to him.

She climbed behind the wheel and turned the key. The engine growled to life. In the seat next to her, Frasier turned to look at the boy.

"Hello, Mr. Robinson. I told you we'd go in the car. Told you."

Frasier stared at the child, a mix of wonder and exasperation on his face. "What's he doing here?" he said to her. "What's happening?"

"We're going to rescue Mark." She turned the wheel and stepped on the gas. The car bumped down the drive to the road.

"Where is he? Where are we going?"

"That way," Stevie said, pointing once again to the southeast.

Eliza turned the car in the direction of the boy's finger.

Frasier said, "Son, Mark is my friend. I have to know you aren't playing a game. Do you understand?"

Stevie turned his eyes on Frasier, the lenses glittering silver. "I *see* him. He's there." His finger pointed again, but wavered in the air. His face changed. "He's hurt. Father and Dr. Smalley and the bad men hurt him."

Frasier bit his lip. He looked at Eliza, his eyes stark.

"We're going to find him," she told him. "Please, trust me."

"Why should I?" Frasier said

"Because I'll do anything to get him back." The road blurred in front of her for an instant before she ruthlessly quelled her emotions.

Frasier was silent, disbelief radiating off of him.

If he knew the panic twisting through her heart, he wouldn't doubt her.

Night was falling, hurried on by the wall of black clouds rushing in from the lake. They drove toward the city glow on the horizon, the powerful car eating up miles of road as she followed Stevie's pointing finger. Glimpses of Lake Michigan glimmered darkly away to the east. She thought of the slime creature living its totally harmless existence out there in the pure, untouched water, until men like Duke poisoned it and turned it into a weapon.

And she thought about why Mark had been taken, and what might be happening to him at that very moment.

60

Light roasted him. It blazed through his lids, stabbed through his skull, seared his skin.

He was lying on his back on a cold, hard surface. His face was a mask of pain, his side and back a white-hot pulsing mass of bruising and cracked ribs. Every breath he took was agony. But the unrelenting light was worse.

He tried to raise his hand to shield his eyes, but was stopped by a hard circle around his wrist. He jerked his limbs instinctively, but metal bit into his wrists and ankles. He was shackled. The cold air crept over him and he realized he was naked, every inch of his skin exposed to the scouring light.

He reached for his power, but it stayed hidden inside him. He was pinned, like an insect to a corkboard. Helpless.

The faintest of shadows fell over him, and his skin drank it up thirstily. But it wasn't enough.

"Ah, you are awake, Subject A," a small, precise voice said.

He knew that voice. He dragged his head up and tried to

321

open his eyes. One was swollen shut, but he managed to get the other open a slit against the blinding glare.

He was in what looked like the basement of an old industrial building, a dank brick room with small windows set near the vaulted ceiling, the windows boarded over. A metal door stood closed in one wall. The space was full of shiny, humming laboratory equipment.

A huge fish tank like the ones in the Shedd Aquarium stood against a wall, four powerful spotlights pointed down into it. Viscous fluid rippled and slurped against the glass, a rubbery wave moving slowly in a circle around the tank like a massive animal pacing its cage.

Seemed he'd found the slime monster.

But he had bigger problems at the moment. There were four more of the spotlights pointed directly at him. He was chained to a metal table. And above him stood Duke's scientist, the man who had shot him with a tranquilizer dart, staring down at him with a lopsided gaze.

The scientist was dressed in a white lab coat and in his white-gloved hand was a scalpel, glittering in the light as he toyed with it between his fingers. He heard Stevie's voice in his mind. *The one-eyed-man. The man with needles and knives.*

"Dr. Smalley, I presume?" Mark grated. It hurt to talk. His lips were split and a few of his teeth felt loose. His jaw was swollen like a grapefruit. How long had he been out? He should have started healing by now, but his power wouldn't work in the glare of the lights.

"How did you learn my name?" the doctor asked.

Mark turned his head and spat out blood. "Lucky guess. Where am I?"

"You're in my laboratory, of course. Where you belong."

"Is this where you created the slime monster for Duke? The thing you've got in that tank over there?"

"Yes. But that was merely a side project while I waited for my true life's work to come to fruition."

"And what's your true life's work? Let me guess. Bottle ship building. No, breeding fancy chickens."

"You are my life's work, Subject A," The doctor said in a low, almost intimate tone. "I made you. You were my first, and so far my greatest creation."

We were both made by Dr. Smalley, Stevie had said. Icy cold rippled over his skin. "I'm the son of Edward and Emily Van Ryn."

"And who do you think was their doctor?"

Mark was silent. A distant ringing in his ears got louder and louder as the small, cool voice kept talking.

"Why do you think you are the way you are, with your ability to dissolve into shadow? It is because of me. Me and my genius."

"You're no genius," he whispered. "You're a madman."

"But I am a genius!" The small voice got higher. "Einstein, Newton? Bah. What are photons and gravity compared to the mysteries of life itself? I studied with Bateson and de Vries, but I was too brilliant even for them to comprehend. They cast me aside. Denied they ever knew me. But I surpassed them all! I alone unlocked the secrets of mutation. I alone devised the formula that created you, a creature with godlike power, when I gave it to your mother."

"You—what—"

"But did I get the credit I deserved? No! I told your father I could make his son a giant among men, and he agreed! He gave his wife my formula willingly, gladly! It was not my fault he did not like the price he had to pay!"

"What price?"

"The life of the female who carried you, of course. She could not withstand the medical regimen that was necessary to bring about your mutation. Females so seldom can."

His ears roared, and the white light turned red. "You killed my mother!"

"Sacrifices must be made for greatness! But your brute of a father never understood that. I kept my end of our bargain, and how did he repay me? He gave me this!" Smalley tapped the tip of his scalpel directly on his glass eye with a small *chink*. "He nearly killed me. Even worse, he destroyed my laboratory! All my notes and equipment, the pinnacle of scientific achievement, gone! It took me years to reconstruct my work!"

The world reeled around Mark, his life cracking in front of his eyes.

"But now, at last, I have you back," the little man crooned. He reached out a skeletal hand clothed in a rubber glove. His cold dry touch landed on the middle of Mark's chest and skated down his stomach, leaving horror in its wake. "A perfect mutated specimen in its prime, mine to explore. Who knows what discoveries I will make when I delve into the mysteries of your body." The hand cupped his thigh, sharp fingertips digging between his legs.

For the first time, true animal terror bit at the edge of Mark's mind. He was thrashing, trying to get the hand off him, trying to get his own fists on this abomination. He heard his voice roaring as if from far away as he strained every muscle against the chains, tearing his flesh on the cuffs. A long time later he fell back, exhausted and panting. His brain swam in his skull.

"There is no point to this ridiculous demonstration," said the doctor, sounding disappointed in him. "You should conserve your strength. We have much work to accomplish over the next several months."

"I'm going to kill you," he panted.

"Yes, much to do," the scientist murmured, ignoring Mark's promise. He turned and pulled up a squeaking metal cart. On top of it was a tray full of scalpels and clamps and saws and needles.

The world tipped crazily again. He hadn't been this helpless since he was a child.

The doctor wetted a sponge with alcohol and started cleaning his scalpel vigorously. "I've been observing you from a distance for the past seven years, you know, through various informants. I bided my time until I knew I was ready to take you in for closer study. There was so much I was unable to discover without thorough testing. I was not even sure you were weakened by the light until that female told me."

Mark's heart seized.

"Though it pains me to admit it, she was invaluable in your capture. She was the one who devised the plan to lure you into the sunlight, Duke tells me." He lifted the wicked blade to his eye and studied it critically. "Quite clever for a female."

Betrayal seared through him, an agony worse than the light. Eliza had told him the truth in the folly. She had tricked him and used him.

"And yet in the end, it was I and I alone who captured you," the little man said smugly.

Mark grappled for control. "What was in that dart you shot me with?"

"A tranquilizer I devised specifically for mutations such as you. In general, I dislike contaminating the tissues of my subjects with foreign chemicals before I study them, but it should have leeched out of you by now. You are fully awake, yes?"

"Go to hell!"

Lightning fast, the doctor laid the scalpel flat against his jugular.

Mark froze.

Smalley ran the cold blade slowly down his throat to his chest. "Where to begin?" He murmured. The tip of the scalpel scraped across Mark's left nipple and rested for a moment over his heart.

Mark didn't dare breathe.

"Perhaps a few skin samples first." The blade continued down his chest to his stomach. "Then, in a week or two, we shall move on to the muscles and bones. And the organs of course. And there will certainly be much to learn from analyzing your glands! But I suspect it is in the brain where we will find the answers to the deepest mysteries." The scalpel skimmed past his groin, lingering over the femoral artery.

"But let us not get ahead of ourselves. The skin first. Just a small sample to start with." The blade slashed deep into his thigh.

He roared in pain, arching, straining against the chains.

"Really," the scientist said reproachfully. "You must be still, otherwise the collection will be much more difficult."

The metal door slammed open. "Stop immediately," Lionel Duke's voice rang out. His tall, powerful shape strode into the searing light, looming over Mark and the scientist.

Smalley's face twitched as he peered up at his boss. "I'm taking samples—"

"You're indulging your perversions," Duke said, his lip

curling. "You utter fool. I cannot have him in pieces when the general comes to view our weapons program!"

"But think of it! If I can discover the root of his power, develop a drug that can replicate the effects, I can make you an army of untouchable soldiers, unseeable spies! Imagine what we will learn if we investigate him, tissue by tissue, and find out how he works!"

For a moment, Duke looked as if he was considering it. Then he shook his head. "It will take too much time. How many years was it before you perfected the slime? Seven, very nearly. I need weapons to show the general immediately. He and the other politicians will be here tomorrow. Our prototype cannot be damaged."

"The prototype is going to kill the both of you bastards," Mark snarled.

Duke finally looked directly at him, eyes hard. "You haven't learned to keep your yap shut yet, have you Mark?" he said, and in his voice was the slum bully boy, not the urbane titan of industry.

Mark showed him his bloody teeth in a grin. "You got a problem with my lip? Let me out of these cuffs, and we'll work it out man-to-man. Or don't you have the balls?"

But Duke had gotten a grip on himself. "Don't be a child. Understand this, Mark. Your life, and your body, belong to me now, and I will do with you exactly as I choose."

61

Eliza drove along a dark street near the open sewer known as Bubbly Creek. Stevie had guided her deep into the city through a warren of tenements and factories, his small finger never wavering. Frasier had leaned near the open window to clear his head and was now watching their surroundings silently and warily.

"There!" The child raised a finger and pointed at a decrepit, three-story factory building rising up through the murk. "I found him!"

The factory looked abandoned at first glance. The brick walls were crumbling, the windows boarded up. But as she drove slowly past, she saw a shadow of movement and a glimmer of light beyond the locked gate. She pulled the car into an alley out of sight of the rotting brick structure. The stench of the nearby canal thickened the air. A few fat drops of rain splashed onto the windshield. The storm was nearly on them.

Frasier turned to the child. "Mark is in there?"

"Yes, and my father and Dr. Smalley and the bad men," The boy said, his voice a monotone. "And there's something in there with them. A big thing. A strange—thing—It wants to eat . . ." His eyelids fluttered, and he swayed, his face turning white.

"Stevie!" Eliza reached into the rumble seat and cupped his shoulders, easing him back. "You mustn't tire yourself, *rebenok*." She exchanged a look with Frasier. They could both guess what the big, strange thing that wanted to eat was. They'd found the creature.

Frasier said, "Okay. Let's say the boy is right, and Mark is in there with Duke, a bunch of his men, and his pet monster. We have to get into the building, get past the guards, find Mark, get him out, and not get shot. Or eaten. We need a plan."

"Not we, me," Eliza said. "I'll rescue Mark. You take Stevie and get away from here." Outside the rain started coming down in earnest, pouring out of the sky in hard sheets.

"Are you crazy? You can't go in there by yourself!"

"You've seen my power. You know what I'm capable of. If you go in with me, you'll only be in my way."

"I'm not just going to drive off and leave my friend in there!"

She could use her poison and force Frasier to comply, but she didn't want to. He'd already suffered enough because of her. "I promise I will get Mark out. But Stevie needs you to protect him. Isn't that what Mark would want you to do?"

He glared at her, furious because he knew she was right. "Where would I take him? Back to Duke's house?"

"No," the boy said, his piping voice eerily calm. "The house is on fire."

Eliza and Frasier turned to stare at him.

"You'll take me to Aunt Martha's house," The boy said. "I'll show you the way, like before."

Frasier gave Eliza a direct look. "You realize I could be accused of kidnapping a rich little white boy. Do you know what they'll do to me if they catch me?"

"They won't catch us," Stevie said. "I *see* it." As if to punctuate his words, thunder cracked, followed by a blast of light. The stink of ozone filled the air before it washed away in the downpour.

"Frasier," Eliza said, "this is the only way."

"Lord help me." Frasier passed a hand over his forehead.

She got out of the car and was instantly drenched.

"This is crazy. Crazy," Frasier muttered to himself as he scooted across the seat behind the wheel. He looked out the door at her. "How will you and Mark get home?"

"I'll take care of it." *Somehow.*

In the back, Stevie said, "She will."

Frasier gave her that measuring stare. "I'll meet you and Mark at his house. If he's not there by tomorrow, I'll—I'll —" He snapped his jaw shut. With one last glare, he pulled the door closed.

She stepped back away from the car. It turned in a tight U, headlights flashing, and roared away into the night.

The wind gushed rain over her, plastering her dress to her legs. She lifted her face to the storm as the lightning cracked across the sky. She closed her eyes and saw it through her eyelids. Blood red. The fiery scent of it filled her lungs. Power boiled in her veins, irresistible.

She opened her eyes and focused on the dim light at the old factory's entrance. Then she was striding through the storm and darkness, her heels snapping against the pavement.

330

62

Eliza slowed her pace to a prowl as she approached the iron gates. In the light cast by one flickering electric bulb, she saw a young tough in a cap and jacket slouched against the wall. Cheap tobacco smoke tainted the air.

He straightened up as she approached, resting a hand on the gun at his hip. "Who's there? What do you want?" he said. But when she stepped into the pool of light, his face went from suspicious to confused.

His eyes roamed over her, and a leer started on the corner of his mouth. "What's doing, doll face?"

Eliza curled her fingers around the bars of the gate and let her poison wreathe through the smoke to him. "Oh, please, sir, you must let me in!"

He stepped closer to her. Eliza reached a hand through the bars and brushed the skin of his wrist. His eyes turned blank.

"Open the gate," Eliza ordered him.

He took a ring of keys out of his coat pocket and unlocked the gate. Pulling it open, he shuffled backward to let her pass, his face slack.

"Where is the man Lionel Duke kidnapped?" she asked him.

He blinked slowly. "The white freak?"

She gritted her teeth. "Where is he?"

"They took him to the laboratory in the basement."

"Is that where Duke keeps his monster?"

Terror ruffled the flat expression on the man's face. "Yes."

"How many men are in the building?"

"Seventeen, including me."

That was a lot of men to try to control. "Are they in the basement too?"

He said in a monotone, "No. The main shop floor. They're cleaning the guns for tonight."

"What's happening tonight?"

"We're hitting Camonte."

Angelique had been right. Duke was preparing for battle, and she would have to get past his soldiers to get to Mark.

But she knew exactly how to do it. It was in her blood. Angelique was right about that, too.

"Take me to them," she ordered the young guard.

He shuffled to the thick wooden door leading into the factory proper and pulled it open. She followed him down a short hall into a vast factory floor. Windows vaulted high above rows of rusted-out pipes and empty vats. Heavy worktables had been brushed off and shoved into the center of the room and guns were scattered across their scarred wooden surfaces.

Men with their coats and hats off were leaning over the tables cleaning the weapons or kicking back in metal chairs, muttering to each other through their cigarettes. A smog of tobacco and latent violence filled the room. She counted thirteen men. Duke, Smalley, and two others must be in the basement laboratory.

The soldiers looked up as she and the guard came through the doorway. The room fell silent as thirteen sets of eyes wandered over her body. Some were hostile, some were confused. A savage scent filled the air. Bloodlust, or just plain lust, even she couldn't tell which.

For an instant, she froze, panic icing her skin. But the poison in her blood rose up, burning the fear away. Her perfume flooded the air. She was Salome. She was Lucrezia. She was every man's nightmare, every man's dream. Their lives were hers to do with as she pleased. She curved her lips softly and secretly, let her eyelashes fall and cocked her hip. "Gentlemen. Good evening," she purred, letting her Russian accent linger in the air.

"Who the hell are you?" one of the standing men barked. He looked tough and grizzled. Probably the boss.

Eliza prowled toward him, every step swaying with inborn grace. She felt a drop of rainwater trickle down her throat between her breasts. The boss man's eyes tracked it. She'd moved in close to him before he knew what was happening.

"Mr. Duke asked me to come and give you boys a show."

"Show?" He blinked at her stupidly. "Like Sally Rand, you mean?"

The legendary burlesque dancer. She smiled. "Exactly like that."

She lifted a hand to his shoulder. His bristly jaw sagged. She gently pressed him down into a chair behind him. His pupils were wide and locked on her. She stepped back. "I got caught in the rain. You gentlemen won't mind if I take off these wet things will you?"

There was utter silence all around. Every stare was riveted on her.

She lifted her hands to her throat to undo the button there, and the next one, and the next one. Her perfume swirled through the air with every motion, roiling the cigarette smoke.

Slowly she glided up to one man cradling a Tommy gun, the length of metal forgotten in his arms. "What handsome fellows you are." She reached out a fingertip and traced it along his shoulder. His eyes hazed over and his mouth dropped open. The gun fell to the floor with a clatter. She stepped in front of the next man, who was sitting in a chair, and kicked off her pumps, pointing her toes delicately. She ran her foot up his leg, and he slumped back in his seat, face vacant.

She glided back and slowly pulled up the hem of her dress, the wet silk sliding over her thigh until it showed her garter. She untied it and rolled the silk down her leg and off her foot, bending slowly at the waist. Grasping hands pawed her bottom. Poison sizzled out of her as she straightened. "Let a girl have some room!" The man grabbing her reeled backward.

She tossed the stocking she had taken off at two more men, sending a wave of perfume crashing into them. They listed over against the table. Six down.

She set her other foot on the chair in between the spread legs of another fellow. "Will you help me with this?"

He dazedly fumbled with her stocking while another grabbed her waist from behind, his breath sawing in her ear. "Hands off, now," she said. The hands on her waist fell limply away. The fellow in the chair let go of her leg, his head lolling backward. She kicked the second stocking off of her foot and reached out to touch the shoulder of the next man looming over her. "My how tall you are. Why don't you have a seat where I can see you?" He immediately sank to the floor, arms and legs sprawled like a rag doll. Nine down.

There were three more men who were still not succumbing to her scent. One of them was actually struggling against it. "What the hell's the matter with youse guys?" he said, looking around at the nine slumped over figures. The other two merely looked confused.

She smiled at the one who'd spoken, gazing deep into his eyes. She was a lamia. And he was her plaything. She stalked toward the three men, brushing her hand over the chest of one, delicately touching the wrist of another. They staggered back, and she eased up to the last holdout, until she was only a breath away from his chin. "Murder and kidnapping is such hard work. I think you boys need a holiday."

His mouth fell open dumbly as he breathed in her poison.

She moved back and looked at the room full of blinking, dazed men slumped over the chairs and tables and slouched on the floor. "All of you, run along home. Leave the guns."

They got up unsteadily, guns falling from lax hands to clatter on the cement. They started wandering to the door, some shuffling, some staggering, some crawling on hands and knees. She watched them go, her poison chasing them out into the night.

As the last of them vanished into the rain, she tipped her head up to sniff the air, searching for the odor that would lead her to the monster. There it was. Acid, mushrooms, and blood.

She followed the thread of scent deeper into the building, winding through a labyrinth of rusted out machinery until she found a hole in the floor filled with a metal stairwell. Her bare feet made no sound on the steps as she stole down them. A few sizzling bulbs shed a ghastly light along a low, narrow corridor at the bottom of the stairs.

Two of Duke's black-suited thugs from the garden party were standing against the wall near a metal door. The terrible scent of fresh blood seeped from behind it. Mark's blood.

The guards caught sight of her and straightened, their hands on their guns before they realized who she was. "Miss Karlova?" one of them said, looking stunned.

"That's right." Eliza prowled toward them. "I've come to surprise my fiancée. Is he in his laboratory?" She pointed toward the door.

"Yeah, but you can't go in there. He's busy," the bruiser said.

She bared her teeth in a smile. "Oh, he's not too busy to see me." She shot out her hands to grab each of the guards by the wrist. Their eyes went blank instantly, their skin sizzling under her fingertips.

"Get out of here," she told them softly. *Before I'm tempted to hurt you.*

She released them and, faces slack, they shuffled away to the stairs. When they were gone, she turned to face the door. Getting past the soldiers had been the easy part. Now came the real battle with the monsters, human and otherwise.

Voices seeped around the edges of the metal panel. She listened, waiting for her moment.

63

"Dr. Smalley, go and fetch my injection for tonight," Duke said, taking off his white linen jacket.

Smalley placed his bloody scalpel on the instrument tray with an angry click and pushed the cart away, rattling and squeaking.

Mark felt dizzy with relief. The room swam around him. Blood was pouring out of the cut on his thigh, pooling on the table beneath him. The damned doctor must have nicked a vein. "What is this place?"

Duke tossed his jacket onto a nearby workbench. "I suppose there's no harm in telling you, since you'll never leave here again except as my soldier."

Mark laughed at that, but let the man continue.

"This is an old soap factory where I used to work as a boy. My father worked here too, for pennies an hour, until the day he fell into a vat of lye. By the time they pulled him out, there was nothing left but bones."

A peculiar smile crept over his face. "Twenty years later I took over this place when I married the owner's daughter. I considered tearing it down, but it proved too useful as a kennel

337

for my creature." He nodded to the tank in the corner where the monster was rippling and sloshing against the thick glass.

"How did your crazy doctor make that thing?"

"Smalley didn't make it."

"Who did then? It sure as hell wasn't you, Oxford."

Duke laughed and punched Mark's broken ribs.

Stars of pain exploded in front of his eyes, and he nearly lost consciousness.

"Mind your manners." Duke took the gold cufflinks off his left wrist and started rolling up his sleeve. "To answer your question, it is my scientific belief that this slime is part of a prehistoric creature that once lived dispersed throughout the Lake Michigan watershed. I say part, because I think that there is a vastly larger portion of slime living in the lake even to this day. But when the city fathers built locks between the lake and the Chicago River, the part of the creature that was caught behind the locks was inundated with the chemical refuse of the entire city.

"It began acting in ways no slime mold ever has, hunting down humans as prey. Sometimes men would fall into the water and never come out again. Sometimes boats would capsize for no reason and the passengers would vanish without a trace, like the wreck of the *Eastland*. But no one ever knew why.

"Until one night I saw the creature eating the industrial sludge in the canal behind this very building. I hunted it when I came back from the War, and after years of work and sacrifice, I captured it. Smalley merely provides me the formula I need to control it."

At that moment, the doctor approached him with a long hypodermic needle. He swiped an iodine cloth over Duke's exposed bicep and shoved the needle in.

Duke didn't so much as twitch, his eyes on Mark and a half-smile on his lips. Smalley withdrew the syringe and carried it away. Duke rolled his sleeve down.

"What was in that needle?" Mark asked, revolted.

Duke refastened his cuff. "A formula we concocted together, Smalley and I. It produces a chemical scent which makes the slime believe I am a part of it, just one of its billions of cells. In essence, I can become one with the creature. I can direct it to go where I go and attack whom I choose. I become its brain, as it were."

"That's not possible."

A cruel light sparked in Duke's eyes. "That sounds like a request for a demonstration. I believe I'll indulge you." He walked to the tank in the corner and climbed the ladder up to the top.

He reached into the tank, scooping his bare hand into the slime, and lifted out a blob of translucent greenish ooze cupped in his palm.

"You see? The formula works just as I said. The creature accepts me as part of it." The slime stirred, tendrils of it creeping over his fingers to the underside of his hand, away from the light. He turned his hand over, and the stuff crawled away from the light again. "Like you, it hates light. An interesting coincidence, is it not?"

"How do you control it when you send it out? You weren't nearby when it ate the first four gangsters."

"My method is quite ingenious, if I may say so." He let the slime play over his fingertips. "I have my men buy the dirty linen of my targets from the laundry before it's washed, and then I toss it in the vat with the slime and add a chemical that signals it to eat. I turn it loose in the drain and let the creature hunt down its prey. It can find its target with only the faintest thread of scent in the water to lead the way."

Eliza's guess about the way the slime hunted had been right. But maybe it was more than a guess. Maybe she knew all along and she'd tricked him and lied to him from the beginning. A surge of agony that had nothing to do with his injuries hit him again. He pushed through it. "How do you get it to come back after it's done the deed?"

"I use the nature of the slime mold against itself. You see, even though this creature can be divided up again and again down to its individual cells, and even though it can live spread out over a vast area, it never forgets that it is one singular entity. When part of it is separated from the whole, it will eventually try to reunite itself. I take out some of the slime and prime it to attack. When the creature is done with its hunt, it comes back, looking for the part of itself still held captive. Simple, yet clever, no?" He started climbing back down the ladder, one hand still cupping his blob of ooze.

Mark blinked hard against the glare that seemed to be growing brighter and brighter. The wound on his thigh wasn't closing. The blood was running out freely, forming a sticky puddle on the table beneath him. He was cold, his heart beating too fast. His thoughts were going blurry. He had to focus. He needed to get answers. "Why target Camonte's outfit?"

Duke came to stand over Mark again. "Because I intend to take over the city and he's standing in my way. And because the good citizens of Chicago won't care if he gets rubbed out. In fact, they'll be grateful. So will the Federal Government. I have it on good authority that they consider the criminal element to be perfect fodder for weapons testing."

"Why are you making weapons for the government? Who are they planning on fighting?"

"Why, anyone. The Germans, the Russians, even the Japanese. The last war was supposed to end all wars, but it was only the beginning." Duke gestured broadly, as if roused to oratory by his own great vision. The slime writhed uneasily around his hand. "The United States Army will need a scientific edge to win the coming battles. I learned that first hand, in the trenches.

"I shipped out to Flanders, a twenty-two-year-old boy, convinced I was fighting for the American Spirit. But I soon learned the great lesson of my life. The American Spirit is worth nothing compared to modern science and the will to use it to its utmost potential. I saw what the new weapons could accomplish. The machine guns. The artillery. The gas. The power of a god at man's fingertips." He looked off into the air at a vision of a battlefield only he could see, his teeth gleaming behind lips curled in grotesque excitement.

"I understood at once that science had truly ushered in a new age, where men with the foresight to seize control of technology would become the new masters of the globe. I came home determined to carve out my own territory in the modern world with weapons man had never seen before."

His glittering gaze focused on Mark again. "You are one of those weapons, Mark. Created by science to work the will of great men. My friends in the Federal Government will want you put to use. Your country demands that you perform any and all tasks I set for you, without question or hesitation."

"That will never happen."

"Ah, but it will. You shall never leave this room alive otherwise. And if you imagine that troglodyte Camonte will save you, you'd best think again. My men and I will mop up the last of his organization tonight. You are my property now, Mark, and you will learn to obey."

"Are you stupid, Oxford? You'll have to kill me first."

"Oh, I won't do that." He held his slime-covered hand over the center of Mark's body, and threads like thin worms started to curl off of it, weaving through the air toward Mark's flesh. "Perhaps I'll let my creature change your mind."

The tendrils of slime licked over Mark's chest, leaving long, raw lines on his skin as it dissolved his flesh and consumed it. It was excruciating. His jaw cracked as he clenched it hard to stop from screaming.

"You see," Duke said, "I don't merely touch the slime, I control it. I can make it eat every scrap of flesh off your bones if I choose. Unless you submit."

"Never happen!" he ground out.

"Ah, a hard case, as they say." Duke withdrew his hand and the tentacles of ooze curled back into his palm with a slurping noise. He turned to a worktable and dumped the slime into an empty beaker. The blob instantly started to slosh back and forth in its container in perfect time with the larger creature in the tank, as if they were indeed one being.

Duke returned to stand over Mark, regarding him with his head tipped to one side. He smiled. "If you won't think of yourself, perhaps you'll think of Eliza."

The name cut deeper than the doctor's scalpel. "Eliza."

"Yes. My future wife. This is very embarrassing for you, of course, but I couldn't help noticing you've developed something of a *tendre* for her."

He forced out a laugh. "A *tendre*? Listen to you, Lionel,

Duke of the South Side." His voice was slurring, haze creeping through his brain.

Duke's voice turned cool with anger. "Fine. Without any sugarcoating, then. If you refuse to obey me, I will see to it that my wife, your dear, sweet Eliza, suffers for it."

Mark didn't answer. His good eye was watering. He shut it against the light.

He heard a rustle as Duke bent over him. The cultured, plummy voice spoke softly into his ear. "I have a gift for rooting out a man's weaknesses, you know. It's why I always win in business and in war. And I've seen how you lust for her beyond all reason. She is your weakness, and I will not hesitate to exploit it to get what I want from you. I believe the doctor told you about the tortures inflicted on your dear departed mother in order to bring about your birth?"

"Did you help him?" Mark snarled. "Did you help him kill my mother?"

"That was long before my time. The doctor and your father dosed her with their super-man mutation drugs all on their own. But you see, I sacrificed my first wife to the same fate when she bore me my son, so don't imagine for a moment that I'm bluffing. If you won't do what I ask, I'll strap my new wife down in your place and unleash the doctor on her. Imagine what kind of scientific atrocities he'll devise for Eliza's soft, innocent body."

Mark sucked in a deep breath. And then he started to laugh, even as his ribs screamed in agony. Blood welled up out of the thin strips the slime had eaten into his skin and trickled down his sides to join the lake of blood on the table beneath him.

"What's so amusing?" The cool smirk in Duke's voice was gone.

"You'll find out," Mark gasped, and laughed some more. When Eliza got through with him, he'd be worse off than dead. Just like Mark.

"Eliza!" Duke said, but instead of coldly threatening, his tone was shocked.

A wave of deadly perfume washed over him. *No.* It couldn't be. Had she come to gloat over him? Could she possibly be that cruel? Mark opened his streaming eye and saw the most magnificent sight of his life.

She stood framed in the doorway, barefoot and bare legged, her slender body clad in a ruined silk dress. Her jet-black hair was slicked wet against her head. Kohl ran in black streaks over her cheekbones. Her red lips were spread in a white-toothed smile.

She looked wild, gorgeous, and terrifying. The air shimmered with her power. She strolled into the laboratory, hips swaying.

"Hello, darling," she said.

64

Eliza scanned the chamber as she strolled through the door. The blood-and-mushroom stench choked the air, billowing out from an aquarium tank in the corner. The murky green liquid inside roiled and pulsed, quivering like flesh under four blazing spotlights. The slime monster.

Along one wall were counters full of gleaming laboratory equipment. Dr. Smalley stood near them, staring at her with his lopsided eyes.

In the center of the room was Mark, chained to a table, his muscular body naked, his white skin bruised and stained with blood. One of his eyes was swollen shut, but the other stared at her with such fury and agony that she had to look away before she lost control.

Lionel Duke stood over Mark. The shock was rapidly draining off his handsome face, leaving his eyes cool and sharp. "Eliza, what are you doing here?"

She walked toward him, her poison seething through the air. In the corner, Dr. Smalley twitched, like a mouse watching a cat padding by. Eliza ignored him, her eyes locked on Duke. "I came to see why you had to leave our engagement party so early, darling. Little did I expect to hear you plotting to torture me."

Duke said, "I'm afraid you've caught me at a rather awkward moment. I don't know how you got in here, but you're leaving. Abel! Newton!" he called toward the door.

"Your men went home," she said, swaying closer. "We're all alone."

He narrowed his eyes at her. She was wreathing him in her scent, but he showed no sign of her influence. "What have you done, little witch?" he said softly. "I knew you were treacherous, but I didn't think you foolish enough to play your tricks against me."

She stilled, a tendril of fear crawling through her heart. Duke suspected what she was. And he was already resistant to her scent. If he was as powerful as Mark, she might lose this battle.

Lose? A voice like her grandmother's hissed in her mind. *You do not lose! You are the scourge of wicked men!* Her poison seethed in her veins and she smiled with abandon. "Why, Lionel, whatever do you mean? Surely you don't think I could do anything to your men, or to you. I'm merely a woman. You're not afraid of me, are you, darling?" She eased closer until she was within arm's reach of him.

"Afraid of you?" He stood with his legs spread and stroked his mustache, his teeth gleaming beneath it. "No. As I was just telling Mark, you belong to me now, and I will use you as I see fit. Shall I take you here, in front of him, to demonstrate?" He languidly reached out and seized the collar of her dress in wide, hard fists. With a sharp yank he tore open the wet silk and dragged it down, exposing her breasts.

She heard Mark roaring in fury, but all her concentration was on Duke. She didn't flinch, standing straight and smiling at him.

Duke grinned and said softly, "Like it rough, do you?" He grabbed a fistful of her hair, wrenching her head back.

Poison burned through her, scent boiling off her skin, saturating the air. She arched her body toward him, her breasts brushing his chest. Then she saw it at last. The sharpness in his gaze wavered.

"Kiss me and find out," she whispered.

His mouth slammed down on hers, his tongue and teeth gouging into her mouth.

She unleashed the full power of her poison. It flooded through her lips and into his, sweet and deadly, searing his flesh. He froze in shock.

She had him. She could kill him, here and now. She'd been planning his death from the start. It was what she was born for. She was a predator, he was her prey. And he deserved it, murderer and torturer that he was. It would be easy.

Easy to prove Angelique right.

She tore her mouth away. He staggered back with a strangled bellow, pawing at his raw, blistering lips, his eyes rolling back in his head. His legs buckled, and he collapsed to the floor, spasming, foam bubbling at the corners of his mouth as he gasped.

The creature in the tank surged against the glass, rippling in agitation. Tentacles of slime started creeping over the top of the tank, reaching sluggishly through the light for Duke.

"Amazing," a voice said. She spun to see Smalley standing by an open cabinet, his face covered by a gas mask, holding a dart gun pointed at her heart. He'd armed himself while Duke and the monster distracted her.

She silently cursed herself for underestimating him. "You don't want to shoot that at me," she said, moving slowly toward him as she poured her scent into the air.

He fired the gun twice.

Sharp pain pierced her left breast and her stomach. She looked down in shock and saw two darts sticking out of her body, the vials attached to the needles emptying into her bloodstream.

She pulled them out, stumbled, and fell to her knees. "How . . . How did you know to wear a gas mask?"

Smalley lowered the dart gun, examining her through the round eyepieces of his mask. "Simple observation and deduction." His voice was muffled behind the long filter. "Lionel started exhibiting unusual patterns of behavior when you and that other female appeared. I suspected biochemical manipulation, but I could find no indication of drugs when I tested his blood. I formed the hypothesis that you were influencing his mind with chemicals in your touch and scent."

Damn. Her family had been right to avoid scientists all these years. She crumpled to the side with her legs folded under her, holding herself up with one arm, her head drooping.

"A natural mutation," Smalley mused. "Quite fascinating. Now I shall have three monsters in my collection."

"I have to t-tell you something," she whispered.

He put the dart gun down and crossed the room to her. His masked face made him look like a man-sized biting insect as he leaned over her. "Tell me what?"

Eliza shot up off the floor and seized the scrawny neck beneath the mask with both hands, poison sizzling in her fingertips. Smalley stumbled back with a muffled scream. He flailed at her with his bony hands, trying to get away, but she held on tight and stared into the eyepieces of his mask. "Your poison darts can't hurt a lamia, fool! I *am* poison!"

He made a bleating noise, his good eye fixing on her in horror for an instant before it rolled back in his head and he collapsed like a puppet with its strings cut. She let him fall, and before he hit the floor she was running to Mark's side.

"Mark!" Her heart quailed at the lake of red pooled on the table beneath his thigh. His eye dragged open, sunken, the color of ash. He'd lost too much blood. "Darling, we have to get you out." She had to search Duke and Smalley for the key to his chains.

She turned back to the two men sprawled on the floor and gasped. Beyond them the slime was bubbling out of its tank, running down to the floor and forming a growing, rippling blob. Long tendrils separated and rejoined as it crawled toward the humans, moving slower than it had under the dim light of the Green Mill, but coming just the same. She had to get Mark out of here before the thing attacked.

"Light," Mark gasped beside her.

Frantic, she grabbed his ice-cold shoulders and shook him. "Mark! You've got to stay awake!"

"Turn off the light," he said, a breath of sound.

She scanned the room. The cables to the spotlights snaked over the floor to a switch plate on the wall.

She bit her lip. Once she threw the light switch, nothing would hold back the slime. But she had no choice. Mark's shadow was the only way to escape before the creature got them.

She ran to the switch and hauled it down, shutting off the electric current. The room plunged into blackness. The afterglow of the spotlights burned in her vision. She heard a soft, sucking noise coming from the direction of the tank and her own ragged breathing.

Then she heard Duke and Smalley scream, two wails of mortal pain, quickly cut off.

"Mark!" she cried out, pressing her back hard against the wall.

A long, slimy tendril crept around her foot, trailing over the skin damply, like a tongue licking her. She screamed.

A naked arm snaked around her waist. "Got you," Mark said as he snatched her up and took them both into darkness.

65

A chaos of shadows whirled around her and abruptly stilled. She was standing clutched to Mark's chest in a Spartan room containing a brass bed, a dresser, a straight-backed chair and a shelf full of books. But there were no lamps, not even a light fixture on the ceiling. This was Mark's bedroom, she realized.

She pushed back from him, her legs trembling under her.

The instant he lost her support he collapsed to his hands and knees on the rug by the bed, an agonized groan coming from between his teeth.

"Mark!" She reached out to touch his bent back. Beneath her fingers his bruised skin seemed to drink in the darkness, whorls of shadow flooding over him and into him, vanishing into the white of his flesh. Before her astonished eyes, the terrible dark splotches on his ribs and back began to fade, the swelling on his face went down, and the vicious cut on his thigh stopped bleeding and started to seal.

"You—you need to lie down," she said shakily. She

hauled him up and tipped him over onto the bed. He sprawled on his back, eyes closed, breath coming harsh through his bloody lips.

She heaved one of his legs and then the other up on the bed. "I'll be back," she said to him.

She ran out of the bedroom into a hallway and found a bathroom a couple of doors down. She looked quickly through the cupboards for medical supplies, but found nothing, not even a sticking plaster. Perhaps he didn't need them, with his evident healing ability. She wetted a washcloth in the sink and rushed back to Mark's side.

He hadn't moved since she left him, his magnificent limbs still spread out on his bed, eyes closed in his stern angel's face. His wounds were healing quickly, the bruises fading from violent purple to yellow, the cuts and scrapes now just red lines. But he was too still, like a bloodstained marble effigy.

With a corner of the washcloth, she carefully cleaned the healing cuts around his left eye and mouth, softly brushing his high cheekbones. She took each broad, long-fingered hand in hers and washed each raw knuckle. She ran the cloth lightly over the purple bruising on his ribs, but felt no worrying give in the hard straps of muscle and bone.

She took a deep breath and lowered her eyes to the wound on his thigh. What had been a wicked gash in his skin was now a pink scar, healing even as she watched. She wiped the blood off his flesh, the muscles like iron bands under the white silk of his skin.

Her eyes slipped sideways toward the organ between his legs. His shaft was long and thick, the skin rosy pink. White hair circled the root of it and ran in a thin trail up his stomach. Beneath, his heavy sack rested against his thigh.

She had held his sex in her hand only hours ago, when it

had been erect and demanding. Now his potency slept, yet was still so primal. So animal.

Her skin felt hot. She twisted the cloth tight in her fingers and resolutely looked away. She found a blanket and spread it over him. He hadn't moved at all as she washed him, except for the rise and fall of his chest as he breathed. He looked much better now, but he was still frighteningly still.

She suddenly became aware of the clammy rags she was wearing, the ruined silk cutting into her skin. She found Mark's closet and threw open the doors, rifling through the hangers until she found a night robe. She took it into the bathroom and stripped naked, draping her torn dress and underwear on the lip of the bathtub to dry. She huddled into Mark's robe and caught a glimpse of her reflection in a small shaving mirror on the wall.

She looked dreadful. Her eyes were glittering, makeup running in dark streaks down her cheeks, lipstick smeared across her mouth. She turned on scalding hot water and scrubbed her face clean with another washcloth, raking her wild curls back ruthlessly with her fingers.

She heard a sound come from the bedroom, a low and terrible moan that was worse than a scream.

She ran back to Mark's side, heart pounding in her throat.

He had thrashed the blanket off, his hands clawing the sheets, his head tossing on the pillow. The terrible groan came again. His long white lashes flickered up, and his eyes were two black pits swirling with darkness, as if his face was merely a mask hiding a being made of endless night.

"Mark!"

"The shadow wants me." Darkness flooded between his pale lips, his mouth a black hole. Dark wisps curled off his skin and vanished, as if the very substance of his flesh was shredding away into nothing.

"No! It can't have you!" She threw herself down on the bed and grabbed his shoulders, her fingers digging into his white flesh as darkness poured off him.

His spine twisted in agony once more, and then he collapsed back onto the mattress and went still. Somehow, that was even more frightening. He seemed less substantial with each breath, his physical body vanishing into the night. Terror seized her heart. Somehow she knew with utter certainty that if Mark gave in to the shadows tonight, he would never find his way back to the real world again.

A sob broke out of her. "Please, Mark, please don't go!"

He was silent and still, the splendid white shape of him melting into the dark. Wildly, she clutched his body to her, holding him as the shadows tried to tear him away. Hot tears spilled from her eyes, falling on the snowy skin. "N-no! You have to stay! Stay for me!"

And then a voice rumbled softly in her ear. "Eliza?" Arms came around her, big hands cupping her head and pulling it up. Mark's mouth found hers in a kiss tasting of night.

She was shocked to immobility. "Eliza," he murmured against her lips, and deepened the kiss, opening her, delving inside. Desire and panic in equal measure rushed under her skin, sizzling through her belly and between her legs as his lips and tongue stroked her.

She tried to push up from him, but Mark's hands fisted in her robe and tore it off her, and suddenly her breasts were cupped in his broad palms, his thumbs brushing over the peaks. His sex was a thick club against her naked thighs. His tongue penetrated her lips again as she gasped.

The world spun, and she was on her back, lying underneath him. Dragging his mouth off of hers he caged her with his arms and loomed above her, his eyes open and flooded with darkness. He was gorgeous and ruthless, a force of nature. "Mark!" she breathed.

He bared his teeth and pushed her legs apart with his knees, spreading her thighs wide. Her sex was weeping with excitement even as she shook in trepidation. He grabbed his thick erection, aimed it at her soft wet opening, and breached her with the slick crown. "Eliza!" he groaned as he shoved inside.

She cried out from the shock of it, her body clenched tight, resisting him, but he wouldn't have it. He withdrew and thrust in again, all the way to his root. It wasn't as painful as she feared, but it wasn't pleasurable.

She grabbed a handful of his thick white hair and yanked it. "Mark! You promised you would never hurt me!"

His big body froze above her even as his organ pulsed within her. In the dark pits of shadow within his eyes, she saw a flicker of awareness. His lips parted and whorls of blackness poured through them. "Hurt you? Never hurt you."

"Then just—just wait," she said, her voice uneven. "For a minute."

His eyes flickered between icy blue and black. He jerked his head in a nod and held himself still, except for his strained breathing and his shaft throbbing inside her.

She tried to relax, to adjust to the strangeness of him filling her, but her legs were restless. She dug her heels into the mattress and moved her hips against the solid body over her. *Oh! That was almost good!* She arched her body up to him again.

His control snapped. He groaned, his hips shooting forward in animal lust. "My God, you're so beautiful."

He captured her shaking legs, folding them up around his waist, and pushed into her in a long, slick glide, his thick shaft rubbing and stroking inside of her. The he did it again, and again and again, until she felt like every thrust of his shaft was pushing her closer to the edge of a towering precipice.

It was too much. She beat on his shoulders with her fists. "I can't! I can't!"

"Yes, you can," he growled with another stroke. "I'm going to make you come. I'm going to make you scream in pleasure. Nothing in this world will stop me."

Lost, helpless against him, she sank her fingers into his straining back and rocked with him, their bodies a tight knot of blazing lust. His pearly flesh was slick with sweat under her fingers, the muscles of his back and stomach rippling with each shove into her. His cock slid in and out of her in hard, long, slow thrusts, winding her tighter and tighter.

He bent his head and kissed her again, tonguing inside of her mouth, biting and licking down her throat. He scooped an arm behind her back, arching her breasts up to his mouth, and sucked her nipples, rubbing his face against them. All the while his hips pumped into hers in that same savage rhythm.

"Mark . . . oh . . ." She was gasping with each thrust, beyond words, but her body begged him, squeezing and gripping him as he drove her toward a peak of terrifying pleasure.

He felt it coming at the same moment she did. His head reared back, his eyes wide with shock as they looked into hers. He shoved home one last time, and they watched each other find glory. She heard her own voice crying out his name, his triumphant roar. A cataclysm swept her up and tore her body to pieces, and she knew she would never be the same again.

She floated for an endless time in stunned bliss, unable to do anything but breathe. Mark collapsed onto his side, pulling her with him. His muscled arms trembled around her, his shaft was still thick within her. She looked into his eyes, hazy with pleasure and wonder. They were blue once more, she saw before his white lashes came down. His flesh was solid and white again, the shadows around him quiet. She held him to her, his skin warm under her fingers. The darkness wouldn't have him tonight.

66

When she woke a faint hint of dawn light was seeping around the window curtains. She was half-lying on top of Mark, her leg coiled over his, her head on his shoulder and her hand over his heart. She could tell by the rise and fall of the muscled chest under her palm that he was awake. But his face was turned away from her.

"Good morning," she murmured.

He didn't turn his head. His voice rumbled softly, "What happened to Duke and Smalley? And the slime?"

"Don't you remember?"

"It's blurry."

"I don't know about the monster. Duke and Smalley . . ." She pressed her face against his skin, trying to blot out the echoes of the men's screams. "They're dead. The slime . . . ate them."

She felt a certain tension loosen in him. But not all. "You came to rescue me," he said.

She nodded against his shoulder. "Yes."

"Why? I thought you wanted me dead."

She raised her head to stare at him. "What?" She scrambled to her knees. "What do you mean?"

He finally turned his head to look at her, his eyes once again the color of ice. "Don't lie to me. Smalley told me about the female who helped him trap me."

"It was my grandmother, Mark! Please believe me, I had no idea of what she and Duke were planning! I would never have betrayed you like that! I've only ever tried to save you. That's why I tried to take your memory away. That's why I said . . . those things to you in the garden. I thought I was protecting you by driving you away!"

"Protecting me? I gave you my heart, and you stepped on it!" The ice cracked with pain.

She dashed away a tear and met his stark gaze. "I'm sorry about what I said. I didn't mean any of it. You're a good man, Mark. You're good to me. I wanted to be good to you. I was just . . . so afraid for you. I still am. The countess said she would set the entire city of Chicago to hunt you down and kill you if I didn't marry Duke. And she can do it! A mob might be on the way here right now for all I know."

His white brows came down.

"And what about my poison?" she said. "What if you're not as immune to it as you think?"

He regarded her for a long moment. "Eliza, I . . . I—" He clapped a hand to his heart. Choking and gasping, he collapsed onto his back, head lolling.

Terrified, she threw herself on him, clutching his shoulders. "Mark! Mark, speak to me!"

He cracked an eye at her and grinned. "Put on my tombstone that I died with a smile on my face."

"Oh! Oh, I *am* going to kill you!" She seized a pillow and started beating him with it.

Laughing, Mark wrestled the pillow away from her and rolled her under him, pinning her wrists above her head. Her breasts plumped against his chest. "For the last time, your perfume can't hurt me, angel."

She looked up into his face. The ice in his eyes had melted into blue flame. The corners of his mouth curled up in a smile. "Mark," she said, suddenly breathless.

He eased his legs between hers and leaned down to rumble in her ear, "There's something else I remember about last night. I remember how it felt to be inside you. The most amazing moment of my life. Eliza . . ." He rolled his muscular hips and eased the head of his penis into her, teasing her opening. "I want back in."

"Wait, Mark. Please. We need to talk," she said, her voice trembling.

He stilled above her. "What do you want to talk about?"

"This," she said, freeing her wrists and gesturing between their bodies. "I've never done this before and it was overwhelming. You have more experience than me—"

He shook his head. "I had no experience at all."

"What?"

"I'd never even kissed a woman before you."

She stared up at him, astonished.

He moved off of her and rolled onto his back with a sigh. "Because of . . ." He made a little gesture that somehow encompassed his skin and hair. His whiteness.

She rolled to her side and stared at his perfectly chiseled profile. How? How could the women of this ridiculous country be so blind? "But Fraser said that you and his sister . . ."

His finely cut mouth quirked. "I was a stupid nineteen-year-old boy, and she was a beautiful girl who had been kind to me when we were children. I thought it meant more than it did. I had all these romantic dreams of spiriting her away to Paris. Turned out she didn't want Paris, or me. She wanted a normal man, and a normal life."

The silly cow. Who would want a normal life when she could have Mark? She thought with a little amazement of herself a few weeks ago when a normal life was all she had wanted.

You silly cow, she told her past self.

But Mark's eyes were starting to darken, and she didn't want talk of the past poisoning this moment. So she leaned up and smiled at him, lazy and slow. "Well. For a man with no experience, you certainly do talk a good game," she said, thinking of the sexy filth he had whispered in her ear when he was moving inside her.

It worked. He grinned, cocky again. "I play a good game too. Natural talent."

She narrowed her eyes at him. "Natural talent, hmm? Now, why do I think you honed your talent through a little voyeurism? Perhaps you whiled away tedious evenings by ghosting into the odd bedroom or two?"

His skin turned from white to bright red, proving she'd hit a bull's-eye. But his devilish grin didn't waver. He lounged back against the pillows, putting a hand behind his head. "I never reveal the details of my personal inquiries."

"Not even under torture?" She ran her fingers over his exposed ribs, startling a laugh out of him.

He captured her hand and pulled it across his chest. She went with it, until she was half lying on him, their smiling faces only a kiss away. "Do your worst," he growled.

She laughed and sat up. His hand fell away, but she left hers where it was, resting on the thick muscle over his beating heart. His small nipple tickled her palm. She ran her hand across the wings of his collarbones, over the solid cap of his shoulder and up the rolling bicep. Back down over his finely shaped triceps and the fine white hair under his raised arm. She rested her hand on the broad ribs she had tickled.

Her gaze roved down the length of his naked body spread out before her. His long, hard legs, one square knee raised a little. The muscle of his calves rolled into balls and set on the straight bones of his shins. His high arched, long-toed feet.

But her attention inevitably swept back up to the vee of his legs, where his thick organ rested along one thigh. It had been hard the whole time they talked, but as she watched it hardened and lengthened further, the heavy sack beneath it tightening with need.

"This *is* torture. Your eyes are burning me up."

Her gaze turned to his face. He was still smiling, but there was a wary note to his voice.

She told him the simple truth. "I love looking at you. You're beautiful."

He blinked and smiled a lopsided, half-amazed smile. As if he couldn't quite believe her, but liked hearing her say it anyway.

It struck deep in her heart, that he was letting her look at him like this. Like he felt no need to hide himself from her, no shame, no fear. Like he trusted her. His knees even spread out a little, and he smiled wider, until he looked easy and smug as a pasha lounging in his harem.

She wanted to caress every crevice of his body, every silky patch of hair, every inch of supple skin with her fingers and lips.

Which gave her an idea.

"Tell me one thing." She eased up onto her knees and spread her hands on his chest. "On any of your excursions into the boudoir, did you see any demonstrations of . . ." She made herself say it. "Fellatio?"

The smile vanished from his eyes, replaced by something hotter, more intense. "Maybe a time or two."

"Good. Because I want to try it. But I'm going to need some guidance, being new at this, you know."

He swallowed. "I think I can manage that."

"Splendid." She looked him over again, dabbing her lower lip with her tongue, suddenly at a loss. But she came from a long line of seductresses, didn't she? Surely she could figure something out.

Experimentally, she leaned down to brush her lips over his. He tried to deepen the kiss but she eluded him, nuzzling his neck below his ear, and then skimming her lips down his throat to his chest when he drew a sharp breath. She touched her tongue to his small pink nipple and was rewarded when his muscular chest contracted. She softly bit the swell of his pectoral, and he growled.

"You like that?" she breathed against his skin.

"I like everything. Anything."

She nipped her way down his breastbone and over the straps of muscle along his stomach, soothing each little bite with a kiss. "And this?" She dipped her tongue into his navel.

"Yes!" he said, his eyes riveted to her. "Don't stop."

Smiling, she wriggled down his body. She shifted to kneel between his thighs, running her palms over the sleek muscles of his legs. She leaned over his shaft, hard and bobbing above his rippling belly, and kissed the soft skin at the crevice of his thighs, nuzzling the tight sack between them. She drank in his heady, musky aroma, and when he caught his breath on a low groan, she slipped out her tongue and lapped at the salty flesh, rough and delicate and delicious, until he was rocking his hips toward her mouth. She skimmed her lips up the straining curve of his penis.

He sucked in a breath, hands fisting in the sheets.

She drew back a little, looking up at him. "Should I keep going?"

"God, yes!"

She bent her head over his organ once more. The tip was slick with his excitement, and she darted her tongue out to catch the drops welling out of his slit. She moaned at the taste of him, opened her mouth and sucked in the plump crown.

He cried out, and his hands flew to her head, cupping it as she loved the tip of him with her mouth. She took his shaft in her hand, so thick she couldn't close her fingers around it. She held him tight, like he showed her before, and suckled him, playing her tongue over him. She looked up and met his ferocious eyes, and she knew she was in trouble.

67

Am I dreaming?

Mark gazed down his body at the most incredible sight of his life. Her skin was as pure as moonlight and as soft as clouds, her hair black as night where it fell across her cheeks. Long, graceful limbs, breasts ripe and full, bouncing, swaying, the nipples rosy and tight as she stroked him with her slender hands and scorched him with her lips.

Could she possibly be real? Did he dare believe it?

She gave him mind-bending pleasure with her touch, not pain.

She called him beautiful.

A brutal sound tore out of him as she took him in her mouth, and he cupped her silky head in his trembling palms, his eyes feasting on the deep curve of her waist flaring out to the perfect shape of her hips and thighs. But the place between her legs was hidden from him. He wanted to see it, touch it, taste it, anything to convince himself that she wasn't a fantasy.

She met his eyes with her soft red lips around his cock,

and he couldn't take it any more. He had to put it inside her, he had to do it hard, and he had to do it now.

He lifted her mouth off him and sat up, clasping his arms around her slim waist. Muffling her indignant gasp with a deep kiss, he eased her onto her back. He scrambled off the bed and stood, grabbed her hips, and dragged her to the edge of the mattress. He folded her legs up and looked hungrily at her rosy sex, the petals of it wet with her dew. He'd like to spend hours kissing her there, but right now he couldn't wait a single second longer. He fisted his shaft and plunged it into the glistening folds.

"Oh!" She cried out, her body arching in pleasure. Her head fell back, shiny black hair fanning across the sheets, exquisite face taut with desire.

He leaned his hands on the bed on either side of her body and started pumping his hips long and slow, the way she liked it. Her lips parted, her dark eyes hazy with pleasure. She spread her legs wide for him, the little muscles inside her gripping him. The only place they touched was his cock working in her tight little opening.

She leaned up on her elbows and they watched together, his shaft glistening with their combined passion as he slid in and out of her. She pulsed around him with each deep thrust, tighter, hotter, until they were one mindless creature of lust. Pleasure raced outward from where they joined, blazing through every vein and nerve.

He felt her orgasm coming, as powerful as the ocean cresting, ready to sweep his mind and body away with her. The lure of the darkness was nothing to this ferocious pleasure. He ground his teeth and held on as his balls tightened and seed boiled in his shaft. He gave one more deep thrust.

She flung her head back, her mouth open in a cry of

need, and the wave broke over him, crashing down on him in a shock, shattering him. His mouth came down on hers, sharing her cries, sharing her breath until the last quake ripped through them both.

She fell onto her back, panting, and curled her legs around his hips, holding him inside her. He stood between her thighs, his knees shaking, his shaft wedged in her, and bowed his head to her breasts.

Her warm, soft arms clasped his head, her lips moving over his hair.

He saw a teardrop fall onto the sweet curve of her breast. He blinked at it, unbelieving, though he felt the trail of wetness on his cheek. He hadn't wept since he was a small boy.

But there it was, the proof that this wasn't a dream. Only reality had this much pain in it, the terrible pain of loving a woman who had the power to destroy him at her whim. She could beat him and betray him and break his heart a thousand times, and he would surrender himself every time for a chance at this moment. He was lost for her, God help him.

"I love you," he whispered against her skin, utterly broken.

A distant sound intruded on his consciousness, a furious knocking echoing through the house from downstairs. Someone was pounding on his door.

His sex-addled mind lurched, and he pulled out of her, making her moan in protest. The deadly world outside his bed rushed back around him. His instincts roared to protect his woman from this new danger, whatever it might be. He spun and ran to his closet and threw on a shirt and pants and shoved his feet into shoes.

Eliza sat up, reaching for him. "Mark, what—"

He strode to her and kissed her silent. "Stay here." He gathered his shadow and sped downstairs to the front door.

68

He looked out the side window to see, not an angry mob, but Detective O'Bannion standing on his stoop. The cop had a newspaper under one arm and a cigarette dangling from his lips. His suit was rumpled and his chin was bristly. He looked like he'd duked it out with a bottle of whiskey and lost.

Of all the bastards to drag him out of Eliza's bed, it had to be this one. He yanked open the door. "What?" he snarled.

"Where the hell have you been? You were supposed to deal with this shit!" O'Bannion snapped open his newspaper and shoved it at him. The headline screamed, *Terror on the River! Industrialist Driven Mad by Scientific Experiment!* The byline was Al Tracy's. Tracy and his photographer must have tailed Duke last night.

Mark grabbed the paper out of the cop's hand. Under the headline a grainy photograph showed the street outside the old factory where he'd been held. Crawling down the middle of the road was the slime creature, a towering mass of jelly three times bigger than when he'd last seen it in the laboratory. Walking inside the blob was the figure of a man, like a fly caught in amber. He could just make out Duke's features. And by the turn of his head, the set of his shoulders, he wasn't terrified or struggling. He looked . . . happy. No, joyful. He was strolling along the street entirely enveloped by a deadly creature, like he hadn't a care in the world.

"Damn," Mark said. Duke was alive. But how?

"You can say that again." O'Bannion barged past him into the house and stumped down the hall to Mark's office.

Mark followed, scanning the article.

This reporter was shaken to the very core to witness the results of science run amok! Lionel Duke, the famed industrialist, has created a monster that has taken him captive and gone on a rampage down the Chicago River.

At midnight last night, Mr. Duke emerged from a secret laboratory in Back of the Yards engulfed by a mountain of venomous crawling slime. Though this reporter witnessed the substance dissolving human flesh, Mr. Duke appeared completely unharmed.

Mark's gaze switched back to the picture. The slime hadn't consumed Duke when it had escaped its tank, it had *incorporated* him. That potion Dr. Smalley had given him to control the creature had worked too well. He read on.

Mr. Duke and the creature walked—or slithered—into the canal and thence into the Chicago River. The monster then swam east to a wharf off of Polk Street where this reporter witnessed it attacking a group of citizens, pulling a delivery van off a bridge into the water and upending a ferryboat. No sign of the passengers in the van or the boat has since been found. They are presumed dead, consumed by the beast.

The van, boat and the missing men are said to belong to a company owned by Gabriel Camonte, the noted businessman.

After the attack, the creature and its unfortunate creator crawled over the lock separating the Chicago River from Lake Michigan. Two police officers and eight innocent bystanders were killed as it made its escape into the lake. Mr. Duke and his creature were last seen swimming east.

The mayor's office has issued a hazard warning and instructed boats in the greater Chicago area to proceed with all due caution.

In related news, Mr. Duke's apartment building and his country house were firebombed shortly after dark last night. Seventeen people have been killed and five injured in the blasts. Chicago's finest at the CPD are investigating.

Hell, Mark thought. Camonte and Duke had gone to war. He'd failed. He looked up at O'Bannion, who was standing by his desk, lighting a fresh cigarette. "How many casualties?"

"Twenty-seven so far, including a fourteen-year-old kid," O'Bannion said through his smoke. "The slime pulled some of them right off the shore and ate them."

Mark rubbed his forehead, which was suddenly aching. *All those people.* He walked around his desk and sat in his chair, tossing the paper on the blotter.

"And worst of all, the World's Fair is opening tonight," O'Bannion continued. "The first lady and the rest of the bigwigs are coming to town today, and we've got a monster on the loose and a gang war!"

"The politicians should have thought of that before they got into bed with a blood-simple killer like Duke," Mark said, disgusted.

"The politicians won't take the blame for this fuckup,"

O'Bannion warned him. "You're the one who's got to clean up this mess."

"Me? I thought you didn't want my help. I thought I was supposed to avoid any freak business during the fair."

"Don't give me that shit. This is what we let you have that private license for. What good are you if you can't handle a problem like this?"

Mark was silent. What good was he indeed? None to the people who had died.

"Where were you when this was happening, anyway?" O'Bannion said, eyeing him suspiciously.

"Mr. Van Ryn was injured in the line of duty last night during a confrontation with Duke and the monster," a cool voice said from the doorway.

69

Mark turned his head to see Eliza standing framed in the entrance, and his breath caught at the gorgeous sight. She was dressed in his shirt and trousers, the sleeves and cuffs rolled up and the waist belted tight, her slender feet bare. But she swept into the room like she was wearing a ball gown, her exquisite face set in an icy expression. She glided around the desk and came to stand behind Mark's chair, resting one slim hand on the back.

O'Bannion stared at her, his forgotten cigarette dropping ash on the floor. "Who's the dame?"

"She nursed me back to health last night after I was attacked," Mark said steadily.

"Nice nurse. What's your name, sweetheart?"

Her perfume wafted through the air as she said coldly, "You don't need to know that."

The cop blinked in sudden confusion. "Right. I don't need to know that."

"O'Bannion," Mark said, drawing his attention back to himself. "What is it you and your bosses want me to do? Tell me exactly."

"Stop Duke. Kill this monster. Any way you have to. Just do it quick."

Mark's face spread in a smile. "Then I'll need some extra juice. I want a contract in writing deputizing me as an official consulting detective on this case."

"Fine, you're our official freak."

Mark idly regarded his thumbnail. "I'm getting to be an expensive freak, O'Bannion. sixty a day, plus expenses."

"Are you crazier than usual?"

Eliza moved around the desk toward him. "You'll be happy you paid Mr. Van Ryn's price when you see how well he handles the case, detective." She held out her hand.

O'Bannion took it on reflex. "Who are you again?" he said, his eyes going hazy.

"I'm no one. You never saw me."

"I never saw you," the cop mumbled.

"And you will see to it that Mr. Van Ryn gets everything he wants, the contract, the money, everything."

"Everything."

"Good. Run along now."

O'Bannion pivoted and marched out the door without another word.

Eliza folded her arms and tipped her chin in the air as she watched him go.

Mark grinned at her. "Was that necessary?"

"Perhaps not. But the man annoyed me. The way he spoke to you, he's lucky I didn't make him hop home like a rabbit."

"I can handle O'Bannion." The grin slid off his face. "Anyway, he was right. I failed. I talk a big game, but when it came to saving lives, where was I?"

"You were recovering from torture." She came to sit on the chair across the desk from him. "You'll do no good blaming yourself. Chicago needs you now. You're the only one who can stop Duke."

His eyes glinted at her. "I'm not the only one. You stopped him last night."

"Not for long, it seems." She picked up the newspaper and scanned it, a troubled look on her brow. "Perhaps I . . ."

"What?"

She met his eyes, hers dark and serious. "I had the chance to kill him last night, but I didn't. If I had, all those people would still be alive."

"Nonsense. You couldn't have done it. You're not a killer."

"But I am, Mark. It's what I was born for. Death follows a lamia wherever she goes. That's the way it's always been." Her face was haunted and pale.

"Don't be so tragic, doll face. You aren't your grandmother. And you aren't responsible for this." He waved his hand at the newspaper.

"No more than you are," she shot back.

"Okay, let's agree to blame Duke, shall we? Now I've just got to catch him."

"I can help. You've seen my abilities. I was able to poison Duke before, and as for the monster, I think I may have an advantage there too."

"What do you mean?"

"Last night, before you took us out of the basement, the slime touched me on the ankle, and—"

He shot to his feet. "Are you hurt?"

"No, that's—"

He rounded the desk and knelt by her chair, cursing himself. He hadn't even thought to check her for injuries last night before taking her like a savage. He picked up one slender bare foot and then the other, pulling up her too-long trouser cuffs to look at her legs. The fine pale skin was unmarred. He let out a breath. "You're all right."

"That's what I'm trying to tell you." She crossed her ankles and tucked them primly under her chair. "The slime wasn't attacking me. It was just . . . well, tasting me I suppose. I think it likes my scent."

Mark remembered the night at the Green Mill when he'd first confronted the monster. It had turned away from its intended victim and crawled straight for Eliza. He hadn't considered why at the time. But her notion that the thing was attracted to her perfume made a certain amount of sense.

"Don't you see?" she said. "This is my chance to use my power for good! I'll lure in the slime with my scent, and you'll trap it."

"Out of the question." He stood up. "A man doesn't put his girl in danger."

"*Your girl?*" She rose out of her chair and looked him in the eye. "I am my own woman, Mark. I always have been and I always will be."

"So last night—" His voice roughened. "Last night meant nothing to you?"

She lowered her eyes. "You know it meant everything to me. But it changes nothing."

"You mean you're still planning on leaving?" A pit opened up inside of him and the darkness roared out of it, hungry. He took a step forward. "Are you?"

Her beautiful face, which had been so open and smiling when she was in bed with him, was wearing a remote look that made him want to bellow in frustration. "My only plan now is to stop Duke."

"And what then?" he insisted.

"I always have to leave, Mark! It's the only way to keep people safe. It's the only way to keep *you* safe."

"Nuts to that! You're making excuses! You're afraid of what's between us!"

She didn't answer, her lips pressed together.

Mark got his reactions under control. "I can't stop you from leaving, so if you're going to run away, then run, right now. Go back to the hotel, pack up your things and leave town. It's the only way *you'll* keep safe from *me*."

"What do you mean? Are you a danger to me Mark?"

"Never." He leaned down to her and said, "But I want you, Eliza. So much it makes me crazy. And if you stay, I'm going to have you. I'll be inside you all night, every night. Because you want me, too."

70

She gasped, her knees quaking with a shock of lust at his blunt words. She swayed toward him, and suddenly she was in his arms, his mouth hard on hers. She moaned in surrender, her head going back as she wound her arms around his neck and tangled her lips and tongue with his.

He palmed her bottom through the fabric of her borrowed trousers and lifted her up, sliding his thigh between her legs, pressing it against the hot, needy place between them. She ground against the iron ridge of his thigh to ease the ache, and he growled in approval. Moving toward the desk, he set her on the edge and stepped between her legs, never ceasing his fierce kiss. The buttons of her shirt came undone at his touch and his hands were inside, cupping her breasts, thumbing her nipples.

She cried out in stunned arousal. He was going to take her here, on his desk. It was mad, outrageous. She should stop him, she thought, but instead she recklessly opened her legs wider and fumbled for the buttons of his pants, eager to get her hands on his shaft again. She slipped her hands inside the opening and wrapped her fingers around the thick, curving length. He groaned, his buttocks flexing toward her. She pulled his organ out of his clothing, stroking it, and aimed the tip of him at the pulsing center of her desire, rubbing his hard flesh against it through the thin fabric of her trousers. The rich scent of arousal flooded the air.

He groaned and took her hands off of him, holding them captive. With his other hand he tore open the buttons of her pants. He seized his shaft and drove it into her, seating himself to the root as she gasped in need.

"God." His mouth found hers again and they kissed frantically. He raked his lips down her throat as he wrapped his arms around her waist and bent her backwards, readying her for his thrusts. He kissed her breasts through the gap in her shirt. "This is where I want to be for the rest of my life. I love you, Eliza. I'll always love you. Stay with me. Marry me."

The deep throb of an engine cut through the air. A car was pulling into the house's driveway.

Eliza met Mark's panicked look. "We have to stop," she gasped.

Mark swore in brutal frustration and withdrew from between her thighs. She almost cried out at the loss of him. He gripped the edge of the desk beside her and hung his head, breathing hard, as she slid to the floor on trembling legs and put her clothes to rights with shaking fingers.

His jaw flexing, Mark fastened his trousers over his shaft and pulled the tails of his shirt down. When he was ready they ran through the house to the back door off the kitchen and peered out the window to see the Duesenberg easing up to the garage.

"Frasier," Mark growled. "If I wasn't so relieved to see him, I'd have to kill him." He pushed through the door and stepped outside, Eliza right behind him.

71

Frasier jumped out of the car as they approached. "Thank the Lord!" He bounded toward them and grabbed Mark into a hug, pounding on his back and grinning. "I can't believe it! You're all right!"

Mark returned his grin a little wanly. "Yeah. 'Course I am."

Frasier turned to Eliza. "You did it! You really did. You . . ." His voice trailed off as he took in her borrowed clothes and disastrous hair. Then he looked back and forth at her and Mark, and his face did something strange, like he wanted to grin and frown at once.

She and Mark both flushed. "Why don't we go inside," she said briskly.

"Here." Frasier reached into the car and brought out the valise she had packed yesterday. She'd forgotten she'd left it in the rumble seat last night. "You might want this."

"Yes, thank you," she said stiffly, taking the case. "Please excuse me. I won't be a moment." She didn't dare look at Mark as she turned and marched inside, the folds of her sex still slippery from his lovemaking as she walked.

She climbed the stairs, intending to go to the bathroom to clean up and change her clothes. But at the top of the staircase she paused, looking along the hallway. It was lined with doors to rooms she hadn't had time to explore last night. She still knew so little about the man she had just given herself to. Certainly less than his oldest friend. Perhaps it was time she learned more. Perhaps he had a Bluebeard's chamber, like Duke.

She started opening doors along the hall, to find nothing but rooms full of bare boards and dust. Then she opened a door on a fully furnished bedroom. It was decorated in a light, feminine style, and was neatly kept. Too neatly. Its pretty fabrics were faded by many years, and the air had the dusty scent of emptiness. No one lived here now. She stepped in the room and looked around curiously.

She saw a photograph on the wall showing a lovely young woman in a wedding gown from the turn of the century posed in a chair, her handsome groom standing behind her. Aside from his coloring, the man in the photograph looked exactly like Mark.

These were Mark's parents. The mother who had died when he was born, and the father who had made him suffer for it. And this was his mother's room, preserved for twenty-six years.

She found her hand stealing up to cover a twinge in her heart. She took one last look around at the shrine to the dead, and tiptoed out, shutting the door quietly behind her.

72

Eliza washed quickly and changed into fresh clothes from her valise. Returning downstairs, she followed the sounds of voices to Mark's office. Mark was sitting behind his desk while Frasier paced the room, waving around the newspaper O'Bannion had left as he talked.

"So then I had to drive through a storm to Wisconsin, guided by a blind little boy," Frasier was saying. "The Lord only knows how we got to his aunt's house safely. The lady was so grateful to have him back she gave me a bed for the night. So I got a couple of hours of sleep, came straight here, and found you neck deep in monsters and mayhem!" He brandished the newspaper.

"Just another day on the job."

"Don't give me that," Frasier said roughly. "For a while there I thought they'd killed you."

"I'm fine." Mark looked over at her as she stood in the doorway. "In fact, I feel pretty great, thanks to Miss Karlova." His eyes were twinkling in a way that made her want to throw something.

Instead she strolled over to his desk and leaned a hip

against the corner, trailing her fingers over the place where he'd set her to make love to her. "You're welcome, Mr. Van Ryn," she purred.

Mark shifted in his seat, the twinkle vanishing.

Satisfied, she smiled at Frasier. "I rescued him, as I promised."

Frasier raised an eyebrow. "So you did. Care to fill me in on what happened after I left you last night?"

She told him about her invasion of the laboratory, her battle with Duke and Dr. Smalley, and the escape from the slime monster. Mark stayed silent as she talked.

"And what exactly happened to Duke and his scientist?" Frasier asked.

"When Mark got us out of the basement, the slime was moving toward Duke and Smalley. I heard them scream. That's all I know."

Frasier examined the photograph on the front page of the newspaper. "Duke, at least, survived. How is it possible that he's inside the creature and still alive?"

"Smalley gave him a drug that made the slime act like he was a part of it," Mark said. "Duke was able to touch it without dissolving his flesh."

"So Smalley's potion worked too well," Frasier said. "The slime absorbed him into itself."

"Maybe," Mark said. "Or maybe it's the other way around. The attacks described in the paper weren't random. He was targeting Camonte's gang. Duke must still be in control on some level."

"Will he send his creature after you through the drains?" Frasier asked.

Mark shook his head. "Duke told me that he has to feed the creature the scent of its prey and a specific formula to make it hunt. I think we're safe from that direction. I'm guessing he'll attack the World's Fair tonight instead."

"What makes you think so?" Eliza asked.

"Tonight is opening night. The first lady and the other Washington politicians will be at Soldier Field Stadium giving speeches. Duke is obsessed with the idea of showing off his new weapon to them, especially a man he called 'the general'. And now that city hall has turned against him, he's going to need support from the feds if he wants to stay out of the electric chair."

"Will the Federal Government protect him, after everything he's done?" Frasier asked.

"I don't know. But if they won't give him cover willingly, he'll try to force them. He has no other play. He'll come to the fair tonight, I'm sure of it. And he's shown he'll kill anyone who gets in his way." He steepled his fingers in front of him. "I have to stop him before that happens."

Frasier's forehead creased in thought. "If Duke and Smalley directed the slime creature by feeding it chemical formulas, we could do the same thing. Devise a compound to control it, or kill it."

Eliza cast him a speculative look. "Yes. I've already begun work on a base formula for the slime's chemical markers. We could start with that."

"Can you whip up this potion by tonight?" Mark asked.

Frasier set his jaw. "We'll have to, won't we?"

Mark shook his head, the spark of hope dimming. "Even if we have the time, we have no laboratory."

"We'll use mine," Frasier said immediately.

"No good. Too many people know about you now, Frasier. Duke or the countess might come after us there. We can't even stay here much longer. We need to go somewhere no one will think to look for us."

"I think I have the solution to our problems," Eliza said.

Both men turned surprised looks on her.

"Wait here, please." She left the office and hurried up the stairs to Mark's room, where she had left her valise. Opening it, she took out the letter Mrs. DeForest's lawyer had given her. She sat on the side of Mark's bed and opened the envelope, shaking the flat lump inside it onto her palm. It was the key to the shop, as she had known it would be.

She weighed the slender piece of metal in her hand for a moment, and then slowly took out the letter. She unfolded the sheet of fine paper and turned it to the faint light behind the window curtains.

My dearest Eliza,

If you are reading this letter, then I have Passed On without settling the future with you. My doctor tells me that I haven't much longer, and so you may not return from your travels until after the Event.

I had hoped to turn the shop over to you while I could still be here to help you on your way. Instead, I may need to be content to leave it to you in my Will. I hope you will run it well and carry our art into the future with pride and joy. Remember my dear, you have a precious gift, and you must share it with the world.

Her eyes blurred. There was more written, but she could read no further. She folded the letter with trembling fingers and put it in her pocket. She bowed her head, tears falling freely down her cheeks.

A rich, dark scent wafted around her. "Mark." She stood up and faced the corner of the room where the deepest shadows fell.

He appeared exactly where she knew he'd be. "I'll never be able to sneak up on you, will I?" He had on a wry smile, but his face changed when he saw that she was crying. He strode to her, his eyes wide with concern and maybe a little masculine panic at the sight of female tears. He took out his handkerchief and patted at her cheeks. "Eliza, don't cry! What's wrong? What happened?"

She took the handkerchief away from him and dabbed her eyes. "Nothing happened."

He cupped her shoulders. "Then what is it?"

She looked up into the melting blue of his eyes, and it all came out in a rush. She told him about Mrs. DeForest, the shop, the perfume, and her self-imposed exile that did no good in the end.

By the time her words finally trickled to a stop, his arms were around her, and her cheek was resting on his broad shoulder. His lips brushed her hair. "She sounds like a lovely woman. I'm sorry for your loss."

She lifted her face to his, utterly disarmed. She had never imagined this tender side of him. For a moment, she let herself drift in the warmth of his gaze. But it couldn't last. "My apologies," she said, pushing away from him firmly. "I didn't mean to carry on so. I have something to show you and Frasier. We should go down. He must be wondering where we are."

He blinked down at her, looking dazed. "Frasier. Right." He passed a hand over his hair and gestured her to precede him out the door.

They returned to the office downstairs, where Frasier was waiting with a shade of trouble in his eyes. She held up the key for him and Mark to see. "The answer to our laboratory problem. My former employer Mrs. DeForest left me her *parfumerie*."

"A perfume shop?" Frasier said. "How will that solve anything?"

"One needs a fully functioning chemistry laboratory to make perfume. And that's what the chemical that controls the slime is, essentially, a perfume that appeals specifically to slime molds. Best of all, Duke doesn't know about this place. Not even my grandmother knows. There's even an apartment above the shop we can use as our headquarters until Duke is caught."

"All right," Mark said. "Show us."

73

Frasier waited as Eliza readied her valise and Mark packed a case of his own, and then the three of them piled into the car. Eliza and Frasier both eagerly offered to drive, but Mark insisted on driving his car himself.

They drove up Michigan Avenue and parked on a side street. Eliza led her companions through the hustling crowds along the avenue to the red door, which she opened with her key. Even though it had only been a few days since the shop had closed, it felt as hushed and empty as an ancient temple. She switched on the lights, which helped a bit.

The two men followed her in. They looked around at the shelves of fragrances in their jeweled bottles with identical expressions of bemusement on their faces.

Despite everything, she smiled. "The laboratory space is this way." She led them through the curtained doorway to the back room.

Frasier examined the equipment on worktables along the walls. "It looks like you have the basics here," he said grudgingly.

"The stairs to the apartment are over there." Eliza pointed to a doorway to the side of the room.

Mark took their suitcases up the stairs to the second floor while Frasier poked around the jars of solvents and emulsifiers.

"I've already created a formula we can use as a base," she said to him. "I started work on it the day we came to your laboratory. All the ingredients should be here."

"Then let's get started." Frasier took off his coat and rolled up his sleeves.

Mark came down the stairs from the apartment and stopped short as he saw his friend tying on one of the shop aprons. A line appeared between his brows. "Frasier, you should go home. Take a sick day or two from work until this is over. You've done enough already."

Frasier cast him an impatient glance. "Brother, don't talk crazy. You know you need my help."

Mark shook his head. "It's your neck, you stubborn —" He cut himself short and clapped his friend on the shoulder.

He looked at Eliza. "I'll only be in the way here. I'm going back to the old factory where Duke was keeping the monster. Maybe I'll find some notes on the formula he was using."

"But it's daylight out," Eliza said.

"This can't wait for dark."

"Are you sure you've recovered from your ordeal?" she said.

He grinned at her. "Positive. I had a very therapeutic night."

She blushed. "But—"

"Don't fret, angel. I'll be back in an hour or two." He walked toward the door.

"Mark!"

He turned to face her from the doorway.

"Be careful."

In two long steps, he was across the room and she was in his arms, being savagely kissed. An instant later, she was on her feet again and he was striding out the door.

She stared after him, silent and flushed.

Frasier cleared his throat loudly. "Let's take stock. Neither of us is a biologist. I'm a water engineer and you're a chemist, of sorts. And we have about eight hours and some basic equipment to devise a compound to control a deadly mutated slime creature."

"That's about the shape of it," Eliza said, marshaling her thoughts.

Frasier grinned. "Swell. I always did like a challenge."

She shook her head. "I agree with Mark. You should go home. On top of all the danger from Duke and the mob, it's simply not a good idea for you to spend too much time near me."

"Think I'm going to fall for you like every other man you meet?"

"No," she said steadily, "I think I might make you ill."

"That's a risk I have to take." He started setting out glassware and racks of pipettes. "Besides, the sooner this monster is dealt with, the sooner you can get out of Mark's life."

"Mark doesn't seem to want me out of his life."

"But you were planning on leaving, anyway, weren't you?"

She didn't answer.

Frasier looked directly at her and sighed. "Look, I don't think you're heartless. Why don't you just end it and go? It would be kinder."

"Why don't you let Mark look after himself?" she returned. "You can't protect him from living his life, Frasier."

He set his jaw. "Let's just concentrate on protecting him from this monster."

74

Mark drove back to the factory where he'd been held and parked in view of the front gate. He watched the place for several minutes, but all was quiet. Crime scene tape was stretched across the entrance, but there was no police guard. That was a bad sign. No guard meant there was nothing in there worth guarding.

He got out of his car and walked slowly through the sunlight to the derelict building. The gates were open, and he ducked past the police tape into the small entryway. The main door was off its hinges, lying in the opening. Punched out from the inside by the creature, it looked like. He stepped over the broken door and slipped inside, sighing in relief at the dimness.

The place was in ruins. The power was off, and the molding brick interior was thick with shadows. The floor was puddled with slimy water that clung to his shoes. Every organic substance seemed to have been chewed by the creature as it passed through. Worktables were in splinters, papers were in shreds.

As for the inorganic stuff, looters had taken care of that.

Everything valuable that could be carried away was long gone.

Mark found the stairs to the basement and descended, the metal of the treads slick under his feet. He walked through the basement hallway to the laboratory where he'd been held.

The room looked like a giant wave had crashed through it. He studied the empty tank that had held the slime, the smashed medical equipment and the overturned flood-lights. The air was still noxious with the dank, pungent smell of the monster. He walked a few steps into the room. His shoes splashed through gummy water and crunched on broken glass.

One foot kicked something small and hard that rolled a little. He crouched and picked up the little round object near his foot, examining it. A white ball with a blue iris surrounding a black pupil. Smalley's glass eye. The rest of him had apparently been eaten.

He held the eye up to his own and looked into that blank gaze. "Count yourself lucky the slime got you before I did."

A distant scuff of footsteps echoed through the shadows from the upper level. He stuck the eye in his pocket and jumped to his feet, listening as the sound drew closer. Silently, he slipped back into the cramped hallway.

Pulling shadow around himself, he crept close to the iron stairwell. Two yellow beams from high-powered electric torches cut through the basement shadows from above. He watched them warily. If the light hit him directly, he wouldn't be able to turn full shadow. They'd have him pinned.

A voice with a cultured Southern accent echoed down

the stairs. "You down there! We saw you come in! Identify yourself!"

"You first," he said.

"We're federal agents with the Investigation Bureau, and we're armed!"

"G-Men, huh? What are you fellows doing here?"

"We're investigating a federal crime. Come out with your hands up!"

"Why don't you boys come down here instead, and we'll talk. There's something you might want to see."

"Identify yourself," the voice said again.

"Name's Mark Van Ryn. I'm a private detective consulting for the CPD on this case. I'm going to show you my license," he said, taking out his wallet. He walked to the edge of the stairwell and stuck the license around the corner for the agents to see. A beam of light fell on his hand, leaching his power. He pulled it back. "Come on down. I have something to show you."

There was a terse, whispered conversation. Footsteps sounded on the stairs. Two figures marched down to the hallway, flashlights and Colt revolvers in their hands. They blasted their lights around the narrow space, but Mark snapped into full shadow and dodged back into the darkness, sliding around the light beams.

"Show yourself," the first figure barked. He was a tall, square-faced fellow with round little eyes. The man behind him was shorter and slighter, but had a mean, whippy look to him.

Mark turned solid long enough to say, "Introductions first."

The beams sliced toward his voice, but he had already darted out of the way into deeper shadow.

"I'm Agent Jones," said the bigger guy. "This is my partner, Agent Smith. Come out and we'll talk."

Mark slid his shadow self up a wall and along the ceiling over the men's heads. He slipped down the wall to the floor behind them and turned solid. "What's the Bureau's interest in this case?"

The agents whirled, their flashlights stabbing into the blackness, but he snapped into shadow and dodged the beams again.

"We're investigating Lionel Duke," Agent Jones said. "Dr. Smalley is our source within his organization, but he's missing. If you know his whereabouts, you must tell us."

He turned solid long enough to say, "Smalley's dead."

The agents slid each other quick glances as they raked the corridor walls with their lights. Their guns were still tracking. "Looks like you *do* have information to share," Jones said.

"Sure I do," he said, flickering in and out of shadow. "Put your guns away and I'll share all you want."

They traded another look.

"If I was going to shoot at you I would have already," Mark said.

They holstered their revolvers. Smith, the scrappy one, kept his hand on the butt. "You can come out of hiding, now," he said. Jones had sounded like a gentleman farmer from Virginia, but Smith's accent came from the western deserts.

Mark let himself go solid and stepped toward them.

Two beams of light swooped around to blast in his face.

Mark squinted into the glare, letting them see his empty hands. "Easy with the lights, boys."

The light beams slid down to his chest. Mark studied the men holding the flashlights, a strange sense of familiarity washing over him. Where had he seen these two before?

Jones said, "How do you know Smalley is dead?"

"He was eaten by the monster Smalley and Duke concocted together. The same thing that killed all those people along the river last night. I was here when it happened." He tilted his head. "See, he kidnapped me yesterday, in order to cut me up for science."

Smith gave a quiver of surprise. Smalley hadn't told them about his capture. Interesting.

"This is an incredible story," Jones said, his small round eyes looking troubled. "Do you have any proof?"

"Yeah. The laboratory where I was held. It's back that way." He jerked a thumb over his shoulder. "But maybe you've seen it already."

The two agents exchanged a glance. Jones said, "I think I should show you some evidence we've found about Smalley." He took a thick white envelope out of his inner coat pocket and held it out to Mark. "Take a look at this and tell me what you think."

Jones was standing on Mark's left side, Smith on his right. So when Mark reached across his body to take the envelope with his right hand, he was half-turned away from the other agent.

Out of the corner of his eye, he saw a slight movement. Feral instinct took over. He darted to the side a fraction of an instant before a gunshot blasted the air. Smith had drawn and fired like a gunslinger.

Fiery pain slashed into Mark's hip as he dove out of the flashlight beams and snapped into shadow.

"Where'd he go?" Smith yelled. Sweat flew off his brow as he looked around.

"He turned invisible, like Smalley said," Jones gritted out.

The agents stood back-to-back, raking the basement with their flashlights. Mark slid up the wall to the shadows under the ceiling, cold fury roiling through his being.

He waited for an opening and raced down to the floor, darting in close to the agents. Turning solid, he popped a fist under Smith's ribs. When the man doubled over he met his chin with an uppercut that sent him wheeling to the floor. His flashlight cracked against the concrete and went out.

Jones whirled on him, the flashlight catching him before he could hide in full shadow. The gun roared. He hurled himself at the darkness but another blaze of white-hot pain caught him in the back. Ricochet. He pushed through it into full shadow. He rushed around Jones and materialized at his back. The agent started to spin just as Mark's fist plowed into the side of his jaw. The big man staggered, and Mark slammed him back against the wall and grabbed his gun hand. He dug his fingers into the nerves of the man's wrist until he dropped the gun.

But Jones jacked up his knee and Mark had to twist aside to save his balls. Jones lunged off the wall and clouted the side of Mark's face with the flashlight.

The sting of blood on his tongue got him good and pissed off. He jabbed a combination into the man's face and ribs, sending him stumbling, the flashlight flying out of his hand. Crazy shadows writhed over the walls as the light rolled on the floor. Jones flailed out with massive fists, but Mark dodged one, blocked the other, and uncoiled a round-house to Jones's temple. The big man dropped like a pile of lumber.

Mark stood panting over the fallen men, darkness

licking at his wounds, the spinning flashlight painting him in light and shadow. The agents were both still breathing. He kicked their guns away and knelt by Smith's side to rifle through his pockets. In his wallet was a federal badge. He had nothing else on him except handcuffs and bullets. The same with Jones. The envelope he had used to distract Mark was full of cash.

He tossed their wallets and the money on the floor and stuck the handcuffs in his pockets. Grabbing the men's collars, he dragged them over to the metal staircase. He snapped a handcuff on Jones, threaded the other side around the iron railing, and cuffed Smith. Jones was fast asleep, head lolling, but Smith was groaning and thrashing weakly.

He knelt by Smith and yanked him upright until he was half sprawled against the wall by the stairs. He gave the man's cheeks a couple of brisk slaps to wake him up. "What was all that about, Agent Smith? I have a mind to be offended. As a general rule, I take getting shot at real bad."

"You're a dead man," Smith gasped, the rims of his eyes showing white. "You attacked federal agents."

"I defended myself against a couple of cowards who tried to shoot me in the back."

"Director's orders. You're a danger to the nation. If you can't be captured, you have to be put down. You and Duke both."

"So why didn't you try to arrest me before you tried to kill me?"

"We were going to take you the night we tossed your house, but your gangster friends showed up before Smalley set the trap."

Mark remembered the three men in the Buick he'd seen

the night of the break-in. "You two and Smalley were the ones who trashed my home?" Mark said softly.

"That's right. We read your files and cataloged your possessions. We watched you with your little Russian birdie in the park. We followed you to the Green Mill. We know everything about you, freak. And we're going to get you. Even if you kill us, more will keep coming."

Mark smiled at him, shadows roiling in his eyes, and watched him flinch. "You know, I swore that when I caught you thieving bastards, I'd string you up in place of my heavy bag and take you apart. And so I did. And it was just as much fun as I thought it would be. When you wake up, tell your boss I want to see him." He slammed his fist behind Smith's ear and watched the man slide limply down the wall to the floor.

75

Mark drove like a maniac back to the perfume shop. He'd never been shot before, and he found he didn't much like it. It was doing something funny to him. He felt flushed, itchy under the skin.

He parked on the street and strode into the shop, through the storefront to the laboratory. He found Eliza there adding drops from a beaker into a flask filled with a pinkish fluid.

She looked up at him as he entered the room, her eyes huge behind a pair of goggles. "Mark!" She set down her chemicals and came toward him, taking off her goggles and apron and stripping off her rubber gloves. A relieved smile lit her face.

He had to force himself not to reach for her and drag her to him. He didn't quite trust himself at the moment. "Where's Frasier?" he asked.

"He went to buy some food for us. I'm so glad you're back! Did you find anything?"

"Would you believe I found even more people who want to kill me?" He told her about the agents, the fight in the basement, and the revelation that he was a public enemy, wanted dead or alive.

She listened with growing outrage and distress on her face. "What are you going to do?"

"I'll do my job. I'll catch the killer." He looked at her steadily. "There's something else. The agents have their eyes on you too. They saw us together at the park the other day. Maybe you should lay low, for now. Go back to the Drake and have a tea party with the Mannerings."

She paled, but her back straightened. "I vowed to do my part to help. I'm going to see this through."

"You'd be safer if you stayed out of it," he said roughly.

She lowered her lashes. "Perhaps we'd all be safer if I left Chicago."

He knew she was right. Danger was closing in on them from all quarters. He should send her away, where she would be safe. But he couldn't do it. The seething darkness erupted within him, and he reached for her. "No! God, no, Eliza, don't leave!" He pulled her body to his and folded her in his arms.

After a startled moment, she hugged him back. But then she drew away sharply, looking at her hand. It was streaked with red. Blood from the wound in his back. The dark gray fabric of his suit had hidden the stain. "Mark! What happened?"

"Oh, yeah. They shot me a couple of times. Nothing to worry about. I've had worse." She was looking up at him with wide eyes and soft lips. His sex hardened in a violent rush, the jittery, hot pressure building. Maybe he ought to leave before he did something he'd regret. "I should let you get back to your work," he said, turning to flee.

She darted around him and stopped him with a delicate

hand on his chest. "Let me see your wounds this instant. Come."

She slipped her hand into his and pulled him toward the stairway to the flat above the shop. He followed her helplessly up the stairs and through a door to the lovely, comfortably worn sitting room. A dainty sofa sat facing a pair of chairs, a fine old Oriental rug beneath them.

She stopped him in the middle of the room. "Take off your coat." She reached out and tugged the lapels off his shoulders. He shrugged it off and tossed it onto one of the chairs. The back was soaked with blood around the bullet hole.

"Now your shirt." She plucked at the knot of his tie.

He turned around so that she couldn't see the fierce erection tenting his clothes. With unsteady fingers, he slipped off his tie, and then unbuttoned his shirt, easing the fabric off his shoulders and down his arms, pooling around his waist. He heard a small thump on the carpet at his feet. He looked down behind him and saw the bullet that had glanced off the basement wall and buried itself in his back. His healing flesh had expelled it.

"My God, Mark," Eliza breathed. Her slender fingers fluttered over the healing wound high up between his right shoulder blade and spine. "You could've—"

"I'm fine." He wasn't fine. His blood was pounding, every nerve was sizzling. He was so hard for her, the fabric of his trousers hurt him where it trapped his organ.

"Mark . . ." her hands ran over the waistband of his pants, around to his front to tug at his belt buckle. "Let me see the wound on your hip."

He shut his eyes. He should stop her. But he wanted her touch too much. He tossed his shirt aside and loosened his belt and pants enough to ease them down, the crusted blood on the fabric scraping his skin. The wound was low on his right hip. The bullet hadn't gone in, merely sliced along the surface. It was nearly healed already, wisps of shadow pouring into it to knit the flesh.

She moved around him again to get a better look at it. Again he felt her soft touch on his healing skin.

He couldn't take it one more second. "Eliza. Does this mean you want to finish what we started on my desk this morning?" He shoved his pants down his thighs, freeing his brutal erection.

Her eyes flew up to his, then down his body to his organ, rising only inches from where her fingers brushed his hip. She snatched her hand away. He saw her pulse beating in her throat. Her skin had a peachy blush, her breasts rising and falling as she breathed. Her little pink tongue touched her lips. "We—we shouldn't. It will only make it more difficult."

"Make what more difficult?"

Her lips parted, but she said nothing.

Sudden fury rushed over him. "Saying goodbye you mean? You're planning on leaving after all?"

Still she didn't answer.

"Go then! But don't forget this!" He grabbed her and kissed her, his mouth hard on hers, demanding, punishing.

For an instant, her lips met his fiercely, giving as good as she got. Then she wrenched away. "Stop."

He stopped, fisting his hands at his sides, his breath coming fast. He was crazed for her, but she held him still with a look and a word.

She was a gorgeous wild thing, hair a tangled cloud, eyes deep and wide, lips red from his kiss. He was afraid to move, in case she fled, or scratched him to pieces.

She raised a hand and placed it over his heart.

He groaned at her touch, his cock leaping.

"Don't forget who's the boss." She gave him a sharp push.

He stumbled backwards, his pants tangled around his thighs, and landed on the elegant sofa on his bare ass.

Eliza stood in front of him. She grabbed the hem of her skirt and hiked it up until he could see her garters. Then higher, revealing her tight black panties. She hooked them in her thumbs and pushed them down her legs, over her stockings and pumps. She kicked them aside.

He got off his shoes and socks and shoved off his pants. He was fully nude, and she was fully dressed, except for the sweet, pink flower between her legs, naked and glistening beneath her rucked-up skirt. It was the hottest sight he'd ever imagined.

In one smooth motion she knelt on the couch and threw a slender leg over his thighs, straddling him. She slipped a hand along his chest, her nails raking lightly over his nipple, and pressed her lips to his. As she slid her tongue into his mouth, he felt her slender fingers curl around his shaft, stroking it luxuriantly. She aimed his organ between her thighs, running the tip of him along the lips of her sex like she was kissing him there, even as she kissed his mouth.

He grabbed her hips under her skirt, his fingers pressing into her firm flesh. He held her above his cock, ready to impale her. "I'm going to make this so good for you," he growled between kisses.

She made a frustrated noise and squirmed. "Then do it!"

"Yes, Ma'am." He shoved up inside her in one long, slick stroke. They cried out together, looking into each other's eyes. She clutched his shoulders and pumped her hips, her flesh trembling around him. He cupped his hands under her bottom and lifted her up and then shoved her down his shaft. Then he did it again. And again, and again.

She rolled her hips and flung her head back, arching her white throat. Her soft lips parted, her inky lashes veiled her eyes. She danced above him, gripping and stroking his cock within her as she used him for her pleasure.

It was agonizing bliss. He was going out of his mind. He needed more. He needed it harder and deeper. So did she.

He wrapped his arms around her back and rolled off the little sofa, cushions tumbling around them. He brought her down onto the rug and forced himself to pull out. She made a sound of protest, but he picked her up and turned her over, pulling her hips up until her face was pillowed on her hands and her bottom was up in the air, her glistening sex begging for him.

He fisted himself, desperate to get back inside her. He shoved in hard as she moaned, pushing back against him. He pumped his cock into her, reaching his hand around her body to the front to find that hot little button at the top of her sex. She cried out as he stroked it, her bottom quaking under him. He drew his other hand down the beautiful line of her back and around to her breasts, kneading the high, firm globes beneath the fabric of her dress.

All the while his cock kept up the same driving rhythm, each thrust making her delicate spine arch, until with a helpless noise she shivered, her sheath tight and hot and quivering around his shaft. She wilted, gasping hard. He slowed his thrusts to long, languorous strokes. "You don't want to leave. You need this," he said, twisting his hips into her. "You need me."

She looked over her shoulder at him, tears streaking her face, and with a liquid movement, she turned over. She was so slippery and silky that his cock stayed inside her as she spun around under him. He bit down on a cry of pleasure.

She looked into his eyes. "I want to watch you come now." Her long legs, still clad in stockings and pumps, wrapped around his waist. Her inner muscles tightened along the length of his shaft.

"God, yes," he groaned. He braced himself above her with his arms and got to work.

She milked him as he shoved inside over and over, deep and soft. His seed was hot in his balls, and he wanted to let it go like he wanted to live. But he had to feel her orgasm again first. He kept a relentless rhythm, caressing her inside with every stroke.

Her eyes widened with surprise. Her hands flew to his arms as he held himself over her. "Yes, oh God, yes, like that," she panted. Her velvety sheath tightened on his cock, pulling him deeper inside, her high heels digging into her buttocks like spurs. "Don't—don't stop."

"I'll never stop! I'll love you forever," he gritted out, his hips pumping faster, harder, out of his control.

She clawed his shoulders, arching her back on a deep cry. It was more than he could take.

He came with an animal roar, his seed shooting out of him in a white-hot rush. The world dimmed, lost to him in a storm of pleasure.

76

Mark came to with his full length pressed against Eliza's softness. He stayed there for a long moment, still inside her, their hearts beating together, the blood pulsing where their bodies joined. He eased out and half-fell, half-rolled off her onto his back.

They lay side-by-side on the rug, panting. "I love our fights," Mark said when he could speak again.

"Who won?"

"I did, of course."

She grabbed a couch cushion and hit him with it. "*Dubi-ina!*" Getting to her feet, she snatched up her discarded panties and stormed off to the bathroom.

He stuck the cushion behind his head, crossed his arms over his chest, and stared up at the ceiling, thinking.

In reality, of course, she had won, and he had lost this war. Conquered and enslaved, that was him. Plenty of monsters and wizards had tried it, but only she had done it. His heart was in her hands and she could crush it any time the mood struck her.

So far, she had shown mercy. She had saved him from

Smalley and Duke. She had given him the sexual experience of his most fevered dreams. And she had anchored him and pulled him back into the real world when the darkness almost had him for good.

But if she left him, the next time the current of shadow running through his body became too much for him to handle, he might not find his way back to the real world. He might not want to.

And if he let anything happen to her, if she got hurt because of him . . .

A yawning pit of darkness opened up inside him, chewing at the edges of his mind. The shadows shifted around him, ready to tear him into nothingness.

Now he knew how his father must have felt, every single day of his life.

With an effort of will, he forced the darkness back into the marrow of his bones. He had to get his head on straight before he went up against Duke and the creature tonight or he wouldn't live long enough to worry about his woman problems.

Rolling to his feet, he walked naked to his suitcase standing against the wall and threw on another gray suit and tie. He gathered up his old clothes and rifled through the pockets for his wallet, keys, and handkerchief. His fingers brushed an unfamiliar round lump in his trouser pocket. Smalley's glass eye. He took it out and clamped it in his fist.

From downstairs in the perfumery he heard Frasier's voice, calling, "Hello? Eliza? Mark?"

"Up here," Mark called back. He left the flat and thumped downstairs, running his hand over his hair to get it looking respectable.

Frasier was standing in the middle of the workshop, a

delicatessen bag in his hand. "Mark! You're back. You look flushed. What happened at the factory? Did you find anything?"

"Yeah, a couple of G-men. They shot me in the back, but I'm okay. Nothing to worry about."

Frasier almost dropped the bag of food. "Did you say they shot you? Are you hurt? Let me see!"

"I told you, I'm fine. Eliza already took a look at it."

"She did, did she? And where is Miss Karlova?"

77

Eliza was hiding in the bathroom, looking into her own eyes in the vanity mirror. *What kind of person are you? Are you a villain, a coward?*

A coward, surely. She didn't even have the courage to go back out there and face Mark, let alone promise him what he wanted. She had tidied herself up, but now she was stalling, finger-curling her hair and applying lipstick. As she smoothed her clothing, she felt the crinkle of paper in her pocket. Mrs. DeForest's letter. She hadn't finished reading it. She drew it out and unfolded it, picking up where she had left off.

Eliza, though you have never spoken of them, I know that you have fears and troubles to bear. But I also know that you have a good heart. Follow it, and it will lead you right. That is what I did, and it led me to my dear Albert, and to you. My only regret is that we had so little time together.

If I had ever had a daughter, I would have wanted her to be like you. Bless you, my dear.

Yours Always,
Gwendolyn DeForest

She hastily put the letter away again before the tears had a chance to start. Follow her heart? Did she dare risk it? And did she dare risk the man she . . . cared for?

A rumble of voices came from downstairs. She sniffed the air. Books and chemicals. Frasier had returned. She checked herself in the mirror one last time. Her face was composed enough, except for a slight rosiness to her cheeks. Not at all the expression of a woman who had just made wanton love on the floor. She left the bathroom and walked sedately downstairs to the laboratory.

"And where is Miss Karlova?" she heard Frasier say.

"Hello Frasier," she said, stepping through the door.

Frasier regarded her for a long moment. He didn't raise his eyebrow, but she could tell he wanted to.

She lifted her chin and returned his stare, though her cheeks were suddenly blazing. "We were just discussing what Mark found in the laboratory where he was held."

Mark's eyes were twinkling again. "Right you are, Miss Karlova." But he turned serious as he told Frasier about his visit to the old factory.

When he finished, Frasier said, "You didn't find any notes on the formula they used to control the slime mold?"

"Nothing. Either the agents took the files already, or the monster ate them. Me, I'm betting on the monster. It ate everything else organic in the building including. . ." He opened his fist to show the glass eye gleaming on his palm. "Our friend Dr. Smalley." He set the eye on the workbench and smiled bleakly down into its blank gaze.

"Good Lord," Frasier said, his face ashen.

"Good riddance." Shadows swirled behind Mark's eyes and curled off his skin. "He killed my mother, and Stevie's mother, and who knows how many other women. Experimenting on them to make monsters. Like me."

Eliza crossed the room and laid her hand on his arm. "Smalley was the monster, not you. And he got what he deserved."

"Yeah, eaten by his own creation. An ironic death, the very best kind." After a long moment, the darkness in his gaze quieted. He took a deep breath and let it out, turning his back on the glass eyeball. "What's the progress on your formula?"

After eying him critically for a moment, Frasier said, "We've analyzed the chemical makeup of the slime fragments in the water sample you gave me, and we've developed a synthetic secretion to trigger its behavior."

"We don't want it triggered, we want it killed," Mark said.

"That's the ingenious part," Frasier said. "If we get this formula right, it will cause the slime to kill itself. We're trying to mimic a chemical slime molds secrete when they're moving to the end of their life cycle."

"Come again?"

"Slime molds have three distinct life stages," Frasier lectured. "First, they live as individual cells dispersed in their environment. Second, the cells conglomerate to form an organism that can hunt around for food. Then finally, they climb to the highest point they can reach, form a fruiting body, and die. Each of these stages is triggered by chemical signals. Right now, Duke's slime monster is in stage two, the feeding stage. If Eliza and I can get our formula right, we can force the slime to switch from feeding to reproduction, the end of its life cycle."

"Will the formula be finished by nightfall?"

"It'll have to be, won't it?" Eliza said.

78

They wolfed down the sandwiches from the delicatessen, and Eliza and Frasier got back to work. Mark went upstairs to the flat to make a telephone call to his police contact.

As Eliza heated a flask, she heard Mark's footsteps pacing above her. His muffled voice grew clear for a moment. "Yes, O'Bannion, I'm sure he'll be at the fair tonight, so the CPD has to be there too. The fair security won't be enough." His pacing resumed and his words became indistinguishable again.

She resolutely focused on her work. She and Frasier sampled and tested and refined and distilled and separated. Acrid and sweet smells filled the air, mingling and reacting and blending.

Mark came back downstairs when he finished his call, but he stayed out of their way, drifting silently through the shadows at the edges of the room. She always knew where he was by his scent, but she tried to ignore him. She had to finish the work before nightfall. His life was in the balance, and the lives of countless others. She refused to be distracted.

When the shadows on the street outside started deepening into twilight, she set a jar full of a pale pinkish liquid on the counter. "Finished."

Mark came out of the shadows and looked at it doubtfully. "This is all you have?"

"All we could make with the raw materials we had to work with," Frasier said. "It will have to be enough."

"Besides," Eliza said, "it's an extremely potent concentrate. Go on, smell it."

He opened the lid and raised the jar to his nose. The odor she and Frasier had concocted poured into the air, animal musk and vegetable growth, a rich soup of life twisted through with a hint of metal and acid. Mark jerked his head away from the jar, eyes watering. "Yeah, potent." He refastened the lid. "You're sure this chemical will trick the thing into ending its life?"

"It should. But we won't know for certain until we test it," Eliza said.

"There's one other problem," Frasier said. "We need a method to deliver the formula to the creature. An aspirator, perhaps, or a pneumatic gun—"

Mark shook his head, tucking the jar into his coat pocket. "No time. Don't worry Frasier, I'll figure out a way to give the thing its medicine. At least now I have a weapon, thanks to you, brother." He reached out and clasped Frasier's shoulder. "Thank you for everything you've done for me."

Frasier's eyes widened, and then turned suspicious. "Why does it sound like you're saying goodbye?"

"It's sunset. Duke and his monster will come out to play any minute now. Time for me to go."

"You mean time for *us* to go," Eliza said. "We're in this fight together!"

Mark kept his face turned away from her. "You've done your part, angel. You can leave Chicago with a clear conscience. I'll let you know how your potion turned out. In person, I hope, or else in my obituary." He strode out of the laboratory into the dim shop beyond.

Eliza ran after him, Frasier right behind her. "Mark!"

He stopped.

"You're not facing Duke alone!"

He turned slowly to look at her, his face a white glimmer amid the shadows. There was a desperate intensity in his eyes, and implacable will in the set of his jaw. He'd never looked more beautiful.

She ran to him, and he caught her in his arms, crushing her to him. His mouth came down on hers with a ravenous kiss.

She clutched his shoulders and kissed him back with everything she had. All her need for him, all her desire, all the feelings she couldn't tell him in her lips, her fingers, her body molding against his.

Then he broke the kiss, pulling back sharply and looking into her eyes. "I love you, Eliza. I can't let Duke get near you again. You have to live. It doesn't matter what happens to me, but *you live*. Go have that future you wanted."

"What makes you think I want a future without you in it!" She framed his face in her bare hands. "I'm ordering you to take me with you!" She poured her power through her fingertips into his skin, a reckless attempt to enthrall him.

For an instant she thought she had him at last. His eyes closed, and he turned his head, pressing his lips against her palm. Then his lashes lifted, and she felt him grin. "Not a chance, boss." Shadows swirled around her, and he vanished. Her arms held nothing but emptiness.

His rich scent lingered for a moment, and then it too was gone.

"Bless it, Mark!" Frasier said.

Eliza whirled on him. "We're going after him."

"Of course we are." Frasier was already putting on his hat and coat. "Mark has the car key. We'll have to take the L."

They left the shop and hurried through the deepening twilight to the Wabash Avenue platform, where they climbed the stairs and caught the train. The cars were packed to the roofs with people hanging onto the straps as the cars jostled and swayed down the tracks. It was all Eliza could do to keep her power under control and not poison the other riders. She found herself leaning forward, willing the train to go faster. Frasier hunched into himself next to her, quiet and stoic.

"I was losing him," Frasier said suddenly.

She glanced at him, uncertain.

"Every time I saw him, he looked fainter. Insubstantial. Like he was fading away in front of my eyes. I was scared that he would just vanish one day, and I'd never see him again. I tried everything I could think of to keep him interested in living. But nothing touched him. Not until you." Frasier turned his head, his eyes meeting hers. "I hope you know what you're doing."

She hoped so too. "I got him back before. I'll get him back again."

Frasier looked away, his jaw flexing.

Buildings flew past the train's scratched windows. The electric glow lighting up the eastern sky grew brighter as they approached the lakeshore. Searchlights sliced across the night, white cones emanating from Soldier Field. They were nearly there.

The train screeched to a halt at the Roosevelt Road stop. Eliza and Frasier pushed out of the car and joined the flow of people crossing the footbridges over Lake Shore Drive, funneling toward the fair's main entrance.

The white facades of the Shedd Aquarium and the Adler Planetarium hulked grandly ahead and to the left, and the Field Museum and Soldier Field Stadium loomed on the right. Between them was the covered entrance to the fairground. Beyond, spreading around the lagoon separating the main shore from Northerly Island, was the Century of Progress.

Buildings in a riot of futuristic shapes and eye-searing colors blazed with light against the windy darkness. The steel struts of the Skyride towers soared hundreds of feet above her head. Past the fair the lake swept into the black distance.

She and Frasier filed up to one of the ticket booths around the circle of blue-and-red monoliths that made up the main gate. Frasier took out a dollar and pushed it over to the man behind the counter. "Two tickets please."

The ticket man gave Frasier a single, disgusted glance, and Eliza an even more disgusted one. "Colored day is next week."

"Sell him a ticket," Eliza snapped. She waved her hand, sending poison through the air to the man.

His eyes glazed over, and he mechanically tore off a ticket and held it out to Frasier. But all around, white faces were turning toward them, staring. A low hiss rippled through the crowd around the ticket booths, the stench of aggression rising. The hair on Eliza's nape stirred. Her scent roiled the air, poison thrilling in her fingertips. But there were too many people, too many of them women. She couldn't possibly control them all if they turned into a mob.

Frasier felt the charge in the air too. He backed away from her, through the thicket of hostile stares, his face set. "Go. Help Mark. I'll meet you back at the house."

It galled her, but she nodded to him as he disappeared into the crowd. She snatched the ticket out of the man's hand and ran for the turnstiles.

79

Mark had to make one stop before the fair. In shadow he raced through the city to the classical limestone hulk of the Art Institute. He slipped inside through a ventilation duct on the roof and wound through the dark corridors to the Medieval wing. Halfway along a gallery full of gleaming weapons and armor, he found what he was looking for. He slipped through the keyhole of a locked glass cabinet to snatch up a two-handed broadsword and take it into shadow. In the middle of the marble gallery, he turned solid and held up his prize.

The rippling pattern of fine Spanish steel glimmered along the blade. He planted his feet and took an experimental swing, slicing through the air. *Yeah, this ought to work better than a barstool.* He tucked the sword under his coat.

A picture of a bloody saint looked on in disapproval.

"Not stealing, just borrowing," he assured the saint, and snapped into shadow. He left the museum and sped through Grant Park to the fairgrounds.

As he approached Soldier Field Stadium, the air above it

burst into light. Arc lights glittered along the top like a crown and searchlights stabbed white fingers into the sky. The first light of the star Arcturus had tripped a sensor, signaling that opening night of the fair had officially begun. Over the roar of the crowd he heard a voice droning from the loudspeakers. One of the Washington politicos, making a speech.

He slipped over the fence near Soldier Field and entered the fairgrounds, moving through the crowds in full shadow. He passed the western tower of the Skyride rising next to the stadium like a gigantic tree of steel struts. Rocket car cables stretched from it across the lagoon to its twin tower on Northerly Island.

The fair closed around him, a dream city come to life. Blue, red, white, silver and black monoliths lined in neon tubes and glittering with arc lights towered above him. The streets roared and heaved with humanity. Light splashed and flowed over the people and around the buildings, draining his power. He was just barely able to keep in full shadow.

Invisible, he wove through the chattering crowd. He passed towering dinosaurs, King Kong, and the president's face grinning down from a two-story tall Time Magazine cover. He slipped through the pavilions and peep shows and freak shows, the Streets of Paris, Darkest Africa, China and Mexico, looking and listening for any sign that Duke was here. But the only screams of terror he heard were coming from the dragon-shaped roller coaster on the midway.

Thousands of faces passed him by, old, young, gaping with wonder and pretending to be bored, each one painted with light and darkness, each one there and then vanished into the ocean of people. Each one completely ignorant of the danger lurking somewhere just outside the glow of electric lights.

But Mark could feel it, a vast, wet, cold presence out there in the dark. He even imagined he caught a ghostly smell of it under the motor oil and popcorn. Mushrooms and blood.

He returned to the main boulevard, a wide street lined with slanted silver flagpoles, long red banners furling from their tips. At the end of the street the Hall of Science rose up like a palace of the future, white pilasters along a curving wall of cobalt blue.

Mark reached the midpoint of the road, where the curve of the lagoon shore brought the water close to the street. O'Bannion was waiting to meet him on the embankment, as they had agreed on the telephone earlier. He was dressed in his blue police uniform, including gun, nightstick, and cigarette dangling from his lip.

Mark turned solid and walked out of the shadow to stand next to the cop. "Evening, O'Bannion."

O'Bannion flinched, but covered it with a sneer. "Where you been, visiting your family at the freak show?" he said, but he was too nervy to put any real venom into it. He did a double take at the broadsword poking out from under Mark's coat. "What the hell have you got that for?"

"This?" Mark brought out the sword and held it with the point low. The razor edge glinted in the electric lights. "This is for chopping up the monster. Guns are worthless against it. I can slow it down long enough for you and your men to get the people away. That'll be your job tonight. Leave Duke and his creature to me."

"You sure he's coming here? He'd have to be crazy," the cop said, cigarette jittering.

"He *is* crazy, and he's desperate. He'll come. You and your boys be ready."

O'Bannion muttered something foul and climbed back up to the road. Mark stayed and looked across the rippling black expanse of the lagoon. "Where are you?" he whispered. The scene was deceptively peaceful, the fair lights sparkling off of the black water, pontoon boats and the visiting ship the *City of New York* ruffling the low waves. On the shore across from him the Federal Pavilion and the agricultural complex rose in geometric towers above the milling people.

But one figure wasn't moving. It stood alone on the shore across the lagoon from him, facing him, legs spread, head bent as if in thought. It was too far away to see any details, but his hackles raised. He knew who it was.

"Duke!" he roared. He lifted the sword, the electric lights glinting off the blade.

80

The figure on the opposite shore stepped directly out onto the water, as calmly as if he were stepping out onto a sidewalk. The water rippled under his feet like a membrane as he started strolling across the lagoon toward Mark. His pace was slow, but something underneath the water was carrying him forward as if he were on a conveyer belt. Soon he was standing on the rippling surface of the water just a few yards off shore in a relaxed posture, faint amusement in the tilt of his head.

It was Duke all right. But every inch of him was coated in viscous greenish fluid. Streams of slime writhed over him, separating and flowing together in an ever-moving river.

Beneath the slime, his hair was plastered to his head in strands. His white suit, the same one he had worn yesterday at the garden party, clung to his powerful body in wet folds. His eyes were wide and unblinking, even as the fingers of ooze slithered across them.

His lips were ruined, raw and blistered from Eliza's poisoned kiss. Bubbles popped at the corners of his mouth as he smiled. "Young Van Ryn, once again inviting yourself to a party." His voice crackled wetly, as if even his lungs were coated in slime.

"My God," Mark breathed.

Duke raised a brow, and slime crawled across his forehead. "Yes. A god indeed. We have become a perfect being. Smalley's injections worked even better than he knew. He put the monster inside the man and the man inside the monster. We are one."

Mark heard a scuffle on the avenue behind him, and the first uneasy murmurs of the crowd. The cops were getting into position. Keeping Duke's attention on him, Mark said, "You need help, Lionel. Give yourself up peacefully. It's your only chance. Maybe we can find a doctor who can fix this."

"Fix perfection? Don't be a fool. We are here to make the government understand that they need us. The nation needs us!"

"The government doesn't need you! They want you put down!"

Duke's blackened mouth opened, and a horrible wet hacking noise came out. He was laughing, Mark realized. "Who'll be the one to do it? You, you useless gimp? We're going to enjoy eating you!" Slime gleamed over his teeth.

He pointed the sword at Duke's heart. "Don't do this! Think of your son! Do you want to make him an orphan?"

"Steven . . ." Slime shivered over Duke's face. "We are beyond unworthy sentiment. What is one life when we hold the fate of millions in our grasp? We are the greatest weapon of the age, the Super-man! Now all will see our power!"

The lagoon behind him erupted in a tower of greenish water fifty feet in the air, the surface rippling like the skin of an animal. It was the slime, a thousand times bigger than before.

Duke laughed over the slurping roar of the monster and the screams of the crowd. "Are we not magnificent? We have joined with the lost part of ourselves in the lake. We are one!" Tentacles shot out of the mountain of poisonous greenish jelly, writhing in the air and creeping over the bank, sweeping for prey.

Panicked noise tore through the crowd on the boulevard behind him as people stampeded away from the lagoon.

A line of cops appeared along the side of the road. Mark snapped into shadow as a fusillade of gunfire destroyed the air. Duke laughed, spreading his arms, and a green wave swept over him. The hail of bullets sank harmlessly into a wall of ooze.

Mark turned solid long enough to bellow, "O'Bannion, get the people out!" He let his power rip through him and raced to a tentacle whipping toward an elderly couple, his sword raised, turning solid to slash through the deadly mass. The tentacle collapsed in a pile of jelly that instantly started oozing back to the main body of the creature.

Mark was already moving fast through the dark to another rope of slime lashing toward a young woman. He sliced it off and sped on to a boy who had fallen in the crowd. He scooped him up and dumped him into the arms of his terrified mother as he spun to slash off another acid green tongue. He dashed right and cut through another. Dashed left, another strike.

He got to a tentacle too late. It tore out a policeman's throat an instant before his sword sliced through it. He darted onward, pulling a screaming, bleeding man out of a coil of slime. He shoved him on and spun to cut through

426

another striking whip of ooze, and another, and another. The world became nothing but the blur of shadow, the slither of the monster and the swing of his blade. It was no good. He was being pushed back, step by step. Duke was walking up the embankment and the slime was crawling along with him up toward the flag-lined street, tentacles reaching for human flesh.

He was headed for Soldier Field Stadium, Mark realized, where the first lady and her entourage were speaking and thousands of people were cooped up together. A killing field.

He planted himself in the middle of the boulevard between the beast and its prey. The giant creature engulfed the line of flagpoles, red pennants and all, and slithered onto the road. Cries of the injured and his own harsh breathing echoed down the street as Duke and the slime came on, inexorable.

Mark could see Duke's shape within the slime's massive bulk. He had to get to him somehow. "Duke! Face me, you coward!"

Crackling laughter and a whip of deadly slime was his only answer.

He dodged the tentacle, but he'd be damned if he retreated farther. Only one option left. He took out the jar of Eliza's chemical and opened it, unleashing the stench of savage blood and twisted growth. But overlaying the smell was a fragrance as darkly sweet as a night flower.

He raised his arm and dumped the jar over his head, letting the thick fluid run down his face, back and shoulders. *He* would be the delivery system for the potion. If the monster wanted to eat him, it would have to eat its medicine too.

He tossed the jar aside and raised the sword. With a

roar he charged through the thrashing arms of slime to the towering main blob and sank his blade into its flank, trying to hack his way through to Duke. Tongues of the slime instantly wrapped around him, licking at his skin, tracing over the drops of the poison he had poured over himself, but not harming him. Not yet.

The thick jelly oozed back into the rifts he'd made, enveloping the sword and wrenching it out of his hands. He let it go and plunged forward into the slime, launching himself at the man inside the monster.

The slime over Duke's face writhed back. He grinned, ropes of ichor stretching between his teeth. "What is this?" His tongue came out, snaking through the ooze on his lips. "Your taste, Mark. We've tasted it before. It is *her* scent. The female. We want her, and we will have her, for she is delicious."

Mark howled in rage and closed with his enemy as the slime enveloped him. He tried to muscle punches through the thick jelly, landing a jab to Duke's temple and another to his chin, but the viscous ooze stole the force of his blows.

Duke shook them off and lunged to coil his arms around Mark's body, jerking him up off his feet. Mark pounded on his head and back, but he had no leverage.

Duke's arms cinched tighter and tighter, crushing Mark's ribs in an inhumanly strong grip. The slime finished chewing through the potion covering him and started on his flesh. Hideous pain seared his skin, his eyes, his mouth, eating him alive. No breath to even scream. He was seconds from death.

One last chance. He opened his entire self to the darkness beyond the puny electric lights, beyond the moon, between the stars, and let the power storm through him. As the black wind tore his body to shreds, he clamped his arms around Duke with all his strength and took him into the shadow.

Howling darkness blasted around him and through him, wanting him, ripping at him. He couldn't hold on to Duke. He could barely hold on to himself.

A soundless scream of insane rage shuddered through the darkness as it tore Duke's essence away from him, a noise that lasted forever, fading infinitely far into the void.

Panic seized him as he realized he had nothing solid to ground him. Duke had lifted him off the earth, and now he was lost in the dark. He clawed through the shadows for a hold on the physical world as torrents of shadow ripped at his essence, peeling it away into nothing.

Come to me, the darkness whispered to him, the music of its voice slicing him to pieces. *Leave the pain. Leave the sorrow, the guilt, the fear. Leave them all and come to me.*

A thread of familiar scent found him. "Mark!" A familiar voice pierced the shadows. He clung to reality with the very last shreds of his will, and through the roiling dark, he saw *her.*

81

She was fighting her way through the terrified mob running from the battle when she saw the two men inside the translucent mass of the creature grapple and vanish. "Mark!" she screamed.

Without Duke's control, the heaving mountain of slime thrashed its tentacles randomly, no longer aiming for the fleeing people. It had stopped in the middle of the flag-lined avenue, its greenish surface shimmering uneasily.

The last of the crowd fled past her, but Mark was still here in the shadows somewhere. He had to be. She smelled him under the stink of the monster. "Mark, where are you?" Her voice shredded in her throat.

The slime stilled. Its tendrils thinned, waving delicately around, as if tasting the air. A tremor rippled through the vast bulk of the creature. With a loud slurping noise, it sent two waves of slime shooting out to either side of her, encircling her.

Eliza spun, heart hammering, and tried to run. Too late. She was surrounded by a roiling wall of slime.

The main mass of the creature rose over her in a huge, cresting wave of acid colored jelly. Inside the quivering blob she could see millions of tiny dots swarming, aggregating together. The nuclei of the individual cells that made up the slime mold, she realized with a shock. The dots bunched together to form a ball at about the same size and height as her head, floating inside the wall of liquid looming over her. She had the horrific notion that the thing was a gigantic eye, looking at her from within the ooze.

Helpless terror held her perfectly still as she and the creature regarded each other. And then the voice in her mind spoke once more, sounding like Mrs. DeForest, and the countess, and every other poison lady who had survived throughout the ages. *Use your gift. Wield your power. Tame the beast if you want to live.*

Power rose up within her. Poison sizzled on her skin. "You don't want to eat me," she whispered. "You don't want to eat anything. You're not hungry anymore." She raised her arms to the monster, flooding it with every particle of her scent.

Tendrils of slime slid out of the main mass from all sides, writhing toward her. A hundred wet tongues started licking her, slithering delicately up her arms and legs, crawling over her body, searching, tasting. She swallowed a scream. If this was the end, by God, she would face it with pride. She had no regrets. Except one. In her mind she saw an angel's face, icy eyes melting warm for her. *I wish I told Mark I loved him.*

She held the thought of Mark to her as an endless moment spooled out between her and the monster. Then the wave of slime crashed down on her, sweeping her away.

Her vision went black, only base survival instinct

keeping her conscious. She thrashed in an ocean of cold jelly, mindless with panic, gagging on the stench of mushrooms and blood. Every time she thrust an arm or leg free the slime oozed back over it. She got her head out for a gasp of air and froze, afraid than any movement would send her under again.

Shapes and lights tumbled past in a blur. The creature was crawling across the fairground, she realized, the flood of slime carrying her around the buildings and over the pathways, headed straight for the western Skyride tower.

Over the slurping, sucking noise of the monster she heard terrified screams as people ran for safety.

The steel lattice of the tower loomed over her. The creature sent long tentacles slithering upward, streams of thick jelly crawling straight up the steel beams, separating and flowing together again as they climbed the tower. One thick coil of slime still enveloped her body, sweeping her along as it crept up the metal struts. Within minutes the thing was climbing onto the observation deck at the top. She was six hundred feet in the air, looking down on the swarming dots of people below, only a membrane of slime between her and a fall to her death.

The creature gathered itself into a blob, the main mass covering the roof while tentacles flowed down over the observation deck, coiling around the steel beams. It stilled for a long, frozen moment, and then it started changing. The substance of it started shrinking, turning hard and rubbery.

Eliza looked up frantically and saw it lengthening into a tall stalk of greenish matter high above her. Slime flowed off of her body, clinging to the metal girders and forming a slick shell. Expelled water cascaded down over her.

Suddenly, she had no support. She clawed for a handhold on the slippery surface of the creature, but her fingers slid off the hardening bulk. In a torrent of water she tumbled down the side of the monster's body and over the observation deck into the air, a scream tearing from her throat as she plunged into nothing.

82

Mark saw her fall from the creature's grip, her body plummeting through space, her scream echoing through the night. No time to think. He launched himself through the shadow, felt her within his reach, and snatched her into the dark.

He held her shadow being to him with all his might as the black void raged around them. He'd saved her, but now the darkness had them both. Terror, anguish sliced through him, shredding his essence into nothing. *Lost. I'm sorry.*

A scent as sweet as the rarest flower and pure as the hottest flame wove through the dark. *We'll never be lost as long as we're together.* There was a tug on his being, like a hand on golden chains binding him. Eliza was pulling him, forging through the shadows and taking him along with her to some destination only she could sense.

He surrendered, following her wherever she might go. He would follow her anywhere, always. They moved through infinite space and endless time, together.

His shadow self brushed against solid ground. In an instant, the black storm eddied, the darkness parted, and the world snapped into focus around him. Eliza had smelled the solid earth and guided them back to reality.

They were at the base of the Skyride tower, surrounded by sodden debris and injured and dazed people tumbled about by the flood of slime. Thousands of gawkers were pouring out of Soldier Field to see what the commotion was about, only to stop and stare upward in bewilderment. Floodlights painted light across the alien creature transforming on top of the steel tower.

But even the most powerful electric lights weren't enough to hold back the night. The howling darkness was rising again, the black wind clawing at his shadow self, trying to wrench him away from Eliza. His grip on her, on the earth, was slipping. He had to take her out of the shadow, now. But when he came back into the physical world, he would face his terrible wounds.

Nuts. This is going to hurt.

With the last scrap of his strength he pulled them both out of the darkness. He landed hard in the real world, every nerve in his body screaming with agony. He sprawled on his back on the grass, a breath from unconsciousness.

His clothing was in shreds, the skin beneath it eaten away in raw patches. His lungs were too damaged even to scream in pain.

He heard the rippling noise of the crowd, panicked, relieved, and confused. Sirens rose in a shattering wail. Roving searchlights blasted him.

A slender shadow fell over him. A voice was sobbing. "Mark, you saved me!" He dragged his ruined eyes open. A pale, beautiful face amid a halo of light.

Eliza. His last thought would be of her.

83

"The poor man. He can't survive."

"It's amazing he's not dead already."

"Such a shame. He was so very brave, did you hear? He fought that monster all by himself! With a *sword*!"

"Landsakes."

Two women talking. Hands cutting away the shreds of his clothing and wrapping him from head to foot in bandages, like a mummy. Bright light blazed down on him, searing him through the gauze.

The agony of his damaged body was as vast as an ocean, but somehow distant. He couldn't speak or move, not even his eyelids. They must have shot him up with a truckload of morphine.

A rattle of a door. A divine fragrance. "Turn off the lights!" *Eliza.*

"Now listen here, young woman, you can't come in here—"

"Please, he's my husband! He's photosensitive! You must turn off the lights or—or you'll hurt his eyes!"

"Dearie," the other nurse said gently, "He won't be opening his eyes again."

"Don't you dare say that!"

"Now, you've got to be practical," the first nurse said.

"Then let me say goodbye to my husband alone!"

"All right dearie. There's nothing more we can do for the poor lamb."

"Yes, and we have other patients to look after. A bad business today was. Bad business," the first nurse said. He heard the sturdy shoes of the two women walking away, and a door closing. The blazing light over his bed clicked off and blessed darkness enfolded him. He still couldn't move, couldn't feel or see. But he could smell Eliza's fragrance, covering him like balm.

And he could hear the tears in her voice. "M-Mark, you can't save me and then expect me to l-live without you. You have to heal, d'you hear me?"

He felt something beyond the pain. Her hand, resting as light as a cloud over his heart. "Mark, please. Please. Come back to me."

He took a rattling breath, drawing in that lovely fragrance. The healing shadow poured through him, knitting his abused flesh together again. "Eliza," he groaned, his throat raw. He pawed at the bandages over his face

"Mark! I'll do it!" Slender fingers plucked at the gauze. When it came off, he blinked open his eyes to look up into her beautiful, tear-streaked face. "This has to s-stop!" she said. "Every time I l-let you out of my sight, you nearly get yourself killed—"

He grasped her head in his mummy-wrapped hands and pulled her down for a kiss.

She gasped in surprise, but clutched him, half-lying on

his chest. Her softness caressed his healing flesh as her lips moved over his.

"Then never let me out of your sight again," he said between kisses. "I was a fool to leave you behind. Forgive me."

She sobbed and kissed him with such heat he nearly passed out again. But she pulled back all too soon. "Mark, you have to let yourself heal," she said breathlessly. "You almost d-died—"

"Don't get mushy on me now, angel face." He wiped a tear off her cheek with his bandaged thumb. "Beat me and abuse me. You know I'm strong enough to take it."

"Oh, you . . . *durak*!"

"That's more like it. Now, kiss me, *wife*."

She gave him a watery look of dignity. "It was all I could think to say to get rid of the nurses."

"No more excuses." He brought her lips to his again, but froze at a scuffle behind the door.

"You can't go in there!" a nurse's voice said outside the room. "Let the poor man die in peace!"

"That bastard ain't going to die. He'll live just to keep pissing me off." Eliza scrambled upright as the door snapped open and Detective O'Bannion stomped into the room. "You call that taking care of a problem?" he bawled at Mark.

"Good to see you're alive too." Mark lifted his head and took his first look around the room. They were in a clapboard cubicle set up with hospital gear. "Where are we?"

"The fair's emergency medical building. Along with about fifty others who got caught in the attack," O'Bannion said.

"How many dead?"

"Seven. Two cops and five civilians."

Mark let his head fall back on the pillow and shut his eyes. "Damn."

"It would have been much worse if not for you," Eliza said. "You're a hero, Mark."

He was no more a hero than he was a gentleman. But he grasped her hand and held it over his heart, and felt a little better.

"What happened to Duke?" O'Bannion asked.

"Duke is dead. Or as good as."

"What do you mean? Where's the body?"

"No body." He opened his eyes and looked straight at the cop. "I took him into the shadow and left him there."

O'Bannion stared at him, his throat clicking as he swallowed. He fumbled a cigarette into his mouth and lit up with an unsteady match. "I don't know what that means, and I don't want to know. So Duke is dead. Great. Now, what do we do about that *thing* sitting on top of the Skyride?"

"You don't have to do anything about the creature," Eliza said. "It's dying. It can't hurt anyone anymore."

O'Bannion squinted at her. "Have we met before, doll?"

Mark jumped in before Eliza put the whammy on the poor bastard. "What's important is that the monster and Duke are taken care of. The fair is saved. I did my job for the city, and I expect to get paid. We had an agreement."

O'Bannion was about to answer when a scuffle of feet and a tense rumble of voices sounded in the hallway.

Four more people crowded through the door, coming to stand over Mark's bed.

84

Two of Mark's visitors were men and two were women.

The first of the men was tall and florid, with black hair and cunning little eyes. He wore an Army dress uniform with two silver stars on his shoulder. His skin was deeply weathered, and he said in a voice to match, "So this is your Public Enemy, Edgar? He doesn't look so tough."

The other man was short and stout, with a pleasant, round face and mousey hair. But his eyes burned cold behind his spectacles. "That's him. He attacked two of my agents. He's more dangerous than you realize, Douglas." He turned to the older of the two women. "It isn't safe for you to be here, Eleanor. You should return to the hotel at once."

"Nonsense," the woman said. She wore an expensively ugly purple dress with a wide white collar, and an equally ugly hat over her salt-and-pepper hair. She was tall and plain-faced, and her blue eyes radiated intelligence and authority as she looked at Mark. "This man apparently saved us from a dangerous madman. I had to come visit him. Besides, the poor fellow couldn't hurt anyone. He's flat on his back."

"But I can hear you just fine," Mark said loudly. He knew who these people were. The general must be Duke's Army contact, the one he was making weapons for. The short man was the director of the Investigation Bureau. And he'd seen the first lady's picture in the papers plenty of times.

The short man pointed a plump finger at him. "Mark Van Ryn, I'm placing you under arrest."

"On what charge?" Mark said.

"Assault. Conspiracy. Wanton destruction of public property. Murder."

"I defended the public and saved innocent lives!"

"You admit to being an outlaw vigilante, then?"

"Every action I took was authorized by the City of Chicago. The CPD legally deputized me as a consulting detective in order to contain Lionel Duke and his monster. Isn't that right, Detective O'Bannion?"

Mark looked over at the cop, who had backed himself into a corner when the others came in. He was smoking like a freight train and casting jittery glances between Mark and his visitors.

"Lloyd?" Mark said softly.

Finally, the cop curled his lip and muttered, "Yeah. He's one of ours."

The lady in purple said, "Then it appears you have no grounds for arrest, Edgar."

"I'll find something to charge him with, mark my words," the director snapped. "The Bureau has been investigating him for weeks. He's a mentally unstable malcontent whose deformities make him a danger to the public."

Mark's cheek twitched.

The director pointed at Eliza. "And she, his female associate, is a Russian national. Possibly a communist.

She's been mixed up in this affair from the beginning. They must both be taken into custody for the good of the nation."

"I agree with Edgar, for once," the general said. "If this fellow is as dangerous as he says, then he needs to be studied and tested. Maybe I can use him."

Mark struggled to sit up, Eliza's arm behind him. "I'm a law-abiding citizen, and I have rights! I won't be locked up, and I won't be used by you or anyone!" He reached for the dregs of his power.

Beside him he felt Eliza doing the same, her poison seething around her, readying for battle.

But before they could move, the lady in purple said calmly, "I have quite something else in mind for you." She turned to the stout, competent-looking younger woman who had been standing silently by her elbow. "Tommy, bring in the reporter, please."

Tommy nodded and hurried out the door.

"What's this?" the director said.

"A bit of public relations for the fair, and the city," the first lady said. "It's the least I can do. I'm very fond of Chicago. My husband was nominated here, you know."

Al Tracy appeared in the entrance, his eyes more guileless than ever. His natty clothes were disheveled, and he had a notepad under his arm and a pencil behind his ear. Behind him was his photographer, camera slung around his neck.

Tracy darted forward to grab the older woman's hand, pumping it vigorously. "Alvin Tracy, *Chicago Tribune*, your first ladyship. It's a real honor. A big, big honor."

The first lady smiled, and winced. "How do you do."

The reporter whipped out his pad and pencil. "Can I get

a comment on the astounding events of the evening, Ma'am?"

"Yes. I've come to visit with the hero of the hour, Mr. Mark Van Ryn. I understand you know him well. He risked life and limb tonight to stop a madman in his tracks. Thanks to his brave efforts, and the fine men of the Chicago police force, The Century of Progress is safe and secure."

Tracy scribbled in his notebook and turned his limpid gaze on Mark. "What were you thinking when you attacked the slime monster with that sword? How did you move fast enough to rescue so many people? How does it feel to be Chicago's new favorite son?"

"Just doing my job," Mark said.

"Talk to me Mark! Tell me about saving the life of this lovely girl." He winked at Eliza. "Lionel Duke's fiancée Miss Elizaveta Karlova, isn't that right? How did you get caught in the middle of the fight, sweetheart?"

She raised her chin. "I've been working with Mr. Van Ryn on this case. I discovered that Mr. Duke had been driven mad by a scientific experiment gone awry. I wanted only to save innocent people from harm."

"And she's not Duke's fiancée," Mark said, taking her hand in his bandaged mitt. "She's mine."

Eliza made a muffled sound and Tracy scribbled on his notepad like mad.

The cameraman inserted a flashbulb into his camera and hoisted it to his eye, training it on Mark and his visitors. "Hold still everybody so I can get a nice clean picture."

Everyone in the room recoiled from the camera like Dracula from a crucifix, except the first lady. She stepped up to Mark's bedside. "I speak on behalf of my husband when I say, thank you, Mr. Van Ryn." She held out her hand to him and gave him the ghost of a wink.

Mark forced out a smile that was more of a grimace and took her hand. "It was my honor, Ma'am."

The camera flashed and clicked.

The shrewd blue gaze turned on Eliza. "And you, Miss Karlova. It seems we owe you a debt of gratitude as well." She offered her hand.

Eliza took it, watching the older woman carefully. "Any good citizen would have done the same."

"You'll make a swell heroine on the front page tomorrow, toots. The boys really go for the wild look," Al Tracy said as the camera fired again. Eliza's hand flew to her hair, which had dried in unruly curls after being soaked by the monster. She obviously wanted to say something foul in Russian.

Tracy grinned down at Mark. "I finally got your picture. Nice outfit, too, kid. I can see the headline now—'Mummy Versus Monster at the Century of Progress!'"

"Funny, Al," Mark said. He tore the bandages off his head and stripped them off his hands. The skin underneath was healing rapidly, the raw red patches fading back to white.

"If you're done with your questions Mr. Tracy, I'd like to speak to Mr. Van Ryn alone now," The first lady said. She looked at the general and the director. "Would you excuse us, gentlemen?"

The two men had been watching the proceedings with identical sour expressions. They were beaten, and they knew it. Mark was now a bona fide hero, injured in the line of duty while saving the city, publicly thanked for his sacrifice by the first lady herself. And Eliza was his brave and doting bride-to-be. They were untouchable. For now. The general stalked to the door, the director close behind. But before he left, the director turned his head toward Mark, his spectacles glinting. "We're not done," he said, and then he was gone.

O'Bannion filed out next.

"Lloyd," Mark called.

The detective paused at the door.

"I left that sword out there somewhere. Find it and return it to the Art Institute, would you?"

The cop grunted once and stumped out, muttering to himself.

"Mr. Tracy," the first lady said. "Would you tell the other members of the press that I'll be with them shortly?"

"Be happy to, Mrs. President," Tracy said, tipping his hat to her, and then to Eliza. "I'll be seeing you around, Van Ryn." He winked at Eliza one last time, and he and the photographer left.

Mark eyed the first lady. "What can I do for you, Ma'am?"

"The question is what can *I* do for *you*. The country owes you a great debt, and I'm quite at a loss how to repay you."

"That's easy. I charge sixty dollars a day, plus expenses. But right now I'll settle for a pair of pants, so I can get out of here."

The first lady's lips twitched. "I think that can be arranged." She turned to her assistant. "See if we can procure some trousers for the gentleman."

Tommy bustled off once again.

Her shrewd eyes turned back to Mark. "Are you certain you want to get up so soon? You were very badly injured."

"I'll be fine. I've been through worse."

"Have you?" Her gaze flickered over his hair and skin. "People can be very cruel to those who are different."

"It wasn't so bad. I always figured no one could make me feel inferior without my consent."

She smiled at that and turned her gaze on Eliza. "Congratulations on your engagement to such a fine young man. I hope you will be very happy together."

"I . . . that is . . . thank you," Eliza said.

Tommy returned just then with not only a pair of pants, but a shirt and shoes and even a cap to hide his hair.

"We'll leave you to get dressed," the first lady said. "Goodbye, until our next meeting."

"Next meeting?" Eliza said.

"Why yes. The government will undoubtedly call upon your services again. And I'm certain you will do your duty admirably." With a last gracious smile, she left.

But Mark swore he heard the whisper, "Or else . . ." trail behind her.

85

After Eliza had gotten Mark out of his bandages and into his new clothes, they slipped out of his room, past a few patients and two shocked nurses, and out the back door of the clinic. Outside, a dazed, confused, and excited crowd was milling on the flag-lined thoroughfare. Every face was turned upward toward the amazing sight of the creature clinging to the top of the Skyride tower.

The blob of slime had transformed into a gigantic growth that looked like something between a mushroom and a flower, a long stalk tipped with a wrinkled oval pod towering a hundred feet above the building. Searchlights played over the slender column as the Goodyear blimp circled slowly around it. As they watched, holes opened all over the dark surface of the pod, like a honeycomb, and thin white dust puffed out.

"What's it doing?" Mark asked.

"It's sporing," Eliza said.

The wind whirled the cloud of dust around the tip of the stalk and out into the night. "You mean—"

"Frasier said this is how slime molds reproduce,

remember? They climb to the highest point they can find, transform, and release their tiny seeds to the wind. After it's finished, it will die. It's over."

"Over? Are you kidding? This is a disaster!" Mark said. "There are five great lakes out there, and thousands of little ones. Now each of them is going to have a mutant slime monster baby living in it!"

"Perhaps," Eliza said. "But I don't think they'll be a problem, if we just leave them alone. The creature would never have bothered with humans if humans hadn't bothered it first."

"I hope you're right."

Above them, the strange flower that had once been the monster was withering. The last of its spores were floating away into the sky. The skin of the thing turned translucent white. The pod caved in and the stem toppled, breaking into cottony pieces and drifting down over the fair in harmless pale flakes that blew away in the wind.

"By morning, it'll be like the creature never existed," Eliza said, reaching out to catch a flake that crumbled to dust on her fingers.

"Yeah. People will have forgotten about it by next week," Mark said. "They always do."

They walked quietly out of the fair, working their way through the masses of people as the strange snow drifted over them. Mark kept his arm around Eliza's shoulders for support. That was his excuse, anyway. She kept her arm wrapped around his waist, also for his support. That was *her* excuse.

They took the footbridge across Lake Shore with a stream of other exhausted fairgoers. When they made it to the safety of the nighttime streets, Eliza said, "What do you think the first lady meant when she talked about 'calling on our services' and 'doing our duty'? She sounded like she was recruiting us to work for the government."

Mark shrugged. "I only work for myself, but I'll do jobs for the government, as long as they pay me my—"

"Sixty dollars a day plus expenses?" she said, fluttering her eyelashes up at him.

"Right you are, angel."

She smiled as they walked on. "I'm glad for you, then. But I don't wish to work for the government. I have my own plans for the future."

The arm around her shoulders tensed. "And what are they?"

"I'm going to reopen Mrs. DeForest's perfumery. I intend to make it the foundation of a perfume empire that will stretch from New York to Los Angeles."

Mark grabbed her around the waist and dragged her to a stop in the middle of the sidewalk. He looked down into her face, his eyes blazing blue. "So you're staying in Chicago?"

Her heart was suddenly fluttering in her throat. She nodded.

"You know what that means."

"I suppose you think I'm going to marry you."

"Of course you're going to marry me."

"Don't be ridiculous darling. I couldn't possibly."

"What's your excuse this time?"

"You never asked me."

"Daffy dame, I've asked you five times!"

"No, you demanded I marry you. Not the same thing at all."

He released her, gave her a hard look, and sank down to the pavement on one knee, taking her hand in his. "I love you, Eliza. I'm yours, body and soul. Will you make me the luckiest man on Earth and marry me?"

She pressed her fingers to her lips, tears flashing down her face as her angel knelt before her. Her future with Mark was there for the taking, if she was brave enough.

Follow your heart and it will lead you right.

She bent down and brushed her lips against his. "Yes! Now get up, for heaven's sake!"

He was on his feet before she finished speaking, and the next thing she knew she was bent backward over his arm, getting thoroughly kissed.

Dimly she was aware of a couple of wolf whistles from interested passersby.

When he set her on her feet again a long time later, her cheeks were blazing. "Not here, you fool!" She walked past him on trembling legs. "Wait until we have some privacy!"

He strolled along at her side, his voice a low growl in her ear, "Privacy. Great idea, angel. As soon as we're alone, we can do it again. Me standing behind you this time."

"You're filthy. Don't forget, I'm a *lady*."

"Ah, but you like it, don't you my lady?"

She slid a smile at him over her shoulder. "I love it. I love *you*."

Before she knew what was happening, she was in his arms once again. His eyes were hot on hers. She suddenly realized he was going to take her through the shadows.

"Mark, no! You shouldn't, you're too tired—"

"So tired I've got to go to bed this instant," he said, and there was a now-familiar blur of darkness.

86

Mark raced through the shadows of the city with the woman he'd been born to love. He had to have her, right now. Even in his shadow form, he was on fire with lust for her.

When they reached the house, though, they weren't alone. Two Lincolns and a limousine were lined up at the curb, and there were about ten guys standing uneasily on the sidewalk. Camonte himself was pacing outside Mark's front door.

Mark materialized with Eliza in a patch of shadow nearby and stepped out into the mobster's path.

Camonte jumped back with a yip of surprise. The gangsters by the cars grabbed for their weapons.

Mark said, "I'm in no mood for you tonight, Camonte. I nearly got eaten, in case you didn't hear."

"Yeah, yeah, it was on the radio," Camonte said, waving away the entire incident with one meaty hand. "Listen, I got a new problem for you to take care of."

"You've got to be joking. The creature that killed your

boys is dead, and so are the men who set it on you. We're done."

The mobster completely ignored him. "You believe this? I'm being audited! They're going to arrest me for tax evasion! *Tax evasion!*" Sweat was beading on his forehead.

Mark laughed aloud. "Do I look like an accountant? What do you want me to do about it?"

"You gotta get in to see the Bureau of Investigation guy. He's here in town with the first lady, right? I want you to put a scare into him and make his boys back off. No pointy-head bean counter with a badge is takin' down Gab Camonte!"

"You're on your own," Mark told him. "I'll fight all the monsters you've got, but I draw the line at the IRS."

Camonte's eyes narrowed. "You're one of my guys," he said in a voice of betrayal.

"I'm no one's *guy*, especially not a two-bit killer like you. You fought a war in the city and innocent people are dead. Now you can take what's coming to you."

Camonte flushed with desperate fury. "You punk! I ought to put you up against the wall right here and now!" Behind him, there was a clicking noise and a ripple of movement as his men raised their guns and trained them on Mark.

Eliza had been standing silently by his side, but now she stepped past him and swayed up close to Camonte, her cloud of perfume around her. "Oh, Mr. Camonte, please don't be angry." She trailed her eyes over his face, her gaze coming to rest on the scar along his left jaw. "So that's the famous scar. May I touch it?"

Camonte stared at her, his mouth folding into a loopy grin. "Sure, dollface."

She reached up and brushed a fingertip along his jaw.

"You've had a difficult day. Why don't you and your friends go get some rest, and forget all about Mark and me."

Camonte's eyes went blank. He pivoted and marched off toward his limousine. "Let's go home boys," he called to his men.

The gangsters looked between each other in confusion as the boss climbed inside his limousine. But eventually they piled into the cars, and the convoy roared off down the street in a cloud of smoke.

Mark crossed his arms over his chest as he watched them go. "I could have fought them," he grumbled.

"I know you could have, darling," Eliza said, tucking her hand into his elbow. "But this way is faster. And weren't you eager to be alone with me?"

He grinned down at her. "Good point, angel." He considered sweeping her into his house on the shadows, but tonight was important, and he wanted to get it right. He unlocked the front door and scooped her up into his arms, carrying her across the threshold as she laughed in delight.

"Welcome to your new home," he said, kicking the door closed behind him. He let her slip down his body to her feet, keeping hold of her waist. "Unless you really don't like the house. We can move, if you want."

She smoothed her palms over his shoulders. "Nonsense. The house suits us perfectly. Though it needs a woman's touch, of course."

"Yeah? So do I. Right now."

"Goodness, how demanding." She slipped her fingers into the opening of his collar to brush his skin, smiling up at him.

He was about to kiss that smile when she stiffened in his arms, her nostrils flaring. Her expression turned horrorstruck. "No!" She whirled and ran to the waiting room, Mark on her heels.

Angelique and Frasier sat on opposite sides of the room, eyeing each other warily. The tinny voice of a radio announcer filled the air between them. When Eliza and Mark burst in, Frasier jumped to his feet, flicking the radio off. "Mark! Thank the Lord! The news reporter said you were hurt!"

"We're fine," Mark said shortly. He kept his eyes on the countess.

The old lady rose up from her chair. Her face was pale and imperious as she looked between Eliza and Mark, her eyes kindling.

"How did you get in here?" Mark said.

"That was my fault," Frasier said. "She made me let her in."

Mark said, "Listen close, old woman. One wrong word, and I will pick you up and put you down outside like a cat."

"You wouldn't dare!" the countess said.

"Want to find out?"

Angelique turned a look of outrage on her granddaughter. "Élisabeth!"

She shrugged. "I'll hold the door for him."

The old lady thinned her mouth. "You will cease this brutish behavior."

"Brutish? That's some nerve," Mark said. "You had me kidnapped and tortured!"

"You are going to have to get over that, *cher garçon*, since we are soon to be kin."

Mark eyed her suspiciously. "That's right, we will. I'm marrying Eliza as soon as the courthouse opens tomorrow morning. Don't try to stop me."

"Stop you? Stupid boy, I would force you to the altar

myself if I had to! No great-granddaughter of mine shall be born illegitimate!"

Stunned silence fell. Mark turned to look at Eliza, his head suddenly light.

Eliza's eyes were wide with shock. Her hands flew to her belly. "No! It can't be!"

Angelique said, "Of course it can, and is! Use your nose, girl!" To Mark she said, "You are not the instrument I would have chosen to carry on my bloodline, but what is done is done. You are to be the father of a new lamia, and —" She drew a breath and her face fell into lines of astonishment. "*Non, c'est impossible!*"

"What?" Eliza cried.

"You are carrying a girl . . . and a *boy*! No lamia has ever carried a boy!"

"Twins?" Eliza whispered, looking down at her flat stomach.

Mark's ears were buzzing. He wondered if he was about to faint. Fortunately Frasier whooped and grabbed him into a hug, pounding on his back and keeping him from falling over.

When he was steady on his feet, Frasier let him go. He went to his bride, taking her hands in his. She looked up at him with a face full of glowing joy, and sheer panic. "Mark, I . . . can't believe it! I'm so happy! But, are you?"

He nodded. "Yes. Anything for you."

"For us. Our family." She brought his hand to her belly. He spread his trembling fingers over the place his son and daughter rested, and looked down into the beautiful brown eyes smiling up at his.

"I'll just be going now," Frasier said cheerfully. He gripped Mark's shoulder. "But don't think you won't get an earful about running off to fight monsters all by yourself, brother."

"You can chew me out when we visit your family for Sunday dinner," Mark said, clasping him back.

Frasier turned to Eliza. "Congratulations. I'm glad for you and Mark."

She looked at him cautiously. "Really?"

"Truly. I thought about what you said, and you were right. Mark can live his own life. You just take good care of him, mind."

"I will. Thanks, Frasier. You're a good friend." She leaned up and kissed the air next to his cheek.

He grinned. "I am. And I'll prove it by taking your grandmother home."

"There is no need," Angelique said crisply. "My driver and Helga are waiting for me in my car."

"Why then, I shall escort you to your car," Frasier said.

"Very well. Come, Élisabeth, we are leaving."

"I'll return to the hotel in a little while. I have something to discuss with my fiancé, alone," Eliza said.

Angelique looked scandalized, but before she could say anything, Mark warned her, "Remember, like a cat."

Pointing a finger at Eliza, the old lady said, "I will see you married tomorrow!"

"Yes, *Grand-mère*. I'm done running."

"Come along, Ma'am." Frasier gestured her toward the front hallway.

She swept past him out of the room, tossing over her shoulder, "That's Countess, to you."

"I'll be back tomorrow bright and early to take you to the courthouse," Frasier said. He winked at Mark, smiled at Eliza, and left, shutting the door behind him.

"Finally we're alone!" Eliza said.

Mark wrapped an arm around her, still trying to find his footing in his new world. "I'm going to be a father."

"Yes, a wonderful father." She went up on her toes and kissed him until he couldn't see straight. "But tonight I want you to be my lover," she whispered in his ear.

He grinned slowly. "You're the boss." He enveloped them in shadow and rushed upstairs to his bed. When they materialized, they were naked. He had left their clothes in the shadow.

"Oh!" she gasped. "That *is* a useful ability you have, darling." Laughing, she clasped his shoulders and raised her knees for him.

"You inspired me to be creative," he said, kissing her. He lowered his hips to hers, and found her already wet for him. "God, I love you so much Eliza." He ended on a groan as he slid inside her. She stopped him there with a hand on his chest over his heart, pushing him back to look into his eyes.

"I love you, Mark. Forever."

He grinned. "Forever."

Tommy,

    Remind me to speak with Franklin about formalizing the status of our interesting new acquaintances in Chicago. I have a notion that they, and others like them, may help us secure the peace and safety of our country during the challenging times ahead, like the National Guard, only stranger . . .

— FIRST LADY E.R., NOTE, JUNE 15, 1933

Acknowledgments

Many thanks to the Bookies, Ann Clement, Julia Gabriel, Victoria Hanlen, and Anna James for your encouragement and good advice.

Thank you Jose and Matthew for a wonderful Chicago adventure.

As always, thanks to my family for your love and support.

About the Author

J.B. Curry is an artist and writer. She has travelled to every corner of the United States, but currently lives in beautiful New England with her family and her vast collection of houseplants.

Come visit her at jbcurry.com.